To Gabriel,

Some of life's greatest rewards
come from pursuing your dreams
and making them happen.

Dan Pekarek

12-4-08

DLPekarek@aol.Com

Mysterious Alcent

Daniel L. Pekarek

Seattle, Washington
Portland, Oregon
Denver, Colorado
Vancouver, B.C.
Scottsdale, Arizona
Minneapolis, Minnesota

Peanut Butter Publishing
an imprint of
Classic Day Publishing
2925 Fairview Avenue East
Seattle, Washington 98102
877-728-8837
ewolfpub@aol.com

Dedication

This story is dedicated to the Waldenbooks' Stores
in which most of it was written.

Acknowledgements

Production of this book was made possible through
the efforts of the following people:

Albert Bjorgen
Storyline and Engineering Consultant

Peter Fisher, M.D.
Medical Consultant

Daniel L. Pekarek
Author and Editor

Joan Pekarek
Assistant Editor and Proofreader

Berk Brown
Assistant Editor and Proofreader

David Pekarek
Cover Image

David Marty
Cover Design

Amy Vaughn
Interior Design

Elliott Wolf
Publisher

Tonya

Chapter One

TIME: Day 43, 5:45 PM

On Alcent, the third planet of Alpha Centauri A, three small groups of interstellar pioneers united to form a new nation. To celebrate their union, they were having an all-day party on the sandy southern beach of Pioneer Island, the home of the Earth people. The other pioneers were from Zebron, a planet orbiting Alpha Centauri B, and Proteus, a planet orbiting Delta Pavonis.

Trang, the Captain of the starship from Delta Pavonis, was sitting at a picnic table with Jerry, the Captain of the starship from Earth. Trang's communicator beeped. After answering it, he turned to his wife Geniya and said, "It's Tonya, she's finally come back from the jungle." Going back to his communicator, Trang said, "Glad you're home honey."

"Dad, I always return safely," Tonya replied.

"I know, but I always worry about you. I wish you would stay in touch with us while you're gone."

"I can't do that. It would break my bond with the jungle. Achieving oneness with the jungle is how I stay alive. I sense where the dangers are and avoid them."

"That's what you always say, but we always worry about you. We wish you didn't spend so much time in the wilderness."

"I love it in the forest. I feel in harmony with the creatures that live there. Using my special telepathic gift, I influence the animals to accept my presence. Sometimes, I can even get certain creatures to befriend me."

"I know you are gifted with special powers, but Geniya and I worry about you when you disappear for weeks at a time."

"This time, you'll be glad I went away, because I discovered something that will blow your mind."

1

"What's that?"

"We aren't the first people to live here. I discovered some old caves that have artwork and script on the walls. The writing could only have been put there by intelligent beings."

"I would like to see those caves."

"I will show them to you, but where are you? There's nobody here. Where is everybody?"

"That's a long story. Great things have happened while you were gone. Our people on Aphrodite have been rescued. We have our starship back and under repair. And our space shuttle is back in operation."

"WOW! How did you do all of that?"

"Some wonderful people have come here from Earth, and they helped us."

"They must be really special. I'd like to meet them."

"You will, because we've united with them and some people from Zebron (B-2) to form a nation. We are going to be working together to build a strong society."

"This is very exciting news, but you still haven't answered my question. Where is everyone?"

"We're having a party on Pioneer Island. This is where the Earth people live."

"Where is Pioneer Island?"

"It's in the middle of Clear Lake. That's the big lake that Mystery Lagoon flows into."

"Now, I know where you are. When are you coming home?"

"Tomorrow."

"Good, I want to take you to the caves I found."

"We also found some caves, and we think they were made by beings with high-tech equipment."

"Really! Where?"

"We flew upriver from the falls in Mystery Lagoon. When we reached the foothills, we found caverns that were cut into a granite cliff."

"You said *we*, who was with you?"

"Jerry, he is the Captain of the starship from Earth."

"When will I meet him? I want to thank him for everything he's done for us."

"Hold on a minute, and I'll find out." Turning to Jerry, Trang asked, "Want to go cave exploring tomorrow?"

"Where?"

2

"Tonya found some in the jungle where we live, and there's artwork on the walls."

"That sounds interesting, and I don't have any pressing plans for tomorrow."

Speaking into his communicator, Trang said, "You will meet Jerry tomorrow. He wants to see the caves."

"Good, I will show both of you my world before we get to the caves."

"What do you mean by that?"

"Hiking through the jungle, it will take us about a week to get to the caves. That will give me a chance to show you my world."

"A week in each direction is too much time. I really can't be away that long. I now have a starship to repair. Maybe we can fly to the caves."

"I am familiar with the jungle, but I don't know if I can find the caves from the air."

"Let's try, because I can't be gone for two weeks."

"Okay, I'll see what I can do, but I do want to show you some of my world."

"Are you familiar with the jungle around the caves?"

"Yes."

"After exploring the caves, you can show us that area."

"That's a deal. See you tomorrow morning."

"Goodbye honey."

Turning to Geniya, Trang said, "I wish she didn't disappear into the jungle for weeks at a time."

"She always comes back," responded Geniya. "You have to respect her survival skills."

"She doesn't just survive," stated Trang. "She actually thrives in the wilderness."

"How does she deal with the lupusaurs?" Jerry asked.

"Tonya is blessed with unique telepathic powers," responded Trang. "She is able to get into the heads of animals better than anyone I've ever known."

"Lupusaurs are intelligent, aggressive hunters," stated Jerry.

"I know, but Tonya is able to sense their presence from a great distance. Then, she can either avoid them or use her mental powers to influence their behavior."

"That's an amazing ability to have. I can see why she feels safe in the wilderness."

"In addition to her mental powers, she's very good at using stealth. In the jungle, she's as hard to find as a shadow on a dark night."

"It sounds like she's the best person to guide us in the forest."

"No doubt about that, but she never wants to take anyone with her. She says people distract her and prevent her from becoming one with the jungle, which is what she needs to do to be safe."

"Why is she making an exception this time?" Jerry asked.

"She wants to meet you and show us the caves."

Jerry turned to his wife Connie and said, "It looks like I'll be going cave exploring tomorrow."

"That should be interesting, but I worry whenever you do something dangerous."

"We'll be armed and alert," responded Jerry.

"And we'll have a very well qualified guide," added Trang.

TIME: Day 44, 7:00 AM

Connie accompanied Jerry to the south end of Stellar Plateau. When they stepped out of the ATV (all terrain vehicle), they embraced warmly. "Be careful today," she said.

"You can count on that," responded Jerry. He gave Connie a goodbye kiss and said, "See you tonight."

Jerry stepped into the open, wooden cage elevator and descended the 150-foot cliff down to South Bay, where he joined his crew and Trang, who were waiting on the beach. They rode a boat out to Jerry's cargo shuttle, which was anchored in the bay.

Jerry went directly to the cockpit and sat in the Captain's seat. He invited Trang to sit in the copilot's seat.

Wanting to depart immediately, Jerry pulled in the anchors, fired up the shuttle's nuclear reactor, and activated the steam turbine. Shifting the marine propeller into gear, he taxied out of South Bay and brought the shuttle up to 40 mph. Now riding on its hydrofoils, the shuttle seemed to yearn for more speed. Suddenly, its NTR (nuclear thermal rocket) thundered into action with a deafening roar that shattered the early morning stillness over Clear Lake. The shuttle quickly accelerated to 200 mph and pitched into a steep climb.

Still standing on the south end of Stellar Plateau, Connie watched the shuttle take off and begin its ascent to space. When it reached the cold stratosphere, the water vapor pouring out of the NTR condensed

4

into a brilliant white vapor trail. Connie beeped Jerry with her communicator and said, "Your climb into space is a spectacular sight."

"We'll be above the atmosphere shortly," he responded.

Two minutes later, Jerry shut down the NTR, and the shuttle followed a ballistic trajectory toward Crater Lake, 1600 miles to the south. Less than 20 minutes after takeoff, the shuttle descended into the upper atmosphere. It made a steep descent to 5000 feet; then, it went into a moderate gliding descent to Crater Lake, where it landed on its hydrofoils at 195 mph. Its hydro-drogues deployed and quickly slowed it to less than 40 mph. Then, the shuttle floated on its hull and came to a stop.

"We're here," Jerry announced. "Let's go to the cargo bay and help Jim get the chopper ready for flight."

"Tonya has never been up in a helicopter," commented Trang.

"Jim is an excellent pilot," stated Jerry, "but he's only 25 and still likes to fly aerial stunts. I'm sure he can make this a thrilling flight for her."

"That may be, but I don't think he'll scare her."

"Why is that?"

"Tonya has a fearless, daredevil personality. With nothing more than a rope, she'll climb a tall tree and then use the rope to swing to a nearby tree."

"It sounds like she and Jim have something in common. They just might get along quite well."

Jerry and Trang went to the cargo bay. Jim was there and had already opened the cargo bay's large upper doors. He pressed a button, and the cargo bay's elevator deck rose to the top of the fuselage, where it served as the flight operations deck for the helicopter.

Turning to Jerry, the highly spirited Jim asked, "Would you mind helping me get this bird ready for flight?"

"Not at all," replied Jerry.

"Count me in," Trang said.

The men went to work on the helicopter. First, they deployed the rotor blades; then, they released the tie-down mechanisms.

"Let's go pick up my daughter," Trang said.

The men boarded the helicopter and flew four miles to the sandstone cliff that Trang and his people lived in. They had excavated caverns in the cliff with entrances well above ground. For extra safety, the entrances had sturdy doors that served as barricades.

Standing in one of the cave entrances, Tonya watched the helicopter land on the rocky open area in front of the cliff. She immediately climbed down a ladder and ran to meet her father, who had stepped out of the aircraft. He ran to his daughter and welcomed her with a big hug. "I'm glad you're safely back," he said.

"I love you dad. I will never let anything happen to me. I will always come back."

"I appreciate that."

"I want to meet your friends from Earth."

"Only two of them are here." Grasping one of Tonya's hands, Trang walked side-by-side with her to Jim and Jerry, who were standing next to the helicopter. Facing them, he said, "I would like you to meet the spirit of the jungle, my daughter, Tonya."

Jerry grinned at the title Trang gave his daughter; then, he said, "My name is Jerry and this is Jim."

Tonya looked into Jerry's eyes to sense his character and personality; then, she smiled broadly and said, "Thank you for helping us."

Returning the smile, Jerry said, "You're welcome."

Tonya turned her attention to Jim, looking into his eyes to explore his inner being. The penetrating gaze galvanized Jim, who couldn't help but notice the youthful beauty of the young woman facing him. He noted her lean, but ample figure, her brown eyes, and black hair. She seemed filled with a vibrant zest for life.

The silent evaluation of each other continued for several seconds until Jim started to sense that maybe Tonya could read his thoughts with her telepathic powers. This possibility made him feel uncomfortable. He didn't want her to know how she was affecting his feelings so soon after meeting her. He decided to break the mental connect. "Would you like to go flying?" he asked her.

"That might be exciting," Tonya responded.

"It's fun, and I can make it as exciting as you feel up for."

"Maybe we should save the wild ride for another time and just go find the caves on this flight."

Sounds like she wants to go flying with me again, Jim thought, as he tingled with excitement. He smiled and said, "Yesterday, you told your father that you didn't know if you could find the caves from the air."

"Since then, I've given it some thought in terms of what might be visible from the air, and I think I can get us pretty close."

"You can sit in the copilot's seat. That will give you a panoramic view of where we're headed. I'll follow your directions."

"Let's go find those caves," stated Jerry.

Immediately after takeoff, Tonya pointed at the distant mountains. "That's where we need to go," she said.

Jim headed the helicopter toward the east as directed. "It's an endless sea of green down there," he said. "It's going to be difficult to find caves in that."

"Around the caves, the jungle is even thicker than it is here," commented Tonya.

"How can it be thicker than that?" Jim asked, pointing at the dense treetops.

"It rains more there than here," replied Tonya.

"That makes sense," commented Trang. "Clouds coming in from the ocean are heavy with moisture. They lose much of that when they rise up to get over the mountains."

"It does rain frequently," Tonya said. "The area is steamy with humidity. Small ponds, marshes, and streams are everywhere. The abundance of water and the warm climate support a lush jungle of plant life, which supports a broad diversity of animal life. There is even a species of small monkeys living there that rarely come down out of the trees."

"I wonder why we never see any monkeys in our area," questioned Trang.

"We don't have the right kind of trees," responded Tonya. "The monkeys are supported by two species of trees; one produces fruit, and the other produces nuts with soft shells that they're able to bite through."

"I suppose you've climbed high into the trees to study the monkeys," commented Trang.

"Of course."

"How did they react to that?"

"I used my mental powers to convince them that I wasn't a threat, and they accepted my presence. In fact, there was one that even seemed to like me."

"How did that one behave toward you?"

"He brought me some fruit and sat on a branch next to me while I ate it."

"I get the feeling you've spent a lot of time with those animals."

"I have, and I even slept a few nights in a tree in their midst."

7

"I'm starting to see why your father introduced you as the spirit of the jungle," Jerry said.

"I am at home in the wilderness."

"Can you telepathically identify the monkey that befriended you?" Jerry asked.

"Yes."

"How far away from the caves does his group live?"

"About a mile to the south."

"Can you telepathically locate them from a distance?"

"I can sense their presence from a half-mile away."

"Maybe we can get close to the caves by finding them."

"It's worth a try," responded Tonya.

Twenty minutes later, Tonya located the monkeys. Jim flew one mile to the north and slowly circled the area. "Do you see anything familiar out there?" he asked Tonya.

"Not a thing. It's just a sea of green."

"Well, this is your backyard, so pick a spot. I'll hover and lower you and your guests to the surface."

Gazing out over the area, Jerry said, "It would be nice if we could find a small break in the trees to drop down through."

With her favorite rope coiled around her left shoulder, Tonya said, "If you're in the mood for a little climbing, I can get us down to the surface from any treetop."

"Those trees might be 200 feet tall," commented Jerry.

"That's true, but they're easy to climb."

"Let's look for a break," Jerry insisted.

"Over there," Trang said, pointing to the right.

Jim turned to the right, and in a few moments, he brought the helicopter to a hover over the opening in the forest. Looking down into the jungle, Jerry said, "There's a large rock formation down there."

"That's where we need to go," stated Tonya. "I think we'll find the caves there."

"Let's go down and take a look," Jerry said.

Jerry, Trang, and Tonya entered the helicopter's cargo bay and stepped onto the center section of its floor, which was detachable and could be lowered to the surface with a ceiling-mounted winch. The floor panel was equipped with safety rails that Jerry deployed to form an open cage. "Is everyone ready to go?" he asked.

"Yes," they eagerly responded.

"We're going down," Jerry said to Jim.

"I'll hold this bird steady," he replied.

Jerry pressed a button, and the floor section released and began dropping away from the helicopter as the winch played out cable. As the trio steadily descended, Tonya's finely tuned senses seemed to meld with the surrounding jungle. Jerry was impressed with the change in her demeanor. She reminded him of a tigress with kittens to protect. She appeared totally focused and alert, but seemed relaxed and ready to pounce. I can see why she thrives in the jungle, Jerry thought.

When the cage landed on the rock formation, everyone stepped out, and Jerry sent it back up to the hovering helicopter. "We'll call you when we're ready to be picked up," Jerry said to Jim.

"I'll be waiting," Jim replied, as he began the flight back to the shuttle.

The rock formation the trio landed on was free of tall trees, but because of frequent rain, it was covered with a thick carpet of moss punctuated by numerous ferns. Toward the west, the rock formation abruptly ended with a 60-foot drop over a nearly vertical cliff. Toward the east, it was buried by a jungle-covered hill that gradually rose nearly 300 feet. It was only 30 to 40 feet from the cliff to the hillside. From north to south, the rock formation stretched only 200 feet before the dense jungle took over.

Tonya led the way to the south and entered the jungle, her senses on full alert. Carefully picking her way through the thick vegetation, it took several minutes to descend a landslide to the base of the cliff. She turned north, and in a few minutes, the trio emerged from the jungle and was once again on a carpet of moss and ferns covering the rocky area at the cliff's base.

Tonya pointed upward and said, "There's a large opening up there that is sealed with a transparent cover. I believe it is the outside end of a skylight that illuminates the five rooms in the underground complex."

"You might be right," Trang said. "The caves we discovered also have skylights."

"It looks like the Ancient Ones started more than one colony on this planet," Jerry said.

"That's possible," agreed Trang, "but why would they divide themselves? It seems like one large colony would be stronger than two or more smaller ones."

9

"Maybe not," argued Jerry. "A natural tragedy could wipe out an entire colony, but if they are divided into several smaller colonies, the tragedy would only take out part of the whole."

"Good point."

"Let's go in and look at the artwork," suggested Tonya.

"How good are your senses?" Jerry asked.

"What do you mean?"

"Do you know with certainty that we aren't going to be ambushed by some wild animal looking for an easy meal?"

"I am familiar with the animals in this area, and there's nothing of consequence in the cave."

"It looks like a good place for lupusaurs to raise their pups."

"There is evidence that it has been an animal den, but it's vacant at present. Are you ready to go in?"

Without waiting for an answer, Tonya headed for the cave entrance. Trang and Jerry followed, but despite Tonya's assurance that the cave was deserted, they were alert with their rifles ready.

The trio entered the tunnel, which was lit by soft, diffuse light from ceiling panels. "This looks like the same kind of lighting system that was in the cave we discovered," Jerry said.

"Apparently, light carrying tunnels extend from these ceiling panels to the outside skylight," noted Trang. "And since it's fairly well lit in here, the tunnels must have mirror finishes to prevent loss of light as they bend and turn to get to these ceiling panels."

Twenty feet inside the cave, the trio came to the first side rooms. The entrances were seven feet high with round tops. Trang and Jerry looked into the rooms, which were 20 by 25 feet. "Nothing here except some old bones with teeth marks on them," noted Jerry.

"All five rooms have old, chewed-on bones in them," stated Tonya. "That's why I think animals have lived in them from time to time over the centuries."

"Have you found any human artifacts?" Jerry asked.

"Everything is gone except for the artwork on the walls in the last room."

"The caves we found were also free of artifacts," stated Jerry. "All we have from the Ancient Ones is a knife and a belt buckle emblem that we recovered from the bottom of Mystery Lagoon."

"How could an ancient, apparently high-tech, people disappear without leaving anything behind?" questioned Tonya. "There should be weapons, tools, pottery... something."

"That's our thinking too," commented Trang.

"Let's go look at the artwork," suggested Jerry.

"It's in the room at the end of the hallway," responded Tonya, as she headed for the room.

On the way, the trio briefly stopped at the other two side rooms, which looked like the two already visited. After a quick inspection, Trang said, "Nothing new here."

Upon entering the last room, Jerry and Trang were surprised at the amount of artwork carved into the stone walls on all sides of the room. One scene immediately caught Jerry's attention. "That's the same scene that's on the belt buckle emblem," he exclaimed, "but a great deal of detail has been added to the wall."

Trang looked at all four walls and said, "My daughter has found a treasure trove of information here. There are not only pictures and diagrams, but also lots of text that might give us some answers if we can figure out how to read it."

"We'll have to do that another time," stated Tonya. "The local pack of lupusaurs is headed this way. We have to leave or deal with them when they arrive."

"I need to get detailed video of this and put it in the computer," stated Jerry. "How much time do I have?"

"I'll go meet the lupusaurs," responded Tonya. "Maybe I can delay them for a while."

"How are you going to do that?" Jerry asked.

"Oh, I have my ways," responded Tonya, as she turned and ran to the cave exit. Once outside, her telepathic powers were no longer dampened by being inside a rock formation. Using her mental gift, she began a search for the lupusaurs. She quickly found and recognized the energy field emanating from the pack leader's brain. She had experience with this pack and its viciously aggressive leader. She had taunted him from the safety of a tree, throwing baseball-sized nuts at him.

Trang followed Tonya out of the cave. She turned to him and said, "Please stay here until I return."

Before Trang could object, Tonya raced into the jungle on a well used game trail. Light on her feet, she moved swiftly toward the advancing lupusaurs. When she was 400 yards away from the cave, she sensed that she was close to the animals, so she stopped to put her plan into action.

She spotted a tree with a large low branch that extended across the trail. A few yards up the trail from the overhanging branch, Tonya dropped her shorts, squatted, and urinated on the trail. With a stick, she spread some of the urine soaked soil across the trail and onto the bushes on either side. On the way back to the tree, she picked up several golf-ball-sized rocks and put them in a pouch attached to her belt. Then, she climbed the tree and made herself comfortable on the overhanging branch, which was only 13 feet above the trail.

In less than a minute, the lupusaurus pack leader trotted around a bend in the trail. Picking up the urine scent, he growled angrily and approached the urine-soaked line across the trail. He stopped and smelled it, recognizing it as the scent of one who had teased and eluded him before. Loudly, he howled out a fierce challenge. How dare this human thing intrude in his territory and mark it as her own.

"I am up here," Tonya screamed. "Come and get me."

The lupusaurus glared at Tonya, barked menacingly, and charged. He jumped as high as he could and snapped his jaws shut, but he was a couple feet short of grabbing Tonya's feet, which were hanging down from the branch. The lupusaurus howled in angry frustration.

Tonya laughed loudly, moved her feet in a dancing motion, and said, "What's bugging you? Is there something in your territory that you can't attack?"

The lupusaurus howled fiercely and glowered at Tonya's teasing movements. He gathered all of his strength and jumped straight up with total determination. The height of the leap surprised Tonya. The animal's jaws snapped shut only inches from her feet.

"That was good," exclaimed Tonya, "but you're going to have to do better if you want me."

Tonya looked into the lupusaur's eyes and felt his hatred and determination. The animal stared back. His jaws rapidly opened and closed several times, while saliva flowed out of his mouth.

"Do I look that tasty? It must be maddening to know that you can't have me."

Being a cunning animal, the lupusaurus began looking for a way to get to his prey. His eyes followed the branch to the tree trunk. He charged toward the trunk, leapt up the trunk, and tried to claw his way up to the branch. But he came up short and fell back to the ground, where he howled and barked in frustration.

The 21 animals making up the rest of the pack were also howling and barking as they milled around under Tonya. The noise was deafening. The pack leader barked out a command, and his pack became silent as all stared at Tonya. They seemed to be thinking about how to get to her.

Tonya noted that the jungle had become deathly still. "It appears that you and your pack have terrified everything into silence except me," taunted Tonya, as she removed a rock from her pouch and threw it at the lupusaurus leader. It struck him on top of his nose.

He howled at the insult and the pain. He became more determined than ever to kill his tormentor. His eyes followed the branch out to its end. Suddenly, the animal charged into the bushes, leapt on top of a boulder, then onto the branch Tonya was sitting on.

Tonya drew her pistol and aimed at the lupusaurus, but she did not fire. Instead, she stared into the animal's eyes, and using her telepathic powers, she projected an image of a large, angry, saber-toothed cat into its brain.

On the ground, a lone saber-tooth could be quickly killed by a lupusaurus pack. But the lupusaurus pack leader wasn't on the ground. He was alone in a tree, and what looked like an easy meal had suddenly become a huge, angry saber-toothed cat. It was a shocking surprise, and the lupusaurus instantly froze in position.

Tonya telepathically projected saber-tooth snarling sounds into the lupusaur's brain to reinforce the saber-tooth image. She began slowly approaching the animal while increasing the strength of her telepathic intrusion into his brain.

The lupusaurus remained frozen in position, determined to stand his ground. Tonya telepathically suggested retreat while continuing to inch closer. She suggested the position of strength the animal could have by being on the ground with his pack.

It was a war of nerves that Tonya was determined to win. Confident in her telepathic ability to control animals, she continued the face-off. She sensed that this lupusaurus was ready to bolt and just needed an extra push, so she added a second saber-tooth to her message. She placed this one on the branch directly above the lupusaurus causing him to look up. Convinced that he was facing two deadly enemies, the lupusaurus jumped off the branch and joined his pack.

Wanting to go back to the cave, Tonya needed to get the lupusaurus pack out of the area. She decided to try appealing to their hunger. Into the mind of the pack leader, she placed an image of a herd of antelope back up the trail from which the pack came.

The strategy worked. Surrounded by his pack, the pack leader barked out a fierce challenge to what he thought were a pair of saber-toothed cats in the tree above him. Then, he turned and headed west in search of antelope. One by one, the pack members turned away from the tree and followed him.

Tonya waited for the pack to clear the area; then, she nimbly dropped to the ground and headed back to the cavern. When she arrived, she found Trang and Jerry waiting for her in front of the cliff.

"Did you find the lupusaurs?" Jerry asked.

"Yes."

"How far away are they?"

"They left the area. They're headed west."

"I thought they were coming this way."

"They were, but I had a little communication session with their leader, and they left."

"Let me get this straight. A pack of vicious hunters were headed this way, and you went out and talked to them, and they left."

"That pretty well sums it up."

"That's incredible. I'd like to know how you did that."

Tonya told Jerry and her father the complete story. When she finished, Jerry asked, "What will they do when they find out that you sent them on a wild goose chase?"

"By the time they figure that out, they'll be miles from here. Anyway, this jungle is so full of life that they'll find something else to kill and eat. They won't be back today."

"You sound very sure about that," noted Jerry.

"I was only 15 when I started making solo trips into the jungle. Since then, I've spent more time in the forest than out of it. I've studied the lifestyles of the creatures that live here, and I have a very good understanding of lupusaurs. This pack will find something to kill and eat. Then, they will contentedly sleep for a few hours."

"Okay, I'll take your word for that, but I'm surprised that your parents allowed you to go into the wilderness alone at age 15."

"We didn't have much choice!" exclaimed Trang. "She had a mind of her own and sneaked off for a few hours at a time. We would've had to lock her up to keep her home, and we couldn't do that."

"I might've been rebellious," stated Tonya, "but I was never irresponsible. I was always tuned in to my surroundings, so that I could avoid danger. I became very good with stealth techniques."

"Geniya and I recognized your capability and sense of responsibility. That's why we gave you as much freedom as we did."

"Well, I'm glad you did. I've become very comfortable in the jungle, and now, I'm going to show you some of its beauties."

Tonya became very still. Her mind was telepathically searching the nearby trees. When she found what she was looking for, she said, "Stay relaxed and don't make any sudden movements."

Jerry and Trang did as requested, and Tonya walked about 20 feet toward a tree. She stopped and extended her right arm. Momentarily, a bird with a 12-inch wingspan and brilliant red and green feathers flew down from the tree and landed on her arm. Tonya turned her head and faced the bird. In just a few seconds, it started chirping a happy song.

Tonya turned her attention back to the tree and extended her left arm. The bird's mate glided down from a branch and landed on her arm. The birds started chirping back and forth with their singing communication. Tonya listened to their cheerful sounds for a couple minutes; then, she lifted her arms a bit, and the birds flew back into the tree.

"That was quite a demonstration," noted Jerry, as he and Trang approached Tonya. "Can you influence all creatures like that?"

"Enough of them to keep myself entertained. Would you like to walk into the jungle and meet more of the creatures that live here?"

"Sounds like fun," responded Jerry.

Pointing down the game trail to the west, Tonya said, "Somewhere down that trail, there is a lupusaurus pack."

"No thanks!" exclaimed Jerry. "I've already had enough experience with lupusaurs."

"Okay, then we'll head down that trail." Tonya pointed toward the north and headed for the trail. Trang and Jerry followed her into the dense rainforest.

Two hours later, they returned to the top of the rock formation. "Have you seen enough?" Tonya asked.

"That was a very interesting nature tour," responded Trang.

"Too bad Jim wasn't with us," commented Jerry. "He would've enjoyed it. Dianne has trained him to be a biologist, and he is keenly interested in the plants and creatures that live on this planet."

"Really!" exclaimed Tonya. "Maybe there are some things he can teach me. Do you need to go back to Pioneer Island right away?"

"What do you have in mind?" Jerry asked.

"I'd like to take Jim on the same tour I just gave you and Dad."

"He'd like that," stated Jerry. "How much time do you need?"

"A couple hours should be enough," responded Tonya with a bright-eyed smile.

Noticing Tonya's demeanor, Jerry said, "I sense that there's more involved here than just a nature walk."

Tonya gave Jerry a silent smile that spoke volumes. He grinned in return and called Jim. "We're ready for pickup," he said.

"I'll be right there," responded Jim.

"We have a tour guide here, who would like to show you some of what lives here. I have to tell you that there's an amazing diversity of life here."

"I'd love to see some of it," Jim said, sounding excited.

Twenty minutes later, the helicopter arrived. Jim lowered the cage into the clearing, and Jerry stepped aboard, but Trang hesitated. "I'd like to do the nature hike again, in case I missed something," he said.

"Dad, I promise, I'll take you into the jungle again, but not now."

Trang grinned and stepped into the cage. "I wonder why she doesn't want me along," he said.

"That's a big mystery," replied Jerry with a smile. Facing Tonya, he said, "Jim will be down shortly." Then, he pressed a button and the winch inside the helicopter started pulling the cage skyward.

When they arrived on the chopper, Jerry took control and sent Jim down. "Call us when you're ready for pickup," he said.

"Will do," Jim replied, as he began his descent. Jim alertly looked into the surrounding trees while steadily dropping into the clearing. However, the leaves were so thick that he couldn't see beyond them. He wondered how many different kinds of creatures lived in the trees. What would Tonya show him?

She was now only ten yards below him. He looked down at her. She was smiling and seemed filled with enthusiasm. Jim returned the smile and thought, she sure is beautiful.

16

Momentarily, Jim landed, stepped out of the cage, and pressed a button to send it back to the hovering helicopter. He turned and began walking toward Tonya, but she didn't wait for him, she met him halfway. They stopped a few feet apart and silently looked into each others eyes. The eye contact was electrifying. Involuntarily, they stepped into a tight embrace followed by a tender, loving kiss. "Welcome to my world," Tonya whispered.

"This isn't the kind of welcome I was expecting."

"I wasn't planning to greet you this way; it just happened."

"I'm very happy that it did," responded Jim, while still holding Tonya in a warm embrace.

"I am too," she whispered softly. Looking into Jim's eyes, Tonya exuded a kind of sweetness that captivated Jim and filled him with desire. Unable to resist her charm, Jim kissed her passionately, freely allowing his rapidly growing desire to flow into the kiss. He felt a mild tremble pass through her. She sighed and seemed to grow weak in his arms. Jim held her with a gentle kind of strength that firmly supported her.

"This is all happening so fast," Tonya whispered. "We just met and you're knocking me off my feet."

"Are we moving too fast for you?"

"No, I like what you're doing to me. You have me churning inside, and I love it."

"What do you think you're doing to me?"

"I know what's happening to you, but I want to hear you tell me."

"You've got me burning up with desire, and I don't know how much longer I can control myself."

Tonya snuggled tightly against Jim. "Who said you have to control yourself?" she asked sweetly.

"No one," responded Jim, breathing hard.

"What are we waiting for?" Tonya asked, with her very being radiating the inner glow of overpowering passion.

"Where can we go that will be safe?"

Tonya closed her eyes and used her telepathic powers to search the surrounding jungle. A half-minute went by. "We'll be safe for a while, and we can go over there." Tonya pointed at some giant ferns. "There's a soft bed of moss in that fern garden. We'll be comfortable there."

Grasping Jim's right hand, Tonya led him toward the ferns at the edge of the forest. The ferns were nine feet tall. Their large fronds were forest green and made a natural umbrella over the moss bed. Pushing the fronds apart, Jim and Tonya entered the secluded natural garden.

A half-hour later, they emerged from seclusion. "I've never been made welcome like that before," Jim said.

"I hope that wasn't a complaint."

"Definitely not, in fact, I'd like to go through the welcoming pro-cedure again."

"So soon?"

"I might need to catch my breath first."

Tonya smiled, "I'm ready anytime you are."

"Why don't we go for a walk in the jungle first?"

"Are you more interested in the jungle than in me?"

"You fascinate me, and the jungle is your home. I will learn more about you if you show me why you enjoy the jungle so much."

"I was only teasing you, but that was a great comeback. What would you like to see?"

"This whole area is new to me, so show me the things that are of greatest interest to you."

"Right now, food is of interest to me. I'm hungry, how about you?"

"I'm starving, what's good to eat around here?"

"Fruit, nuts, berries, and mushrooms are plentiful. Some plants grow tubers that are quite tasty. Streams and ponds have fish in them, but that requires a campfire. I'm not into eating raw fish."

"Let's save the fish dinner until we get to Pioneer Island."

"Did you just invite me to the island?"

"Yes, do you want to come?"

"That depends."

"On what?"

"On what kind of welcome I will get."

"What kind of welcome do you want?"

Tonya smiled invitingly.

"It's going to be difficult for me to top the welcome you gave me, but I'll try."

"Okay, I accept your invitation. Now, let's find something to eat."

Holding hands, Tonya and Jim walked to the north end of the clearing. Several squirrel nut bushes were growing in a sunny area at the edge of the forest. They were healthy and loaded with nuts. "Let's start with these," Tonya said.

A few minutes after they started eating the delicious nuts, Jim's communicator beeped. It was Jerry. "I hope I'm not interrupting anything, but an emergency has come up, and we need to go back to Pioneer Island. How long will it take you to get to the clearing?"

"We're in the clearing," Jim replied.

"Good, we're on the way."

"What's the emergency?"

"I'll explain after we pick you up. See you in 20 minutes."

"We'll be ready."

Speaking to Tonya, Jim asked, "Are you ready to visit Pioneer Island?"

"Will I be with you?"

"Yes."

"Then, I'm ready. Why are we leaving so soon?"

"I don't know. All Jerry said was an emergency has come up, and he would explain later."

"I hope it's not serious."

"He sounded like it is."

Twenty minutes later, Tonya and Jim heard the sound of a hovering helicopter. They looked up and saw the cage descending. When it arrived, they stepped into it and were lifted to the helicopter.

Jim entered the cockpit. "What's the big emergency?" he asked Jerry.

"We have to go to Alpha Centauri B."

"Why?"

"Rex called. There are terrorists operating in his area, and they've kidnapped his wife, son, and daughter."

"What do the terrorists want?"

"I think they want our starship."

"Why do you think that?" Jim asked.

"They've told Rex that he has to find them a ride back to their homeland, or he'll never again see his family alive."

"The Great War totally destroyed Rex's country, so they have no way to return the terrorists to their homeland."

"That's the point, and the terrorists know that. They also know, or should know, that Rex and his wife Shannon have been in daily contact with us. They should know that Rex will ask us for help. If we agree to help, that will bring us and our starship to them."

"And you think they want revenge for what we did to them?"

"That's a possibility," stated Jerry. "We did blast their chemical warfare weapons out of existence."

"Revenge might be their objective, but they still have the problem of getting to our starship, which will be in orbit. How are they going to do that?"

"That's what we have to figure out. When we get home, we'll have a meeting to brainstorm that question and develop our strategy."

"You need to have your chief engineer at that meeting," stated Trang. "I have direct experience at confronting his military mind, and he's good."

"Mike and his wife Michelle will be there," responded Jerry. "Michelle has been in daily contact with Rex and Shannon. She understands their language and has taught them English."

Chapter Two

TIME: Day 44, 5:30 PM

After returning to Pioneer Island, Jerry called a meeting to discuss the emergency on Zebron, the second planet of Alpha Centauri B. This planet was originally designated B-2 by the earth people before they learned its name from Zeb.

When everyone was present, Jerry faced his colleagues and said, "As most of you already know, Rex's family has been captured by terrorists. They're demanding that Rex provide them with a ride to their homeland, or they'll kill his family. The problem Rex has is that his country was destroyed by the Great War, and he has no way to meet the demand. Rex's only option is to ask us for help, and I believe the terrorists know that. That's why I think their true objective is to bring us back to Zebron, so they can capture our starship."

"The Great War is over," stated Michelle. "Maybe they do want nothing more than a ride home."

"No way!" exclaimed Zonya. "Those people are fanatics. For them, the war will never be over. They don't want to go home. They would rather stay in my homeland, so they can kill and destroy."

"She's right," declared Zeb. "Jerry's conclusion is justified."

(Note: Zeb and Zonya are from Rex's country on Zebron and are not yet fluent in English. Michelle has learned their language from Rex and his wife Shannon. In this dialog, Michelle is the translator for Zeb and Zonya.)

"We have to rescue Shannon and her children," Michelle pleaded. "They are our friends."

"Do you think we should attempt to rescue them even at the risk of losing our starship?" Mike asked.

"How are they going to get to the Challenger?" questioned Michelle. "It will be in orbit, and they'll have no way to get to it."

"We don't know that for sure," responded Mike, "but if their country does have a way to fly into space, I can easily destroy their spacecraft."

"I don't think they would try to get to us that way," Jerry said. "They already know the destructive power of our antimatter particle-beam gun."

"That's true, so how can they possibly capture the Challenger?" Michelle asked.

"I don't know," replied Jerry. "Because we just simply will not allow them to capture it, but they must have a plan that they think will work. And we have to figure out what that is."

"I know how they could put us in a difficult position," stated Mike.

"Let's hear it," Jerry said.

"Suppose we agree to their demand for a ride home, and they come out of hiding. To make sure we do what they want, they've attached bombs to Shannon and her children. That would force us to comply with their wishes and board our shuttle for the journey to their homeland. But before we take off, they tell us that they don't want to go home, and demand to be taken to our starship."

"That would present us with a tough choice," acknowledged Jerry. "We either take them to the Challenger, or we watch them blow up Rex's family."

Michelle cringed and said, "That would be horrible. How can people be so evil?"

"When it comes to infidels, these people are ruthless, cold-blooded killers," stated Zonya. "They will stop at nothing to accomplish their goals."

"Capturing the Challenger has to be their objective," Zeb said. "With its antimatter particle-beam gun, they could wipe out all opposition."

"That means all of us," stated Zonya. "They've already destroyed Zebron, so after killing us, they could use the Challenger to transport their fanatical followers to this planet. Then, they could plunder the life that's here."

"We have to outsmart them and find a way to rescue Rex's family without putting our starship at risk," Jerry said.

"That means finding the terrorists and killing them before they have a chance to kill Rex's family," stated Zonya.

"Does Rex have any idea where they are?" Mike asked.

"He thinks they have a base hidden in the jungle south of his home," replied Michelle.

Tonya's face lit up when she heard the word jungle. "If they're hiding in the jungle, I can find them," she said. "Then, I can use the natural hazards of the jungle to defeat them."

"Are you volunteering for the mission?" Jerry asked.

"Yes."

"It will be extremely dangerous. You could be killed."

"They can't kill me if they don't know where I am."

"Yes, they can! You could step on a mine or trigger any number of different kinds of lethal devices they may've planted around their base."

"That's true, but when I'm one with the jungle, I sense things that are out of place, and I will find and avoid their booby traps."

"I don't like this," stated Trang. "We know nothing about them. They might be highly trained professionals with the skills that elite Special Forces soldiers have. You're not familiar with their weapons and what they're capable of doing."

"It's going to take a couple weeks to get there, and I can be given intensive training during that time."

"I still don't like it. They're expecting us, and they'll have concealed sentries around their base. They might spot you before you even know where they are."

"But Dad, I've often heard you say that in the jungle, I am as hard to find as a shadow on a dark night. Using my stealth techniques and telepathic powers, I will find them, but they will be unaware of my presence."

"You are very capable," Trang admitted, "but we don't know the capabilities of the enemy. One or more of them might also have telepathic skills."

"I can sense that ability in other people and guard against it," argued Tonya.

"And I can sense that you are determined to do this no matter what I say."

"It has to be done, and I am the best person for the mission."

"I will go with you," Jim said.

"I appreciate your offer to help, but I can't take you along. You distract me too much, and you do know what I mean."

Seated next to Tonya, Jim put his right arm around her and silently looked into her eyes for a few moments. Then, he said, "I believe we have something special, and I don't want anything to happen to you."

"We do have something special. We're in love and wildly excited about each other. There's no way I could tune in to the aura of the jungle with you at my side."

With the memory of the fern garden encounter still fresh in his mind, Jim said, "You're right. I can't be on the ground with you, but I will support you in other ways."

"I have a plan for doing that," stated Mike.

"I do too," responded Jim, "but what do you have in mind?"

"You are an excellent helicopter pilot with daredevil skills, and we need to create a diversion. We need to convince the kidnappers that we're planning to come after them with a commando raid. Planning a defense for that will keep them busy while Tonya carries out her mission."

"First we have to locate them," stated Jerry. "The jungle is a very big place. We need to get Tonya close enough to the terrorists' hideout, so she can find them. On the way to B-2, we'll figure out how to do that."

"When are we leaving?" Mike asked.

"Just as soon as we determine what equipment to take along and who will be on the mission."

"Count me in," stated Trang. "I have a score to settle with those people."

"What do you mean?" Jerry asked. "They've never been here."

"They haven't, but their country sent the people here who shot up my shuttle and grounded it until you came along. Two of my people were almost killed in that attack."

"You're welcome to join us. After the gutsy way you captured me with empty guns, I have to believe that you have a few tricks up your sleeve that we can use."

Trang grinned at Jerry and said, "You can count on that."

"I also have a few tricks up my sleeve that you might be able to use," offered Geniya. "En route, I will discuss them with Mike to see if he can build what I need."

"Don't you need to stay here?" Trang asked. "We need to begin the rehabilitation of our people that we rescued from Aphrodite."

"Akeyco and the rest of our medical staff should be able to handle that. If any problems come up, they can call me, and we can discuss them."

"That's a good plan," agreed Trang.

Speaking to Jerry, Zonya said, "I realize these terrorists aren't the people who caused so much grief for Zeb and me, but their fanatical religion is to blame. We must destroy them, because they will strike again if we let them live."

"The purpose of our mission isn't to destroy the terrorists," stated Jerry, "it is to rescue Rex's family."

"I know," responded Zonya, "but these people are fanatics and they will kill and destroy until they are dead. We must kill them and rescue Rex's family. And I can help."

"How?" Jerry asked.

"I grew up near Rex's home, and I am familiar with the area. I speak Rex's language and the language of the enemy."

"Are you prepared to be a member of our commando team?"

"Yes, and I am qualified. I had military training before leaving Zebron to come here. Also, while living alone on this savage planet, I found a way to survive in the jungle and raise two babies to adulthood. I believe my record speaks for itself."

"You've definitely demonstrated the tenacity to overcome all hazards," stated Jerry.

"You need to take me along too," Zeb said. "I am also from Rex's country. I speak the language, and I am fluent in the enemy's language. I've also had military training."

"You can't go into combat," stated Connie. "Your ankle is still in a cast. It'll be a couple weeks before it's healed."

"It's probably going to take two weeks to get to Zebron," argued Zeb. "My ankle should be healed by then."

"That's possible," admitted Connie.

"If it's not healed, I can still be on the Challenger and play a support role. While orbiting Zebron, we'll be weightless, and my ankle isn't going to slow me down any."

"He's right about that," Jerry said to Connie, "and he does have skills and knowledge that we'll need."

Connie nodded, and Jerry said to Zeb, "The doctor has given her okay. You're on the team."

"I also have to be on your team," declared Connie. "You're going into combat and you might need my medical skills."

"I hope we don't, but I do want you along."

"Are you actually going to carry out a commando raid?" Michelle asked. "I'm worried. I don't want to lose Mike."

Mike and Jerry made eye contact; then, Mike said, "We can't guarantee that we won't lose anyone, myself included, but we are going to try to anticipate all contingencies. We will outsmart the enemy, and we have an awesome array of technology and equipment to work with."

"But are you actually going to carry out a commando raid?"

"That depends on how successful Tonya is, but we do have to put the forces in place to convince the enemy that this is our plan."

"All of my people are good with weapons," stated Trang. "But there are three guys who are exceptionally good at sneaking around in the jungle, and they are good trackers."

"Let's take them along," responded Jerry. Turning to Mike, Jerry asked, "How many people do we want on the ground?"

"That question would be easier to answer if we knew more about the enemy: like, how many are there and what kind of weapons do they have?"

"Their numbers don't have to be very large to carry out what we think their mission is. Five or six highly skilled, well-armed people would be adequate. Their force could, of course, be much larger than that. We just don't know."

"It could even be smaller," commented Mike. "A devastating 30-year war was fought. It seems like all terrorist cells would've taken part in that war and suffered casualties. It seems very unlikely that there could be any large cells left."

"For planning purposes, let's assume a minimum of three and a maximum of ten to fifteen," stated Jerry.

"If that's the case, I think two six-member commando teams can do the job. Anyway, our objective isn't to defeat them with numerical superiority; our objective is to defeat them with strategy, technology, and superior weapons."

"Jim can insert the teams with the helicopter when we figure out where to put them," stated Jerry. "And that brings me to the next problem. We need to find a safe place to land our shuttle that's within helicopter range of Rex's home."

Mike displayed a large area on the video screen. "This might be a secure place to operate from," he said, pointing at a large lake. "It's about 12 miles wide by 16 miles long. Because of the totality of the Great War, I doubt the terrorists would have access to the kind of weapons that could reach us at the center of that lake. It seems like missiles and artillery would've been expended long ago."

"That might be a dangerous assumption," Jerry said. "However, that lake is 90 miles from Rex's home. Because of the infrastructure destruction, it seems like the terrorists have to be on foot, which means they're not likely to be at that lake planning to ambush us."

"You might be right about them being on foot," stated Moose. "When I explored Zebron with radar, I did not find any moving vehicles: no aircraft, no ships, no trucks, no cars, nothing. I did find plenty of destroyed bridges and neglected highways."

"The long war also took a very heavy toll on animal life," noted Dianne. "It's possible that they don't even have horses to ride."

"If we assume they're on foot, their hideout should be near Rex's home," commented Jerry. "We have excellent recon data for that area. Back when Rex was telepathically communicating with Dianne, we tried to pinpoint his location. Now we can use that data to try to locate the terrorists' camp."

Speaking to Moose, Jerry said, "I want you to look at the topography and identify the ideal places to locate a base camp."

"You got it," replied Moose. "But in addition to being on foot, there is another possibility we need to consider."

Moose paused briefly while he reduced the land area shown on the video screen to a one-mile radius around Rex's home. "As you can see, there is a river near Rex's home that flows from north to south. With a couple canoes or small boats, the terrorists could easily have gone downriver 50 miles or even 100 miles or more."

"What you're saying is possible," Michelle said. "But Rex told me that he thinks the terrorists have a base camp in the jungle south of his home."

"But that could be 50 to 100 miles south of his home," argued Moose. "As you can see, there is jungle all along this river. Has Rex ever been more specific about where he thinks the terrorists are?"

"No, he hasn't, so maybe he just doesn't know."

"Or he might know and just isn't saying," commented Jerry. "He might be worried the kidnappers are listening to our communication and doesn't want to give away anything."

"Rex has good reason to be worried," stated Michelle. "When the kidnappers captured Shannon, they probably ended up with her communicator."

"Would Rex know that?" Jerry asked.

"He most likely would, because Rex and a friend were on a field trip when the kidnapping took place, and Shannon always wore her communicator when Rex was in the jungle, so she could stay in touch with him."

"Does Rex make a lot of field trips?" Jerry asked.

"Yes, he does. He's a veterinarian and a scientist. He studies the life that survived the Great War."

"That being the case, he should be familiar with the countryside and have some idea where the terrorists are."

"I believe he does," Michelle said. "I wish he could tell us."

"Maybe he'll find a way to let us know," Jerry said. "Let's try to read between the lines in all of his messages. There might be some hidden meaning there."

"Good idea," replied Michelle. "When are we leaving?"

"I'd like to leave yet tonight."

"Does your starship have enough fuel?" Trang asked. "Mine is crippled, but it is fully fueled. We can transfer some to your ship if need be."

Jerry turned to Mike and said, "I want to accelerate at 1g until we're halfway there and then decelerate the rest of the way. Let me know if we need more fuel and how long it will take to get there."

Mike reached for his communicator and accessed the Challenger's flight control computer. In just a few seconds, he said, "Zebron is currently 2.45 billion miles from here, and it will take 14 days and 16 hours to get there. Also, our fuel reserves are low."

Speaking to Trang, Jerry said, "I accept your offer. Let's make the fuel transfer tonight."

Speaking to everyone, Jerry said, "I want those who are going on this mission to be onboard our shuttles by 8:30 PM. We'll take off at that time and go to the Challenger. The personnel shuttle will come back down. The Challenger will rendezvous with Trang's starship to take on fuel; then, we'll leave for Alpha Centauri B."

"Two weeks is a long time," Michelle said. "How do we persuade the terrorists to not torture Shannon and her kids until we get there?"

"Send a message to Rex. Tell him that we'll be there in 18 days and that we'll give the kidnappers a ride home if their captives have not been harmed."

"But Mike just said that we'll be there in 14 days and 16 hours."

"I don't want the terrorists to know that. Tell Rex 18 days."

"Okay," Michelle replied.

TIME: Day 45, 4:00 AM

Captain's Log entry:

"We have just ignited our antimatter engines, and we are accelerating at 1g. We are going to Zebron, a war-ravaged planet orbiting Alpha Centauri B. Our mission is to rescue Rex's family from terrorists.

"Due to the urgency of this mission, everyone onboard has been up all night preparing for the earliest possible departure. We will now have a ten-hour rest period; then, we will begin detailed planning and preparation for action on Zebron."

TIME: Day 46, 8:00 AM

Captain's Log entry:

"We have reached a speed of 615 miles per second and have traveled 31 million miles. We are on schedule to arrive at Zebron in 13 days and 12 hours.

"Rex has informed the terrorists that we are on the way and will give them a ride home, if his family has not been harmed. He demanded that his wife and kids be allowed to speak to him, but the terrorists refused. They said no communication would be allowed until their ride home arrived."

After completing his log entry, Jerry went to the cafeteria with Connie. When they arrived, they found Trang and Mike sitting at a table eating breakfast.

"Mind if we join you?" Connie asked.

"Please do," replied Trang.

Connie and Jerry ordered breakfast from Moose, the on-duty chef. Then, they sat down with Trang and Mike.

"We've been discussing Rex's latest message," Mike said.

"What did you come up with?" Jerry asked.

"There are two obvious reasons why the kidnappers would deny communication between Rex and his family. In the worst case, Rex's family is dead, and the terrorists are trying to keep that secret, so they can bluff us into coming to Zebron."

"I find it hard to believe that they would've killed them," stated Trang. "Living hostages are far more valuable than dead victims."

"That brings us to the possibility that the terrorists have split up," commented Mike. "Perhaps, they have a spokesperson, who is in contact with Rex from a location that is close enough to Rex, so that his activities can be observed, while the main group is holding his family at a more distant location. Communication between Rex and his family cannot be allowed because the origin of the radio signal could be located, and that would reveal the hideout."

"I think we should assume that to be the case," stated Jerry. "It is what makes the most sense."

"I agree," Mike said, "and that means the terrorist in contact with Rex will see our arrival."

"How do we use that to our advantage?" questioned Jerry. "What do we want him to see? How can we mislead him?"

"Give me some time to think about that, and I'll give you some good answers."

"How much time do you need?"

"I'll get back to you by early afternoon."

"Good."

"There is something about this that worries me," Connie said.

"Like what?" Jerry asked.

"Rex's telepathic powers are truly phenomenal. He should be able to communicate with his family telepathically and find out if they're okay. Since he's not able to reach them, they might be dead."

"Not necessarily," argued Trang. "If they're being held deep underground, they would be cut off from telepathic contact. Also, Rex lives in a very hilly area. A large hill between Rex and his family would make telepathic contact difficult."

"There is another possibility," suggested Mike, "and that's deception. Rex might suspect that some of the terrorists have telepathic powers. If he attempts telepathic contact, they would detect it. He might not want them to know about his ability, so he demanded permission to talk to his family."

"That makes sense," agreed Connie, "but when Rex's family was captured, they were traumatized. Their emotional energy would've been sky-high. Rex should've been able to sense that and the direction they went. He might even know where they are."

"That's possible," responded Mike, "but he can't tell us because the terrorists might be listening."

"If he knows where they are, why doesn't he attempt a rescue?" Connie asked.

"The obvious answer is that he has decided that he doesn't have the capability to be successful," Mike replied. "A failed attempt would most likely get his family killed."

"It must be ripping his heart out to not be able to do anything except sit there and wait for us," commented Connie.

"He's in a tough situation," agreed Mike, "but he is a coolheaded thinker, and he will have some rescue plans worked out by the time we arrive. And he probably has some key information that he's holding until we get there."

"Without that information, we can't finalize our rescue strategy until we land and talk to Rex," stated Jerry. "What we need is a spy on the ground to sneak in and make contact with Rex without the terrorists knowing about it."

"Zonya is the only one who might be able to pull that off," Mike said. "She grew up in that area."

"Our helicopter was designed for quiet operation," stated Jerry. "So we should be able to insert her without being heard. The problem will be to avoid being seen. We'll have to look at the terrain and plot the best path to the best insertion point."

"I can do that," volunteered Moose, who had been listening to the conversation.

"You need to work with Jim on that project," stated Jerry.

"Will do."

"Just don't bring the chopper in over the terrorist hideout."

"How do I avoid that when we don't know where they are?"

"All you can do is avoid the areas that look like good places for a base camp and then trust to good luck."

"It might not matter if we fly over them," Mike said. "They can't react to our over-flight without revealing their location. They can't even call the person spying on Rex to let him know we're on the way. If they make that mistake, we'll know where they are."

"Just the same, I'd like to keep our arrival secret from all of them until after we talk to Rex."

"I'll take a look at the terrain and see what I can do," Moose said.

"There's another possibility we need to consider," stated Trang.

"What's on your mind?" Jerry asked.

"We've been assuming that most of the terrorists are at their secret camp with their captives and that only one or two are spying on Rex. What if we're wrong? What if only one or two are guarding the captives and the rest are staked out around Rex's home?"

"That would mean they plan to ambush us when we arrive," responded Jerry.

"But Rex has very good telepathic powers," argued Connie. "He would sense their presence and warn us."

"What if Rex and his family are being held captive in their home?" questioned Trang. "What if the terrorists control Rex's activities by threatening to torture his family?"

"Then, Rex could not warn us," responded Connie. "The terrorists would probably kill his family if he did that."

"There's no *'probably'* about it," stated Mike. "The terrorists would kill Rex and his family if Rex sounded a warning. They are being used to bring us to the scene. If Rex does anything to keep us from showing up, then he and his family would no longer be of any use to the terrorists."

"That would present Rex with a tough choice," Connie said. "He could play along with the terrorists' plans to kill some of us and capture our starship, or he could sacrifice himself and his family."

"I believe that he would play along with the terrorists," stated Jerry. "He would assume that we are smart enough to figure out all possibilities and plan for them."

"There is one very bad possibility that we have to plan for," stated Trang. "And that is the possibility that their only goal is revenge. You did destroy their doomsday chemical weapons and the people operating them. Revenge might be a very important part of their dogma. Their mission might be to kill as many of us as possible, even at the cost of their own lives. They might be on a suicide mission."

"If revenge is their objective, Rex and his family will be killed when we arrive," Jerry said. "Then, they'll start killing us in a fierce suicide attack with all weapons at their disposal. This possibility makes it more important than ever that we get a spy into the area without being discovered."

"We'll figure out how to do that," Moose said.

"Also, we need to arm our helicopter with some devastating firepower," stated Mike. "And I will do that."

"There is one more thing I want you to do," stated Jerry. "I want you to arm our shuttle; just in case, they do have the ability to attack us in the middle of the big lake that we'll be operating from. I want smart weapons that can reach well beyond the shores of the lake."

"I will design and make some."

At that moment, Geniya arrived. Facing Mike, she said, "I have a project I need your help with."

"I hope it's something I can do."

"I've heard that you have a habit of making the difficult look easy."

"Uh oh, it sounds like I'm being set up for a tough job."

"Maybe, maybe not, how good is your nanotechnology?"

"That's a wide-open question. What do you want me to make?"

"My daughter wants to defeat the terrorists using the jungle's natural hazards. I want to give her some tools to supplement what the jungle has to offer."

"I recall you saying that you had a few tricks up your sleeve. I sense that they might be something deadly."

"They could be, but I'm also thinking reconnaissance. I want to build mechanical replicas of a couple large insects that are common on Zebron. I need some mechanical hornets to deliver drugs and some mechanical dragonflies to gather information."

Mike's brain quickly raced through the possibilities. "What a brilliant idea!" he exclaimed. "Dragonflies and hornets are common in Rex's area. I've seen them in some of the video he has sent us."

"So how advanced is your nanotechnology? Can you make a mechanical dragonfly with cameras for eyes and microphones for ears?"

"I have only two weeks to design it, build it, and test it. But if I'm successful, all we'll need is an open door or window, and we'll be able to fly into Rex's home and look around."

"That's half of my project. The other half is a mechanical hornet to deliver a potent drug that I've brought along."

"I hope it's very potent, because a hornet will only be able to inject a few drops."

"That's all that is needed."

"What effect will the drug have?"

"It will destroy an individual's ability to fight for at least a day, maybe two."

"How does it do that?"

"It causes the injected person to go into a state of hibernation. Body temperature drops dramatically and pulse goes down to five or six beats per minute. Blood pressure also drops."

"How did you come up with a drug that does that?"

"It's produced naturally in our bodies. Here's a case that you're familiar with. Twelve days ago, when Akeyco sustained a serious head injury, she dropped into hibernation. It's a natural self-preservation mechanism. In her case, it slowed down the swelling of bruised brain tissue. We've been able to isolate and concentrate the chemical that induces hibernation. We've also made a synthetic version that's even more potent."

"How fast does the drug take effect?"

"A few minutes after injection, a patient starts to get sleepy. A couple minutes later, the patient passes out and begins dropping into hibernation."

"I see some super possibilities here," Mike said. "I see a terrorist feeling a sting on the back of his neck. He sees the hornet fly away and thinks he's the victim of a bee sting, so he cusses and ignores it. Most important, he does not sound an alarm. When he starts to get sleepy, he sits down to rest and is soon out cold."

Speaking to Jerry, Geniya asked, "Does this qualify as one of the tricks up my sleeve that I promised you?"

"It definitely does. If we can get these bugs operational on time and combine them with Tonya's talents in the jungle, we should have the winning edge that we need to neutralize the terrorists without getting Rex's family killed."

"I have lots of projects to do and only two weeks to do them in," stated Mike. "But we have some amazing equipment in the shop, so I should be able to get everything done."

"Trang and I will help you."

"I can help too," offered Moose.

TIME: Day 52, 12:05 PM

Captain's Log entry:

"We have reached a speed of 3,863 miles per second and have traveled 1,225,000,000 miles. We have just started 1g deceleration, which will continue for seven days and eight hours. At that time we will arrive at B-2.

"We have been in contact with Rex several times each day, but we have gained no new information, at least not directly. We have asked him numerous questions in an attempt to get answers where we could read between the lines for hidden messages. Some of his responses seem to be carefully scripted, like he's being told what to say. We are becoming convinced that Rex and his family are being held captive in their home and that we will be ambushed when we arrive.

"Mike has designed and built mechanical bugs, and we are flight testing them to find and correct design problems. One innovation was to make their wings out of paper-thin solar cells. The tiny batteries in the bugs allow only several minutes of operation, so the solar cells are necessary to recharge the batteries.

"Tonya and Zonya will be our spy team, and they are training intensely for their mission. Zeb and Zonya are working hard to improve their English skills. The rudimentary understanding of the language they came into this mission with could lead to communication errors and catastrophe in a combat situation."

TIME: Day 58, 8:00 AM

Captain's Log entry:

"To divert the terrorists from our real plans, we've decided to convince them that we plan to land on Lake Jamalya, a small lake near Rex's home. We believe they are planning to ambush us when we arrive, so if we can convince them that we will land on Lake Jamalya; then, their ambush plans will be made around that, and they won't be prepared for our covert action."

At a meeting in his office, Jerry said, "We need a convincing misinformation strategy. We need to feed them incorrect information in a way that sounds authentic. Above all else, we must be careful to not oversell it, because that could create suspicion."

"Why don't we just tell Rex that we would like to land on Lake Jamalya," Mike suggested.

"Have we ever told Rex that our shuttles operate from water?" Jerry asked.

"My wife has had extensive communication with Shannon and Rex. She did tell them that we live on an island that our shuttles land next to. Rex responded with a list of questions about our shuttles that I answered."

"So if we tell Rex we want to land on Lake Jamalya, he'll believe us because he knows how our shuttles operate. If the terrorists are holding him captive and question him, he'll be able to give them a believable, matter-of-fact explanation about the need to land on water and how it's done."

"I believe he can, so I will send him a message telling him we plan to land on Lake Jamalya. I will ask him if the lake is at least fifteen feet deep throughout and if the river ever brings any large floating debris into the lake. Then, we'll see what response we get."

TIME: Day 58, 9:30 AM

Message received from Rex:

"If you stay at least 50 yards away from the shoreline, Lake Jamalya is never less than 20 feet deep. The lake is currently free of large driftwood, but the river sometimes does bring in large pieces. I will keep you posted."

Jerry listened to the message and thought, Rex's English is getting pretty good, and that makes me wonder about the terrorists. Even if Rex is their captive, he should be able to tell us anything he wants to, because the terrorists can't possibly understand English. Unless, one of them was a trusted friend of Rex and Shannon, and was privy to their communication with us, and has learned enough English to know what Rex is telling us. Then, Rex could only tell us what he's being told to tell us.

Maybe Rex and his family are being held by a power hungry colleague who put together a gang of locals to capture my starship. In that case, the enemy I must defeat might not be a group of skilled professional terrorists. If they aren't fanatics from the other side in the Great War, it might not be necessary to kill them. There has already been too much death and destruction on Zebron.

TIME: Day 59, 2:00 PM

Captain Jerry Jerontis assembled his troops in his office to discuss mission details. After everyone was seated, he said, "In a few hours we will arrive at Zebron, a full three days ahead of our advertised arrival time."

On a large video screen, Jerry displayed a map of the region Rex lived in. It was made from reconnaissance images stored in the computer. He pointed at a large lake 90 miles east of Rex's home. "This is the lake we hope to land on," he said. "We've named it Lake Shannon in honor of one of the people we're here to rescue. Because of the distance involved, we should not encounter terrorists there. However, we'll do everything we can to avoid detection, just in case they do have spies in that area.

"The first thing we'll do is land a marine explorer on Lake Shannon during the nighttime darkness. It will only take the marine explorer a few hours to determine if the lake is suitable for a shuttle landing. If it is we'll land at night coming in from the east."

With a pointer, Jerry drew a line on the screen to a hilltop located six miles from Rex's home. "Jim will fly our first team to the valley east of this hilltop and then return to the shuttle. We have no reason to believe that terrorists will be waiting for us in this area, but we must be prepared for that possibility."

Tonya raised her right hand to get Jerry's attention. Then, she said, "If there are terrorists there, and if they are above ground, I will be able to telepathically sense their presence."

"Is that guaranteed?" Jerry asked.

"I have never met a human that I couldn't detect telepathically."

"Good, Jim will fly the approach that you need to check out the area. When you are satisfied that it's clear, you and your team will be lowered to the ground."

Speaking to Tonya, Jim said, "Get together with me after this meeting, and we'll work out a flight plan."

"That won't be a problem. We're together all the time anyway."

"At this time tomorrow, we won't be together, and you'll be in grave danger."

"I can handle it. In fact, I'm looking forward to the challenge."

"Don't take the challenge lightly," Jerry warned. "Your life will be on the line. Any mistake you make could be fatal."

"I know, but I will prevail."

Looking into Tonya's eyes for a few moments, Jerry sensed the depth of her conviction and admired her courage. "I believe you will be successful," he said.

Tonya smiled in appreciation of Jerry's confidence in her and said, "We'll rescue Rex and his family, and we won't lose anyone."

"Mission success depends largely on your ability to get the information we need. We have three days for this part of the mission, so I urge you to use utmost patience and not take any unnecessary risks. If you run into an insurmountable problem loaded with too much risk, I want you to withdraw, so we can discuss a new approach."

"Understood."

"Your first task will be to scout a path to Rex's home and lead your team as close as you think they can go without being discovered. Then, you will scout Rex's vicinity on your own to get the information we need to develop a rescue plan. Our second team will remain on the shuttle until you complete your intelligence mission. Is there anything about this that you want to discuss?"

"No, I will be in the jungle, and I will be at home there."

Jerry made brief eye contact with each of his troops; then, he asked, "Does anyone have any questions or comments?"

"How well do you know Rex?" Geniya asked.

"Why do you ask that question?" Jerry asked.

"After we rescue Rex and his family, what if Rex says it's too dangerous to continue living on Zebron, and he asks you to bring him and his family to Alcent?"

"I see no reason why we can't do that."

"What if this whole kidnapping thing is a setup to misdirect our suspicion? What if Rex is the terrorist leader?"

"No way!" Michelle exclaimed with conviction.

"Can you absolutely guarantee that?" Geniya asked with equal conviction.

"I've been in constant communication with Rex and Shannon for several months, and there's no way that you can convince me that Rex is a terrorist."

"I'm not trying to convince you that he is. I'm just saying that it's a possibility that we have to consider."

"He just doesn't fit the terrorist profile," argued Michelle. "Rex and Shannon are my friends. They've been friendly and cooperative, and like I said, we've had constant open communication."

"And that means they are fully aware of this starship's capabilities," responded Geniya. "They know what they could do if they possessed it."

"That's true, but Rex does not have aggressive ambitions. He's not power-hungry."

"I hope you're right, but we can't possibly know that for sure."

"I know that for sure," Michelle shot back.

The room fell silent while everyone thought about the exchange between Geniya and Michelle. Eventually, Jerry broke the silence. "It would be an incredible hoax played on us if this whole kidnapping thing is a setup to bring us into the hands of a group organized by Rex, but we have to be aware of that possibility while we carry out our rescue mission."

Jerry made eye contact with Tonya. "I will keep that in mind while I investigate Rex's home," she responded. "I will look for clues to prove or disprove that possibility."

Jerry nodded and scanned the facial expressions of everyone else. "Are there any other questions or comments?"

After several seconds of silence, he said, "This meeting is adjourned. Let's get our mission done."

TIME: Day 59, 8:00 PM

Captain's Log entry:

"We have arrived at Zebron. To avoid being seen by the terrorists, we will enter an orbit that will not take us over Rex's home. Our announced arrival time is three days from now. By then, we need to determine what the terrorists have planned for us.

"The first thing we will do is land a marine explorer on Lake Shannon. It will be delivered by a landing capsule arriving from the east."

TIME: Day 59, 10:45 PM

On the Challenger's flight deck, Mike Johnson was monitoring the landing of the capsule carrying the marine explorer. The capsule was suspended below a para-wing that was currently 100 yards above Lake Shannon in the last leg of its approach glide. When the capsule had descended to just a few feet above the water, the para-wing pitched up into a stall that killed most of its velocity. With a splash, the capsule settled into the water, and its flotation collar quickly inflated.

A hatch in the side of the capsule popped open, and the tightly packaged marine explorer was ejected. Its pontoon inflated and its instruments came to life.

Underwater cameras, sonar equipment, an electric motor, and a battery pack were attached to the bottom of the pontoon. Solar cells, cameras, an instrument pod, a computer, and communications equipment were mounted on top the pontoon.

The automated explorer beamed a narrow, highly-directional signal to the communication satellite in geosynchronous orbit high above Zebron. The satellite was placed in orbit on the Challenger's previous visit to Zebron, so that Rex and Shannon could communicate with the earth people on Alcent.

While reviewing the initial data, Mike said, "We have a healthy marine explorer with all instruments functioning normally. And we have a deep lake, 360 feet at this location."

"And the sonar doesn't show any floating logs or other debris of consequence," added Jerry.

"It's all very encouraging," commented Mike.

"By morning, we'll have a pretty good picture of the central part of this lake," stated Moose, who had volunteered to stay up all night to explore Lake Shannon.

"I want to land when it's still dark," stated Jerry. "We'll come in from the east, and we could touch down right where the capsule landed if it's safe to land there. We need to find out, so I want you to run the explorer three miles west and then circle back to where you are now. If there aren't any hazards, I'll use the explorer for my landing beacon."

"You got it," responded Moose.

Chapter Three

TIME: Day 60, 3:35 AM

Jerry and Mike were seated at the controls in the cargo shuttle, which had just dropped below 30,000 feet on its way to Lake Shannon. Suddenly, the darkness was replaced by blinding light when a brilliant lightning bolt split the sky open in front of them. At that instant, the shuttle flew into a powerful updraft that violently jerked it upward, only to be hit almost immediately by an equally powerful downdraft that slammed it into freefall. Two seconds later, the shuttle was again shoved upward.

"This is bad!" Mike exclaimed. "I hope we survive this storm."

"Don't worry," responded Jerry. "This shuttle was designed to take punishment and keep right on going."

"I know, but the forces of nature can be rather frightening."

"Actually, the scattered thunder showers are a stroke of good luck. Hopefully, the sonic boom we're creating will be passed off as a thunderclap and be ignored by anyone who hears it."

"Since supersonic aircraft haven't operated on this planet for a good many years, that should be the case," agreed Mike.

"We don't know if the terrorists even have any agents in this area, but if we can land undetected, it won't matter if they do."

"I can't imagine anyone spotting us. Except for an occasional lightning bolt, it's pitch-black dark outside. Besides that, why would anyone be out and about at this time of the day?"

"I don't know. Stargazing is certainly out of the question."

Mike chuckled at the absurdity of stargazing during a drenching thunderstorm. Then, he said, "I guess the terrorists could be out looking for us if they happen to be suspicious about our announced arrival time and think we might be coming in early."

"I suppose they could be suspicious, but I'd sure hate to be down there trying to spot us in this weather. Without radar, it would be an impossible feat."

"I don't believe they have radar. We've been listening to all frequencies, and we haven't detected any."

"That means we should arrive undetected," Jerry said.

Several minutes later, the shuttle was over Lake Shannon. Looking out the side window, Mike said, "I still don't see anything, except the darkness."

Jerry sent a fifty-millisecond radio signal to the marine explorer. It responded with an equally brief signal that the shuttle's flight control computer instantly located and set course to land 200 yards beyond.

Mike deployed the shuttle's hydrofoils, which entered the water a minute later with the shuttle flying at 195 mph. The hydro-drogues deployed and quickly slowed the shuttle to less than 40 mph, causing it to settle into the water and float on its hull.

"We're here," announced Jerry, "and we have just enough darkness left to insert our first team."

Jerry flicked a switch to unlock the upper cargo bay doors and a second switch to open them. Mike remained in the cockpit while Jerry headed for the cargo bay. Jim was already there. While waiting for Jerry, he raised the elevator deck to its top position, where it would serve as a takeoff and landing deck for the helicopter. Jim, Jerry, and Trang prepared the helicopter for flight.

The first team boarded the helicopter. It was made up of Tonya and Zonya who would sneak into the area around Rex's home to scout the situation. They would operate from a base camp secured by Trang and his two best fighters. Also, Zeb no longer wore an ankle cast, so he would work with Trang and his people. Zeb's ankle was not yet 100 percent, but his fluency in the local language made him an important team member. Geniya was on the team to provide medical services if needed.

When the helicopter was ready for flight, Jim entered it and spoke to his passengers. "Make sure you're securely belted it. This could be a rough flight. There are numerous storm cells in the area and plenty of turbulent air. I will fly around the thunderstorms, but it's impossible to miss all the turbulence."

Jim sat in the pilot's seat and tightly fastened his seatbelt. Tonya sat in the copilot's seat where she could use her telepathic powers to search for terrorists who might be planning an ambush. The plastic bubble enclosure gave her excellent telepathic visibility.

"We still have enough darkness left to get there without being seen," commented Jim while starting the turbine.

"They could have night-vision goggles," responded Trang, who was sitting behind Tonya.

"That's possible," Jim admitted, "but I doubt it. The long war has destroyed most manufacturing, and the batteries needed to power night-vision goggles might not even be available."

"Good point," conceded Trang.

With the turbine now at full power, Jim lifted off and said, "Our greatest risk of being seen is when the sky is lit up by a lightning discharge, so I'm going to avoid the storm cells as best I can."

Jim headed west while climbing steadily to gain cruise altitude. To avoid the worst of the turbulent air, he flew a zigzag course around storm cells. Even so, the helicopter was knocked around by turbulence.

"This is a rough flight," commented Trang. "I hope this bird holds together."

"Don't worry," responded Jim. "It's rugged and can take lots of punishment."

"I hope that's also true for our commando squad. They're not going to be very effective when we arrive, if they're shook to pieces and banged up."

"My guess is that they're enjoying this rough ride. Personally, I think it's a blast."

"Jerry did say you enjoy stunt flying."

"Unfortunately, I can't do much of it. This is the only chopper we have, and we can't subject it to unnecessary risk."

"This mission is risky," stated Trang. "In the worst case, we could get shot down."

"Tonya has assured me that she can detect the enemy and keep us out of trouble."

"I sure can," she responded, "and I recommend we make the rest of the flight in silence, so I can concentrate without being distracted by your conversation."

"You got it," responded Jim as he looked at a map displayed on a video screen. His destination was denoted by a small red X on the map. His current location was denoted by a small red helicopter that was steadily moving toward the X. The coordinates for the planned insertion point had been programmed into the flight control computer, and the helicopter's inertial navigation system kept track of its position in spite of the buffeting and zigzag flight path. Even with the darkness and bad weather, Jim knew exactly where he was and where he needed to go.

As the minutes slowly passed by, the rough weather took its toll. It thoroughly shook up everyone, and the thrilling pleasure of being on a wild ride disappeared. It was replaced by a desire to stand on solid land.

Finally, after nearly an hour of zigzag flying, Jim and his commando team were only three miles from their destination. Despite the danger posed by the turbulent weather, Jim was now flying a low-level approach, staying well below the hilltops. The flight path had been plotted to keep hills between the helicopter and Rex's vicinity. If one of the terrorists had special telepathic powers, this flight path would make it difficult to detect the people approaching in the helicopter.

Tonya used her powers to search the surrounding hilltops and the valley below and ahead. She found nothing except a few animals.

Shortly, the helicopter was over the insertion area. Wearing night-vision goggles, Jim looked for a place to land and spotted a small meadow a couple hundred yards to his left. He headed toward it while Tonya intently searched the area with her telepathic powers. "It's clear," she said.

Jim flew over the meadow and dropped to a hover only a few inches above the ground. Wearing night-vision goggles, everyone hopped out with their equipment, and Jim quickly left the area following the same course that he came in on. The eastern sky already had the faintest tint of light, and the thunderstorm squall line would soon be out of the area. Jim wanted to be well away from the insertion point before he lost his cover.

On the ground, Trang led his commando team into the forest. Stringing a cord between two trees, they threw a canvass over it and staked its corners to the ground. This quickly provided a shelter for them and their equipment to ride out the remnants of the storm.

Tonya had a different plan. Speaking to the team, she said, "I am going to check out this area. I'll be back in a few hours."

"Want me to come along?" Zonya asked. "I am familiar with this territory."

"Thanks for the offer, but I need to do this first scouting trip by myself. I need to get a feel for the aura of this jungle, and I am better able to do that when I'm alone."

"Don't take any unnecessary risks," warned Trang, with Geniya at his side.

"Dad, the jungle is in my blood, and I know how to use it to my advantage."

"That's true, but I know you well, and I am concerned that you might try to do this rescue on your own. Remember that your objective is to gather information, so we can plan a rescue."

"Don't worry Dad; I'll get the info we need."

Geniya grasped Tonya's hands and said, "Our prayers are with you. Just be careful, and you will do just fine."

"Thanks, Mom."

With her concerned parents looking on, Tonya removed the bulky coveralls she had worn for the flight. Wearing only shorts and halter top, she quietly disappeared into the jungle, carrying her backpack and weapons.

Tonya moved slowly, stopping frequently to look around and investigate every little thing. Her night-vision goggles gave her excellent visibility.

She listened intently to the sounds made by various insects. She listened to the water dripping from the trees. In the distance, she heard the faint sound of a river flowing over rapids.

Tonya smelled the air. It had a rain-washed freshness to it. There was the scent of wild flowers, and the musty smell of the rain-soaked forest floor.

Telepathically, Tonya searched her surroundings, looking for the faintest indication of life. She wanted total familiarity with the aura of this jungle, so she could sense anything that was out of place.

Progress was slow, but Tonya steadily put more distance between her and camp. By the time she was a mile away, the storm system had blown through, and the sky was relatively free of clouds.

Tonya approached a small open area on the east side of a hill and searched it from within the forest using all of her senses and powers. When she was sure that it was safe, she entered the area, which was strewn with boulders, vines, and low-lying shrubs.

Spotting a large boulder, Tonya scrambled to its top and faced the eastern horizon. Alpha Centauri B was just beginning to peek over the treetops. Its orange rays colored the sky with an orange hue. This is beautiful but kind of eerie, she thought.

The gorgeous sunrise held Tonya's attention for several minutes while she soaked up the sights, sounds, and scents of her surroundings. When she felt that the aura of the area was imprinted on her mind, she decided to move on. But before going back into the forest, she took another look at the sky directly overhead. I'll never get used to this orange hue, she thought. It's just too alien. I much prefer the blue sky back on Alcent.

Entering the forest, Tonya headed downhill toward the sound of running water. She wanted to investigate the stream and find out what lived in it and next to it.

Several minutes later, she arrived at the bottom of the hill and found a small river flowing through rapids. The water looked so refreshing that Tonya was tempted to drink it, but Jerry had given strict orders not to drink this planet's water. It had been poisoned by monstrous chemical warfare weapons operating on the Equatorial Continent. Mike and Jerry had destroyed them with the Challenger's antimatter particle-beam gun creating hate-filled enemies who wanted revenge. Their agents were holding Rex's family.

Tonya continued to gaze at the rapids. The sight and sound of the rushing, splashing water was soothing. This is relaxing me in an almost hypnotic way, she thought. The water looks so good, and I am so thirsty. I've lived in the jungle for weeks at a time, and I've always drunk the water. It's been four months since Jerry destroyed those poison machines. It should be safe to drink the water by now, but Rex had said that it took six months for the poison to completely deteriorate.

Tonya thought about the incredible cruelty of the people who built and operated the chemical weapons. How could anyone indiscriminately poison an entire continent, she wondered. The poison did not affect all species. It killed people and the mammals that needed to drink water regularly. Most birds, insects, and cold-blooded creatures were not affected by the poison.

Being a jungle girl, Tonya had a deep respect for nature. She seethed with anger at the thought that people could be so fanatical that they were willing to kill much of the animal life in order to kill the few survivors of the Great War. But the people living on this continent were considered to be infidels, so they had to be killed at any cost.

The more Tonya thought about the situation, the more angry she became. "I will destroy the criminals holding Rex and his family," she declared. Then, she reached for the canteen hanging from her belt and drank from it.

Tonya followed the creek in the downstream direction. In 100 yards, the rapids came to an end, spilling into a slow moving pool. A small fish leapt out of the water and grabbed a dragonfly that had ventured too close. I am glad the poison didn't kill fish and insects, Tonya thought. At least there's some life that wasn't killed.

Backtracking a bit, Tonya found some rocks that she could use for stepping stones. Hopping from rock to rock, she crossed the creek. Looking up and down the creek, an open avenue between the trees caught her attention. The avenue was about 25 feet wide.

Why are there no trees growing in this lane, she wondered. Since the Great War, this planet's plant life has overrun everything. Rex said that genetic mutations caused by radioactivity produced some very aggressive, fast-growing plants, so why do I see a lane with no trees?

Tonya stepped to the center of the lane, dropped to her knees, and dug into the leaves. Just a few inches down, she found a hard surface. There's an old highway buried here, she concluded. When was the last time vehicles used this road, she wondered. Shannon had told Michelle that 99 percent of the population had been killed in the Great War, so it's possible that there hasn't been a vehicle on this road in 30 years. And it looks like no one has walked on it in quite some time either, because this litter of leaves has not been disturbed. This old road might be an easy route to Rex's home, but can I walk on it without leaving an easy-to-follow trail?

Walking softly and using great care to not drag her feet, Tonya walked back to the pool at the end of the rapids. There, she found a bare spot on the old road. It looked like asphalt. Looking downstream, Tonya noted that the creek and the road turned to the right.

She reached into her backpack and pulled out a map, which was made from orbital reconnaissance photos taken on Jerry's previous visit to Zebron. The hilltop near the landing site was marked on the map. Judging her distance from base camp and relating it to the map, Tonya fixed her position. The map had enough detail to show the rapids and the bend in the creek, which flowed into Jamal River a mile north of Rex's home. Jamal River flowed into and out of Lake Jamalya, which was only 200 hundred yards from Rex's home.

Can I safely follow these rivers to Rex's home? Tonya wondered. What are the terrorists expecting us to do? Where are their sentries? How many are there? Do they believe we aren't going to arrive for three more days? Do they think we're going to land on Lake Jamalya? What is my best route to Rex's home? Should I go back and get Zonya or should I do this alone?

Tonya thought about her options for a few moments. She knew what her father would want her to do, but an inner voice seemed to be urging her on.

I have to go forward on my own, she decided. I am going to follow this creek for a while and see how close to Rex's home I can get before I detect any of the enemy. Without any additional thought, Tonya slowly headed downstream, taking great care to not leave a trail or make any noise.

Three hours later, Tonya was halfway to Rex's home. So far, I haven't detected any large animals, she thought. But Rex said that most species are on the verge of extinction. What a contrast to the jungles on Alcent where animals are plentiful. All I've seen here are lots of birds and small animals. Apparently, they get their water from the food they eat and never drink the poisoned water.

Hearing a soft background buzz, Tonya noticed multitudes of insects, which just seemed to be busily doing their thing everywhere she looked. Their numbers mean that my mechanical bugs are not going to attract any attention, she concluded. The only risk is they'll be attacked by hungry birds.

Tonya entered a thick patch of brush near the creek. She sat down on a rock, closed her eyes, and listened to her surroundings. Then, she tuned out the sound and listened telepathically. The first thing she detected was the aura of a snake. It was getting stronger. It must be coming toward me, she thought. I wonder if it's poisonous.

Opening her eyes, Tonya looked in the direction the aura was coming from. Shortly, she saw the snake slithering toward her. It stopped and looked at her with its tongue rapidly darting out and back in. The snake coiled. Its fangs were dripping a milky fluid.

Uh oh, it's poisonous and it feels threatened, Tonya quickly concluded. Sitting perfectly still, Tonya telepathically transmitted calming thoughts to the snake, causing it to gradually become less agitated. Then, she switched to suggestions of drowsiness, and the snake gradually became placid. Its tail went limp and settled down. Your head is becoming extremely heavy, Tonya hypnotically suggested. You are very sleepy. The snake struggled to keep its eyes open and its head up. Tonya's telepathic, hypnotic onslaught continued. Soon the snake closed its eyes and its head settled down on top of its coiled body. Still, Tonya did not relent. You will sleep soundly until I wake you. Telepathically, Tonya entered the snake's brain ever more deeply. She planted a wakeup signal. You will sleep until you hear this signal.

When she was satisfied that the snake was out cold and would stay that way, Tonya stopped the hypnosis. Looking at the coiled snake, she judged it to be four to five feet long. She picked it up and placed it in her backpack. It's good that you're sleeping, she thought. I might have a job for you, and I want you to be well rested.

Tonya shouldered her pack and resumed following the creek. She stopped frequently to tune in to the jungle, but she detected nothing unusual.

An hour later, she came to a juncture in the creek where a stream flowed into it from the north. Tonya looked at her map. Rex's home is only a mile-and-a-half southwest from here, she determined, and Duck Lake is three-fourths of a mile to the north. And 100 yards ahead, I should find an old bridge crossing this creek.

A few minutes later, Tonya came to the bridge and saw that it was made out of wood that appeared to have been treated with a dark-colored preservative. This bridge looks like it hasn't been driven on in years, she noted. It's littered with leaves, but there's a footpath down the middle that's largely free of leaves. I haven't seen any animals, so that means that the people in this area must be using this bridge. But I haven't seen or detected any people either.

Telepathically, Tonya intently listened to her surroundings in an attempt to find people. This is really strange, she thought, I'm not detecting any people. Where is everyone? Did they leave with the arrival of the terrorists? Could it be that the only people currently using this bridge are the terrorists? But why aren't I detecting them? Maybe it's because there's a hill between me and Rex's home, and his home is partly underground. But it seems like the terrorists should have some sentries out and about; unless, they believe that we won't be here for another three days.

Tonya dropped to her knees and studied the foot trail leading to the bridge; then, she crossed the bridge and again studied the trail. This trail has been recently used, she concluded. Maybe the terrorists pass through here regularly. Maybe they're holding Rex's family in the Duck Lake area. It's close enough so that they could easily hike back and forth to Rex's home. Even a slow, lazy hike would take less than an hour.

Tonya had a decision to make. Which way should I go? She wondered. She stared in the direction of Rex's home for a few seconds; then, she took several steps in that direction and stopped. My inner voice is screaming at me. I need to explore the Duck Lake area before I scout Rex's home.

Tonya looked up the trail as far as she could see. Can I safely use this trail, she wondered. I'm not detecting anyone, so there must not be any sentries, but the trail could be mined or rigged with warning devices to set off alarms.

With no further thought, Tonya left the trail and picked her way through the jungle, heading toward Duck Lake. She moved slowly, using great care to not make any noise and to stay concealed. She stopped frequently to sense the aura of the jungle, but everything seemed normal.

After an hour of slow travel, Tonya arrived at Duck Lake. Its scenic beauty grabbed her attention, so she gazed out over the lake for a few moments to appreciate its natural beauty. Then, with sadness in her heart, she thought, what a tragedy that the water is poisonous to people and mammals. I must punish the agents of those responsible, and I know that some of them are here. I am not detecting them, but I know that they're here. I feel their presence. But where are they? Where would I hide if I were them? To conceal myself from telepathic detection, I would hide underground, and I would camouflage the entrance to make it difficult to see. So how can I find them? My best strategy might be to wait for a while. Maybe they will reveal themselves by coming out for some fresh air, or maybe they travel between here and Rex's home.

Tonya found a cliff overlooking the lake. Concealing herself among some bushes, she set her pack down and made herself comfortable, prepared to wait for several hours.

Alpha Centauri B was now high in the midday sky, and Tonya was hungry. Sitting on the leaf-strewn cliff top, she ate her lunch. Then, the drowsiness that sometimes comes after the midday meal hit Tonya, so she stretched out on a carpet of leaves to rest for a few minutes. Looking straight up, she thought, I don't think I could ever get used to this eerie orange sky.

It was a warm, pleasant, peaceful day in the Duck Lake area. The thunderstorms had moved on, and the sky was now filled with cumulus clouds. A gentle breeze blew through the trees, rustling the leaves. Birds were cheerfully singing against the background noise of a chorus of insects. Always at home in the jungle, Tonya drifted into a deep sleep. She had been up all night, and now, the lack of sleep caught up to her.

Two hours later, Tonya was abruptly jolted out of her sound sleep by screaming women. She did not understand the language, but she understood the emotions. She telepathically felt fear and anger coming from two women. The anger was coming from an older woman, and the fear seemed to be coming from a child.

Urgently, but carefully, Tonya crawled to the edge of the cliff and peered over it from behind a bush. She saw a woman struggling with a man. Tonya recognized her instantly; it was Shannon. A second man was ripping the clothes off of a struggling girl. It was Shannon's daughter, Kristi. She was trying to fight off her attacker, but he was husky, and Kristi was only twelve.

Tonya instantly became extremely angry at what was obviously a rape scene unfolding only 30 feet below her on the sandy beach of Duck Lake. She quickly drew her pistol, but decided she could not shoot. The risk of hitting Kristi or Shannon was too great. She shoved the gun back in its holster and opened her pack. She removed a box that contained six mechanical hornets and two control units.

With one control unit in each hand, Tonya launched two of the hornets and put them into a steep dive. She pulled them out of it only a few feet above the beach.

Kristi was the most urgent problem. She was so young, and her attacker was a big brute, who was only seconds away from raping her.

Tonya landed one of the hornets on a rock and flew the other one to Kristi's attacker. She guided the hornet to the man's right temple and injected the drug. He cussed at the stinging pain.

It would take a few minutes for the drug to work, so Tonya needed to distract him. She flew the hornet in front of the man's face and went for his right eye, but missed. The stinger hit the thin flesh on the cheek bone. There wasn't any drug left to inject, but the man again cussed as he swatted at the hornet. He missed because Tonya had already flown the hornet behind him. The bug was now buzzing between his legs heading for his testicles. This got his attention real quick, and he jumped to his feet to fend off the hornet attack. Kristi scrambled to her feet and ran toward her mother, who was still on her feet, but in the grip of her attacker.

With Kristi safe for a few moments, Tonya used the other hornet to sting Shannon's attacker in the back of his neck. He swatted at the hornet, but it had already flown away. The momentary distraction gave Shannon the opportunity she needed. Being held by only one hand, she was able to struggle free. Backing up a step, and being light on her feet, she jumped and did a double snap kick to the man's groin. The excruciating pain caused him to double over. Shannon quickly did a second double snap kick, this time to his face, stunning him for a few seconds. Before he could recover, Shannon grabbed a fist-sized rock and hit him in the head as hard as she could. All of her anger went into the blow, knocking the man unconscious.

The man who had attacked Kristi was violently angered by what Shannon did to his buddy, so he charged Shannon, hoping to knock her to the ground. But Shannon was too quick for him. She nimbly side-stepped away from the charge and stuck out one foot to trip the man, who went face first into the sand. Shannon attempted to strike him in the back of his head with the rock she still held, but he rolled over and grabbed her. Being very strong, he had complete control. He rolled over, pinning Shannon to the sand. He raised his upper body and was about to punch Shannon in the face, but Kristi jumped him from behind. However, Kristi was just a kid, and the brute of a man shrugged off her attack. Shannon struggled, but the man pinning her was just too heavy. She could not free herself. Kristi charged the man again, but he simply knocked her aside. Kristi fell next to the unconscious man and saw a hunting knife in his belt. She pulled the knife and circled behind Shannon's attacker, who saw the gleaming knife and jumped off Shannon to meet the attack. But he staggered on his feet and seemed to be disoriented. When he turned to face Kristi, his knees gave way, and he crumpled to the sand. He struggled to get up but could not. Consciousness faded; he was out cold. The drug injected by the mechanical hornet had done its job.

Shannon ran to the base of the cliff and picked up one of the rifles leaning against it. She chambered a cartridge and pointed the gun at the man who had attacked her. But she didn't pull the trigger because she saw the horrified look on Kristi's face and decided not to kill in front of her daughter.

Turning her attention to Kristi, Shannon saw that her naked daughter was battered and shaking. "This was a terrible thing for you to go through," Shannon said while putting her right arm around Kristi to comfort her. Speaking in a soft tone, Shannon gently asked, "Did you get raped?"

"No, but I almost did. It was horrible. Those men are evil." Kristi looked at her attacker, who was crumpled on the ground, out cold. Kristi became aware of the knife that she was still holding. She clenched it tightly, held it up, and looked at it. She moved closer to the unconscious man, stared at him, and angrily kicked him in the head. Then, she dropped to her knees next to the man and raised the knife above his neck. An inner struggle went on in Kristi's mind. Try as she might, she was unable to plunge the knife into her attacker's neck.

With tears streaming down her face, Kristi stood up and stepped into her mother's arms. Shannon tightly embraced her.

When Kristi regained her composure, she collected her torn clothing and put it on while Shannon looked at the unconscious men in thoughtful silence. Then, she asked her daughter, "How did you get away from your attacker? He's so big."

"At the moment he was about to rape me, a bee stung him in the head, and then headed for his eyes. He jumped up to swat at it."

"A bee also stung the man who was attacking me. It's strange that two bees would show up and go after the men who were attacking us. Why didn't we get stung?"

"I don't know, Mom."

Looking at the unconscious men, Shannon said, "I hit that one on the head with a rock, but why is this one unconscious? Did you hit him?"

"No, I only tried to get him off of you. When he stood up, he just fell down."

"There has to be a reason. Maybe he had a heart attack or a stroke. He's really out. It looks like he's barely breathing."

Shannon dropped to her knees next to the man and checked his pulse. "His heart is beating very slowly," she said.

After checking the other man's pulse, Shannon said, "His heart is also beating very slowly, and he's barely breathing. There is something very strange about this. It's almost like they've been drugged in preparation for surgery."

Kristi held up the knife she had taken from the man and said, "Maybe we should do some surgery."

"What do you have in mind?"

"They tried to rape us. Maybe we should cut off their testicles."

"That would serve them right, and revenge would feel good, but I think we should focus on our big problem, which is rescuing your father and brother."

"How are we going to do that?"

Up on the cliff top, Tonya was intently watching the scene, wondering if she should reveal her presence. They have to have information that I can use, she decided, but if they know I'm here, that will increase the probability of the enemy finding out about me. Their minds might be susceptible to telepathic probing.

What will Shannon and Kristi do now that they're free? I have to assume that they'll try to rescue Rex and Jeff. Should I shadow them and lend assistance if they need it? Or should I talk to them and get the information they have?

My mission is to gain information and take it back to camp, so we can plan a rescue using all of our assets. But what just happened complicates the problem. Shannon and Kristi have to act before the terrorist leader discovers what just happened, and that means they might not have much time. But if they fail, they could be killed or captured and then tortured. If I join them and we fail, then Jerry's rescue mission might be put in jeopardy, because the terrorists will connect me with Jerry and know that we are already here.

Maybe there's another alternative. We could kill those two thugs and hide their bodies in the jungle. Then, I could take Shannon and Kristi back to camp, and we could plan a rescue with info from them. The terrorist leader would find out that Shannon and Kristi are gone, but he would not know for sure that we have them. If we leave the right clues, he might think that his thugs ran off with the women for the purpose of making sex slaves out of them.

It seems like the best thing for me to do is reveal my presence and talk to them. Then, we can decide what to do. But how do I contact them? If I do it telepathically, I might be heard by the enemy. If I stand up and announce my presence, I could get shot. After what just happened, Shannon might be trigger happy. She might shoot me before she realizes that I'm not the enemy.

An idea came. Tonya removed the map from her pack. On the margin at the top of the page, she wrote in English, "We are here to help you." Then, she folded the map into a glider.

Being a jungle girl, Tonya was skilled at imitating the songs of various birds. From the concealment of the bush she was hiding behind, Tonya watched Shannon and Kristi while she loudly chirped out the song of a bird common on Alcent but not present on Zebron.

The unfamiliar bird call immediately got Shannon and Kristi's attention. When they looked up, Tonya tossed the paper glider over the bush, and it sailed out over the beach. It twisted and turned sailing aimlessly to and fro. Surprised by its appearance, Shannon and Kristi watched its descent. By chance, it landed practically at Shannon's feet.

"There has to be someone up there," Shannon quietly said to her daughter while alertly staring at the bushes above her.

"Are we in danger?" Kristi asked, fearfully.

"I don't think so. They only threw a piece of paper at us."

Shannon reached down to pick up the glider. Even before unfolding it, she recognized the English words on the map. She smiled because she knew that there was only one place this could have come from. "Jerry is here," she said.

"Does that mean we're going to be rescued?" Kristi asked.

"I think so." Shannon looked up at the cliff top wearing a hopeful smile.

Seeing this, Tonya stood up, smiled back, and waved. "I'm coming down," she said.

A minute later, Tonya was on the beach. She walked up to Kristi and her mother and said, "Hi Shannon! Hi Kristi! My name is Tonya."

"We are so happy you're here," responded Shannon with a warm greeting. "We've just been through a nightmare." Pointing at the unconscious men, Shannon continued, "They tried to rape us."

Tonya noticed that Shannon trembled while speaking, so she offered a consoling remark, "That was a brutal attack, but they failed, and now you don't have to worry about them."

"We fought tooth-and-nail to beat them off, and it seems we were helped by a couple bees that showed up at the right time."

"I can explain that. Take a look at that rock over there. What do you see?"

"Two bees sunning themselves."

Tonya set her pack down and removed a control unit. "Hold out your hands," she said to Shannon.

Working the controls, Tonya flew one of the hornets to Shannon and landed it on her right hand. Shannon's eyes opened wide as she realized what had happened.

"I guess I don't have to tell you what we've been through," she said. "You saw everything, and you used your bees to save us from the attack. I don't know how I can ever thank you enough. My daughter is only twelve, and you saved her from a brutal rape."

"Your appreciation is enough. I'm glad I arrived in time to help you."

"Just the same, when this is all over, we'll find a way to do something special for you. We owe all of you so much for coming here to rescue us."

"I appreciate your sentiment, but we haven't yet rescued all of you. There are some things I need to know, and I don't know how much time we have, so I'm going to start asking questions."

"We'll answer them as best we can."

Pointing at the unconscious men, Tonya asked, "Is there regular communication between these guys and the people holding the rest of your family?"

"They have the communicators that Jerry gave us, but they haven't been using them."

"Why?"

"They're worried about the communications equipment Jerry gave us to stay in touch with him on Alcent. They think it's tuned in to the communicators, so they don't use them out of fear that you'll hear their conversations. And they don't want to turn off the equipment, because they're afraid that Jerry will then believe that Rex is also a captive."

"So how do the people holding Rex and Jeff stay in contact with these guys?"

"The leader rotates his personnel. Every day, in the late afternoon, two men arrive and the two that are here go back."

"That means that they're going to be here soon."

"If they stay on the schedule they've been using, it will be a couple hours before they arrive. But if the schedule has changed, they could be here anytime."

"If that's the case, I need to set up a warning system." Tonya removed a video headset and a small RPV from her pack. She put on the headset and flew the RPV down the trail toward Rex's home. Three hundred yards out, she parked the RPV on a fork in a tree branch where it had an excellent view of the trail. She programmed the headset computer to sound an alarm if the RPV spotted movement on the trail; then, she said, "We now have a warning system in place, so let's plan a welcome for them."

"What kind of welcome do you have in mind?"

"After hiking all the way up here, they might be tired, so I think we should be considerate and put them to sleep for a while."

"How many hornets do you have?"

"Six and I have a bottle of the drug, so I can reload them."

"How long are these guys going to be out?"

"At least 24 hours, and if all goes well, we'll be gone by then."

"It sounds like you have a rescue plan all worked out."

"No, we don't. I came here to gather information, so we could develop a rescue plan. But I had to save you and Kristi, so we now have a big problem. We have to do the rescue ourselves before the terrorists find out that you've been freed and that we're already here."

"We have a dangerous job ahead of us."

"I know, but we can get it done, so let's drag these guys off the beach, get ready for their replacements, and plan a rescue."

The women dragged the men into a thick patch of bushes. Then, with tree branches, they brushed the sandy beach to smooth out the sand and eliminate all signs of the struggle.

When the job was done, Tonya asked, "Do you know where Rex and Jeff are being held?"

"In our home, I believe."

"You sound uncertain."

"I know only what I've heard our guards say," responded Shannon, "They've openly discussed their plans in our presence. Apparently, they believe that there's no way we could pass along the information to Jerry."

"And you've heard them say that Rex and Jeff are being held in your home?"

"Yes."

"And you believe them?"

"Yes."

"Why?"

"Because they need Rex to respond to messages from Jerry, and

57

the communications equipment is in our home. Jeff has to be there too, because they can control Rex by holding a gun to Jeff's head."

"Even so, they could be lying."

"But why would they? The only reason to conduct a false conversation in front of me would be to mislead me. Why would they do that? What could they hope to gain by misleading me?"

"You're right; it makes no sense for them to mislead you unless they think that we can contact you. Then, misleading you would result in you giving us incorrect information."

"I don't believe that's their objective."

"Why?"

"Right there, inside that cliff, there's an old bomb shelter. They've been holding us inside it, because they don't think you could ever find us there. That strategy might've worked if our guards hadn't been sex-starved. You found us only because they wanted to rape us on a warm, sandy beach."

"And if I hadn't been here, even that would not have led to us finding you."

"I think we should take their conversations at face value and see where that leads us."

"Okay, what else have you heard them say?"

"They've been talking about ambushing and capturing your people when they come here to help Rex get us back. They think they can get control of your starship if they capture enough of you."

"We've figured out that capturing our starship might be their ultimate objective."

"The terrorists want you to think Rex is free, so that you'll just walk right into our home to help him get us back. They have elaborate plans to capture your people. Then, if Jerry doesn't meet their demands, they'll start executing your people, one at a time, until Jerry gives in."

"If they have a cleverly planned ambush set up, it's going to be difficult for us to rescue Rex and Jeff from your home."

"We do have several things going for us," stated Shannon.

"Let's discuss them and see if we can come up with a plan."

"Our biggest advantage is surprise. The terrorists don't know that you are here and that Kristi and I are free. Also, they don't know that two of their fighters are out of action."

"There will soon be two more of them out of action. Do you know how many are in their gang?"

"I believe there are eleven."

"That means there might be seven of them at your home for us to deal with."

"That's too many. We have to find a way to tip the odds in our favor."

"If they have a sentry on duty, I can use one of my hornets to put him to sleep. That will get their numbers down to six."

"That's still too many."

"I know, but it's a start."

"If they have a sentry, how will you find him before he sees us?"

"I need to scout the area around your home by myself. I am very good at quietly sneaking around in the jungle, and I have phenomenal telepathic ability. I can sense the presence of an active mind."

"What if he's sleeping on the job?"

"Then, I will find him by other means. But I need to know the layout of your home and the area around it. Maybe we can figure out where it makes the most sense for them to put their sentries in terms of setting up an ambush. Also, I wish I knew how telepathically capable our enemies are."

"That I don't know, but I can tell you that my husband is a gifted telepath. His ability is unique."

"Are you saying that Rex is the only person you know who has telepathic ability?"

"No, nearly everyone on this planet has that ability to some degree, but Rex is unique. He can telepathically transmit images into another person's mind at great distances, and he can reach out and see images in the other person's mind."

"That's awesome. I wonder if there's some way we could telepathically contact him without the terrorists knowing."

"That would be risky, because I don't know how telepathically capable they are."

"It's too bad we don't have a risk free way to contact Rex. What I'm getting at is Rex has to behave because he thinks you and Kristi are captives. If we could tell him that you've been freed, then he might look for an opportunity where he and Jeff could slip away, like sneaking out the back door. Does your home have a back door?"

"Yes, it does."

"I thought you lived in an underground home that's dug into the side of a hill. How can that have a back door?"

"Part of our home is above ground. It's built over the entrance to an old underground bomb shelter that was used during the early phases of the Great War."

"Tell me about the back door."

"The bomb shelter has two entrances. The main entrance has the above ground part of our home built over it; the other entrance is 50 yards north of our home and hasn't been used in years."

"Is it open or closed?"

"It's closed."

"Can it be opened?"

"I have opened it, but it is a heavy concrete door that was designed for blast protection."

"How do you open a heavy door like that?"

"There's a metal crank you can turn that slowly opens the door."

"Does the door make noise when you open it?"

"Some."

"Would it be heard by the terrorists?"

"It would probably be heard by anyone in the bomb shelter."

"What if we were to create a diversion in front of your home to draw them out? Would they hear it when they're outside?"

"There is thick forest between the two entrances, but they still might hear it. I guess it would depend on the diversion we create and how fully it occupies their attention. What did you have in mind?"

"What would happen if a terrorist outside your home were bitten by a poisonous snake?"

"That might work, but how would we make that happen?"

Tonya reached into her pack and lifted out the sleeping snake. At the sight of it, Shannon and Kristi cringed with fear.

"That one is bad medicine," stated Shannon. "They're very aggressive and usually strike anything that gets close to them. Fortunately, they are rare. Where did you get this one, and how did you get it to sleep so soundly?"

"I have a special telepathic gift. I am able to get into the minds of animals and influence their behavior."

"If there were some way to deliver that snake to my front yard, it will strike whoever is there. But if they see it before it strikes, they will shoot it."

"Is its venom deadly?"

"It's worse than deadly."

"In what way?"

60

"People who are bitten don't die; they suffer. The toxin causes painful inflammation, but worse than that, it causes hallucinations and paranoia. This happens as soon as some of the venom gets into the victim's blood and gets carried to the brain. Usually, it's just a matter of a half-minute or so."

"Is there any antidote?"

"None that we know of. This snake is a genetic mutation that came into being after the initial phase of the Great War."

"What is the medical treatment?"

"All you can do is draw as much venom out of the wound as possible. But the most important thing is to restrain the patient. Because of hallucinations and paranoia, the patient is very dangerous and might even try to kill those around him because he sees them as enemies."

"How long does the paranoia last?"

"It will last until the patient's liver is able to cleanse the toxins out of his system."

"How long does that take?"

"That depends on how successful you are at sucking the venom out of the wound, but usually the patient needs to be restrained for at least three days."

"The only problem I see with using the snake to create a diversion is that they'll use Rex to treat the victim," Tonya said.

"That's true, but when the victim starts hallucinating, everyone's attention will be totally occupied, and I will be able to get into the bomb shelter. There are places where I can hide. If you can create a second diversion, I will be able to get Rex and Jeff out."

"I can do that," stated Tonya. "But there's something that bothers me about you going in the back door, and that is, it could be rigged with an alarm or even a bomb. You could be killed."

"There is definitely risk involved, but I need to get my husband and son back. Besides, leaving them where they are is also risky."

"That's true, so let's consider some other plans and see if we can find something with less uncertainty."

At that moment, the headset computer sounded an alarm. Tonya quickly put the headset on. "We've got company," she said. "Two men are walking this way, and they're taking their sweet old time."

"Good, that means they don't know what has happened to their comrades. How do you want to greet them?"

Pointing at the cliff top, Tonya said, "Let's go up there."

Tonya took three hornets out of her pack and put them on three different rocks near the trailhead. Then, she followed Shannon and Kristi to the cliff top, where she made herself comfortable behind a bush above the trailhead.

"Your ambush and our rescue plans could be put in jeopardy if they telepathically detect your presence," whispered Shannon.

"That will be difficult for them to do, because I am very good at making myself telepathically invisible. But what about you and Kristi, can they detect you?"

"It doesn't matter if they detect us, because we're supposed to be here."

"Okay, let's not talk, so I can concentrate on putting these guys to sleep."

A few minutes later, the men walked out of the forest and onto the beach. Tonya launched one of the hornets and stung the second man out of the forest on the back of his neck. He cussed at the hornet and swatted at it as it flew away. The other man turned around to see what the problem was. When he saw his buddy swatting at a hornet, he laughed and made fun of him for being so upset over such a minor pain as a bee sting.

But his laughter was short-lived because he felt a sting in the back of his neck. Now that he was the victim of a bee sting, it didn't seem quite so funny anymore, and he cussed and swatted at the hornet. But it flew up just out of his reach and circled his head as if it was going to strike again.

Now it was his buddy's turn to laugh and make derogatory remarks. Tonya kept the hornet buzzing around above the man's head. She teased him with it, keeping it just beyond his reach. She wanted to keep him busy until the drug took effect.

Soon, both men sat down because they felt groggy. Tonya kept the hornet in front of their faces to keep them occupied, so they wouldn't sound an alarm, in case either man became suspicious about the hornet attack. The strategy worked. The men passed out while feebly swinging at the hornet.

"Four down and seven to go," stated Tonya with a smile.

"We don't know that for sure," Shannon said. "There might be more or less than seven. But you know what; the rescue would sure be easy if we could take them all out with the hornets."

"I've thought about that, but it could be risky. If the terrorist leader saw that his men were dropping in their tracks, he might suspect that we're here and drugging them. He might kill your son as a warning to make us stop."

"He could not do that if we could find a way to take him out first. If I could get into our home through the back door, I might find an opportunity to capture or kill him."

"I don't think you should take that risk. The back door has to be guarded, booby trapped, or rigged with an alarm. We need to find another way."

"You're probably right," Shannon reluctantly agreed. "Let's drag those guys into the bushes and take away their guns. Then, let's discuss our options."

"I also need to reload my hornets and charge their batteries. How much time do we have?"

"The terrorist leader will expect the first two men you drugged to return before dark. If they don't, he'll be suspicious."

Tonya noted the position of Alpha Centauri B and said, "It looks like we have about three hours to plan and carry out a rescue. We'd better get busy."

Meanwhile, back at the base camp, Trang was starting to worry about his daughter. "It's already late afternoon," he said. "It seems like she should've been back by now. She said she would only be gone a few hours."

"You know how she is when she goes into the jungle," commented Geniya. "She's so at home there that she just loses track of time, but she always comes back."

"That's true, but this jungle has armed terrorists in it."

"Our jungles have packs of vicious lupusaurs in them. Can the terrorists be any more dangerous?"

"That's a good point, and Tonya does know how to stay out of trouble. But I'm concerned that she might try to do the rescue on her own, instead of bringing back information, so we can put all of our forces into action."

"I realize our daughter is independent minded, but she is blessed with intelligence and common sense. She's just not going to do anything stupid."

"But something unforeseen might've happened," argued Trang. "Maybe we should move closer to Rex's home, so we'll be in position to help her if she needs it."

"If we're spotted, that would let the enemy know we're here, and that could make Tonya's job and ours much more difficult."

"That's a good point."

"I think we have to sit tight and trust our daughter to make sound decisions and stay out of trouble."

"You know me. I have a hard time sitting here and doing nothing. Let's take another look at the map and see if there's a place that makes sense to go to."

"What will Tonya do when she returns and we aren't here?"

"You're shooting down every idea I come up with."

"That's because you're getting personally involved with Tonya's mission. If you had sent a specially trained soldier out on a scouting mission, you would trust him to use his skills and get the job done. But since it's our daughter, you're worried. You have to just relax and trust her on this. She is very skilled at staying alive in the jungle. She's been doing it for years."

Trang thought about his wife's remarks and said, "You're right, but I'm going to study the map some more anyway. There might be something that would make sense for us to do."

Six miles away, Tonya, Shannon, and Kristi were cautiously moving closer to Shannon's home, where they hoped to find Rex and Jeff. They had three miles of hiking to do and decided to use the trail for the first two miles. It followed the valleys between the hills.

Tonya was a full 100 yards ahead of Shannon and Kristi. She used all of her powers to search for sentries, stopping frequently to sense the aura of the jungle.

Time dragged on. Eventually, Tonya was only three-fourths of a mile from Shannon's home. She stopped and listened intently to the sounds of the jungle. She listened telepathically. She let her mind bond with the jungle. This is strange, she thought. I'm not detecting anything out of order. Where are they? I don't like this.

Tonya visually searched every inch of what lay in front of her. Then, she backtracked until she met Shannon and Kristi.

"I'm not sure what's going on," Tonya said, "but I'm not detecting anyone. My telepathic ability is very good, and I should be sensing them, but I'm not. Let's hide in the bushes and discuss this."

Tonya led the way. When she found a thick patch of brush to hide in, she said, "We can see the approaches to this thicket, so we should be safe here. What do you think is going on?"

"There might be a simple explanation," replied Shannon. "Maybe everyone is in the bomb shelter, which is under our home. Then, you would not be able to detect them."

"Why would all of them be in there? Why don't they have a sentry or two on alert?"

"What kind of messages has Jerry been sending Rex? Specifically, when did you tell Rex you would arrive?"

"Three days from now."

"Maybe they believe that and don't have sentries out yet. Did you say anything about where and how you would arrive?"

"We told Rex that our shuttles land on hydrofoils, and we asked him how deep Lake Jamalya is and if there are any floating logs."

"When did you do that?"

"Several days ago."

"That explains this," stated Shannon, while holding up a communicator.

"Where did you get that?"

"I took it off the brute that tried to rape Kristi. Starting several days ago, one of our guards always had one of these. Apparently, the terrorist leader thought you might arrive early and land on Duck Lake, and he wanted an immediate warning."

"Have you ever seen them use the communicators?"

"No, because they think the communications equipment Jerry left here might be tuned in to the communicators, but once Jerry arrives, they wouldn't have to worry about that. Getting a warning would be essential."

"Maybe that explains why I can't detect a sentry. They might only have one or two overlooking Lake Jamalya, because we said that's where we're going to land. And there were two at Duck Lake in case we landed there, but where is the rest of the gang? If they're all in the bomb shelter, why are they in there?"

"Maybe they plan to do their ambush from there, or maybe they're having a meeting to discuss strategy."

"I will have to look around inside the bomb shelter and see if anyone's in there."

"How are you going to do that?"

Tonya opened her pack, took out a mechanical dragonfly, and

said, "This thing has cameras for eyes and microphones for ears. Is there a way I can fly it into your home and then down into the bomb shelter without attracting attention?"

"Dragonflies are common here, so it should not attract attention. If we can get close to my home without being discovered, I can show you how to get it inside."

"With no one outside, we should be able to get close without being detected, unless they've rigged a bunch of alarms around your home."

"I know the land around our home, and I think I can get us there without setting off any alarms."

"Carefully concealed alarms can be hard to spot. And since there aren't any sentries, we have to assume that there are alarms in place."

"That's possible, but you have to remember that this country was destroyed by the Great War. There's almost no manufacturing left. Batteries, generators, video cameras, and electronic motion detectors just aren't available. What we have to look for are trip wires, land mines, and concealed pits that we could fall into. I think I can spot those."

"I will help you, but we'll need to move silently. Even so, there is the risk that we could be telepathically detected. Maybe Kristi should stay here. If we all go, that will increase the risk of detection."

"I want to come along," stated Kristi. "After what those horrible men tried to do this afternoon, you have to let me help."

"I'd rather leave you here where you'll be safe," responded Shannon.

"How do you know I'll be safe here? They could find me, and I definitely don't want to be alone."

"Can you handle a rifle?" Tonya asked Kristi.

"I could point it and pull the trigger."

"I don't think that's good enough for defending yourself." Turning to Shannon, Tonya said, "I think we should take her along. Part of the gang might be away from your home, and if we can figure out how to rescue Rex and Jeff, we might have to leave in a hurry before they return."

"All things considered, I think you're right," agreed Shannon. "We should stick together."

Kristi had been carrying one of the military rifles taken from the men at Duck Lake. Now, Shannon, once again, showed her how to use it. She showed Kristi how to hold it, how to chamber a round, how to turn the safety on and off, how to aim it, and how to fire it. When she was sure that Kristi understood, she turned to Tonya and said, "That's the best we can do without target practice, so let's go rescue my husband and son."

Shannon led the way. She stayed off the main trail and followed an old trail that hadn't been used in years. Progress was slow because parts of the trail were grown over. In the vicinity of her home, the trail was totally grown over, so Shannon didn't think the terrorists knew about it.

One hundred yards from her home, Shannon stopped in a clump of bushes. "Have you detected anyone?" she asked Tonya in a soft whisper.

"No," Tonya whispered back. "And this is weird. It's almost as if they're not here. I need to sneak up to your home and investigate this. I want you and Kristi to wait for me right here."

"What do you want us to do if you're captured?"

"I don't expect to be captured, because I don't think they're here."

"Some of them have to be here or at least nearby, so they can respond to messages from Jerry in a timely manner."

"Where do you think they are? You live here. What are the possibilities?"

"Let's assume they believe that Jerry's coming in on a shuttle that lands on water, and I think that's a safe assumption because Jerry has to land some place, and there aren't any open areas here except for the water. It's all jungle."

"Okay, let's also assume that they don't know we're already here, and that they believe Jerry will arrive in two or three days. Where does that take us?"

"There are only three places nearby where a water landing is feasible. One is Duck Lake, and we've already put those people to sleep. Three miles north of here, the river widens into a marsh that is two miles long and a mile wide. There is open water down the middle of the marsh. That straight stretch of open water is 30 to 40 feet deep and could support a shuttle landing. Two of the terrorists could be up there watching it."

"Why two?"

"They could suspect a night landing with your people floating down river in the darkness for a surprise arrival. It would take two people to watch the water around the clock."

"Why can't I detect their presence?"

"This is a hilly area, and most of the hills have caves dug into them that date back to before the war started. The sentries might be in a cave overlooking the river."

"Unless they're in a deep cave, I would still be able detect them. My telepathic ability is very good."

"What if they're sleeping on the job?'

"I cannot detect an inactive mind."

"Okay, let's assume there are two up there, and for whatever reason, you're not able to detect them. That still leaves five that could be here, who could capture you."

"If they're all in the bomb shelter, I will see them before they see me. Capturing me will be difficult for them."

"They might not all be in there. They have to watch Lake Jamalya."

"Where is the best location for that?"

"They could hide in the forest anywhere around the lake and spot a shuttle landing without being seen."

"What if they're good with rifles and want to have a clear shot at Rex and our people? What if they want Rex to know that?"

Shannon thought about the questions for a few moments; then, she said, "There's only one place that fits those requirements, and it's 300 yards south of our home."

"What can you tell me about it?"

"It's a cave dug into the side of a hill, and it's fortified with concrete. It's actually an old bunker, and from it, there's a clear view of Lake Jamalya and its beaches, especially the eastern shore. That's where your people are probably expected to come ashore with Rex standing there to greet them."

"Maybe there's one terrorist in the bomb shelter with Jeff. Maybe the rest are at the bunker showing Rex what a clear shot they have at anyone on the beach, just to make sure Rex knows that rifles will be aimed at him and Jerry when Jerry arrives."

"That has to be what's happening," stated Shannon. "It just makes sense from their point of view."

"Okay, I think we've done all the speculating we can. Now, it's time for me to investigate your home and see what I can find out."

"What will happen if things go wrong and you're captured?"

"Is there a way I can disguise myself to look like I'm from this planet? Then, the terrorists won't know that Jerry's already here."

Shannon closely evaluated Tonya's appearance; then, she said,

"There's a race of people living far to the north that look like you. Those people are very hardy and prefer the arctic region, but some have moved south since the war. You could easily be mistaken for one of them."

"Do they speak the same language as you?"

"No, each tribe has its own dialect."

Tonya spoke a few sentences in her native tongue and watched for Shannon's reaction.

"That sounds just as foreign as the languages the northern tribes speak," commented Shannon.

"What style of clothing do they wear?"

"Your clothing will pass, but your high-tech gear will give you away."

"What about my backpack?"

"That should pass. It's made out of plain looking material."

Tonya removed a headband from her pack and put it on. It was decorated with what appeared to be a few polished pebbles that were earth tone in color. "Will this pass?" she asked.

"Yes, and it looks good on you."

"Thanks. What about my headset?" Tonya asked, as she put it on.

"It looks like a pair of ordinary, everyday sunglasses."

"That might be, but this is a piece of high-tech equipment. When turned on, the lenses are actually video screens that allow me to see what my dragonfly sees. When turned off, I can see through them like ordinary clear plastic. Also, I can darken the lenses if the day is too bright. The arms of this headset have little speakers at the ends, which puts them near my ears."

"Your headset won't give you away, but the control units with their joysticks will."

"I can leave them behind."

"How will you control your bugs?"

"Take a good look at my headband. What do you see?"

"I see a knitted headband decorated with objects found in nature. It's attractive on you, but it is a rather common headband."

"It doesn't look high-tech?"

"No."

"Good, because it's very high-tech." While putting her fingers on them, Tonya said, "These objects over my left and right temples look like polished agates, but they are high-tech electronic units. They sense my brain waves and translate my thoughts into electronic signals that are transmitted to my hornets and dragonflies. In effect, I can telepathically control my bugs using this headband."

"Are you saying that you can control your mechanical bugs with your thoughts?"

"That's right."

"Wow!"

Tonya opened her pack and took out everything that could connect her to Alcent. She kept her bugs, because she might need them, and they looked too real to arouse suspicion. Tonya took off her gun belt and laid it next to her rifle. "Have I missed anything?" she asked.

"Not that I can see," replied Shannon, "but what about that snake?"

"He's going to stay in my pack. I might need him."

"How much longer is he going to sleep?"

"Until I wake him up."

"I can't believe he has slept through everything."

"I keep telepathically reinforcing the sleep state I put him in."

Shannon crushed some leaves in her hands and added some green stain spots to the seat of Tonya's shorts. Then, she added some dusty soil to Tonya's legs and to her shorts. "Now you look like a hiker who's been on the trail for a few days," she said.

Tonya shouldered her pack and said, "It's time to go check things out. Wait for my return."

"What if you get in trouble and need help?"

"I will contact you."

"How?"

Tonya explained to Shannon the various ways that she could contact her depending on the situation she found herself in. Then, she cautiously headed toward Shannon's home.

A few minutes later, Tonya arrived at the edge of the clearing that made up Shannon's front yard. She searched it from the concealment of the bushes that she was hiding behind. There's no one here, she noted, and I'm not detecting anyone in the house either. Where are they?

Maybe I can find some clues in the house. Since there's no one here, why do I need to investigate it with my dragonflies? Maybe I can safely go in and look around. I suppose the place could be booby trapped, but why would it be? We aren't expected for two or three days, and they can't get our starship by killing us. They need to capture us and control us. I suppose the house could be rigged with alarms, but that doesn't seem likely. The front door isn't even closed. Why is it wide open? Did they leave in a big hurry, or do they not care about Rex's property?

At that moment, Tonya telepathically detected an individual south of her, then a second one, then a third one. They must be coming out of the concrete bunker and it must be steel-reinforced, she thought. Within seconds, Tonya detected a total of seven individuals coming her way.

Suddenly, Tonya sensed alarm in the minds of two of the people. Uh oh, we've been telepathically detected by the terrorists, Tonya concluded. To protect Shannon and Kristi, Tonya quickly decided on a bold plan. She stepped out of the forest and ran to Rex's home. Stepping through the front door, she found herself in an entry room. Passing through it, she entered the kitchen/dining area. She set her pack against the wall just inside the doorway and untied the flap covering the compartment with the snake in it. Quickly, Tonya placed her hornets in high places where they weren't visible. She put her headset away because she did not need it.

Facing a decorative mirror, Tonya fussed with her hair, so that it covered much of her headband. She did not want it to attract unusual attention and be taken away. Next, Tonya repositioned her halter top to better show off her breasts. I have a nice figure and after what I saw earlier today, some of these terrorists might be sex-starved. I look pretty good, so I should be able to get their attention long enough to wipe them out. I'm not armed, and I'm alone, so they should not see me as a threat; which means they should not kill me, especially, if they see me as a sex object to be used at their whim.

Tonya found a kitchen knife and put some cuts in the bottom of her shorts. Then, she ripped them part way up, almost to the point of showing pubic hair. Viewing herself in the mirror, she surmised, if I don't get their attention now, I don't know what will.

Tonya found some fresh fruit, which looked like apples, on the kitchen table and decided to eat one of them. She wanted to look like a hiker who had done nothing more than stop by for food and rest. She sat on the north side of the table, so she could see out a south window across the table.

Shortly, the terrorists began to emerge from the jungle. Two of them held guns on Rex and Jeff. Seeing this, Tonya thought, they don't know who I am and what I'm doing here, so they're holding

71

guns on Rex and Jeff to make sure I behave. Also, they might think there are three of us here, which means I have to take them out before they go looking for Shannon and Kristi.

Tonya pushed back from the table a bit and angled her chair 45 degrees to the table. By turning her head to the left, she could look out the south window. By turning her head to the right, she could see the entry door.

What would an all-day hiker do right now? Tonya asked herself. Well, I have been hiking all day, and my legs are tired. Tonya backed away from the table a bit more and placed her left leg on top the table. This feels good, she thought, and it seems normal. She leaned back in her chair to get as relaxed as possible. Her right leg relaxed off to her right a bit. Assessing her pose, Tonya thought, my legs are spread just enough to be provocative, but not so much as to be obvious as to what I'm up to.

Tonya picked up one of the apples and waited a moment; then, she bit into it just as the terrorist leader burst into the room with two of his henchmen right behind him. Their guns were pointed at her.

Acting surprised, Tonya faked an expression of fear. She dropped her apple, opened her eyes wide, screamed, and raised her hands high. She cowered backwards as much as her chair allowed. In the local language, she pleaded, "Please don't shoot me." Zeb and Zonya had given Tonya a crash course in basic conversation words.

Tonya's provocative posture, along with her helpless vulnerability caught the terrorist leader's attention. His eyes roamed her body for a few seconds. "Where are you from?" he demanded.

"Far to the north," Tonya responded. To emphasize the point, she rapidly rattled off a couple sentences in her native language.

"I don't understand that crap," he responded angrily. "I never did like your people, but you look like you might be useful to me and my men. Why are you here?"

"Eat and sleep."

The terrorist lustily surveyed Tonya's body and turned to his men. "I think we should let her sleep here tonight," he said with a lustful laugh.

Both men laughed, and one of them said, "She ain't gonna get much sleep."

The laughter didn't last long. While the men leered at her, Tonya telepathically woke up the snake in her pack. It stuck its head out from under the flap. With its tongue darting out, it sensed the warm legs before it and quickly crawled out of the bag. It struck with lightening speed, burying its fangs in the calf of one of the legs.

The bitten man's laughter turned into a screamed line of profanity when he felt the painful bite. He quickly spun around, spotted the reptile, and yelled, "Demon Snake." He fired his pistol at the snake, but missed. The snake struck again, but this time, its fangs only broke skin because they hit the man's shin bone in his right leg.

Now, all three terrorists were frantically shooting at the snake, and some of the bullets found their target. During this commotion, a hornet stung the terrorist leader in the back of his neck, but he was so busy that he ignored the minor pain of the sting. He grabbed the snakebite victim and plopped him into a sturdy armchair in the corner of the room. "We have to tie him down before he goes crazy," he shouted.

The leader and his unbitten henchman urgently ripped off their shirts and used them to tie the victim's arms to the chair's arms. While they were frantically doing this, a hornet stung the leader's assistant, and he didn't even notice it.

The crescendo of gunfire at the snake caused the two terrorists who were outside guarding Rex and Jeff to come running in. They brought Rex and Jeff with them.

Facing Rex, the terrorist leader yelled, "You have medical skills! And you will treat my man for snake bite! Get busy, right now!"

The terrorist who had just escorted Rex into the dining area felt a sting in the back of his neck. He spun around and cussed at the hornet while swatting at it.

Suddenly, the snakebite victim started yelling out warnings about alien invaders who were out on the lake. The snake venom was starting to enter his brain inducing paranoia and hallucinations.

"Do you have anything to sedate him with?" the leader asked Rex.

"I'll see what I can do, but we don't have much."

Only one terrorist hadn't yet been stung, but he was holding a gun on Jeff to make sure that Rex would behave. Seeing this, Tonya thought, I have to be careful with this one. If he has a nervous trigger finger, a hornet sting might result in Jeff getting shot.

Tonya flew the hornet past the man's face about three feet in front of him. He watched it go by, but then, the hornet circled back and landed on his left upper arm. He quickly shoved his pistol into its hol-

73

ster, so he could swat at the hornet. But he was too slow; Tonya activated the sting mechanism the instant the gun wasn't pointed at Jeff. However, the man was quick enough to hit the hornet before Tonya could fly it away. He cussed at the sting and then examined the insect that had stung him. He wanted to see what it was. Momentarily, he said, "This is a strange bee. I hit it hard, but it's not squishing goop like a bug does when you smash it."

The terrorist leader was irritated. "I have a man hallucinating. My men are late coming back from Duck Lake. And you bother me with a bug."

"I think this is important," the man insisted.

"I'll look at your bug later. Right now, I'm tired. I will sit down and rest." The leader sat down at the table. He put his arms on the table top, rested his head on his arms, and passed out.

"Why is he so tired?" questioned the man with the smashed hornet. "I've never seen him conk out during the day."

Observing the man's inquisitive attitude, Tonya thought, he sure is suspicious. I hope he passes out before he figures out what I've done here. I don't want to get shot when I'm so close to success. What can I do to distract him until the drug takes effect?

At that moment, the second terrorist that Tonya stung wobbled unsteadily on his feet. He struggled to stay standing, but he lost the struggle and slumped to the floor.

"Something is wrong here!" exclaimed the man with the squashed bug. He faced Tonya. "What do you know about this?" he demanded.

"Nothing, I stop to eat and sleep."

"I don't believe you. We find you here, and a Demon Snake bites my friend. Our people are passing out, and I have this hornet that doesn't squish."

"My hands are up since you walked in."

"She's a witch," yelled the hallucinating man.

"Witches don't exist and neither do bugs that don't squish," stated the man as he presented the smashed hornet to Tonya. "Tell me about this."

"It's a dead hornet. I don't know anything more."

"Maybe this knife will help you know something," stated the man while pulling his knife and holding it against Tonya's face. "A few scars and you won't look so pretty."

Trying to buy time, Tonya telepathically placed calming emotions in the man's mind. She hoped this would slow down his demands and calm him down a bit. It stayed his knife briefly, and then, the only other terrorist still standing collapsed.

By this time, Rex figured out what had to be happening, and he came to Tonya's assistance. Using his unique telepathic ability, he placed an image of a coiled, ready-to-strike Demon Snake in the man's mind. The image placed the snake on the floor behind the man. His reaction was instantaneous. He jumped on top the table and pulled his feet up with him. He leaned forward and looked over the edge of the table.

At his point, Rex changed the image to that of a snake coiling around one of the table's legs and climbing it to the top. Rex used the full power of his brain to project the image into the man's mind. It was so convincing that the man drew his pistol and aimed it next to the table leg. He fired the gun repeatedly until it was empty. Then, he passed out.

Meanwhile, the hallucinating man was still screaming, "She's a witch!"

With Rex watching, Tonya launched her last hornet and stung the man on his neck. She faced Rex and said in English, "In a few minutes, he'll be out cold. Is this all of them or are there more?"

Upon hearing English words, Rex became electrified with excitement because he knew what this meant. He responded in English, "There are two more a few miles upriver, and there are four at Duck Lake holding my wife and daughter."

"Those four are out cold, and Shannon and Kristi are here."

"Where are they?"

"They're hiding in the jungle about a hundred yards north of here."

Rex immediately made telepathic contact with Shannon and Kristi. Then, he and Jeff went to meet them.

One more time, the hallucinating man screamed, "You are a witch!" Then, he passed into dreamland.

Tonya stood up and looked around the room. "Not a bad day's work," she said to herself with a sense of satisfaction. "Guess I should call my father and report the results of my scouting mission."

Chapter Four

Tonya needed a communicator, so she turned to the unconscious terrorist leader and reached for his. Looking at it, she noted, this will do the job. It's one of those that Jerry gave to Rex.

Tonya entered her father's number. When he answered, she said, "Hi Dad, how are you?"

"Never mind how I am! I want to know how you are. You've been gone all day, and I've been worried about you."

"Dad, I'm fine."

"Thank God you're okay. You went out on a dangerous scouting mission that was only supposed to last a few hours."

"I know, but I ran into an urgent situation that I had to deal with. Then, I had to figure out how to complete the rescue."

"Are you saying that Rex and his family are already free?"

"That's right, and all the terrorists except two are out cold."

"Where are those two?"

"We think they're three miles north of here watching a wide area of Jamal River. They're supposed to sound an alarm if Jerry lands there. Hopefully, they don't know that we're already here."

"Where are you?"

"I'm at Rex's home with him and his family."

"I'll bet they're happy to be free and back together."

"They're overjoyed."

"Have any of them been hurt?"

"They're okay."

"That's great news, but you need to be on guard, in case the other terrorists return and try to rescue their comrades."

"I don't think they know what has happened to their comrades, so there's no reason for them to come here on a rescue mission."

"That's probably true, but you should not take that for granted."

"You're right. I'll talk to Rex, and we'll make plans to defeat anything they might try."

"Good, that's exactly what I want you to do. You've had a great day, and I'm proud of you. Now, you have to safeguard your success until we get there."

"When will that be?"

"I'll call Jerry and find out; then, we'll let you know."

"Thanks, I'll be here."

Tonya looked around the room and thought; I need to collect their weapons, in case they wake up a lot sooner than they are supposed to. Going from man to man, she took away their rifles, pistols, and knives. She carried them out the front door and stacked them against the house.

When she finished the job, she turned toward the north and saw Rex and his family approaching. They were all smiles and rapidly talking in exuberant tones. Seeing their happiness overwhelmed Tonya, causing tears of joy to fill her eyes and roll down her cheeks. A heartfelt sense of satisfaction welled up deep inside of her, and a radiant smile beamed from her face.

Rex and his family surrounded Tonya. All tried to hug her and thank her at the same time.

"You risked your life to save us," stated Shannon. "How will we ever repay you?"

"That's not necessary. What I did was the right thing to do."

"That might be, but it took a lot of courage to put yourself into their midst and rescue my husband and son."

Wearing a radiant smile and feeling like she had gotten away with something, Tonya admitted, "It was risky, but it was the thrill of a lifetime. Defeating the evil ones while they thought I was their victim has given me the biggest natural high I've ever been on."

"We're pretty high right now too," stated Rex. "We need to have a party. Where's Jerry?"

"He's in the cargo shuttle 90 miles east of here."

"This is the second time he has come to our assistance. We need to find a way to thank him. We sure can't have a party without him."

"I know you're in the mood to celebrate, but it might be too soon to have a party. We still have two terrorists to worry about, and we have to decide what to do with the guys I drugged."

"You're right," agreed Rex. "How long will they be out?"

"If they react to the drug the same way my people do, it will be at least 24 hours before they come to."

"That's plenty of time to figure out what to do with them."

"If you decide to continue living here, we'll have to deal with them in such a way that they never again bother you."

Surprised by Tonya's comment, Shannon asked, "What do you mean by if we decide to continue living here?"

"Jerry is going to offer you the opportunity to leave this planet and live with us on Alcent."

Rex and his family were stunned by Tonya's statement. After a few moments of silence, Rex said, "We've never considered leaving here, but maybe we should. The society I grew up in is gone, and it's going to be centuries before this planet's people recover from the Great War. I am a veterinarian and a scientist, but it's impossible to get the most basic things I need to treat animals and do research. Also, we're living off the land and what we find in old buildings that survived the war."

"Rex is trying to say that living here is difficult," stated Shannon, "but we've adjusted to it, and this is home. We've never considered leaving here, because we've never had a way to leave, but now we do." Turning to Rex, Shannon said, "We have a big decision to make."

"Yes we do, and I think we should make it quickly. If we decide to leave, and do so before these terrorists wake up, then we can just leave them here."

"Won't they be surprised if all of us are gone when they wake up," commented Shannon.

"They would be even more surprised if they woke up far away from here," Rex said. "They would not know where they are and would have no clue as to how they got there."

"That idea has great potential," responded Shannon with a malicious grin. "There are some places on this planet where staying alive is far more difficult than here."

While facing Shannon and Kristi, Tonya said, "There are two of them that we might want to deal with more harshly than the others."

"They all need to be dealt with harshly," responded Shannon, "but especially those two."

"I agree," stated Rex, as he turned to Tonya and said, "Thanks for saving my wife and daughter from that brutal attack."

"I am so happy that I was there at the right time to do that."

"I am impressed by the clever way you took them out. They never knew what hit them. And then, you did the same thing to the ones holding me and Jeff. They bought your helpless act, and you methodically took them out without them even knowing what you were doing to them. They had no clue. Only one of them became suspicious, and by then, it was too late."

"I did what I had to."

"But you were so professional. You made it look easy. There's no doubt in my mind that you are one cool cookie with nerves of steel."

Tonya grinned and said, "I've never been described that way before."

At that moment, Tonya's communicator beeped. It was Jim. "Hi honey, I'm on the way. I heard you had a pretty exciting day."

"I sure did! I knocked out nine terrorists, and I rescued Rex and his family!"

"How did you do all that?"

Still on an adrenaline high, Tonya spewed out words at warp speed, quickly giving Jim a detailed account of what she had done. When she finished her story, she said, "I wish you were here."

"I'll be there in less than a half-hour."

"Where will you land?"

"Images taken from the Challenger indicate that the clearing in front of Rex's home is big enough for me to land the helicopter in. Maybe you could check it out for me."

"What do you want me to look for?"

"Lawn furniture, tools, anything that might be a hazard to my landing. Ricocheting debris could damage a rotor blade."

"We'll prepare the area for a safe landing."

"Thanks, see you shortly."

Tonya relayed Jim's request to Rex. He and his family were excited about the helicopter already on the way, and they eagerly went to work preparing the clearing for it to land on.

Tonya went into the forest to retrieve the high-tech gear that she had left behind. When she came back from the forest, she said, "I am starving. I need to sit down and eat."

"We'll join you," responded Shannon.

"First, we have to drag the sleeping terrorists out of our dining area," Rex said. "I'll do that while you put some food on the table."

"I haven't been here for several days," Shannon said. "Do we have anything to eat?"

"We have fruit, vegetables, and smoked fish. Our captors forced me to keep them supplied with food, so now we can eat some of it."

Several minutes later, the happy group finished eating their quickly improvised meal, as they heard the sound of a helicopter landing. Even though they were excited by its arrival, they stayed inside until the rotors wound down to a stop. Then, Tonya rushed out with everyone else in pursuit. Jim hopped out of the helicopter, and Tonya stepped into his arms for a tight embrace. "I am so happy to see you," Jim said. "I was worried about you all day."

"I would be disappointed if you weren't. I would think that you don't love me anymore."

"I don't believe you'd think that, because you know that I'm hopelessly in love with you."

"I'm happy that you are, because I've decided to marry you."

"I haven't asked you yet."

"I know, but you will."

Jim smiled into Tonya's love-filled eyes. Then, they broke off their embrace, so Tonya could introduce everyone to Rex and his family. She started with Jerry. Presenting him to Rex, she said, "This is Captain Jerry Jerontis."

Extending his right arm for a firm handshake, Rex said, "I am pleased to meet you. I thank you for everything you've done for us. We owe you a very big debt of gratitude."

"There is something you can help us with," Jerry responded, warmly.

"Name it," stated Rex.

"Back home on Alcent, we are looking at a life-filled planet that we need to explore and understand. Since you are a scientist, you might come to Alcent with us and help us with that project."

"If I can bring my family along, you got yourself a deal."

Jerry looked at Shannon, Kristi, and Jeff. They were expectantly smiling and their eyes were filled with hope. "I believe we can find room for them," stated Jerry.

"How much time do we have to pack?" Shannon asked.

"I'd like to leave as soon as possible. How much time do you need?"

"That depends on how much stuff you let us bring along."

"You should limit your packing to personal items and things of sentimental value. We can make anything else you need."

"In that case, we won't need much time to pack."

En route to Rex's home, Jim had stopped at base camp to pick up

Trang and his team. Now that Jerry had taken care of the pressing business, Tonya introduced them to Rex and his family.

Speaking to Trang and Geniya, Rex said, "You need to be proud of your daughter. She is an amazing young woman."

"We are proud of her," Geniya said. "But over the years, there have been times when her disappearing act caused us lots of worry."

"That's true," agreed Trang, "but her ability to survive alone in the jungle for weeks at a time made her the best person for the mission she carried out today."

"She handled herself very well," stated Rex. "The terrorists bought her helpless act completely, and then, she did them in. Now we have to decide what to do with them."

"Do you know any of them?" Jerry asked.

"No, in fact, I've never seen them before."

"How did they find out about me and my starship?"

"That is also something I don't know."

"Maybe they found out from one of your neighbors," suggested Jerry.

"We live alone in this area. Our nearest neighbors live 20 miles away. We've only had two visitors since you landed communications equipment here, and both of them are long-time family friends. In fact, one of them is a colleague."

"Do you trust both of them?"

"Yes, of course, but who knows how many people they've talked to. Your arrival from the Solar System was, and still is, the biggest news event of all time. It proved to us that people exist on other planets. Also, you destroyed the chemical warfare weapons, giving us hope for a better future. This kind of news story is so exciting that it would travel far and fast just by word of mouth."

"You're right; it wouldn't take long for the news to reach the wrong people. Then with a little investigation, they could find you. But where did they come from, and who do they work for?"

"I don't know. They could be a group of opportunists or they might be deeply entrenched agents left over from the Great War."

"The fact that we know nothing about them worries me," stated Jerry.

"In what way?" Rex asked.

"To start with, how do we know that there are only two that haven't yet been taken out?"

"I've only seen eleven, and Tonya has put nine of them to sleep."

"But there could be two groups: one group to kidnap you and

your family to bring us here on a rescue mission, and a second group to capture us in the event that we take out the first group."

"That's possible," admitted Rex, "but I haven't heard them say anything that would even suggest a second group."

"They could not say anything in front of you, because they would then lose the element of surprise."

"Good point, but it does take a lot of discipline to avoid an occasional slip of the tongue."

"That's true, but if there is a second group, where do you think they might be hiding?"

"This is a hilly area covered with thick forest. They could be anywhere."

"I was afraid you'd say that."

"If there is a second group, it would be hard for them to surprise us," Trang said. "We can scout the vicinity and post sentries."

"We're also well armed and have night-vision equipment," stated Jerry. "We can certainly defeat an attack, but one or more of us could be killed. Also, a lucky shot could ground our helicopter."

"It only took a few bullets to ground my shuttle for 30 years," stated Trang. "And two of my men were almost killed. We did win the battle, but the price was high."

"We cannot allow ourselves to get stranded here," stated Jerry. "We came here on a rescue mission. That mission has been achieved, so let's not give a possible group of enemies a chance to attack us. Let's leave as quickly as we can."

Speaking to Rex, Jerry asked, "How soon can you and your family be ready to leave?"

"We'll meet your schedule."

"If there is a second group, they'll probably sneak in and attack during the night when they expect most of us to be sleeping, so we need to leave before it gets dark."

"Alpha Centauri B has already set," stated Rex. "Alpha Centauri A will set in three hours, and it'll be dark a few minutes after that."

Turning to Jim, Jerry asked, "Can we evacuate the area with one flight or do we need two?"

"If we take only people and leave everything else behind, we could all leave at once, but we would be dangerously overloaded."

"I don't want to take that risk, and I don't want to leave anything behind that these terrorists can use, so we're going to make two trips. If you leave in a half-hour, you can be back well before second sunset."

Jerry turned to Shannon, but before he could say anything, she said, "We'll grab the things we value the most and be onboard in a half-hour."

"Good, you and your children will be on the first flight out."

Turning to Rex, Jerry said, "I want to take along all the communications equipment I gave you the last time I was here. That way the terrorists will have no way to contact us after we leave. If they can't talk to us, they can't bring us back by taking hostages. Consequently, there'll be no incentive for them to try that."

"I'll put that stuff on the chopper."

"Jim will help you and your family get things loaded."

"What are we going to do with the terrorists?" Trang asked.

Before Jerry could respond, Zonya said, "I recommend we execute them, so they will never again prey on innocent people."

"That's a very stiff sentence to carry out against people we don't know anything about," responded Jerry.

"We know that they captured Rex and his family and held them for ransom," argued Zonya. "That forced us to undertake a dangerous rescue mission. Some of us could have been killed and still might be."

"You are right, but no one was killed, and execution is a penalty normally reserved for premeditated murder. We don't know if these terrorists have ever murdered anyone. We don't know if they would've killed Rex and his family if we had refused to come here. We don't even know if they are terrorists working for the Equatorial Continent. They may be power-hungry locals, who seized upon an opportunity to try to capture my starship. If they are, then when we leave, that opportunity will be gone, and they might simply return to whatever life they came from. Some of them might even have wives and families to go back to. We just don't know."

"You are very persuasive," Zonya admitted, "but these people did commit a grievous crime against Rex and his family. They should be punished for that."

"What do you propose we do to them?"

"We could start by going to Duck Lake and castrating the two that tried to rape Shannon and Kristi."

"That would be a fitting punishment, but it would take time to do that. We don't know if there is a second group of terrorists planning to attack us, but if there is, then the longer we stick around here, the more danger we face. We've completed the rescue. Rex and his family are unharmed, and none of us have been injured. I think our best policy is to just leave as quickly as we can."

"Again, you are very persuasive, but let's at least take a look at each terrorist and see if there is anything we can learn about them."

"That's a good job for you and Zeb, since you are from this planet."

"We'll do that right now."

A few minutes later, Zeb and Zonya eagerly approached Jerry. Filled with excitement, Zeb exclaimed, "We know the leader! His name is Borg. More than 30 years ago, he and I were Air Force fighter pilots training to be astronauts. We both wanted to be on the mission to Alcent, but I won the position."

"How did Borg react to that?" Jerry asked.

"He was upset, and I never trusted him after that. I felt like he was looking for an opportunity to rig a serious 'accidental' injury to me to get me off the mission. I was always on guard."

"He also lost out in another competition," added Zonya. "He was filled with desire for me, but I was in love with Zeb, and that bugged him to no end. He was so obsessed with me that I sometimes felt like he was stalking me. I was always alert for trouble. Borg never took kindly to not getting his way."

"It sounds like both of you knew him well," noted Jerry. "Did either of you ever suspect him of being an enemy agent?"

"Just the opposite," responded Zeb. "He hated the people from the Equatorial Continent. He did a pretty good job of keeping that hatred concealed, but now and then, his feelings slipped out. That hatred was a big factor in him not being accepted for a position on the joint mission to Alcent."

"According to Rex, the people on the Equatorial Continent started the Great War that destroyed this planet. If that's true, it seems like Borg would now hate them even more than when you were his colleague long ago."

"It's hard to say what he's like today," commented Zeb. "People do change. But my guess is that his hatred would now be stronger than ever."

"Based on what you're saying, it seems safe to assume that his demand that we give him and his henchmen a ride back to the Equatorial Continent is a cover-up for his real objective."

"No doubt about that," stated Zeb. "I believe he wants to capture your starship."

"That would be one way to realize his thwarted ambition of going into space," noted Jerry.

"I believe there's more to it than that," stated Zonya. "Unless he's changed, Borg is a power-hungry man. With your starship, he could rule what's left of this planet and Alcent too."

"Why would he want to rule a planet that's been devastated by war?" Jerry asked. "There just isn't much left here to rule."

"But you have to look at his limited choices," argued Zonya. "Living here has to be very difficult. With your starship, he and his henchmen could live a life of luxury."

"It looks like these thugs might not be enemy agents left over from the Great War," stated Jerry. "They might be nothing more than a gang of thieves trying to steal a starship."

"I can certainly envision Borg wanting to steal the Challenger," stated Zeb. "Even though he was rejected for the mission to Alcent, he was an astronaut who flew on some of our manned spacecraft. He had a passion for being in space. By stealing the Challenger, he could return to space."

Geniya and Trang were quietly listening to the conversation, but now, Geniya interrupted them. "If you want to question Borg, I have a drug in my medical bag that will wake him up."

"It might be dangerous to wake him up," Trang warned. "If he has telepathic ability and if he has a reserve group, he could alert them to attack us."

"Good point," Geniya agreed.

"I'm not sure he would tell us anything of value anyway," commented Zeb.

"I'd like to question him," insisted Zonya. "We could learn a lot just by seeing how he reacts to various questions."

"We should not awaken him here," argued Trang.

"We could take him to the shuttle for questioning," stated Jerry. "But I don't want to do that unless there is something specific that we hope to learn that will benefit us in some significant way."

Speaking directly to Zonya, Jerry asked, "What do you hope to learn by questioning Borg?"

"I don't know. I just want to confront him with Zeb at my side and see how he reacts. It should be quite a shock for him to face us after all these years. He hates us, and I'd like to mislead him into thinking that Zeb and I are the ones responsible for thwarting his current ambitions. We should gain a wealth of information by just watching how he reacts and listening to his initial comments. Maybe we can even provoke him into mouthing off about how and why he organized this whole kidnapping plot."

"That would be great information to have, but I don't know that it would be worth delaying our departure."

"Maybe not, but when you're fishing for information, you never know what you're going to learn. Borg could surprise us with something unexpected that is significant."

"If he's willing to talk," commented Jerry.

"I could help with the interrogation," offered Geniya. "Not too long ago, you were our guest, and we had no problem getting you to talk."

"What do you mean, guest? I was your captive. And yes, I'll have to admit that you and Akeyco got everything out of me that you wanted to know."

"You might've been our captive, but you were well treated."

"That's true," Jerry admitted. Then, he turned to Zonya and said, "Let's put the interrogation on hold for a little while until we see how smoothly our evacuation goes. If we can work it into our schedule without much delay or risk, we'll give it a shot."

Jim approached Jerry and asked, "Have you decided on a passenger list for our first flight out?"

"Shannon, Kristi, and Jeff, plus all cargo; I'd like to keep the rest of us here, in case there is a second group that attacks. If all of us are here, we can have a strong defense. Are you going to have a problem taking the rest of us out on the next flight?"

"I thought this might be how you would want to do it, so I've already worked out the numbers. According to the book, we'll be overloaded a little, but I don't think it will be a problem. We'll still be within the safety margin."

"It sounds like it would be better if you took one additional person along on this first flight. Why don't you take Tonya along. She's already done her job, and the rest of us can hold down the fort until you return."

Jim's eyes lit up at the thought of getting Tonya safely out of the area and back on the shuttle. "I can see that you approve," Jerry said with a smile.

"Is it that obvious?"

"Yes."

"Well, she is dear to my heart, and I'd like to get her out of here. Besides, she can entertain Shannon and her children during the chopper flight. They've never flown before, and it's going to be an exciting ride for them."

"Promise me you won't do any aerobatics," requested Jerry.

"I won't have to for them to be thrilled."

"I believe you're right about that. How long before you're ready to take off?"

"Ten minutes, maybe fifteen."

"Good, you'll be back here well before second sunset."

Ten minutes later, the things that Rex and Shannon decided to take to Alcent were on the helicopter and tied down. They had packed quickly because of the urgency of the situation.

Super excited about going flying, Jeff was already onboard with his seatbelt fastened, but Kristi needed a little encouragement. So Jim patiently took her by the hand and helped her step aboard. He explained to her that he had flown many times and that it was perfectly safe. Kristi seemed doubtful, but her fears went away when Tonya entered the helicopter and sat down in the copilot's seat. Tonya had become Kristi's heroine and needed to be emulated.

Jim waited for Shannon to enter the helicopter; then, he closed the doors and took his place in the pilot's seat. When everyone was clear of the area, he started the turbine. A high pitched whine and a muffled roar could be heard inside the helicopter.

Jeff's excitement rose to a feverish pitch as his childhood dream of flying was about to come true. He looked outside and saw the helicopter's rotor blades starting to spin.

Jim gave the turbine engine maximum throttle and it rapidly came to full power. The rotor was now spinning at top speed, but there was no lift being produced because the blades were still at zero angle of attack. An obvious expression of anxiety appeared on Kristi's face, but it was too late for a change of heart, because Jim pitched the rotor blades to optimum angle of attack for takeoff, and the helicopter suddenly jumped off the ground with authority. Very quickly, it was 100 feet above the treetops. Jeff's eyes opened wide when he was suddenly looking down on the trees that surrounded his home. "This is fun!" he yelled.

The view of his home didn't last long, because Jim tilted the helicopter forward and part of the lift produced by the rotor was now used to gain speed. The helicopter rapidly reached Jim's planned cruise speed of 180 mph, and he dropped down a little closer to the treetops. He wanted to leave the area at low altitude to minimize the possibility of being seen by a possible second group of terrorists.

Skimming along the treetops at 180 mph provided a thrilling sensation of speed that Jeff had never experienced before. "This is wild!" he screamed. "We're flying much faster than the birds."

"This is scary!" Kristi yelled. "But it's fun!"

Tonya didn't say anything to Rex's family, because her mind was totally focused on a telepathic search for a possible second group of terrorists. After five minutes passed by, the helicopter was well out of the area, and Tonya discontinued her search. She left the copilot's seat and sat down next to Jeff, who was only ten years old and filled with the kinds of questions that come from childhood curiosity. "Will this chopper take us to the stars?" he asked.

"No, we have a starship for that."

"Is Jim taking us to the starship?"

"No, we're going to our space shuttle, and it will take us to our starship."

"How fast can the shuttle go?"

"It can go fast enough to take us into space."

"Is the starship in space?"

"Yes."

"What's it like in space?"

"You'll find out tomorrow, because that's where we're going."

"Wow! That's going to be super wild."

Meanwhile, back at Rex's home, Trang's commandos were searching the vicinity with RPVs to guard against surprise attack. One of them announced, "There's a canoe coming up the river with one man in it."

Trang put on a headset and looked at the imagery coming from the RPV. Then, he handed the headset to Rex and asked, "Have you ever seen that man before?"

"That's Reecho," responded Rex. "He's one of my colleagues. He was here two months ago. We spent several days discussing our research and the problems we have here on Zebron. At that time, he told me he was going on a research expedition and wouldn't be back for at least a year. I wonder why he changed his mind."

Sounding suspicious, Trang said, "That might be a good question to ask him."

Sensing Trang's suspicion, Rex said, "Surely you don't mistrust Reecho. He's been a colleague and trusted friend for 20 years."

"His travel plans have changed, and he's showing up here at a critical time. Do you think that's purely coincidental?"

Rex thought about Reecho and the relationship he'd had with him over the years. He racked his brain searching his memory for anything of concern. Finally, he said, "I can't think of any reason to mistrust him."

"Very well," responded Trang, "but I think we should test him. Right now, I don't trust anyone who approaches this area."

"Not even one of my long-term friends," protested Rex.

"Deeply entrenched enemy agents, the so-called sleepers, are trusted members of society. All I want to do is test Reecho."

Jerry was quietly listening to the conversation, but he now asked, "What kind of test do you have in mind?"

"You've raised the possibility that Borg and his gang might be an expendable decoy group and that the real terrorists might be waiting for the opportune time to strike. What if Reecho is Borg's boss and he has a backup group waiting to attack? Since Reecho is Rex's friend, he could show up here to check on Borg's situation without Rex being suspicious of the true nature of his visit."

"That's a possibility," admitted Jerry, "but we don't have any evidence other than Reecho is showing up at a critical time. How do you propose to test him?"

"I'm getting to that. Let's assume for the time being that Reecho is Borg's boss. What would he be expecting to find when he arrives here?"

Jerry's face lit up at what was implied by Trang's question, and he said, "I see what you're getting at. We show him what should be a total surprise and watch how he reacts."

Turning to Rex, Jerry said, "We need to drag Borg and his henchmen into the bomb shelter, along with their weapons and anything else that would indicate that they've ever been here. All of us need to get out of sight except you and Zeb. When Reecho knocks on your front door, I want him to find only you and Zeb. You will introduce Zeb as a long lost friend who showed up this morning. Then, we'll see how Reecho reacts."

Trang grinned at Jerry and said, "You and I think alike. That's exactly the test I have in mind. If Reecho is Borg's boss, he'll be so surprised at not finding the gang here that he should react in some detectable way."

"That's a great test," Rex agreed. "But I believe that we'll find that Reecho is innocent."

"Either way, we need to know," stated Trang.

"We don't have much time to set the stage," Jerry said. "He should be here in 15 minutes, so let's get busy."

"There is one thing that bothers me about hiding in the bomb shelter," stated Trang.

"What's that?" Rex asked.

"If Reecho has telepathic power, he will detect us in there, and he might even know how many of us there are."

"There's a room in there that he won't be able to detect you in."

"Is it big enough for all of us?"

"Yes."

Fifteen minutes later, Reecho walked into the clearing in front of Rex's home. He was on camera because Jerry had parked an RPV in a place where it could not easily be seen. Video and sound from the RPV were transmitted into the secure room where everyone was hiding. Jerry, Trang, and Zonya watched Reecho walk across the clearing. He looked from side to side as he walked.

"He seems puzzled," commented Jerry. "Is that because he expected to find Borg and his gang?"

"No way to know," responded Trang. "He might just be looking for Rex or a family member."

Reecho continued walking toward Rex's front door. When he reached it, he knocked and said, "Anyone home?"

Rex went to the front door, looked at Reecho, and acted surprised. "Reecho! What brings you up this way? I thought you were on a one-year research trip."

"Something else came up that I needed to take care of first."

"It must have been something very important, because the research trip we talked about sounded pretty interesting to me. Are you still going?"

"I plan to, but I have some new ideas I want to discuss with you first."

"It's a pleasant evening. We can sit down here on the front porch and talk about it."

"If you don't mind, I'd rather go inside."

Back in the bomb shelter, Zonya was translating the conversation into English, so Trang and Jerry could understand it. "I think Reecho wants to check out the inside of the house," commented Jerry.

"We don't know that for sure," argued Trang. "There are lots of reasons why he might want to go inside."

Jerry switched from the outdoor RPV to signals coming from one concealed in Rex's home. "My guess is Reecho will check the place over as carefully as he can without being obvious."

Reecho followed Rex into the dining room, where Zeb stood up to greet them. Rex introduced the two men. Speaking to Reecho, Rex said, "Zeb is an old friend I haven't seen in so many years that I assumed he was a casualty of the war. Earlier today, he showed up unexpectedly with some friends, and now, you make a surprise appearance. How many more people will surprise me yet today?"

"He concealed it well," commented Jerry, "but it looked to me like Reecho flinched at that question."

"It was subtle," agreed Trang, "but I saw it too. He might be planning to come back with an armed group, and Rex nailed it with that question."

"Do you have any reason to expect more visitors?" Reecho asked Rex.

"No, but I didn't expect Zeb. I thought he was dead. And I sure didn't expect you; I thought you were on a research trip. So I'm just wondering how many more surprises I'll get yet today."

"Maybe your friends from Earth will stop by; you know, the ones that are living on Alcent."

"That would be an awesome surprise, because they're busy building a home and exploring a planet. They really don't have time to come here."

"That's true, but I'll bet they would show up here if they had a compelling reason to."

"I suppose they probably would," admitted Rex. "They are nice people. If we had a critical problem that we needed help with, I'm sure they would help us. Do you have something in mind that you want to bring them here for?"

"Why would I want to bring them here?"

"I don't know; I just asked."

Deep in the bomb shelter, Jerry said, "It looked to me like Reecho flinched again."

"I think he's hiding something," stated Trang. "He was fishing for info about you, but Rex turned it back to him, and he flinched."

Quickly changing the subject, Reecho asked, "Where's your lovely wife and family?"

"They took off with Zeb's friends. I'm not expecting them back tonight, so we have the whole place to ourselves."

"Actually, I'm not planning to spend the night. I'm camped downriver with some friends. I told them I'd be back before dark, but if you don't mind, I'd like to come back tomorrow and bring my friends along."

"That will be fine. Maybe tomorrow, you can tell me what came up that's so important you had to delay your research trip."

"No problem, I plan to hit you with that and enlist your help."

"You got it."

"Maybe your family will be back by then, so I can visit with them."

"I definitely expect to see them tomorrow."

"Okay, it's a plan," stated Reecho as he stood up to leave. Turning to Zeb, he said, "Maybe tomorrow, we can visit for a while. I'd like to find out where you're from and what you experienced during the war."

"Trading war stories should be interesting," responded Zeb.

Facing Rex and Zeb, Reecho said, "See you guys tomorrow." Then, he turned and left.

"I don't trust him," stated Jerry. "We need to watch him."

Trang turned to the commando who had spotted Reecho coming up the river and ordered him to follow Reecho with an RPV while using care to keep the RPV out of sight. Then, he asked Jerry, "Do you think Reecho bought Rex's act? Or do you think he suspects we are already here?"

"If he's involved in the kidnapping of Rex and his family, then he came here expecting to find Borg and his gang. Since he did not find them, he could assume that we're already here and that we've rescued Rex and his family. Also, since Rex did not tell him about any of this, he would have to assume that Rex believes that he's involved and doesn't trust him. If he assumes that, then he's not going to wait until tomorrow to return. He and his friends will be back tonight, probably as soon as they can get here. I hope we're gone before they arrive, or we'll have a battle on our hands."

"If Reecho's involved, all of that makes sense," agreed Trang. "If he's not involved, he probably believed everything Rex said and is planning to come back tomorrow with his friends. We'll be gone, but Borg and his gang will be here."

"If Reecho's not involved, we don't want him and his friends hanging around when Borg and his gang wake up. They could become victims of Borg, especially if some of them are women."

"I have him under surveillance," stated Trang's RPV pilot. "I'll stay with him, so we can take a good look at his camp and friends."

"Good," acknowledged Trang.

At that moment, Zeb entered the room and said, "I believe he's guilty."

"How did you reach that conclusion?" Jerry asked.

"When Rex was visiting with Reecho, I attempted to telepathically listen to Reecho's thoughts, but I was unable to because he built a mental shield around them. Why would he protect his thoughts unless he's trying to hide something?"

"It's possible that he didn't trust you," responded Jerry. "He doesn't know you. He might've built a mental wall around his thoughts just to avoid giving you access to them. That would make it nothing more than a privacy issue."

"That's a reasonable explanation," acknowledged Zeb. "But the mental ability to completely shield one's thoughts is rare. It's a special ability that requires intense training to develop, and when I was living here, it was usually found only in spies."

"Are you convinced that he is a spy?" Jerry asked.

"Yes."

"If you're correct, we still don't know if he's an enemy agent. He could just as easily be a domestic intelligence officer."

"Either way, he would be well trained and very dangerous. If he wants your starship, we have a formidable opponent."

Jerry put on a headset and tuned in to the transmission from the RPV. "Reecho is in his canoe paddling downriver as fast as he can," Jerry said. "I wonder how far away his camp is and why he's in such a big hurry."

"Maybe he suspects what's going on here and wants to get back before Jim does," responded Zeb.

"How could he possibly know that Jim has been here and is coming back?" Jerry asked.

"I don't know, but skilled spies are able to spot the smallest clues and figure things out from them. I saw everything that Reecho did in the house and when he left, but I did not see him when he approached the house. I would like to look at the video of him stepping out of the forest and walking across the front yard."

Jerry handed Zeb a headset, and he put it on and pressed the replay button. Zeb watched Reecho's every move right up to the front door.

"Anything grab your attention?" Jerry asked.

"Yes, why was Reecho puzzled when he looked from side to side while walking across the front yard?"

"I assume it's because he expected to find people out and about and was surprised that the place was deserted."

"There might be some other reason," Zeb suggested.

"What do you think caught his attention?"

"I don't know, but I think we should retrace his steps and see if we can discover something."

"Okay, let's do it, and let's take Rex along."

When the small group stepped out of the front door, Zeb said, "Let's walk around the clearing and step out of the forest in the same place that Reecho did."

A few minutes later, everyone was in the forest at the west side of the clearing. Following the same trail that Reecho used, Zeb stepped out of the forest and slowly walked toward Rex's front door. He looked from side to side without slowing down. Whatever caught Reecho's attention must have been obvious thought Zeb, because he never slowed down.

Halfway across the clearing, Zeb stopped dead in his tracks. A big grin spread across his face because he knew what it was that put the puzzled expression on Reecho's face. Zeb turned around and motioned his friends out of the forest.

When they arrived, Zeb said, "Look around this spot where we are standing and then let your gaze move toward the forest. Then, do the same thing in the opposite direction and tell me what you see."

The men did as requested, and Rex was the first to speak. "My front yard has undergone a rather dramatic change," he said.

"In what way?" Jerry asked.

"My front yard has never been anything other than a clearing in the forest. It has always had a wild, untamed, natural look with leaves and twigs lying around. What do you see now?"

"The whole area is clean," responded Jerry. "The leaves and twigs have been swept to the edge of the forest. It's almost as if you used a powerful blower to put them there."

"A helicopter landing and taking off could do that," stated Rex.

"And you think Reecho noticed this change in your front yard, was puzzled by it, and maybe even concluded that a helicopter was here."

"Reecho has been here often enough over the years to know what my thinking is in regard to my front yard. He would've noticed the change."

"Also, he is as old as I am," stated Zeb. "That means he could've had military training and spy training back before the war. He would definitely be familiar with helicopters. After being surprised by the change in Rex's front yard, he could have concluded that a helicopter had been here. At that point, he would've been puzzled, because helicopters haven't flown on this planet in a good many years. If he's involved in the kidnapping scheme, he would have to conclude that we're already here and that we have a helicopter."

"And he probably concluded that you are part of the rescue team," stated Jerry. "And that's why he shielded his thoughts from you."

"If he's smart enough to figure all that out, then he's probably concluded that Rex's family has already been evacuated," stated Trang. "This means he's assuming that the chopper will soon be back for the rest of us, so he's paddling his canoe as fast as he can. He intends to rally his troops and get back here right away, because he sees his chance to grab a starship slipping away."

"Why doesn't he just communicate with them telepathically?" Jerry asked.

"Don't forget that telepathic communication is a line-of-sight thing," responded Zeb. "Out of necessity, he's had to keep his troops concealed from telepathic detection, which means that he can't communicate with them telepathically."

"I must say that I am deeply disappointed in my friend Reecho," stated Rex. "I don't want to believe that he's involved in this, but it sure looks like he is."

"So far, it's all speculation," stated Jerry, "but it seems to add up."

"We'll know shortly," added Trang, who had just put on a headset. "It appears that Reecho has reached his camp. He's just beached his canoe."

"I need a headset," stated Rex. "I need to see what he's up to."

"You can use mine," offered Jerry while handing it to Rex. Even though Rex was filled with anxiety for what he might see, he quickly put it on.

Shortly thereafter, Rex said, "You guys are right. Reecho is talking to a large group of men. There must be at least 20 of them, and they're all carrying rifles and pistols. I even see some machine guns. Where did he get all those men and military-style guns?"

"He has definitely put a major effort into this," stated Trang. "It's not only a large force, but what's especially ominous is that they look like well trained professionals. It's too large a force for us to fight. We would take casualties, and we might even lose."

"What if we ambush them?" questioned Jerry.

"Reecho's telepathic ability is so good that he would detect us before we could pull it off," responded Rex. "We need to retreat, and do it quickly, because they are already on the way, which means that Reecho has concluded that we are going to be picked up yet tonight. When will Jim be back?"

"In about an hour," replied Jerry.

"Reecho and his men will be here in less than a half-hour," stated Rex. "We have to run for it. We can take the trail toward Duck Lake. When we reach the old highway, we can head east on it. With a half-hour head start, we should be able to keep ahead of Reecho, and Jim should get to us before Reecho catches up to us."

"I believe that's our best option," agreed Trang.

"We're going to have to move fast," stated Rex. "These guys are trotting up the trail at a pretty good clip. They're obviously in pretty good shape. Even with our head start, they might still catch us. Can Jim get back here any faster?"

"I'll call him and tell him about our situation," stated Jerry. "He'll quickly refuel and race back here."

"Let me call Tonya," suggested Trang. "Just in case Reecho stole a communicator, he'll never understand my language."

"Good idea," Jerry agreed.

Trang quickly made the call while Rex, Zeb, Zonya, and Geniya headed down the trail. After completing the call, Trang said, "They understand our situation. Jim will complete refueling and take off in a few minutes. He expects to be here in 40 minutes."

"Good, now we need to get going, but to make our retreat successful, we have to always know where Reecho and his men are. We have RPVs, but they're hard to fly while running."

"My commandos can fly an RPV in relays if we give them each a control unit. They're both young, fast, long-distance runners, and they'll have no trouble keeping up with us."

The commando currently flying the RPV said, "I'll stay here and fly it for a few minutes; then, my buddy can take over while I sprint down the trail to catch up. Then, I'll relieve him."

"I don't like leaving you here alone," responded Trang. "But I don't see any alternative. No one else is fast enough or has the endurance to keep up with either of you."

"We'll be okay. We'll stay alert and out of sight while flying the RPV."

One commando flew the RPV while the other sprinted down the trail. Trang and Jerry followed as fast as they could, but the young man quickly outdistanced them. When he was far enough ahead, he stopped, put on a headset, and took control of the RPV. A couple minutes later, Trang and Jerry passed by him, and he reported, "Reecho and his men are still coming on strong. I wish this RPV had a grenade I could drop to slow them down a little."

"Our grenades are too heavy for the RPVs to carry," responded Jerry while running by. "But we could plant some on the trail and use a signal from the RPV to detonate them."

"If they get too close, that should buy us some time," agreed Trang.

A few minutes later, the other young commando ran past Trang and Jerry. When he was far enough ahead of them, he stopped and took over the RPV.

Twenty-five minutes after the RPV relay started, the entire group, except for the commandos, was together and jogging eastward on the old highway that Tonya had come in on earlier in the day. To catch their breath, they slowed down to a fast walk.

Jerry put on a headset and reported, "Reecho and his troops have reached Rex's home. Reecho is walking toward the front door, and his troops are surrounding the place while staying hidden in the forest."

"It's not going to take him long to find out that we're gone," stated Trang. "But he has no way of knowing that we're still in the vicinity. His first thought should be that the helicopter came back and picked us up."

"He'll consider that possibility," agreed Zeb. "But if Reecho is a highly capable enemy agent, he will also look at other possibilities. He might even figure out where we are."

"How will he do that?" Jerry asked. "We left on a well used trail, and we took care not to leave a track in the first 100 yards. He can't detect us telepathically, because there's a big hill between us and him."

"He will not give up until he is sure that we are gone," stated Zeb. "If necessary, he'll climb to the top of that hill and do a telepathic search from there."

"That will take time," Jerry said.

"We must use that time to put more distance between us and him," stated Zeb. "We need to keep moving as fast as we can."

"Jim will be here in less than 20 minutes," stated Jerry.

"Reecho's best men could be here in 15 minutes," argued Zeb.

"In that 15 minutes, we could easily be at least a mile-and-a-half farther down the road," stated Jerry. "We need to keep moving and stay ahead of them until we meet Jim."

A few moments later, Jerry said, "Reecho has just entered Rex's home, and he's come right back out. Now, he's walking briskly toward the center of the clearing. He's just bent over to pick something up. It's a leaf. He's quickly looking in all directions. He's pointing at the trail we left on and barking out orders. His men are charging down the trail."

"He guessed right," stated Zeb. "And he must have dropped that leaf on his way out earlier as a simple way to know whether or not our chopper returned."

"Let's hit it," yelled Jerry. "We're in a race for our lives."

While running, Jerry pressed a button on his communicator, and it began sending out a signal for Jim to home in on. Yelling at Rex, Jerry asked, "Do you know of any clearings two to three miles ahead of us that our chopper could land in?"

Before Rex could answer, Trang said, "We must be at least halfway to the base camp we set up this morning. There is a clearing there that Jim has already landed in twice."

"I know where that clearing is," stated Rex.

"Can we get to it before Reecho's men catch us?" Jerry asked.

"There is a hill just west of that clearing," replied Trang. "We need to be gone before Reecho's fastest men get to that hilltop. They would have a clear shot at us from there if we're still around."

"Hopefully, we'll be gone by then," responded Jerry.

Ten minutes later, Jerry noticed that Zeb was falling behind. Jerry slowed down a bit, so he could talk to him. "They're gaining on us faster than I expected," Jerry said. "We can't slow down now; we need to pick up the pace."

"It's my ankle," Zeb said. "It's healed, but it's not yet back to 100 percent, and it's starting to slow me down. But don't wait for me. If I fall too far behind, I'll fight a delaying action for the rest of you."

"We're not leaving you behind," Jerry stated, adamantly. "I'll stay with you and mine the trail with grenades if need be."

"I'm with you guys," stated Trang, who had also dropped back.

"Thank you both," responded Zeb. "I'm still too young to die."

Ten minutes later, Zeb was hurting badly. He was making a determined effort to run anyway, but he was running with one leg and limping with the other.

"They're going to catch us before we get to the clearing," Jerry said. "So let's keep our eyes open for a good place to plant some grenades."

"You got it," replied Trang.

"Jim should be at the clearing in five minutes, but it's going to take us ten to get there."

A few minutes later, one of Trang's commandos dropped back to join the trio. "The ten fastest runners in Reecho's group have split up," he said. "Three of them are heading for the hilltop overlooking our pickup point. They must be familiar with this area and have guessed where we're going. The other seven are going to catch us."

Jerry made a quick call to Jim to warn him about snipers on the hilltop while Trang looked for a place to plant some grenades. Pointing down the trail, he said, "Right there is a good place to set them."

The trio planted eight grenades on a 50-yard stretch of trail. Then, they ran 40 yards forward on the trail and Trang said, "We can hide behind this boulder. They won't be able to telepathically detect our presence, and when we detonate the grenades, we'll jump out and shoot the survivors while they're in shock."

"That's a good plan," agreed Trang's commando, "but I have a suggestion. Let me and my buddy do the ambush. We are fast enough to outrun the rest of Reecho's men. You and Jerry can catch up to Zeb and help him get to the clearing."

"He's right," Jerry said to Trang.

Trang nodded and his commando parked the RPV on top the boulder with its camera pointed at the grenade-seeded trail. Then, wearing a headset so he could watch the trail, he made himself comfortable behind the boulder with his automatic assault rifle ready for action.

Jerry and Trang headed for the clearing as fast as they could run. Before they caught up to Zeb, they encountered Trang's other commando, who was running toward the boulder to be part of the ambush.

Then, Jerry's communicator chirped. It was Jim, who said, "I've landed in the west side of the clearing. There are some trees there, and I am as close to them as I could safely land. Snipers on the hilltop have no shot at me at present. The danger will come when we take off."

"You will have an opportunity to use your daredevil flying skills to give them a difficult shot."

"I'll work out a takeoff strategy that will make it tough for them. How long before I have everyone onboard?"

"I'm guessing five minutes. Zeb's ankle is slowing him down. He's hurting, but he's still moving faster than we could go if we tried to carry him."

"He's a tough old bird," responded Jim. "He'll make it."

"We've just caught up to him, and he's still hobbling along. We'll be there in a few minutes."

"Zonya and Geniya have just arrived. And Rex is right behind them. They're taking up defensive positions just inside the forest to the west."

"Good," responded Jerry.

At that moment, the simultaneous explosion of eight grenades echoed through the forest, followed immediately by the sharp staccato of automatic weapons fire. "Sounds like your men did their job," Jerry said to Trang. "I hope they weren't hit."

"They're very good," stated Trang.

Less than two minutes later, Trang's commandos came racing down the trail. "We got those seven," one of them said. "But the rest aren't that far behind, so we need to watch for them."

"We're only a minute or two away from the clearing," stated Trang.

The two commandos performed rear guard duty while Jerry and Trang supported Zeb to speed up his progress. Shortly, they arrived at the waiting helicopter and scrambled aboard. Rex, Zonya, and

Geniya ran out of the forest and jumped in, followed immediately by Trang's commandos.

"I need everyone tightly belted in!" Jim yelled.

The helicopter's turbine engine and rotors were already running at full speed. Expecting to be shot at, Jim wanted a maximum power takeoff with the nose of the helicopter pointed toward the suspected sniper location. This would make it nearly impossible for the snipers to score a hit on the helicopter's turbine engine. Also, during the voyage from Alcent, Mike had manufactured some rocket-propelled grenades with sophisticated guidance systems. They were heat seeking missiles that could home in on the hot gases coming out of guns that were being fired. Best of all, their microcomputers had collective intelligence in that the missiles could communicate with each other and decide which target each missile would take out.

Jim pitched the helicopter's rotor blades to optimum angle of attack, and it leapt off the ground with authority. However, Jim was quick on the controls, and before he cleared the treetops, he had the helicopter's nose and guided missiles facing the suspected sniper location. Immediately upon clearing the treetops, Jim rolled hard left. He did not want to give the snipers an easy shot, but they were good, and several bullets hit the chopper. One of them hit Jim, but with total determination, he maintained control while three missiles instantly launched themselves. The gunmen were only 400 yards away, and the missiles quickly found their targets. The fragmentation warheads exploded, and the gunfire abruptly stopped.

"I've been hit!" Jim yelled at Jerry, who was sitting in the copilot's seat. "You have to take over. I'm bleeding badly from my left shoulder."

Being the lead onboard medical doctor, Geniya quickly went to work. "I need you stretched out on the floor," she said to Jim, who managed to comply.

"I'm feeling pretty weak," he said. "I think I'm going to pass out."

"I'm going to save you," Geniya assured Jim, as she ripped his shirt to expose the bullet wound, which was rapidly bleeding in pulsing spurts. Geniya urgently removed a hemoscope from her medical case. She very quickly inserted the end of the scope into the bullet wound. While watching a monitor, she guided the scope deeper into the wound. The end of the scope was instrumented with sensors that could home in on the source of flowing blood.

In just a few seconds, Geniya said, "I found it, and it's a severed artery."

With meticulous precision, Geniya guided the end of the hemoscope an inch into the artery and inflated a tiny balloon on the end of the hemoscope. After checking for leakage around the balloon, she detached it from the hemoscope and said, "I've stopped the worst of the bleeding."

While Geniya was finding and closing the severed artery working from Jim's left side, Zonya was urgently at work on him from his right side. She found a prominent vein in his right arm and began injecting an oxygen-carrying blood substitute. "How fast can I safely pump this stuff into him?" she asked Geniya.

"We need to go beyond the recommended limit. He's lost a lot of blood, and we have to get oxygen to his vital organs quickly, or we're going to lose him."

"How fast?"

"Double the recommended limit."

"You got it."

"Is he going to survive?" Jerry asked, sounding very worried.

"His condition is critical," responded Geniya. "His blood pressure is way down, and his heart is beating very weakly."

"Can you save him?" Jerry demanded.

"The next several minutes will tell the story," stated Geniya. "His heartbeat should get stronger as his heart receives the oxygen that it needs, and a stronger heartbeat will deliver oxygen to his other vital organs."

"Is there anything I can do to help?"

"Get us back to the shuttle as quickly as you can. We need the medical lab to do the microsurgery that Jim needs for a full recovery."

"That request tells me that you believe Jim will make it."

"He will make it if I can keep his heart beating long enough for the blood substitute to refresh his vital organs, especially his heart. The next few minutes are critical."

"You have to keep him alive."

"I will pour my heart and soul into keeping him alive."

"That's all I can ask. And it looks like I have enough fuel for a full power, maximum-speed return flight. We should be there in 25 minutes."

A few minutes later, Geniya announced, "His pulse is getting stronger. That's a good sign, but we're not out of the woods yet."

"Thanks for the update," responded Jerry.

"I'll call Connie, so she can get the lab ready."

When Geniya finished her medical discussion with Connie, Tonya took over the conversation. "Mother, you have to keep Jim alive. He's a wonderful man, and I love him. How bad is he hurt?"

"He has a bullet wound in his left shoulder, and he's lost a lot of blood, but his condition is slowly improving."

"I wish I could talk to him."

"I know you do honey, but he's unconscious."

"I wish I could be at his side, so I could put my hands on him and offer him comfort."

"We'll be there soon."

"Will he be conscious then?"

"I don't know. His system is in shock, and that's one of nature's ways to shut out pain."

"Please keep him alive."

"I will honey."

"Is he getting better?"

"His condition is continuing to slowly improve, which means the blood substitute we're pumping into him is doing a good job delivering oxygen throughout his body."

"I'm so happy to hear that. Thanks, Mom."

Less than a half-hour later, Jerry landed the helicopter on the shuttle. In just a few seconds, Tonya was at the chopper, closely followed by Mike, who was carrying a stretcher. Jim was soon on the stretcher and on his way to the medical lab.

In the lab, Connie started a blood transfusion to begin replacing the blood that Jim had lost. The blood substitute had done its job. It kept Jim alive by providing oxygen to his vital organs until real blood could be given to him.

Using sophisticated ultrasound equipment, Connie, Geniya, and Zonya began evaluating internal damage. They quickly located the bullet and two fragments.

"I think we should remove the bullet and fragments right away," Connie said. "And we should reconnect the severed artery."

"This sure is a nasty wound," stated Geniya. "We have lots of repair work to do."

While looking at the bullet image on the monitor, Connie said,

"The nose of the bullet is smashed flat. It must have collapsed when it struck the helicopter's windshield."

A worried Jerry, hovering in the background, confirmed Connie's conclusion. "The windshield could collapse a lead bullet," he said. "It's hard enough and tough enough to withstand a 250-mph collision with a 20-pound bird."

"Smashed bullets inflict terrible damage," stated Connie. "It's going to take some time to fix this."

"How much time?" Jerry asked. "What I'm trying to find out is how long will it be before we can take off?"

"I have to remove the bullet and fragments, repair the damage, and bring his pulse and blood pressure back to normal before we subject him to the g-forces of returning to orbit."

"What's your best time estimate?"

"Sometime tomorrow."

"Okay, I want you and your medical team to take all the time you need. The rest of us will provide security."

Jerry left the medical lab and went to the helicopter deck. There he found Mike, Trang, Rex, and Zeb. "We're going to be here until tomorrow," Jerry announced. "We have to get Jim off the critical list before we can take off."

"Your comment implies that he's going to make it," noted Trang.

"There's a lot of repair work to do, but my wife believes Jim has a good chance for a full recovery. But we have to stay here at least until tomorrow, and that means we have to worry about security."

"We've destroyed half of Reecho's force," stated Trang, "and I don't believe the other half has any way to get here."

"There hasn't been any land vehicle or air travel here for more than 20 years," stated Rex.

"Are there any forces locally that we have to worry about?" Jerry asked Rex.

"I don't think so, but I can't be positive. Let's face it; I was surprised by Reecho's troops. I had no clue about them or Borg."

"Here in the middle of the lake, we are several miles from land in any direction," stated Mike. "We've had sonar going all day. Plus, we've been listening to the sounds of the lake, and we've detected nothing but fish. Our radar has detected only birds. I've explored the lake with an RPV, and I found only a few small fishing boats, but they stayed close to shore. We should be safe here, but if need be, we have the firepower to destroy anything that threatens us."

"We'll take turns sleeping and doing guard duty," Jerry said.

Meanwhile, in the medical lab, Tonya placed her hands on the sides of Jim's head. Telepathically, she entered his mind and expressed her love for him. Then, she focused her mental energy into his mind to give him extra strength to help him deal with the stress the traumatic injury was subjecting him to. And she concentrated on stimulating his body's natural healing forces.

Connie removed the bullet and two fragments. Then, she tied the severed artery and removed the balloon that had stopped the bleeding. With this done, she installed a short piece of artificial artery to replace what had been smashed by the bullet. This reconnected the artery, and Jim's left arm began receiving the full supply of blood that it needed. The arm's light, anemic color began to disappear and it took on a healthy flesh tone.

The piece of artificial artery installed was a product of genetic engineering. It was made out of living tissue that was neutral and would not be rejected by Jim's body. The splicing junctures were sealed with genetically engineered glue, and in just a few days, Jim's repaired artery would heal itself to the artificial artery.

Starting at the deepest part of the wound, Connie began splicing torn tissue together. Eventually, she reached the bullet's point of entry and closed the skin on the upper left part of Jim's chest. Three hours after the beginning of surgery, it was over.

Using her hypnotic ability, along with her telepathic powers, Tonya had kept Jim in a state of deep sleep while the surgery was in progress. She did this even while charging his brain with mental energy.

Tonya had maintained the telepathic contact for the entire three hours of surgery, and she was now mentally exhausted. But before breaking contact, she decided to be a bit devious. She induced a dream in Jim's mind. She placed a scene in his mind in which he asked her to marry him, then a joyful wedding ceremony followed by a happy home life. With this done, she broke contact and left the medical lab.

Tonya found a cot and collapsed into a deep sleep. Being well past midnight, it had been a very long, active day for her, and her last bit of energy was gone.

Chapter Five

TIME: Day 60, Early Morning.

It was two hours after sunrise, and Alpha Centauri B was casting its orange light onto Lake Shannon. The orange hue reflecting off the lake created an eerie alien scene, but it was calm and peaceful around the shuttle with only small ripples on the water.

In the medical lab, Tonya and Connie were standing on either side of Jim. "His vital signs are normal and stable," Connie said. "I believe we can expect a full recovery."

"I am so happy that he's going to be all right. Is it okay for me to wake him?"

Connie looked into Tonya's eyes, beamed a warm smile, and said, "I think he needs to wake up to some tender loving attention. Do you have any idea where he can get some of that?"

"I know where he can get plenty of that." Facing Jim, Tonya leaned over him and placed her hands on his head. Telepathically, she entered his mind and slowly brought him out of the deep sleep that she had induced during her previous telepathic intrusion.

When Jim opened his eyes, the first thing he saw was Tonya's love-filled, smiling face. She tenderly kissed him and said, "Good morning, how do you feel?"

"I have a dull, sore ache in my left shoulder. I remember being hit by a bullet. Was anyone else hit?"

"No, you were the only one."

"Was our helicopter badly damaged?"

"No, just a few bullet holes."

"Where are we?"

"We're still on Lake Shannon. We had to fix you up before we could leave."

Jim sat up and said, "Except for my shoulder, I feel pretty good." Swinging his feet off the gurney he was sitting on, Jim stood up.

Facing Tonya, he warmly embraced her using only his right arm. He affectionately placed his left hand on her right hip. Not wanting to aggravate Jim's left shoulder; Tonya returned the embrace with a gentleness that expressed tender love. "I was worried sick about you," she said.

"I am sorry that I put you through so much worry, but I wasn't planning to get shot."

"I know, and I'm so thankful that I didn't lose you. We have so much to live for."

"We did come close to losing our future," Jim admitted. "A few inches to the right and a little lower, and that bullet would've smashed into my heart."

Tonya trembled at the thought. "My life would be empty and very lonely without you," she said. "Our future is so filled with promise. It would be so sad to lose that."

"I think we should start living our future real soon," Jim said.

"What do you mean?"

"When we get back to Alcent, we should get married and begin a family."

"Are you asking me to marry you?"

"Yes, but why do you sound so surprised?"

"I'm not surprised. I'm just trying to clarify what you said," Tonya teased.

"What's confusing about what I said?"

"Nothing, but it didn't sound like you were asking me to marry you. It sounded more like a suggestion."

Jim smiled at Tonya's playful teasing. Then, while looking into her eyes, he popped the big question, "Will you marry me?"

Returning the loving eye contact, she responded with a heartfelt, "Yes!" Then, she passionately kissed him and held onto him in a long, loving embrace.

At that moment, Jerry walked into the medical lab. "I hope I'm not interrupting anything," he said, while smiling at Jim and Tonya.

"It's just another romantic encounter in the medical lab," commented Connie.

"As I recall, that's how our love life got started," responded Jerry. "And our marriage has worked very well."

"We just decided to get married," Jim proudly announced to Jerry. "And our marriage is going to be great too."

"Congratulations, when's the big day?"

"We haven't set the date yet, but it will be soon," stated Tonya.

Speaking to Tonya, Jim asked, "Do you want to get married on our starship, or do you want to wait until we get home?"

"Getting married in space on the observation deck would be romantic, but I think we should wait until we get home, so all of our friends can come."

"I agree," Jim said. Turning to Jerry, Jim asked, "When are we leaving?"

"As soon as your doctor says you're fit for takeoff and climb."

Jim looked at Connie questioningly, and her response was quick in coming. "Medically speaking, you should be able to handle the g-forces involved in returning to orbit," she said.

Turning to Jerry, Jim said, "I'm ready to go."

"Good, we'll take off in a half-hour."

"That's going to be an eye-opening experience for Jeff and Kristi," commented Tonya. "They're so young and impressionable."

"Make sure they have window seats," Jerry said. "Let's also seat Rex and Shannon next to windows, so they can enjoy their first space flight."

"Great idea," responded Tonya. "They're probably going to be just as thrilled as their children."

A half-hour later, the shuttle was ready for takeoff. Its marine pro-peller began churning the water under its aft end. Then, its nuclear reactor throttled up and poured high-pressure steam through the tur-bine powering the propeller, rapidly bringing it up to full power. Like an awakening giant eager to flex its muscles, the shuttle quickly accelerated to 45 mph and rose up on its hydrofoils.

Thrilled by how fast the water appeared to be rushing by, Jeff and Kristi sat with their faces pressed against their windows. Totally engrossed by the sensation of speed, they were unprepared for the acceleration that suddenly pressed them back into their seats when the NTR (Nuclear Thermal Rocket) thundered into action. But not wanting to miss anything, Jeff and Kristi struggled to return to their windows, where they saw the water appear to rush by with an ever increasing speed until it became just a blur. Then, they saw the water appear to rapidly fall away as the shuttle pitched into a steep climb. In a matter of seconds, the shuttle broke above the few low-lying clouds in the area as it rapidly gained speed on its near-vertical climb toward space. Soon, the clouds were far below as the shuttle streaked through the stratosphere. Shortly, it was above the atmosphere, and the blackness of space provided stark contrast to the colorful planet far below.

A few minutes later, the shuttle reached orbital speed, and the NTR shut down. The sudden silence and feeling of weightlessness snapped Kristi out of her mesmerized mental state. "What happened?" she asked, sounding alarmed. "Are we falling?"

"Everything is okay," replied Tonya, who was sitting next to Kristi. "We're going as fast as we need to go, and our rocket has been shut down."

"But I feel like I'm falling."

"Don't worry, you're not falling. You're just weightless."

"I don't like being weightless. It feels weird."

"You'll adjust to it," Tonya assured Kristi.

"I think it's fun to be weightless!" exclaimed Jeff, who was sitting behind Kristi.

"It's weird," Kristi said, "But Tonya will help me adjust to it."

"Flying in space is wild," declared Jeff. "When will we get to the starship?"

"In a few minutes."

"Will we be weightless there too?"

"Only until we begin accelerating away from this planet."

"How long before we leave?"

"Jerry hasn't decided yet, but it will be soon."

"Good, I want to fly through space to your planet and see the dinosaurs."

"Are the dinosaurs scary?" Kristi asked.

"Some of them are."

"I want to see the scary ones," declared Jeff.

"But they could eat you," warned Kristi.

Jeff considered the possibility for a few moments; then, he said, "We could see them from a safe distance."

"That's a good idea," agreed Tonya.

"I see the starship," exclaimed Jeff, while pointing at it. "It's over there."

"It doesn't look very big," commented Kristi.

"It looks small because we're not very close to it," explained

Tonya. "Here in space, it's hard to judge size and distance because you don't have any familiar reference points to use."

As the minutes passed by, the shuttle gradually closed in on the Challenger. At a distance of 50 yards, Kristi exclaimed, "It's huge."

A few minutes later, the shuttle was in the hangar bay and secured to its berth. The hangar doors were closed, and the hangar bay was pressurized.

At that moment, Jerry floated out of the cockpit and into the passenger section. Facing Rex and his family, he said, "Welcome to my starship."

"Believe me, it's a pleasure to be here," responded Shannon. "I feel like I'm living in a dream. It's hard to believe that we've been rescued from the terrorists and that we've left our war-torn planet for a better life. We owe you a lot."

"I have a feeling that you and your family will become cherished members of our society. You have much to offer. Just sharing your life's experiences with us will greatly enrich our lives."

"I'd like to work with Michelle and write our life's stories."

"She's already working with Zeb and Zonya to write their stories. Adding your story to that will give us some good insight into what life has been like on Zebron."

"A big part of our story is the suffering inflicted on us by the chemical warfare weapons you destroyed the last time you were here," stated Rex. "I'd like to see that destruction."

"I plan to do a thorough recon of this planet before we leave," Jerry said. "Those chemical warfare bases are top of the list. I want to make sure they stay out of action."

"I really appreciate that," stated Rex. "The people and animals that are still alive deserve a chance to recover."

When the very excited Jeff was finally able to get Jerry's attention, he said, "Flying in space is fun. How high are we?"

"Our altitude is 230 miles," replied Jerry.

"Wow! Does your starship have any windows? I want to look down."

"We sure do."

"When can we go to the windows?"

Speaking to Tonya, Jerry asked, "Would you mind taking our guests to the observation deck?"

"I'd love to," she replied.

"I'll go with," stated Jim.

"Not so fast," Connie objected. "I need you in the medical lab for a checkup."

"But I feel fine."

"I'm happy that you do, but I want to make sure that the takeoff g-forces didn't cause any problems for you. The checkup will only take a few minutes; then, you can go to the observation deck."

"Okay," agreed Jim.

"Speaking to Rex and Shannon, Jerry said, "In 45 minutes, Mike and I will conduct a meeting in my office to discuss our recon of Zebron. Zeb and Zonya will be there, and we would also like to have your input."

"We'll be there," stated Rex.

Facing Rex and his family, Tonya said, "Let's head for the observation deck."

"How do we get there?" Jeff asked.

"Follow me," replied Tonya, as she led her guests to an open door in the side of the shuttle. Then, she pointed at an elevator 25 yards away and said, "We're going to take that elevator."

"How do we get there?" Kristi asked. "Being weightless is weird. I feel like I'm falling. I keep tumbling, and I can't walk."

"I know how to get there," exclaimed Jeff. "We can fly like birds." Jeff briefly stared at the elevator, fixing it in his mind as his destination. Then, he pushed off with his legs. Screaming with delight, he spread his arms to imitate a bird in flight. Before arriving at the elevator, he rolled and tumbled a few times. After grabbing a handrail next to the elevator entrance, he faced his sister and yelled, "That's how it's done."

"If my brother can do it, I can too," declared Kristi. Then she pushed off and floated to the elevator while gracefully imitating a bird in flight.

"It sure didn't take them long to figure out how to move when weightless," commented Shannon, feeling pride in her children.

"You can go next," suggested Tonya. "You can show off your style to your children."

"I don't know if I can do as well as they did."

"There's only one way to find out."

Shannon did not adjust to weightlessness as quickly as her children, but she could not allow them to outdo her, so she struggled to get control of her sense of balance. With no sense of up and down to cling to, it took a supreme act of willpower to overcome the vertigo she was feeling. Her disorientation bordered on the edge of motion sickness, but her determination was strong, and she managed to gain partial control of her churning stomach and dizziness. Gently, she pushed off and slowly floated toward her children. When she reached them, Kristi said, "Flying like a bird is fun."

Still struggling to control her vertigo, Shannon responded weakly, "I am pleased that you and Jeff are enjoying this so much, but I'm having a hard time getting used to it."

"You can do it Mom," encouraged Kristi. "Just relax and don't fight it. Just pretend you are a cloud floating in the sky. You are no longer tied down by your weight. You are free to just drift wherever you want to go."

"It's fun Mom," stated Jeff. "You'll get used to it."

With her stomach still churning, Shannon smiled weakly and said, "Thanks for the pep talk."

When Rex arrived, closely followed by Tonya, all five entered the elevator. "Plant your feet on the floor," requested Tonya. "We are going to feel some acceleration."

All did as requested, and Tonya started the elevator on its ascent to the observation deck. During the few seconds of acceleration, Shannon's feet were firmly pressed to the floor, and she felt a sense of up and down. This brief break from weightlessness was all she needed to establish control. When the acceleration stopped, and she was again weightless, she said to Jeff and Kristi, "I think I'm going to be just fine."

"Good, now you can have fun with us," stated Kristi.

"Your first test will come shortly," stated Tonya.

"What do you mean?" Shannon asked.

"We have to decelerate to bring this elevator to a stop. When we do that, the ceiling will become the floor. I need everyone to flip over and put your feet on the ceiling right now."

Everyone quickly followed the request, and almost immediately, the elevator engaged its brakes. Everyone's feet were firmly pressed against the ceiling, which now felt like the floor. The elevator came to a stop, and everyone again felt weightless.

The door opened. "Welcome to the observation deck," Tonya announced.

Jeff's eyes opened wide when he drifted out of the elevator and found himself on a large circular deck with a crystal-clear plastic hull all the way around. "This is awesome!" he exclaimed. "I can see Zebron down below and lots of stars everywhere else. And space is black."

Alpha Centauri B did not flood the observation deck with its brilliant orange light because the Challenger's tail was pointing directly at it. Alpha Centauri A, however, was above Zebron's horizon, and its yellow light did pour into the observation deck. But it was soft light because of the star's distance. Zebron's moon was also visible from the observation deck.

Pointing at Alpha Centauri A, Jeff asked Tonya, "Is that where your dinosaur planet is?"

"Yes."

"It looks pretty far away. How long will it take us to get there?"

"A little over two weeks."

"You mean we're going to be in this starship for two weeks!" Jeff exclaimed, very excited. "I want to spend a lot of time on this deck, but where will we eat and sleep?"

"When we leave this deck, I'll show you to your rooms and the cafeteria."

Kristi quietly floated right up to the transparent plastic hull and put her hands against it. She gazed down on Zebron. Looking at its curved horizon, Kristi gained a true appreciation for the fact that she had been living on a spherically shaped planet. She looked at the atmosphere that blanketed the planet and noted the difference between it and the blackness of space. Brilliantly lit by Alpha Centauri B, the atmosphere glowed with a soft orange hue. Even the cloud tops directly below were colored with a soft pastel orange. Kristi noted the huge ocean that they were passing over. It reflected the soft orange hue of the atmosphere. Kristi had never seen an ocean before. Flying over this one gave her an appreciation for its immense size. She noted several groups of green islands set off by the orange hue of the ocean.

Rex and his family gazed in total fascination at the constantly changing scenes presented by the planet far below, which was surrounded by the star-filled blackness of space. "I could stay here for hours," Rex said, "but Shannon and I have a meeting to go to."

"We'll take you there," responded Tonya, with Jim at her side. "On the way, we'll show you the cafeteria and your rooms."

"Can we come back here later?" Kristi asked.

"We sure can," Tonya assured Kristi.

"All of us are going to want to come back," Shannon said.

"My guess is that it will be a day or two before we leave this planet," Jim said. "That will give you plenty of time to enjoy the scenic views from here."

Using the stairway, Tonya led the small group up to the next deck, which was the medical lab. After a brief stop, they took the stairway up one more deck to the cafeteria. All picked up a beverage and a snack.

Back to the stairway, Tonya led the way up to the next deck, which was one of the Challenger's four decks equipped with staterooms. A hallway stretched across the circular deck with the stairwell on one end and the elevator on the other end. Three apartments were located on each side of the hallway. Pointing at the first two doors on the right, Tonya said, "Jim and I live in those two rooms." Pointing at the three doors on the left, she said to Rex and Shannon, "Those three staterooms are for you and your family."

Tonya opened the first door and took them into the room. "Your three rooms are connected," she said while pointing at a door. "That door leads to the center room and it's connected to the far room."

"I think we should live in the center room," Rex said to Shannon. "Jeff and Kristi can each have one of the other rooms."

"I like this room," exclaimed Jeff. "Living on a starship is going to be fun. And the cafeteria and observation deck are really close."

Kristi went to her room, inspected it briefly, and returned. "I'm ready to move in," she said.

With the living arrangements decided, Jim said to Rex and Shannon, "It's time to go to our meeting."

"I'll stay with Kristi and Jeff," Tonya said. "I think they might like a tour of the rest of the ship."

Their eyes lit up. "Let's go," Jeff said, with Kristi eagerly agreeing.

"Why don't you start with the flight deck," Jim suggested to Tonya. "We can all go up there together." Turning to Rex and Shannon, Jim said, "The Captain's office is next to the flight deck, which is located in the nose of this ship."

Everyone boarded the elevator. Shortly, they were on the flight deck. Jim briefly explained it to everyone; then, Tonya, Jeff, and Kristi left.

Jim, Rex, and Shannon entered Jerry's office, and the informal meeting came to order. "I don't expect to return to this planet for quite a long time," Jerry said. "So before we leave, I want to update our reconnaissance information. We'll start by taking a look at the chemical warfare bases we destroyed the last time we were here. Also, we'll fill the gaps in our recon database from back then. And I am open to suggestions from each of you."

"I'd like to see if there's anything left of the military bases I was stationed at before the Great War," stated Zeb. "As you know, I was a fighter pilot and a test pilot before becoming an astronaut."

Mike called up a map of the Northern Continent and asked Zeb to pinpoint the base locations. After this was done, Zeb asked for a map of the Equatorial Continent. On it, he marked the location of the space complex involved in the interstellar mission to Alcent.

"We'll get detailed data for those locations," Jerry assured Zeb. "Then, I'd like you to help us interpret the data."

"That I will do," responded Zeb.

Jerry turned to Rex, who said, "My request is of a more personal nature, but if it's not too much trouble, I'd like the opportunity to check it out."

"What do you have in mind?" Jerry asked.

"I have a brother who is 20 years my junior. That would make him 30 years old, if he's still alive. I'd like to look for him. If I'm able to find him, I want to tell him that I'm leaving this planet."

"Do you have any idea where he might be?"

"Ten years ago, Zack left my home with two friends. They planned to hike all the way to the west coast."

"That's a very long journey to be making on foot," Jerry said.

"I know, but they had no other way to make the trip, and they didn't care if it took them a few years to get there and back. But it's been ten years and they haven't returned."

"And now, you'd like to look for your brother."

"Yes."

"It's 3000 miles from your home to the west coast and ten years have passed by. I don't mean to be pessimistic, but this seems like an impossible search."

"I agree that it is, but there are some places along the way that they wanted to check out. There is one place in particular that Zack wanted to investigate, and that's where I want to look first."

"Where is that?"

"There are some cave dwellings in the Desert Southwest that were inhabited by an ancient civilization thousands of years ago. Zack and his friends read about them in an archaeology book and were intrigued by the technology that they must have possessed to excavate caves in solid granite. If Zack and his friends made it to the caves, they may've decided to live there because they wanted to do an extensive investigation. Their hope was to determine where those people came from and what happened to them. Our best scientists were never able to solve the mystery, but Zack and his friends were determined to solve it. So they might still be there."

Mike's ears perked up at the phrase 'excavate caves in solid granite'. He turned to Jerry and said, "Those caves might be something that we need to investigate before we leave here."

"I agree," responded Jerry. "It sounds like there's a possibility they were inhabited by relatives of the mysterious Ancient Ones that we're investigating on Alcent."

"Looking inside those caves won't delay our departure more than a day or two," Mike said. "All we have to do is deliver an RPV to the site with a small landing capsule. Then, we can fly the RPV inside and get some good video."

"What Ancient Ones are you guys talking about?" Rex asked.

Using a large video screen, Mike displayed images of the knife and belt buckle emblem found on Alcent that were believed to be 123,000 years old. Then, he showed the granite cave complex above Rainbow Falls. Last, he showed the caves Tonya had discovered and the writing on the walls of one of the caves.

The writing instantly caught Rex's attention. He studied it intently. "I've seen similar writing," he said. "It's in the caves Zack went to investigate. Is it possible people came here from somewhere else and they also settled on Alcent?"

"We think so," responded Jerry. "It's a mystery that we'd like to solve, so we need to investigate those caves. Maybe we'll even find your brother there."

"That would be great. I'd like to see him before we leave here."

Turning to Mike, Jerry said, "Before we check out those caves, I want to update our reconnaissance database for this planet. I am especially interested in the military situation. I don't want any nasty surprises, so let's make sure nothing of consequence has happened since the last time we were here."

"The recon satellite we left here hasn't detected any military activity during our absence," stated Mike. "But it doesn't have the capability the Challenger has, so I'll work out a plan to detect anything that it may've missed."

"Good!"

Two hours later, the Challenger was in the optimum orbit to investigate the previously destroyed chemical warfare bases. Still at an altitude of 230 miles, it was approaching the northernmost base from the north.

On the flight deck, Mike said, "I'll be surprised if we find any activity at any of these bases. Our antimatter particle-beam gun rendered such complete destruction that I just don't believe anything could've survived."

"I agree," Jerry said, "but we have to check them out anyway."

To show Rex what the base looked like before its destruction, Mike displayed imagery of it on a large video screen. The 3-D video showed a dormant volcanic peak stretching to above 30,000 feet with a large chimney protruding from its top. A thick black jet of material was blasting out of the chimney directly into the stratosphere, where it was picked up by the jet stream. Much of the chemical poison was carried to the Northern Continent where thunderstorms milked it out of the air and dropped it into streams, rivers, and lakes.

"Those are the poisons that killed so much of the life in my country," stated Rex with a heavy heart.

Mike removed the video and brought up an image of what the chemical warfare base looked like after its destruction. After studying it for a few seconds, Rex said, "You delivered some awesome destructive power to that mountain. It looks like you removed several hundred feet from its top."

"Six hundred feet," stated Mike, "and we created a crater at the top."

"I can see that you caused some huge avalanches that most likely contained mud, rocks, ice, and snow."

"It's time to look at the mountain in its current condition," Mike said, as video was beginning to come in on an adjacent screen. Everyone watched in silence while visually switching back and forth between the two screens.

Mike was the first to comment. "The most obvious change is that the crater at the top has started to fill up with snow, and snow fields are starting to form on the mountain's sides. Eventually, some of them will turn into glaciers."

"The base of the mountain looks like the aftermath of a volcanic eruption," noted Rex. "It's a wasteland, but eventually, life will return."

"The destruction is regrettable," Jerry admitted. "But the evil fanatics running the chemical weapons buried inside the mountains were indiscriminately killing unsuspecting people and most mammals on two continents. They had to be brutally shut down."

"Life on the Northern Continent and the Southern Continent now has a chance to recover," stated Rex.

While reviewing the data coming in from the Challenger's various reconnaissance instruments, Mike said, "I see no indication of any military activity. I believe we delivered complete destruction, and this base will never again operate at any capacity."

"That's also my conclusion," agreed Jerry.

Shortly, the Challenger passed over the second destroyed chemical warfare base, then the third, fourth, fifth, and sixth. "I see no military activity at any of them," Mike said. "I think we can safely assume they are permanently out of action."

Speaking to Jerry, Rex said, "Once again, I want to thank you for destroying those chemical warfare machines. Now that I've seen the destruction, I can understand why Reecho wants the Challenger and its antimatter particle-beam gun."

"No one is going to get the Challenger while I'm alive," declared Jerry, adamantly.

"You will have lots of help keeping it out of the wrong hands," stated Mike.

"I appreciate that," responded Jerry. Turning to Zeb, Jerry said, "Your former military bases are next on the agenda. We'll find out if there's anything left of them."

"The Great War was very thorough in its destruction," Rex said. "I doubt that we'll find anything."

"All of the bases I worked at had extensive underground facilities," argued Zeb. "Some of that may've survived."

"We'll be over one of them in 45 minutes," stated Mike. "If there's anything going on, we'll spot it."

Mike displayed a map on a large video screen showing the base's location. While looking at it, Zeb said, "I was a test pilot at that base. Top secret new aircraft were tested and developed there, and we had large, hardened underground facilities that were designed to survive everything except a direct hit from a bunker-busting nuclear bomb."

Rex also studied the map. "That base was located in a highland desert," he said.

"That's right," responded Zeb. "The altitude was 6200 feet, and it was isolated by the surrounding desert, which made it a good place to develop secret aircraft."

"The ancient cave dwellings that Zack went to investigate are located 150 miles south of that base in what is currently a semiarid lowland desert at 1400-feet altitude. Climatologists think the area was lush with vegetation in ancient times, which would've made it a good place to live."

"We're going to pass over that cave complex a half-minute before we pass over the military base," stated Jerry. "But I do want to spend a day checking out the military situation on this planet before we start investigating those caves."

"I appreciate that," responded Rex. "But I could use the first over-flight to make a telepathic search for my brother."

"If he's there, will you be able to find him?"

"Only if he's outside. He could just as easily be in one of the caves; in which case, I won't find him."

"While you're telepathically searching for your brother, we'll search the area for indications that people are living there."

"Thanks," responded Rex. "If you don't need me for anything here, I'm going to the observation deck. This is my first spaceflight, and I'm eager to do some sightseeing."

"I believe we've discussed everything we need to for now," Jerry said.

Facing Rex, Zeb said, "I'll join you. I grew up on this planet and have been away for a long time. I can't pass up this opportunity for some nostalgia."

"Mind if I tag along?" Zonya asked.

"Please join us," replied Rex with Zeb nodding in agreement.

A half-hour later, on the observation deck, Rex said, "I'm only a few minutes away from possible contact with my brother."

"You must be excited about that," commented Zeb. "I know how happy I was when I telepathically found Zonya from this observation deck after a 30-year separation."

"That was a stroke of good fortune," stated Rex.

"It sure was," agreed Zonya while giving Zeb a hug.

"I hope I can be as lucky in my search for Zack," Rex said. "I realize that finding him is a long shot, but I'm happy to have the opportunity to look for him."

"I know how you feel," Zeb said. "I faced the same uncertainty in my search for Zonya. I didn't even know if she was alive."

"Zack might not be alive. Anything could've happened, but the biggest problem he faced was drinking water. There was the constant problem of poison rain."

"How was he planning to deal with that problem?"

"When the poison rain first started, many of our people were killed because we didn't know that our water was being poisoned. When the poison was identified, we discovered that it was more volatile than water. We found that boiling water for ten minutes was long enough for the poison to evaporate out. Zack and his friends planned to boil their water, but matches have been unavailable for a long time, so they had to use other means to start fires. I just hope they never got careless about boiling their water."

Gazing down on the planet far below, Rex noted, "The coastline is directly ahead, and the ancient caves are only 110 miles north of there, so it's time to start looking for Zack."

Rex stared at the lowland desert and focused his mind on the cave location. Using his mental power, he telepathically reached out searching for Zack's mental signature.

While Rex did his search, Zeb stared intently at the lay of the land, searching his memory trying to recall what the terrain looked like when he was a young man flying high-altitude experimental aircraft over the area. He noted that even though much of the planet had been overrun by plant life since the Great War, the desert below was still brown.

Directly over the cave complex, Rex said, "I'm not detecting Zack or anyone else."

"I'm sorry to hear that," replied Zeb, "but we have something very interesting directly ahead at the secret projects base."

Looking at the area, Rex said, "I see what you mean. There are lush green areas there. How can that be in the middle of a desert?"

"Irrigation is a possibility, but that means people must be living there."

"But where is the water coming from?"

"The airbase had a vast underground complex equipped with several deep wells."

"We must search for people," stated Rex.

Immediately, Rex and Zeb focused their minds in a telepathic search of the area. In a few seconds, Rex said, "I've found Zack."

"I've found several people," stated Zeb. "It looks like we have a viable community down there."

Rex quickly hit Zack with a telepathic message. "Hi Zack! This is Rex. I'm happy that you're alive. I need to visit with you."

When the message entered Zack's mind, he was driving a jeep pulling a small trailer loaded with freshly harvested potatoes. He stopped the jeep and looked around expecting to see Rex, but he was nowhere to be found.

Rex expected Zack to react in this way, so after pausing a few moments to let Zack discover that he wasn't nearby, he sent a second message. "You won't find me down there, because I'm in a starship directly overhead."

Zack was shocked by the unexpected message from Rex, and now, he was even more shocked to find out that Rex was on a starship. Quickly focusing his mind, Zack beamed a telepathic message straight up. "How did you get onto a starship, and where is it from?"

"It is from Earth, a planet orbiting the Sun. How I got on it is a long story that I need to save for later. I want to know what your situation is before we lose contact. We'll soon drop below your northern horizon."

"I've joined a self-sufficient community that is maintaining the technology we had when the Great War started. Everything is underground. Our leader is General Kayleb, but he dropped the title long ago. He insists on just being called Kayleb. Okay, that's my story. So how did you get on a starship?"

"That story will have to wait. I want to know if you discovered anything in the caves."

"Maybe."

"What do you mean by maybe?"

"There is a sealed chamber, or I should say that I'm convinced there is. We were unable to open it, but we believe it's there."

"I will tell Jerry about that."

"Who is Jerry?"

"He is the Captain of this starship. We are going to lose contact in a matter of seconds, but we'll be back in a couple hours."

"I will tell Kayleb about you. He will have more questions than I do."

At that moment, contact was lost, and Rex asked Zeb, "Does the name Kayleb mean anything to you?"

"He was my commander when I was a test pilot at that base. Why do you ask?"

"He's in charge of the community we just passed over."

"I don't know what he's like today, but he was a good man back when I knew him."

"We need to go tell Jerry what we've discovered."

A few minutes later, Rex, Zeb, and Zonya arrived on the flight deck, where they found Mike, Jerry, and Trang looking at high-resolution video of the community just passed over. On the screen, there was a jeep with an open top pulling a small trailer. The jeep stopped, and the driver looked around, appearing puzzled. Then, he looked up. Seeing the man's face, Rex exclaimed, "That looks like my brother. Can you get more resolution?"

Jerry froze the image, zeroed in on the jeep, and asked the computer for maximum detail. "That's Zack!" exclaimed Rex. "And he looks healthy."

"Were you able to establish contact?" Jerry asked.

In response to the question, Rex and Zeb revealed everything they had learned while on the observation deck. Zeb concluded his comments with, "I'd sure like to visit with Kayleb and find out what's going on down there."

"I'd like to talk to Zack and find out what he's seen and done since leaving home," stated Rex.

Turning to Mike, Jerry said, "We need to get some communications equipment down there. How soon can you have it ready to go?"

"All I have to do is pack a video phone in a small capsule and plug in the landing coordinates. If I go do that now, we can drop it on our next approach."

"The release point is less than an hour away. Can you have it ready that soon?"

"It'll be ready," replied Mike, while leaving the flight deck.

Turning to Rex and Zeb, Jerry said, "On our next pass, you can let the people down there know that a capsule is on the way and that it will use a para-wing to glide to its landing point. We don't want them to think they're being attacked."

"I'll bet Kayleb will be looking for telepathic contact on our next pass," stated Zeb. "I'll make sure he knows what's happening."

"With the arrival of a starship over his community, I can imagine he'll be filled with questions," Jerry said. "If I were in his place, I'd want to know what our intentions are and if we pose a threat."

"I'll put his mind at ease," stated Zeb. "I'm sure he remembers me."

"He'll remember both of us," commented Zonya. "We were part of this planet's first interstellar mission. Our names and pictures were constantly in the news."

"When he finds out we've come back from Alcent, he's going to want to talk to us," stated Zeb. "He'll want to know everything that happened on the mission and how we came to be on this starship. We could sit at a conference table with him all day and still not have enough time to answer all of his questions."

"That would certainly be an interesting meeting," commented Jerry. "I have lots of questions I'd like to ask Kayleb. A tour of his underground facilities might even be interesting. But after the narrow escape we just had, I'm not sure going down there would be a wise thing to do."

"Kayleb was an honorable man when I worked with him," Zeb said. "But that was a long time ago. He may've changed since then."

"I can find out from Zack what life is like in that community," offered Rex. "That will give us an indication of what kind of leader Kayleb is."

"The images we have suggest that there is a smoothly functioning community down there," commented Jerry. "That suggests Kayleb is an effective leader. But we don't know what he would try to do to us if we go down there. He might think capturing us would be a good way to grab a starship."

"In view of what my family just went through, there's no way we can rule that out," stated Rex. "We were terrorized by a man I thought was a friend, a trusted colleague. After that, I'm just not willing to trust anyone down there except for my brother."

"We need to be cautious," responded Jerry, "but a horrible war was fought here, and people have suffered much tragedy. Now there appears to be a thriving community down there. Maybe with just a little help from us, they could be the foundation on which this society rebuilds itself."

"They might not need any help," commented Zeb. "Their underground facilities were extensive, and it looks like everything survived. There are only three bomb craters down there, and they appear to be way off target."

"Those are pretty big craters," noted Jerry. "The nuclear bombs that made them must've had a yield of at least one megaton."

"Kayleb and his people are fortunate those bombs were off target as far as they were," stated Zeb. "I don't know how large that community is, but when I was stationed at that base, there were 3500 men and women there. And everyone lived underground."

"Apparently, they still live underground," speculated Jerry. "We haven't spotted any homes. Agricultural activities appear to be the only thing going on above ground."

"It's amazing that they would still be living underground 30 years after the nuclear exchange," commented Trang.

"When I worked for General Kayleb, he was a very cautious man," stated Zeb. "With the ongoing poison rain, he would've kept everyone underground to guard against the possibility of the enemy having the ability to make and deliver more nuclear weapons."

"Providing Kayleb with current intelligence data is one way we could help him right now," Jerry said. "He would probably love to have detailed recon data for the Equatorial Continent."

"Just knowing that the poison rain will never come back will be a big relief for him," stated Rex. "Even though he lives in a semiarid desert, it does rain occasionally, so I'll tell Zack that you destroyed the chemical weapons."

"If he'll tell Kayleb, that should put his mind at ease as to what our intentions are," Jerry said.

"I will also tell Kayleb," stated Zeb. "I should say I will tell him if I'm able to make telepathic contact with him."

Jerry's communicator beeped. It was Mike. "I have the capsule ready to go," he said.

"That was quick," responded Jerry.

"I had to be quick. We're only a few minutes away from the release point."

"Thanks for getting the job done in a hurry."

"You're welcome."

"I think it's time for us to go back to the observation deck," Rex said to Zeb and Zonya.

A few minutes later, the trio arrived on the observation deck. Lost in their own thoughts, they quietly observed the planet below as the Challenger moved northward at its orbital speed of about five miles per second. Zebron had a serene peaceful appearance. Casual observation offered no evidence that a tragic planet-wide war had been fought.

Soon, the secret projects military base appeared on the northern horizon. "It's time to establish contact," Rex said as he began focusing his mental energy in a telepathic search for Zack. Very quickly, Rex found his brother and began relaying pertinent information.

Zeb and Zonya attempted to telepathically contact Kayleb, but as the minutes ticked by, they did not find him. Soon, the starship passed over the military base and dropped below its northern horizon. Telepathic contact was no longer possible.

Turning to Zeb and Zonya, Rex said, "They now know that communications equipment will be landing shortly."

"That's good, because we were unable to establish contact with Kayleb," Zeb said.

"There's a reason for that. Zack told me that Kayleb suffered a head injury in an accident a few years ago. He has recovered his health but the injury damaged the part of his brain that makes telepathic communication possible. Kayleb was with Zack during our conversation and coached him. Kayleb is thrilled that communications equipment is on the way, and he is eager to talk to both of you."

"Let's get back to the flight deck, so we can talk to Kayleb in Jerry's presence," suggested Zeb.

"Good idea," stated Rex, as all three headed for the elevator.

Meanwhile, down on the military base, Kayleb, Zack, and many other people searched the sky. Zack was the first to spot the red, white, and blue para-wing with the landing capsule hanging below it. "There it is," he yelled while pointing at it.

Following Zack's direction, everyone located the slowly descending para-wing, which was nicely contrasted against the soft orange hue of the late afternoon sky. Excitement grew in each person's mind while they watched the para-wing circle the area in its tight spiraling descent. Kayleb thoughtfully expressed what was in everyone's mind. "What an awesome surprise this is," he said. "We have interstellar visitors. I've always believed that the Universe is filled with life, but I never expected anyone to come here."

Onboard the Challenger, Mike deployed the landing capsule's video cameras. He spotted the large group of people looking up and decided to land the capsule near them.

Instruments on the capsule reported wind direction and velocity along with the capsule's altitude. Using this information, Mike skillfully piloted the capsule's para-wing. When it was only a few hundred feet above ground, Mike put it into a tight turn heading it into a gentle breeze for its final approach glide.

The group on the ground intently watched the para-wing glide directly at them. Only a few moments before reaching them, it veered away, pitched into a stall, and fell straight down for the final few feet of its descent. The para-wing collapsed to the ground next to the capsule.

"They landed it practically at our feet," exclaimed Kayleb. "They must have some awesome technology to drop a capsule from an orbiting starship and land it so close to us."

Knowing that the capsule contained communications equipment, Kayleb turned to Zack and said, "Let's go meet our visitors."

Side-by-side, Zack and Kayleb walked toward the capsule, which was only 50 feet away. As they arrived, a door with a video screen mounted on its inside swung open. An image of Rex appeared on the screen. "Hi Zack," he said. "I'm happy to see that you appear to be in very good health."

"I am," replied Zack, while staring at the video camera on top the capsule. "Kayleb and his people have welcomed me into their community, and life has been good."

"When do I get to meet Kayleb?"

"He's standing to my right. Can you see him?"

"Yes!"

Turning to Kayleb, Zack pointed at the video screen and said, "This is my big brother Rex." Facing Rex, Zack said, "This is Kayleb."

Rex and Kayleb nodded toward each other's video screen image and said, "Pleased to meet you."

"I want to thank you for taking care of my little brother," stated Rex.

"He and his friends have been good additions to my community," responded Kayleb. "They've definitely earned their keep. But I want to know about you. How did you manage to get yourself onboard a starship from the Solar System?"

"My family and I were captured by terrorists, and the people on this starship came here from Alcent to help us. Using a bold strategy, they defeated our captors and rescued us. Captain Jerontis invited us to join his community on Alcent, and we accepted his invitation."

"Captain Jerontis must be a very special friend that he would come here from Alcent just to rescue you and your family. I would like to meet him."

Rex's image disappeared from the screen and Jerry's image appeared. "This is Captain Jerontis," stated Rex.

After formally greeting each other, Kayleb said, "Thank you for rescuing Zack's big brother and his family."

"They are our friends," responded Jerry. "In our position, you would've done the same thing."

Kayleb's facial expression made it obvious that he was honored by the compliment. "That's true," he said, "but we've only just met. How could you know that about me?"

"I have a man standing at my side who was one of your test pilots back before the war. He has spoken quite highly about you."

Reacting with complete surprise, Kayleb said, "That could only be Zeb."

"That's who it is," responded Jerry.

"This is truly a great day. First I was shocked by the surprising arrival of a starship. Then, I find out that a respected colleague that I thought had perished on our first interstellar mission is not only alive but has made a triumphant return on your starship."

"It's even better than that. Two of your astronauts are with me," stated Jerry as his image was replaced by Zeb and Zonya.

"Both of you look really great!" exclaimed Kayleb. "It's good to see that you're both alive and healthy. I never dreamed that I would ever see either of you again."

"We've had some close calls," responded Zeb. "And we were separated for 30 years, but Jerry brought us back together. We have a daughter and a son-in-law who are both 31 years old, and we have two grandchildren. We are now living with the earth people."

"It sounds like Jerry has been busy rescuing people," commented Kayleb.

"More than you can imagine," stated Trang, who appeared on the video screen. "He also rescued half of my people."

"Who are you?" Kayleb asked.

"My name is Trang, and I am the Captain of a starship from Delta Pavonis. Some of us are also living with the earth people."

"It looks like Jerry has brought people together to form an interstellar community."

"That's true," stated Jerry, after he reappeared on the video screen.

"Is the community open to new members?" Kayleb asked.

"It definitely is. What do you have in mind?"

"We are a small community struggling to rebuild a nation that was destroyed by a brutal war. We are determined to be successful, and so far, we have been. But there might come a time when we'll need help, and we would find a way to compensate you for helping us."

"I believe that we'll be able to work something out. Looking at the long-term big picture, I would like to build a strong interstellar community based on a union between Zebron and Alcent. We are currently updating our recon data for Zebron, but so far, your society is the largest social unit we've found, and that makes you the prime candidate to represent Zebron."

"When Zeb left this planet many years ago, I never dreamed that his mission would one day lead to us being considered for membership in an interstellar union."

"It might be an easily workable union," Jerry said. "Based on what Zeb has said, it appears that your values are compatible with ours."

"That's something we need to determine," responded Kayleb. "We really do need more information about each other to find out what we have in common and to identify and work out our differences."

"That should be easy. The communications equipment we just landed will enable you to communicate with us even after we've returned to Alcent."

"That's great, but if we're going to unite, I think we should meet face-to-face before you go back to Alcent. I would be honored if you would come down here and be my guest for a few days before you leave."

"Thanks for the invitation. How about tomorrow morning?"

"That will be great. Will you bring Zeb and Zonya along?"

"I can't imagine coming down without them. If I leave them behind, they might never speak to me again."

"That sounds like the Zeb I remember, but I can't speak for Zonya. I've never met her."

"You will, tomorrow morning."

"Good."

"Zeb has some questions for you, so I'm going to turn this over to him. I will see you in the morning. If you need to speak to me before then, you can call me."

"Thanks."

Eager to catch up on events with an old friend, Zeb took over the communications. Jerry went into his office, taking Trang, Mike, and Rex with him. "We have an opportunity to cement a relationship," stated Jerry. "But there are some risks involved." Jerry made eye contact with each man and waited for their comments.

Trang was first to speak. "I believe we can trust Kayleb," he said.

"I think so too," Jerry said, "but when we go down, we'll be at his mercy. We'll be a small group, and we'll be vastly outnumbered by his people."

"That's true," acknowledged Trang. "But I don't think Kayleb wants your starship. I think he's dedicated to rebuilding his country and wants to be friends with you, so he can call on you if he ever needs help."

"If we take him at his word, that is what he wants," agreed Jerry.

"My little brother thinks the world of Kayleb," stated Rex. "In fact, Zack is inspired by Kayleb's total determination to rebuild our country."

"Of all the things that Zack said about Kayleb, what caught your attention more than anything else?" Jerry asked.

"Zack likes Kayleb's political philosophy, which emphasizes personal freedom and responsibility. He also likes the way Kayleb treats everyone with courtesy and respect."

"That confirms what Zeb has said about Kayleb," Jerry said. "With Zack and Zeb speaking up for Kayleb, we have two excellent character references for him. What we see going on down there also speaks well for Kayleb. I am willing to gamble that his intentions are good, so let's go down tomorrow morning and treat Kayleb with utmost respect and see where that takes us."

Chapter Six

TIME: Day 61, Early Morning

One hundred ten miles south of the cave complex, Alpha Centauri B peeked over the eastern horizon and began casting its orange rays onto the saltwater bay and landscape. Greeted by the sunrise, the big cargo shuttle arrived with its hydrofoils splashing into the bay. Captain Jerry Jerontis sat in the pilot's seat, and Mike Johnson sat in the copilot's seat.

"It sure is a beautiful morning," commented Jerry as the big shuttle taxied to a stop five miles offshore. "I wonder what surprises this day will bring."

"It sounds like you're expecting some," responded Mike.

"We haven't had very many surprise-free days on Alcent or here on Zebron."

"Today certainly has lots of potential for unexpected things to happen. We don't know what we're going to find in the caves, and we don't know what Kayleb has planned."

"There is another possibility that you haven't mentioned."

"What's that?" Mike asked.

"One of the biggest surprises in my life was being kidnapped by aliens while guarding this shuttle."

"Are you suggesting that might happen to me today?"

"No, but you will be guarding the shuttle, and we are on an alien sea."

"That's true, but you were alone, and I have two sharpshooters with me who are well trained in security matters."

"They are good," acknowledged Jerry, "but you need to be very cautious anyway."

Mike nodded and checked the sonar data. "The water here is 190 feet deep," he said. "And there's nothing in it except fish." Using the shuttle's radar, Mike checked the surrounding air and surface of the water. "There's nothing in the air except a few birds," he noted, "and there are no boats in radar range."

"It looks like you won't be hit by any surprises today, but I trust that you'll stay alert and take good care of this shuttle."

"You can count on it."

"It's time to board the helicopter and go visit Kayleb," stated Jerry as he opened the upper cargo bay doors. Then, he and Mike headed for the helicopter.

After they prepared it for flight, Jerry wished Mike a great day and entered the chopper, where he sat down in the pilot's seat. Trang sat next to him in the copilot's seat. Sitting in the passenger seats were Connie, Rex, Zeb, Zonya, and Trang's best two commandos.

Jerry started the helicopter's turbine, brought it up to full power, and took off. He headed north while steadily climbing to 5,000 feet, his planned cruise altitude.

Meanwhile, on the shuttle, Mike closed the cargo bay doors and filled the wing tanks with water. Then, he checked all systems to make sure that the shuttle was ready for takeoff. If any threat to the shuttle materialized, Mike planned a quick takeoff and return to orbit where he would await Jerry's request to come back down.

Ninety minutes after taking off, Jerry and his passengers arrived over Kayleb's base. Having already descended to 500 feet, they circled the area and spotted the agreed upon landing site. Shortly, Jerry brought the helicopter to a soft landing. Its rotors and turbine wound down to a stop.

A large crowd was gathered 50 yards away. The arrival of inter-stellar visitors was a momentous occasion that no one wanted to miss. Kayleb and Zack were at the front of the crowd.

Jerry looked at the group and noted that there weren't any guns visible. "If they're armed, they're keeping their weapons out of sight," he said. "Our best policy might be to leave our guns onboard. Wearing side arms might create the impression that we don't trust them, and I don't want to do that. If their intentions are bad, we could not defeat such a large group anyway."

"Just the same, we don't want them crawling all over our helicopter out of curiosity," Trang said. "Why don't I post my commandos next to it to act as an honor guard?"

"That should be acceptable to Kayleb. Having once been a general, he should understand that."

"I would hope so," Trang said.

"Before we post the guards, let's give them Zeb and Zonya. I believe they might have a hero's welcome planned for them."

Jerry entered the passenger section and directed Zeb and Zonya to greet the welcoming party. While looking at the crowd, Zeb said, "They look rather subdued."

"I believe there'll be a dramatic change in their demeanor when they see you and Zonya."

"I'm not sure about that. We've been gone for such a long time."

"The suspense in that crowd is building. Are you going to make them wait all day? I'm beginning to think you might be a reluctant hero."

"I lived alone for 30 years and became accustomed to a very quiet life."

Speaking to Zonya, Jerry said, "I think you should lead the way. Your husband seems to be suffering from stage fright."

Zonya laughed and said, "I've never known him to be shy, but that is more people than we've seen in a very long time." Then, she opened the door, and together, she and Zeb stepped out. They stood straight and tall, and waved at the crowd. Most of the people recognized them and a loud cheer rang out. Zeb and Zonya continued waving, and the cheering took on a celebratory tone. It lasted a full three minutes.

Still inside the helicopter, Trang said to Jerry, "You were right about the hero's welcome. These people are really jacked up."

"They've been through a horrible war, and some homegrown heroes to be proud of just might give them a huge emotional boost."

"Every society needs heroes to be proud of," stated Trang.

When the cheering subsided, everyone else stepped out of the helicopter. Connie and Jerry stood on Zeb and Zonya's right. Rex and Trang stood on their left, and the commandos stood behind them. With Zeb and Zonya in the lead, everyone except the commandos began walking toward Kayleb and Zack, who left the crowd and met their visitors halfway.

Grasping Zeb and Zonya's hands, Kayleb said, "Welcome home!"

"We're pleased to be here," they responded.

Zack greeted his big brother Rex with a warm embrace. Then, Zeb formally introduced everyone to Kayleb, who welcomed each person. Since Kayleb and his people did not understand English, Zeb and Rex took on translator duties.

After warmly appraising each of his visitors, Kayleb said, "I hope you're all hungry because we've prepared a feast. Your visit is the most exciting event that has ever happened in our lives, and we need to celebrate. We're going to have an all-day party. We can discuss business as we go along."

"We have a lot to discuss," responded Jerry. "And I like the idea of doing that in a relaxed atmosphere."

Kayleb led his guests to a rickety old bus. "We'll ride this to the picnic area," he said. "I apologize for its age, but we don't have any new equipment. It's a constant challenge to keep our old equipment running because parts aren't available. We have to make them."

"I'm amazed that you can keep anything running without the support of an industrial base," commented Jerry.

"Rebuilding our industrial base is my top priority," stated Kayleb. "Our nation has been destroyed, but there must be pockets of survivors. If we could find them and connect them with a transportation system, maybe we could rebuild enough of our industrial base to manufacture some simple basic equipment and parts for the old equipment. If we fail, we are destined to return to the pre-industrial age, and I can't allow that to happen."

"We might be able to help you," offered Jerry. "My starship has vast reconnaissance capability."

"Our people have been living underground for a long time," responded Kayleb. "They're going to be hard to find."

"Even though they're living underground, there have to be telltale signs. Your community was easy to spot because of your agricultural activity. Irrigated fields in a desert are hard to miss."

"Granted, communities like mine would be easy to find, but most of our nation has been overrun by aggressively growing plant life. How will you find an underground community hidden in it?"

"Individual families living off the land would be hard to find unless they happen to build a campfire for some reason. But you're not looking for lone families. What you're looking for are communities large enough to tie together to build an industrial base."

"And you can find them when they're living underground in the jungle?"

"If a group of families are functioning as a community, they'll have to gather and process food. That usually means fires for cooking or smoking, and I can spot them. If they have fields or gardens, I can detect them. They'll have a different spectral signature than the surrounding jungle."

"And you're willing to do this for us?"

"Sure! I mean, why not?"

"How do we repay you? We still have our pride, and we don't want to be a charity case."

"Let's not worry about pay right now. We're going to be interstellar neighbors, and I'm sure there'll come a time when we'll need your help with something."

"That's a deal I can live with."

At that moment, the creaky old bus, with its brakes squeaking, came to a stop in the picnic area, which was next to an apple orchard. Several dozen outdoor tables had been set up. Four large tables were loaded with a variety of tasty-looking food. Five barbecue pits were in operation.

Jerry assumed that most of the welcoming crowd was coming to the feast. They were only a half-mile away, an easy hike.

After getting off the bus, Kayleb led his guests to the largest food table. There, they were met by a nice looking, middle-aged woman. Presenting her to his guests, Kayleb said, "This is my wife Giselle. She insisted on being in charge of preparing our feast. She is an excellent cook, and preparing specialty dishes is one of her hobbies."

Facing Giselle, Jerry said, "It looks like you've prepared a feast fit for a king."

"We don't very often receive interstellar guests," she responded. "We're trying to make a good impression, and we're trying to make you feel welcome."

Jerry surveyed the abundance of food arranged on the four large tables and gave Giselle a smile of approval. "You've accomplished your objectives," he said.

"Thanks for the compliment."

While displaying obvious pride in his wife's accomplishment, Kayleb said, "We can't let all this food set around. Let's eat."

Realizing that his guests weren't familiar with the various dishes, Kayleb decided to lead the way. He picked up a tray, a large plate, a small plate, silverware, and a large cup. His guests followed his example as he walked around the tables selecting his favorite dishes. Giselle explained the various foods to her guests while Rex, Zeb, and Zonya acted as translators.

Connie was especially interested in a meatloaf kind of dish that was made with eggs as the main ingredient. The loaf was light and fluffy. It was filled with bits of ham, red and green peppers, and onions. After tasting it, she said, "This is delicious. Where did you get the eggs?"

"We are an agricultural community," responded Giselle. "We have several kinds of animals, but laying-hens are the mainstay. They're easy to care for, and each hen lays an egg almost every day."

Recalling the ordeal she went through to get a few eggs in the wild to put in a meatloaf, Connie smiled and said, "We could use some laying-hens."

"How many do you want?" Kayleb asked.

"How many can you spare?"

"We could let you have a couple hundred."

"With that many hens, we would end up with a lot more eggs than we need. I believe 100 hens would be enough. If we could have a few roosters, we could get some fertilized eggs and hatch some chicks to replenish the flock."

"Before you leave Zebron, we'll fix you up with 125 healthy hens and a couple dozen roosters in their sexual prime."

"That should take care of our poultry needs," responded Connie. "Thank you."

Speaking to Kayleb, Jerry said, "I knew it wouldn't take long to find something you could do for us."

"A few chickens doesn't seem like enough in return for what you're planning to do for us."

"Since we don't have any, it's a pretty big deal for us," responded Connie.

"That may be," noted Kayleb, "but if there's anything else we have that you need, let me know. Maybe we can share it with you."

"How tasty are the apples hanging on those trees?" Jerry asked. "They look just like the apples I used to eat back on Earth."

Without saying a word, Kayleb stood up, walked to the nearest tree, and selected two choice apples. Upon returning to the table, he cut one into quarters, removed the core, and handed a piece of the fruit to Jerry. He bit off part of it and savored the flavor while chewing it. "This is delicious," he said. "It's crisp, sweet, and juicy."

"Would you like to take a couple hundred pounds home with you along with some potted young trees?"

"That would be great."

Zeb patiently waited for the food negotiations to run their course; then, he asked Kayleb, "Are any of the X-planes I used to test fly still around?"

"We have them stored in dry underground hangars. They haven't been flown in years. Our problems are more down-to-earth, and we just don't have any need for hypersonic aircraft."

Openly showing how surprised he was, Jerry stared at Zeb and exclaimed, "You never told me you flew hypersonic aircraft!"

"I wasn't trying to keep a secret. It's just that the subject never came up."

"Zeb was my best test pilot," stated Kayleb. "I hated to lose him to the astronaut corps, but he wanted to go into space, and I couldn't hold him back."

"I'm impressed that you flew a hypersonic X-plane," Jerry said to Zeb. "I'd like to see that bird."

"I'd like to climb into the cockpit and take it up," stated Zeb.

"After all these years, it might need a little refurbishing before you could do that," responded Kayleb.

"That's undoubtedly true," agreed Zeb, "but I have a good memory and a vivid imagination. I could sit in the cockpit and visualize Mach six at 100,000 feet, and the thrill would come back."

Jerry and Kayleb noticed the sparkle in Zeb's eyes. "I think we'd better take a look at that airplane just as soon as we finish eating," stated Kayleb.

"Thank you," responded Zeb as he started eating faster.

"Slow down a bit," suggested Kayleb. "We need to enjoy this feast. The airplane isn't going to go away."

Realizing that he had unconsciously started racing with his meal, which was meant to be a slow-paced welcoming feast, Zeb smiled broadly and said, "You're right, but that airplane was an exciting time in my life."

"It seems to me that your present life is even more exciting," commented Kayleb. "You're back together with Zonya, and you've come home on a starship that came from Earth. Most of us can only dream about interstellar flight, but you've done it."

"You'll never hear me complain about my life," Zeb said, sounding happy.

Speaking to Trang, Kayleb said, "Rex tells me that your youngest daughter played a key role in the rescue of him and his family."

"She sure did. She even surprised me with her courage. I am proud of her. She is a very special young woman."

"You should've brought her along, so we could properly honor her for what she did."

"Her fiancé Jim got shot during the rescue, so she stayed behind to be with him."

"I hope he's going to be okay."

"Thanks to the miracle of modern medical technology, he's going to make a full recovery."

"There's more to it than that," stated Jerry. "Jim is alive only because of instant, on-the-spot, highly skilled treatment by Geniya and Zonya."

"I've already met Zonya," stated Kayleb, "and I would like to meet the rest of the team."

"Jim is going to be in recovery for a while," Jerry said. "So if you want to meet him, you'll have to visit my starship."

Kayleb's face lit up like a Christmas tree. "I am honored to receive such an invitation," he exclaimed. "I've often dreamed of going into space, but I never thought I'd ever have the opportunity. I accept your invitation."

"You'll be more than just a tourist," Jerry warned. "I am going to put you to work."

"Now, you've got me curious. What will I do on a starship that's advanced far beyond our technology?"

"My starship has vast recon capability, but your country is big. Finding pockets of survivors will be easier if I know where to look."

"And you want me to show you where to look?"

"You know your country better than I do."

"You're right, and there are several locations I want to search. When do you want to start?"

"That depends on how long you keep us busy with this party."

"You're doing me a big favor, so I need to live with your schedule."

"I've never been one to leave a good party before it's over, so why don't we have fun today and get down to business tomorrow."

"I like that plan."

A short time later, when it became obvious to Zeb that everyone was stuffed with food, he turned to Kayleb and said, "I'd like to see my favorite X-plane."

"Let's go," responded Kayleb as he led the way to the old bus.

Wanting to visit with her new friends, Giselle joined the tour. "We still live underground," she said. "So after we look at Zeb's airplane, I'll show you our home and tell you how we live."

"Is it difficult to live underground?" Connie asked.

"We're fairly comfortable, but I'm tired of living in what's basically a bomb shelter. I want a house on the surface. But there are so few people left alive in our country that it's essential that we survive. We can't move to the surface until we're positive our enemy can no longer attack us. We're grateful to you for destroying the chemical warfare weapons. Now, we no longer have to worry about poison rain."

"Before we leave Zebron, we're planning to do a thorough recon of the Equatorial Continent," Connie said. "If we find any intercontinental weapons of mass destruction, we'll destroy them."

"That's wonderful! Then, we can build homes on the surface."

Shortly, the creaky old bus with its squeaky brakes came to a stop next to an entrance to the underground world. While stepping off the bus, Jerry looked closely at the heavy concrete doors that were upright in their wide open position. When closed, they would be level with the concrete tarmac they were part of. From the air, or from space, this entrance would be difficult to spot when the doors are closed thought Jerry. That would make targeting next to impossible. It's little wonder that this base survived the war.

Kayleb led the way down five flights of concrete stairs, descending 50 feet. At the foot of the stairs, everyone boarded an open tram with Kayleb sitting in the driver's seat. With the soft hum of electric motors, he headed the vehicle through an open blast-protection door and into a tunnel that headed downward on a fairly steep grade. After descending 500 feet through several open blast-protection doors, the tunnel leveled out. Now 550 feet below ground, Kayleb drove by several side tunnels with open blast-protection doors before making a right turn into a side tunnel. One hundred yards down the side tunnel, Kayleb drove into an aircraft hangar and brought the tram to a stop next to a sleek aircraft.

"That's my baby!" exclaimed Zeb while hopping off the tram. "I'd sure like to take it up one more time!"

Standing next to Zeb, Jerry stared at the advanced aircraft in obvious admiration and said, "I can see why you enjoyed flying it. This bird looks like a high-tech dream Machine."

"Back when I flew it, there was no doubt in my mind that it was far and away the most advanced aircraft on this planet. Several revolutionary new concepts were developed and tested on this aircraft. The combined cycle turbo/ramjet engines were a huge step forward."

"It looks like you have two of those engines buried in the fuselage with a huge inlet just ahead of the wing on both sides."

"Big inlets are needed because the air is thin at 100,000 feet, and that's where this X-plane was optimized to cruise. On one test flight, I flew this plane to 150,000 feet before I had engine flameout. My speed carried me above 200,000 feet before I pitched down into a dive. At 140,000 feet, I was able to restart the engines."

"I'm amazed that an airplane with air breathing engines could take you right to the edge of space like that."

"It's even better than that. On another flight, I went all-out for altitude, and I reached 247,000 feet, an all time record. Two weeks after that flight, I set a speed record of 4785 mph at 112,000 feet."

"What an amazing career you've had," commented Jerry. "You went from speed and altitude records to space travel, to living in a cave with stone-age weapons, back to space travel, and now, back to this X-plane. That's definitely going full circle, career wise."

Grinning at Jerry, Zeb admitted, "I have lived a full life, but I'd sure like to take this bird up one more time."

Facing Zeb, Kayleb said, "It's an awesome airplane, and I understand how you feel, but these days, our needs are more down-to-earth, like trucks, tractors, farm equipment, and highways."

"I guess I'll have to climb in the cockpit and be happy with a pretend flight." Closely followed by everyone, Zeb walked around the aircraft and gave it a visual inspection while answering the many questions that came from Trang and Jerry.

After completing the walk-around, Zeb had a question. He turned to Kayleb and asked, "When was the last time anyone did a systems checkout on this bird?"

"Even though we no longer have a need for this airplane, that has been done on a regular basis."

"Why?"

"Your maintenance crew chief survived the war, and he could not allow this amazing Machine to deteriorate. He visits this plane frequently. Keeping it healthy seems to be his number one passion in life. It's his dream that this plane will fly again. He refuses to accept the tragedy that the horrible war wreaked on our most advanced aero-space technology. He refuses to let it die."

"As I remember him, the chief was a very determined individual. Where is he now? I'd like to visit with him."

"He and five young men left town two weeks ago on a fact-finding trip. They haven't returned yet."

"Where did they go?"

"Before the war, there was a mining town 350 miles north of here. They made cast iron and steel. Chief went up there to find out if there's anything left of that town and its manufacturing ability. We need some steel."

"How are they making the journey?"

"They have two four-wheel drive jeeps pulling small trailers with extra fuel and supplies. It's mostly highland desert between here and there, so Chief thought they could make it on the old highway, but I'm starting to worry. I thought they'd be back by now."

"Do you have any operational aircraft besides this one? I could fly up there and look around."

"Unfortunately, all of our aircraft are in various states of disrepair. Most of them saw combat. Even though experimental, they were pressed into service. Many were lost fighting Special Forces soldiers that infiltrated our society before the war started. By the time we defeated them, we were combat weary and our resources were worn down. The resources we had left were used for survival. We had to develop a farming community so we could eat. But this X-plane is Chief's pride and joy. He's obsessed with it. He's poured his heart and soul into maintaining it. Even so, it has not flown in 30 years and might need more refurbishing before it could fly again."

"If you don't mind leaving me here for a few hours, I'd like to do a pre-flight systems check and find out what's working and what isn't."

"You've been away from it for a long time; do you still know how to do that?"

"Don't forget that this X-plane was also my pride and joy. Now that I'm standing next to it, my last flight is so fresh in my mind that it's almost like I flew just yesterday."

"You are welcome to check it out."

Having received the approval of his former commander, Zeb's face lit up, and he quickly walked to an electrical substation. After flicking a few switches, he noted that power was available. He removed a heavy-duty, electrical-power cord from a cabinet and plugged one end into the power substation. Holding the other end, he dragged the cord to the X-plane, where he crouched under the right wing landing gear well. Reaching up into the gear well, he plugged the cord into the X-plane's external power receptacle.

Coming out from under the wing, Zeb walked forward to the cockpit area. He opened a small panel in the side of the fuselage and flicked a switch to the 'on' position. An electric motor came to life, and the canopy rose to its fully open position. With his adrenaline flowing and his excitement growing, Zeb smiled broadly at his spectators and winked at them. Then, he retrieved the cockpit entry ladder from the nearby support station and hung the ladder from the cockpit. With a spring in his step and a sparkle in his eyes, Zeb climbed into the cockpit, where he made himself comfortable and began turning on systems. As they came to life, Zeb's pulse quickened, and he gave his spectators a thumbs-up signal; then, he put his head down and went to work.

Being an experimental aircraft designed to push technology to revolutionary new levels, the flight control computer was loaded with diagnostic systems checkout software. On the computer monitor, Zeb selected avionics checkout and opened the program. Then, he started checking out the X-plane's electronics.

Kayleb climbed the cockpit ladder, faced Zeb, and said, "I'm going to show my guests more of our base. We'll be back in a couple hours. Have fun."

"You can count on that," Zeb said, acting like a child with a new toy.

Next, Zonya climbed the ladder. She looked into her husband's eyes and said, "You are determined to fly this bird, aren't you?"

"Maybe, but right now, I'm just checking out the possibilities."

"That non-committal answer doesn't fool me. I know you better than that."

Zeb silently smiled at his wife, but the smile said more than words. It revealed an inner glow, an inner excitement, an inner determination.

"That look confirms my suspicions. I sure hope you don't get yourself killed. After being apart for 30 years, I sure don't want to lose you now. We have lots of living to catch up on."

"Don't worry; I'm not going to do anything foolish. Right now, I'm just trying to find out if this aircraft is flyable."

"I don't want you to be offended by what I'm about to say, but I need to express a note of caution."

"Uh oh, I think I know what's coming. You're going to tell me I'm getting too old to fly."

"Well, you are in your 60's, and you've been away from flying for a very long time. The sharply honed skills you once had might be getting rusty."

"I understand your concern, but flying is in my blood. Most of the snap decisions I used to make as a test pilot were instinctive. My mind is still as sharp as ever, and living in the wild for 30 years has kept me physically fit."

"I can't argue with any of that, and I know that you're going to invent some compelling reason to take this thing up."

Zeb looked into his wife's eyes and didn't say anything, but she telepathically read his mind and knew what he was up to. "I'll see you later," she said, and then, she returned to the tram.

Speaking to Zonya, Kayleb said, "What an amazing transformation your husband just went through. I could swear he looks 20 years younger than he looked before he climbed into that airplane."

"He's definitely fired up."

"We'll check on him in a couple hours," stated Kayleb while driving away.

Speaking to his guests, Kayleb said, "We have a large, sprawling underground base. It was carved out of bedrock using mining equipment and explosives. When this base was built, the threat of war was hanging over our heads. This base was designed to survive a war and preserve enough people and technology to rebuild our nation. We are basically an underground city complete with all the facilities that make a city function. We even have oil wells and a small refinery. Fuel was never shipped here. We made our own and still do. We have extensive Machine shops and can manufacture parts to keep our Machinery running. But we're running out of raw materials like the basic metals. We desperately need steel."

"We'll be doing extensive reconnaissance of your country tomorrow," responded Jerry. "If you could provide me with a map that shows where various resources came from, we could take a look at those areas and see if there's anything left of those communities."

"Providing you with a map is the easy part."

"If there's anything going on at the locations you call to my attention, we'll discover it."

Kayleb's tour lasted four hours. He drove the tram on a network of tunnels that connected all the facilities that made up the sprawling underground base. He stopped at each facility for as long as it took to answer the questions that his guests asked. Finally, he stopped the tram at the front door of his home. "This is where Giselle and I live," he said.

Stepping off the tram, Giselle said, "I'll show you our home. It isn't very large, but we are comfortable here."

Kayleb opened the door and stepped back, so his wife could lead the way into their home. It was nothing more than a cavern cut out of rock, but the cavern was partitioned into four rooms. There was a kitchen/dining room, a bedroom, an office, and a bathroom complete with tub and shower. The walls, floor, and ceiling were attractively decorated.

"We don't have much space," Giselle said, "but we do have a complete home. That's because my husband was the General in charge of this complex when it was a military base. Most of our people live in small dormitory bedrooms and share community kitchens and bathrooms. So we feel fortunate to have a complete home; even though, it is small. But I think you can understand why we're eager to have a house on the surface."

"We lived in a small apartment on our starship for nearly seven years," responded Connie. "We're very happy to now have a home on Alcent. We enjoy the great outdoors."

At that moment, Kayleb's radio phone rang. He reached for it and said, "Hello! Kayleb speaking!"

"Kayleb, this is Chief! We'll be there in an hour, and we've brought with us as much steel as our jeeps and trailers can haul."

"That's good news."

"I also have some bad news."

"Hit me with it."

"The mining community no longer exists. There are several families living up there, but nowhere near enough people to operate a mine, a smelter, and a steel fabrication plant."

"So where did you get the steel you brought back?"

"There's a warehouse that's partially intact, and we selected some stock from it to meet our most critical needs. We need to get a couple large trucks in shape for the round trip, so we can get more."

"What about the people up there? Were they friendly?"

"They were excited by how much technology we still have. The people we met would like to join our community."

144

"I'm sure something can be arranged, but before we talk about that, I have a surprise for you that will knock you off your feet."

"What might that be?" Chief asked, sounding very curious.

"Zeb and Zonya have come back from Alcent."

There was a brief period of total silence; then, Chief said, "What did you say?"

"I said Zeb and Zonya are back."

"That's what I thought I heard you say, but I had a hard time believing my ears."

"Well your ears are still functional. They are here. Zeb is sitting in your X-plane doing a pre-flight systems check. He could hardly wait to get to that plane."

"Is he going to take it up?"

"He'd like to, but I don't know if it's flyable."

"It's flyable," stated Chief.

"Assuming you're right, what would Zeb's mission be?"

"Seeing that plane in flight would be an awesome morale booster for our people, especially those living in outlying areas who don't know how well our base survived the war. Zeb could even drop leaflets explaining our objectives. If we could find some communities that have several hundred people, we could use that airplane to get all of us united. We could be the center around which our nation rebuilds."

"We'll start looking for those communities tomorrow."

"How are we going to do that?"

"There's a starship from the Solar System orbiting Zebron, and the Captain has offered to help us."

"Wow! That's great news! First, you hit me with Zeb, now a starship. What else has happened during my absence?"

"Zack's brother is here."

"How did he get here?"

"That's a long story that I'll have to save for later."

"Okay! When we arrive, my men will deliver the steel to the main supply room, and I'm going to look up Zeb. We have a lot to talk about. We'll be there soon."

"I'm glad you guys are okay. Thanks for calling. See you later."

Speaking to his guests, Kayleb said, "I'm greatly relieved that they're back. Now, I don't have to worry about them anymore."

"It sounds like they found some steel for you," Jerry said.

"They found enough to meet our needs for a while, so now, I need to locate sources for all the other basic metals."

"We'll begin that search tomorrow morning," responded Jerry.

"You can't imagine how much I appreciate that. Rebuilding this nation is a huge job that's going to take a few generations. All I can do is build the foundation and get the process started."

"You and I have nation building in common. On Alcent, we are laying the foundation for a new civilization that's going to take many generations to build."

"I'm trying to rebuild a shattered nation. You're trying to build a new nation. Whose challenge is the toughest?"

"I don't know, but we have many of the same problems, like locating resources, for example."

"But you have one problem I don't have, and that's contending with dinosaurs. How are you handling that challenge?"

"We're looking for places that humans can live without confronting the big dinos. We're showing great respect for the life that's already on Alcent. Coexistence is our prime objective."

"I like that approach. It is in stark contrast to the poison rain created by our enemies."

"Only sick, evil fanatics could do what your enemies were doing."

"I am glad you destroyed them. Rebuilding this nation would be impossible with those chemical warfare weapons in operation. We owe you a great debt of gratitude."

"You don't owe us anything. Some things just need to be done, because they are the right thing to do. Your enemies were creating poison rain to indiscriminately kill people and animal life on half a planet. That's akin to planetary genocide, and it is evil beyond comprehension. We had the means to destroy them, so we did."

"It appears that you and I think alike in many ways," Kayleb said, while looking into Jerry's eyes. "I feel good about the future."

"You should. Your base has all the essentials. All you need are raw materials and communications with surviving groups of people, and we'll begin addressing those problems tomorrow."

"I'm looking forward to that, but right now, I think we should go check on Zeb. For all I know, he could be airborne by now."

Everyone hopped on the tram, and shortly, they were back at the X-plane. Zeb was standing next to it. "Chief did an excellent job maintaining this bird," he said. "Everything I can check from here is operational. Now, I need to take it topside, so I can ground test the engines."

"Chief will be here shortly," Kayleb said. "He's very excited about your return, and he'll want to get in on testing the engines."

"That's great!" Zeb exclaimed. "Now I know I can get this thing airborne."

"My husband's glowing with enthusiasm," commented Zonya.

"He should be," stated Kayleb. "He's been reunited with his favorite toy, and he and Chief say it's flight ready."

"That may be, but I think we should go eat before we take the airplane topside for the engine test," Zonya suggested.

"Now that you mentioned it, I'm hungry too," acknowledged Kayleb. "And we have lots of food, so let's go eat."

Zeb seemed reluctant to leave his X-plane, so Kayleb said, "You may as well join us. You can't test the engines until Chief gets here, and he's going to be hungry too."

"Okay, but I do want to do the engine test yet today."

"I think that's a workable plan, so let's go eat."

A short time later, everyone was back at the picnic tables. Chief and his party arrived and joined the mid-afternoon feast.

Zeb and Chief had a difficult time eating because they had so much to talk about. Each needed a rundown on major events in the other's life. But most of all, they had an engine test to plan, followed by a flight test. Finally, after an hour of talk, Zeb could not contain himself any longer, and he said, "I'm full. Let's go test those engines."

Chief turned to the man and woman who had helped him maintain the X-plane. "Our years of effort are about to bear fruit," he said. They nodded enthusiastically and joined Chief and Zeb. With eager anticipation in their hearts, the foursome headed for the X-plane.

Speaking to Chief, Zeb asked, "Do you still have fuel in stock for the X-plane?"

"We sure do! Nothing else runs on the special formula developed for that bird, so we have a pretty good supply."

"Good! I plan to burn some of it."

"I've waited a long time for this day," exclaimed Chief. "Seeing the X-plane in flight will give people hope for the future. It will inspire their imaginations and motivate them to rebuild the country we once had. We must not lose our technology and fall back into the Stone Age."

"I've had a taste of Stone Age living," stated Zeb. "That's how I survived for 30 years, and I can assure you that you don't want to go there, so let's get the X-plane flying."

"First, we need a successful engine test."

A short time later, the foursome arrived in the X-plane hangar. "Before we take this bird topside, I'd like to cycle the landing gear a few times," stated Zeb.

"Good idea," agreed Chief. "We haven't done that in quite some time." Walking to the control panel at the side of the hangar, Chief turned on three ceiling-mounted winches that rolled out cable. His assistants climbed on top of the X-plane, opened three panels, and hooked the cables to hard points. Chief turned on the winches and lifted the X-plane two feet.

Sitting in the cockpit, Zeb retracted the landing gear and said, "My readout indicates a complete retraction."

Chief ducked under the plane and did a visual inspection. "The gear doors are closed," he confirmed.

Zeb lowered the landing gear and said, "I'm showing the gear locked in the down position."

After a visual inspection, Chief said, "Affirmative!"

Zeb cycled the gear up and down three times; then, he said, "I'm satisfied. Let's fuel up."

Chief lowered the X-plane until it rested on its wheels. His assistants unhooked the winch cables; then, they fastened fuel lines to the receptacles in the wheel wells. Fifteen minutes later, the tanks were 60 percent full, and Zeb said, "That should be more than enough for the tests I want to do."

The external power cable and fuel lines were disconnected. Chief backed a tractor up to the X-plane, and his assistants hooked a drawbar to it. Everyone climbed onto the tractor, and chief began towing the X-plane to the nearest elevator. When they arrived at it, they parked the X-plane on the elevator deck and seated wheel blocks against all wheels. Chief turned the elevator on, and the 500-foot ascent to the surface began.

Seven minutes later, they reached the tarmac. Unusual activity on the runway grabbed everyone's attention. Zeb was first to speak. "There are hundreds of people on the runway!" he exclaimed. "What are they doing?"

"It looks like they're inspecting the runway and clearing debris," responded Chief. "Apparently, Kayleb is expecting your engine test to turn into a taxi test."

"He knows me well."

"We'd better not disappoint Kayleb and all those people working on the runway."

"You're right," responded Zeb. "Let's park on the south end. They seem to be done with that part of it."

With the appearance of the X-plane, the people on the runway turned to stare at it. Then, a loud cheer rang out.

Speaking to Zeb, Chief declared, "You need to get this thing off the ground. Nothing more than just a few low speed passes over the field would be enough to fire up this crowd."

"It looks like they're already fired up," noted Zeb.

"They should be. They've been beaten down by a terrible war that has destroyed our country, and now, you've returned. You are a hero in their eyes. Not only that, but this airplane represents the pinnacle of our technology. Seeing a returning hero fly it would be a huge morale boost for them. It would be loud and clear proof that we haven't lost everything."

"I'll see what I can do, but we must make sure all systems are go. A crash would be a horrible downer for them, not to mention what it would do to me."

"I always did appreciate your sense of humor."

"What do you mean? I didn't say anything funny."

"It's the casual way you mentioned your possible death as nothing more than just an afterthought."

"I was once a top-of-the-line test pilot. Death is always a possibility when test flying a hot new experimental aircraft. I just never gave the possibility more than a passing thought. I was always confident that my skills would keep me out of trouble."

"You were definitely the best test pilot we had," stated Chief.

"Thank you! Very soon, I am going to find out how much of that skill I still have left."

Driving the tractor, Chief reached the south end of the runway and turned onto it. His assistants unhooked the drawbar, and Chief drove the tractor away from the X-plane. Zeb climbed into the cockpit, and one of Chief's assistants removed the ladder.

Zeb looked down the long runway in front of him and noted that groups of people were leaving it. Apparently, they've finished their inspection, he concluded.

Zeb recalled the many times he had gone roaring down this runway in this X-plane. That was a long time ago, he noted, but it seems like it was just yesterday. This bird has been dormant for a long time, and so have I. Now, we're back together. Can we both still perform? It's time to find out.

Zeb started a small turbine, which powered a generator that produced electrical power for all of the X-plane's systems. After verifying that the generator was operating normally, Zeb locked the wheel brakes and started the number one engine. While watching its performance parameters on a video screen, he slowly throttled it up to full power, then, back down. Everything is normal here, he concluded. With the number one engine idling, Zeb started the number two engine and gradually brought it up to full power. Hearing the roar of the jet engine and feeling the X-plane straining against its brake-locked wheels sent a wild thrill up and down Zeb's spine. "I have awakened a beast!" he exclaimed. "This bird wants to fly, and this engine's performance is also normal." Satisfied that the engine had met its test, Zeb throttled it down to idle.

Turning his attention to the flight control computer, Zeb directed it to do a pre-flight systems checkout. In just a few minutes, it checked the operation of all control surfaces and instrumentation. He monitored the systems check with keen interest. When it was complete, he concluded: everything is operating as it should be. But what else could I expect; Chief was the best maintenance technician ever, and he put his heart and soul into keeping this aircraft flight ready. Now, it's up to me to show him that his work wasn't in vain.

Looking down the runway, Zeb noted that it was clear of people. Looking to his left, he saw a rickety old bus parked next to the tractor that Chief was still sitting on. Standing next to the tractor were all the people that meant the most to Zeb. I think they're expecting more than a taxi test, Zeb concluded. I think they want to see this bird fly. And why not? As far as I can tell, all systems are in perfect working order.

Zeb smiled at his friends and gave them a smart military salute. The salute was returned by Kayleb and Chief. Everyone else gave Zeb an enthusiastic thumbs up signal.

After releasing the brakes, Zeb quickly brought the engines up to full power. With only a 60 percent fuel load, the powerful X-plane rapidly accelerated down the runway. Quickly reaching flight speed, Zeb pitched into a steep climb. With his adrenaline flowing, he noted that all systems were performing normally. "I love this bird!" he exclaimed. "Wow, is it ever good to be back home! I feel 20 years younger!"

Ninety seconds after takeoff, Zeb was at 35,000 feet. What a thrill this is, he thought. Now, it's time to give my fans a thrill. Zeb pulled the stick all the way back to loop over backwards. Simultaneous with the loop, he deflected the ailerons to roll the X-plane 180 degrees. This loop-roll combination put the X-plane in a dive along the climb-out path. Zeb pulled out of the dive 5,000 feet above the base and did a flyby at Mach 2. Doing a 360-degree roll, he looked down on the old yellow bus. My sonic boom is going to jolt their senses, Zeb thought, but I have to let them know the X-plane is back in action.

Two miles past the old bus, Zeb pitched into a vertical climb while throttling the engines back to 25 percent power. He wanted to lose a lot of speed. When velocity dropped to 200 mph, he flipped over backwards, rolled 180 degrees, and put the X-plane in a shallow dive. He leveled off 1,000 feet above the base and circled it twice at 350 mph. Then, he dropped down to 500 feet and flew over the old yellow bus in a northerly direction. He waggled the wings, briefly looked down, and noted that people were waving.

Five miles beyond the north end of the runway, Zeb banked into a tight turn and headed back toward the runway. He reduced his speed and deployed the leading and trailing edge flaps into their landing configuration. Then, he lowered the landing gear and adjusted his glide path.

A half-minute later, Zeb was over the runway. He throttled the engines back, reducing thrust and speed. Then, he pitched up a few degrees, which increased the drag and reduced the X-plane's speed. In just a few seconds, Zeb felt a gentle bump and heard tires squeal as the main gear hit the runway. Then, the nose gear hit the runway. Immediately, Zeb popped up the spoilers to create drag and kill the remaining lift. Then, he applied the wheel brakes. The 200 mph landing speed was soon dissipated, and Zeb taxied to a stop at the south end of the runway. While the turbines wound down to a stop, Zeb opened the canopy and removed his flight helmet.

Whooping, yelling, and cheering, people swarmed toward the X-plane. For the second time in the same day, a hero had landed.

The crowd surrounded the X-plane, admiring it and Zeb, who was still sitting in the cockpit. Zeb waved at them, and the cheering grew louder. Several minutes passed by before the pandemonium subsided.

Speaking in a loud booming voice, Zeb said, "We were once a great nation. You've endured a long brutal war, and you survived. While you endured the war, I was deserted and left to die. But I lived in a cave and survived. Zonya ended up on a small island on a dinosaur planet with two infants to care for. She not only survived, but she also raised a family. We are all survivors because we are a tough determined people. We can rebuild the great nation that we once were. Tomorrow, we'll begin the search for other groups of survivors. We'll tie people together with a communications network, and nation building will begin. For now, let's all go back to the party. We have much to celebrate."

Zeb's impromptu speech resonated well with the fired up crowd. Applause and loud cheering broke out anew.

Turning to Jerry, Kayleb said, "My people have always worked hard, but I've never seen them so charged up. My nation building project just got a little easier."

"Enthusiasm is a powerful force," agreed Jerry, "and they are definitely fired up. Now, we have to find some groups of survivors for them to connect to and work with.

"There might not be any groups," noted Kayleb.

"We'll find out tomorrow," stated Jerry.

Chapter Seven

TIME: Day 62, Late Morning

The previous day's festivities had run well into the night, because Kayleb's people considered Jerry's visit to be a turning point in history, a very special occasion worth celebrating in a big way. By the time the party wound down, it was so late that Jerry and his people slept over as honored guests of Kayleb. But now, it was time to return to the Challenger. However, Zeb and Zonya decided to stay on the base until Jerry came back down to explore the caves. Kayleb, Giselle, and Zack joined the rest of Jerry's crew for the flight to the Challenger.

Everyone going to the Challenger was onboard the helicopter except Kayleb. He was standing next to it facing Zeb. "This is an exciting day for me," he said. "I've dreamed of going into space, but I never thought I'd ever have the opportunity. Do you have any suggestions for me?"

Zeb smiled and said, "Just relax and enjoy it. Zonya and I are going to enjoy exploring your base. We've been away for a very long time."

"I expect that you'll get the V.I.P. treatment wherever you go."

"I'm not used to that."

"Just relax and enjoy it," responded Kayleb. "You've earned some V.I.P. treatment."

Zeb nodded and Kayleb turned and stepped aboard the helicopter. When Zeb cleared the area, Jerry started the turbine, and the helicopter was soon airborne.

Giselle and Kayleb looked down on the base with great interest. They noted the fields, gardens, and orchards. The agricultural development was extensive, and this was their first aerial overview. For the benefit of his passengers, Jerry circled the area once; then, he headed south.

An hour after taking off, the helicopter was over the cave complex. Speaking to Rex, Zack said, "We need to unlock the mysteries in those caves."

"They were inhabited by people a long time ago," responded Rex. "What's mysterious about that?"

"For starters, what happened to those people? Did they die out, or did they move on? And where did they come from? Where did they get the tools needed to excavate caves in granite?"

"How do you expect to get answers to all those questions?"

"I don't know, but I'm convinced there's a sealed chamber in that complex."

"Why?"

"I drew a floor plan of the cave complex in an effort to figure out if the caves were randomly cut or if they followed a systematic pattern."

"What did you find out?"

"There is a definite pattern, but there is a glaring exception to the pattern in that there's no cave where there should be one."

"That's pretty flimsy evidence for the existence of a concealed chamber. There are lots of reasons why they might have deviated from the design."

"That's true, but I believe there's a sealed chamber there."

"But why would they seal a chamber in a way that there's no evidence of its existence other than your floor plan?"

"There might be evidence. It might be high-tech evidence that can't be discovered without the right technology."

"But why would they do that?"

"Maybe they locked up a treasure trove of high-tech information that can only be used by a society that has achieved a high enough level of technology to know how to use it. If that's the case, the info would have to be locked up in such away that treasure hunting thieves or vandals could not get to it and intentionally destroy it because of not knowing the value of it."

"Jerry and Trang think the Ancient Ones came here from another star. That's one way they could've had high-tech info to lock up for a far-in-the-future civilization. But why didn't they just give that info to the colonists they planted here?"

"Maybe they did, but maybe they feared that their colonists would revert to living off the land because life was easy. That way, their technology would've been lost in a few generations. But as the society grew over thousands of years, they might've been expected to also grow technologically. Then, one day, they could open the time capsule and recover the knowledge of the Ancient Ones."

"I can see that you've put a lot of thought into this," Rex said.

"Those caves represent a mystery that bugs me to no end. I want to solve that mystery."

"You're not alone. Jerry is planning to explore them before we leave here. There are similar caves on Alcent. He's hoping to learn something here to help solve the mystery back home."

"I look forward to that," stated Zack. "When is he planning to go to the caves?"

"When we finish the recon for Kayleb, we'll come back down and take a look at those caves. It shouldn't be more than just a few days."

"Good! I can hardly wait."

"The time will fly. You've never been in space, and you'll have a large starship to explore. The observation deck alone will take hours of your time as you watch the ever-changing views of the planet far below, not to mention the fabulous views of the Universe that are unobstructed by the planet's atmosphere. You are going to have the time of your life."

While viewing the landscape as far as he could see, Zack said, "There's no doubt in my mind that you are right."

Meanwhile, on the cargo shuttle, Mike watched the blip of the approaching helicopter on a radar screen. Using radar and sonar, he verified that there was nothing threatening in the area except for an approaching storm system in the south. The storm concerned Mike. It towered high into the stratosphere, and its upper levels were filled with violent turbulence. If those strong winds descend to the surface, we are going to have problems, Mike concluded. We could be looking at waves big enough to make a shuttle takeoff very hazardous. I need to go outside and look at this thing.

Mike opened the upper cargo bay doors, and raised the helicopter landing deck to its top position. Then, he left the cockpit and went outside to the landing deck, where he visually searched the surrounding sea. It was still calm, and there were no dangers present. Mike stared at the towering storm cell. That thing is huge, he noted, and the lightning bolts are spectacular. We sure don't want to get hit by one of them.

Mike went back inside and headed for the cockpit. There, he probed the storm with radar at various frequencies. This thing is worse than I thought, he concluded. All the conditions are right for producing one or more tornados. Large hail stones are also possible.

Mike contacted Jerry and said, "We have a large, violent storm coming in from the south. It would be very dangerous to weather this one. I've clocked your progress and that of the storm, and you need to get more speed out of that chopper. Can you do that?"

"I am cruising at a fuel-efficient speed. Cruising at full power will dangerously deplete my fuel reserves. How bad is that storm?"

"We need to be out of here before it arrives. I am five miles offshore, but I'm going to cruise four miles to the north and meet you one mile offshore. That will buy you an extra 20 minutes at the storm's current rate of progress. It's coming this way at 12 mph, but that could change."

"Keep me posted on that. I will fly at full power for a while, but if fuel gets too low, I'll have to throttle back a bit."

"I will track your progress and that of the storm."

Ten minutes later, Mike was one mile offshore and called Jerry. "It looks like you're going to arrive six minutes ahead of the storm," he said. "That's cutting it awfully close. How's your fuel supply?"

"It's getting low, but I think I'll make it."

"When you arrive, we're going to have to tie that chopper down and nest the rotor blades in a hurry. My guards will be in position to do that."

"I will help them."

"I will have all systems ready for immediate takeoff."

"Good!"

Using the flight control computer, Mike did a pre-flight systems check. It showed the shuttle ready to go.

Next, Mike looked at the storm using his multi-frequency radar. He immediately called Jerry and said, "This thing is growing more violent, and it looks like a funnel cloud is forming."

"I see it, and it looks ugly, but I have you in sight. Right now, I need some of Jim's daredevil flying skills, so I can make a quick landing without crashing."

"Good luck on that."

Jerry came up on the shuttle at full speed. At the last possible instant, he pitched the chopper into a steep angle of attack, so that the lift produced by the rotor quickly slowed the chopper to near zero forward velocity. Jerry's timing was perfect, because the helicopter came to a hover just a few feet above the shuttle. Jerry turned the helicopter a bit to line it up with the landing deck. As he cut power for the landing, the turbine flamed out because the last drop of fuel was gone.

Mike's guards quickly secured the chopper to its deck. Then, they went to work nesting the rotor blades. Jerry hopped out of the chopper to help them while Rex quickly escorted Zack, Kayleb, and Giselle to their seats inside the shuttle.

When Jerry and his assistants finished nesting the rotor blades, windblown raindrops and hailstones were already pelting them. Jerry hit the switch to lower the helicopter operations deck into the shuttle and simultaneously began closing the upper cargo bay doors. Even before the doors were completely closed, Mike brought the marine propeller up to full power and began the takeoff run. By the time the shuttle reached hydrofoil speed, the upper cargo bay doors were locked shut, and Mike fired the nuclear thermal rocket (NTR), while Jerry and his assistants struggled against the acceleration to get to their seats in the passenger section.

While climbing out, Mike announced, "Nice work guys! We narrowly escaped the brunt of the storm. Radar indicates hailstones up to golf ball size are falling where we used to be. A mile behind that, the funnel cloud has touched down, and a waterspout has formed. That storm is a monster!"

Using Rex as a translator, Kayleb said to Jerry, "I guess we should've gotten up a little earlier this morning. Then, we wouldn't have had to race with that storm."

"Racing the storm was exciting," responded Jerry. "Besides that, we were having too much fun last night to go to bed early. We had to sleep in a bit today."

"For me, the fun is just beginning," stated Kayleb while looking out the window at the landscape that appeared to be rapidly falling away. "This shuttle has awesome acceleration. We'll soon be in space, and it's my first time."

"I still remember my first flight into space. I was so jacked up that my whole being was operating on a higher plane fired by adrenaline flow."

"That's me at the moment!" exclaimed Kayleb. "I'm living a dream that's coming true."

Mike's takeoff was to the north because the Challenger was currently moving south to north in its polar orbit. A few minutes after takeoff, the shuttle, which was still accelerating, passed over Kayleb's base at an altitude of 100 miles.

"My base looks pretty small from up here," Kayleb said.

A minute later, the shuttle passed over the remains of the mining community that Chief had visited. "From this distance, it's hard to tell that a horrible war was fought down there," noted Kayleb. "Everything looks so inviting that it looks like a good place to live."

"That just might be part of the answer to your nation building project," noted Jerry. "You might relocate some of your people to that mining community with the idea of getting it partially back in operation."

"If we can assure ourselves that our enemy no longer has intercontinental WMDs (weapons of mass destruction), we can move to the surface and branch out. We haven't done that because there aren't very many people left in my country, and we just can't risk large loss of life. It's possible that my community is the largest remaining group. Therefore, it's imperative that we not only survive, but we must also remain a healthy, functional social group."

"We'll do a thorough recon of the equatorial continent, but I think it's doubtful that they'd still have ICBMs or long-range aircraft 30 years after the end of major combat. If they had them, it seems that they would've used them years ago. But if they do have any, we'll find them or the evidence that they exist."

"I greatly appreciate that. If the search comes up negative, we can get busy with the serious task of nation building."

"If the search is positive, we'll destroy any weapons we find, and you can still get serious about nation building."

"The recon of what's left of my country will help me decide on how best to rebuild it."

At that moment, the NTR shut down, and Kayleb suddenly experienced weightlessness for the first time in his life. Taken by surprise, he exclaimed, "Wow! This is weird! I knew this would happen, but even so, I'm not prepared for it."

"There is no way to prepare for being weightless," commented Jerry. "You've lived with gravity your entire life, so this is a very unnatural state for you to be in."

"If I could get my stomach out of my throat, I'd be okay."

"Just relax and give your system a chance to adjust. You should be okay in a few minutes; if not, we have a drug that will help you."

"That won't be necessary. I am strong-willed, and I will control this mentally."

"That's an attitude I can relate to."

A half-hour later, the shuttle caught up to the Challenger. Mike piloted it into the hangar bay, where it was secured to its berth.

Jerry and Connie gave Kayleb and Giselle a tour of the Challenger with Rex and Shannon acting as interpreters. And of course, Zack tagged along for the tour, which ended in the cafeteria.

Facing Kayleb, Jerry asked, "Has your stomach settled down enough so that you can enjoy lunch in this weightless environment?"

"My disorientation has gone away, and I feel pretty good. In fact, I'm enjoying floating around."

"I've always enjoyed the sense of freedom that comes with being weightless."

A few minutes later, after eating his first bite of steak, Kayleb said, "This is delicious. What kind of animal is it from?"

"That's an imitation steak made by our food processors," responded Jerry. "Our life-support equipment is used to grow the ingredients used by the synthesizers to make the things we eat."

"It's hard to believe that this is imitation steak. It's more tender and delicious than the real thing."

"Delicious food is one of the things that made our long journey through interstellar space tolerable."

"I can understand that," responded Kayleb. "Poor quality food over an extended period of time can have a bad effect on morale."

"You sound like a man speaking from experience."

For a few moments, a distant look of sadness overcame Kayleb; then, he said, "We've endured a long and terrible war. There was a time when food of any kind was hard to come by. Thank God we survived that era. Things are better for us now. We are a thriving agricultural community. Hopefully, we aren't the only such community in my once great nation."

"We'll start searching shortly," Jerry said.

"I'd like to find some large groups of people," stated Kayleb, "but I don't have much hope for that. In their long hike across the country, Zack and his friends never encountered groups larger than just a few families."

"We'll do a thorough search," stated Jerry. "If large groups exist, we'll find them."

"I may've already found two such groups," stated Tonya, who had overheard Jerry's remark while entering the cafeteria with Jim at her side.

Tonya's remark instantly grabbed Jerry's attention. Rex translated the remark to Kayleb and also explained the role that Tonya played in rescuing him and his family.

Kayleb eyed the beautiful young woman he was introduced to. Then, he gave her a broad smile of approval and praised her for her courage and the skillful way she did the key part of the rescue.

"Thank you," responded Tonya while vibrantly glowing from the compliments.

"Why and where do you think you've found two large groups?" Kayleb asked.

"I am gifted in that my telepathic powers are exceptionally good. Since completing the rescue mission, I've practically lived on the observation deck watching the ever-changing views of Zebron and telepathically listening for life. There are two places where I think sizeable communities exist. One is on your west coast, and the other is on your south coast. The Southern Community is only a couple hundred miles east of where the shuttle spent the night."

"I am excited by the possibilities," stated Kayleb. "If that Southern Community is where I think it is, there is great potential there. We once had a large industrial complex in that area. There were even dozens of oil wells and a refinery there. I wonder if any of that manufacturing capability survived the war."

"I wasn't able to determine that from what I saw in the minds of the people I detected. But for the most part, they were in a positive upbeat mood, which might mean they are content with life. I don't believe the kind of contentment I detected would exist unless they have a thriving community and hope for the future."

"That makes sense," agreed Kayleb. "I can hardly wait until we get our recon data for that area. What can you tell me about the community on the west coast?"

"There seem to be just as many people there, but they're not as upbeat."

"Some people bounce back very quickly from the tragedy of war," Kayleb said. "Others are emotionally scarred for life. It's possible the people in that community have nothing going for them and are struggling just to survive. Maybe communication between them and my people would give them hope. We could give them access to the technology we still have. Agricultural technology and medical help might make a big difference in their lives."

"We'll do some extra recon of that community and the one on the southern coast," stated Jerry. "We'll try to find out what's going on down there and what kind of help they might need."

"I greatly appreciate that," responded Kayleb.

A half-hour later, when all had finished eating, Jerry took his guests to the flight deck to begin the reconnaissance project. Kayleb looked around with great interest and asked questions about everything. Being proud of his starship, Jerry eagerly answered the questions.

When the questions seemed to reach a pause, Jerry said, "While we look at the areas that you want to check out and the groups that Tonya found, I will update our database for your country. Then, our computer can compare it to the database we generated the last time we were here. The kinds of changes that could be the result of human activity will then be investigated. We're going to start with your west coast because that requires only a small adjustment in our current orbit."

Jerry ordered the change in orbit to be made. Then, he sounded the warning klaxon and said, "Prepare for acceleration! Our engines will be ignited in three minutes."

TIME: Day 64, Late Afternoon

Rex, Jerry, and Kayleb were on the flight deck discussing the results of two days of searching for groups of war survivors. On a wall-sized video screen, Jerry displayed a map of Kayleb's country. Red dots marked the location of cooking fires and agricultural activity.

"It looks like your community is by-far the largest in your country," commented Jerry.

"Unfortunately, I think you're right," agreed Kayleb. "But I do need to reach the groups that are in key locations. For planning purposes, I'd sure like to have a copy of that map."

"I'm planning to provide you with all the info that we've collected these past two days."

"I appreciate that," responded Kayleb. "The data will be very helpful, but I must admit that I do feel discouraged. I'd hoped we'd find more people. Rebuilding this nation is going to take many generations, lots of hard work, and some luck."

"But the era of poison rain is almost over, and it looks like you no longer have an enemy to worry about. We found no large groups of people on the Equatorial Continent and no evidence of intercontinental WMDs."

161

"That means we can confidently live a normal life on the surface, which will make life easier for us."

"Also, you do have a very well equipped base to work from, and we can give you some key technology that will be helpful."

Kayleb's ears perked up, and he came to full attention. "What kind of technology are you talking about?" he asked.

"Your most pressing problem is communication, and that can be fixed with some rather simple technology. We already have a communications satellite in geosynchronous orbit over the hemisphere your country is located on. We can drop small capsules loaded with communications equipment into the communities you want to connect with. Then, all of you can work together to achieve common goals."

"That's definitely the first step in putting my country back together," responded Kayleb, who began studying the map to determine where best to drop the capsules. Then, he said, "We need to start with the two communities Tonya discovered."

Kayleb highlighted nine additional communities on the map and said, "This is my wish list. How many of these can we do?"

"I have a high-tech machine shop that is capable of making whatever we need to repair any malfunction on this starship. Making landing capsules packed with communications gear is a simple task. It'll take a few days, but we can make eleven of them."

Facing Kayleb, Rex said, "There is something you might want to think about before you drop those capsules."

"What are you concerned about?" Kayleb asked.

"All of my problems started a couple months after Jerry dropped communications equipment into my front yard. Some slime-balls captured me and my family and used that equipment to try to capture this starship. Some of the people who find out about all the good things you have going for you on your base might be scoundrels. They might not be interested in your nation building project. They might be interested only in using you and your people to their advantage."

"Unfortunately, that possibility does exist," acknowledged Kayleb. "But I have a military base that was designed to survive nuclear war. Our security systems are extensive, and we still have some very well trained Special Forces people to defend the base."

"That's good, but you don't always know who your enemy is. The slime-ball in charge of the group that caused me so much grief was a colleague, a trusted friend for 20 years."

162

"You make another good point, but I am serious about rebuilding this nation, and that starts with communication. We'll just have to be alert for all possibilities when we reach the various groups that I want to contact."

"I can help you get started," Rex offered.

"What do you have in mind?"

"My telepathic ability isn't as good as Tonya's, but it's far better than what most of our people have. I can contact each group that you want to reach, let them know what your objectives are, and that communications equipment will be sent down if they want to participate in your nation building project."

"Why wouldn't they?" Kayleb asked.

"I don't know; it's just a possibility. I will try to learn as much about each group as I can. It's possible that you might want to avoid some of the groups we've located. Some of them might be selfish, trouble-making agitators. The scars of war affect people differently, and we just don't know what's going on down there."

"Have you contacted any of them yet?"

"No, but like Tonya, I have listened to the sounds of life, and I am intrigued by that community on the south coast. They seem to be quite content. I think we should start with them. They might be fun to work with."

"I agree. Also, they are nearby, and transportation between us and them would be easy." Turning to Jerry, Kayleb asked, "When will we pass over that community again?"

"I can adjust our orbit so that we pass over them in about an hour."

"When can we drop a communications capsule?"

"If Rex is able to contact them an hour from now and arrange the drop, we can do it on the next orbit, which will be about an hour-and-a-half later."

"If they're out and about, I will establish contact," stated Rex, "but the person I reach might not be connected with those in authority. It might take a few over-flights to reach the right people."

"In that event, we'll drop the capsule sometime tomorrow."

"And then, the get-acquainted dialog will begin," stated Kayleb.

An hour later, the Challenger was approaching the Southern Community from the south. Rex and Tonya were on the observation deck to attempt telepathic contact. They planned to have Rex play the lead role in the attempt, because Tonya was not yet fluent in the language. She would play a support role by tuning in to the emotions of individuals living in the community.

When the community came into view to the north, Rex and Tonya focused their minds to begin telepathically searching for human life. In less than a minute, they located a group of people on the ocean beach. Telepathically, Rex looked at each individual attempting to determine if anyone was in a position of authority.

"They're all in a party mood," he said to Tonya.

"You're definitely right," she responded. "I wonder what the occasion is."

"I don't know, but I have an idea on how to add some excitement to their party."

"What do you have in mind?"

"It looks like it's just beginning to get dark down there. If I introduce myself and let them know I'm up here, they should be able to see this starship. It should look like a bright star moving across the sky."

"Spotting a starship in the evening sky will definitely blow them away," stated Tonya.

Rex selected the individual in the most boisterous mood and hit him with a strong telepathic command, "Look up now!"

The message hit the man hard, and he impulsively looked up. "What do you see?" Rex asked.

"I see a bright star moving across the sky," the man exclaimed while pointing at it. Everyone immediately looked up.

"It isn't a bright star," responded Rex. "It's a starship. My name is Rex, and I'm on this starship. General Kayleb is also onboard."

Rex detected a sense of surprise and dumbfounded disbelief in the man's mind. "How can that be?" he asked. "General Kayleb died in the Great War, and the only starship we ever had went to Alcent and never returned."

"This starship is not ours. It is from the Solar System. The Captain's name is Jerry Jerontis, and he wants to help us begin the rebuilding of our nation. General Kayleb is not dead. He is very much alive. His base survived, and he has a thriving community of 3,000 people. He wants to unite with your community and other communities to build a foundation for rebuilding our nation."

"This is great news, but how do I know it's true?"

"We plan to drop a communications capsule, so that your leader can communicate directly with Kayleb. The equipment will have audio and video capability. We need to know where to land it, so that it will be convenient for your leader to use."

"My name is Tawambi, and I am the leader. I've just been elected to another four years in office, and we're having a victory celebration that's likely to run well into the night. But your news is so sudden, so unexpected, and so shocking that I still don't know if I should believe it. It seems like just too much to hope for."

"Well, it's true. Where do you want the capsule to land?"

"How big is it?"

"It's less than a hundred pounds."

"In that case, you can land it right here on the beach, and we'll move it to a convenient location. Wow! This is wildly exciting news. I still can't believe this is happening. First, I get re-elected, and now this. Wow!"

"You are having great weather and a full moon. That works well for us, so we'll drop the capsule on our next orbit, which will be in about an hour-and-a-half. We are about to lose contact. I will be back in touch on our next orbit."

"Thank you!" responded Tawambi.

Turning to Tonya, Rex asked, "What do you think?"

"He's genuine. He is someone that Kayleb can work with."

Ninety minutes later, the Challenger was again approaching the Southern Community from the south. Rex and Tonya were on the observation deck preparing for telepathic contact with Tawambi. When contact was established, Rex said, "The communications capsule has been released and is well into its descent. I will probably lose contact with you before it lands, but if all goes well, it will automatically activate itself."

"What a great day this is," responded Tawambi. "You people are adding a special touch to my victory celebration."

"Shortly, you'll be able to share that with Kayleb."

"That's great. I have a million questions for him."

"He has a few for you too."

"I'm ready."

Rex explained to Tawambi how to use the communications equipment that he would soon have. By the time Rex finished answering questions, he lost contact with Tawambi, who had already begun searching the moonlit southern sky for the capsule.

Shortly, Tawambi spotted the flashing strobe light that Mike had mounted on the capsule. He pointed at it and yelled, "There it is!"

Suspended from its para-wing, the capsule slowly circled the area in its spiraling descent. Eventually, it entered its final approach glide heading directly toward Tawambi forcing him and his people to scramble out of the way. Moments before touchdown, the para-wing pitched into a stall, killing its forward velocity. The capsule thumped down in a gentle landing, immediately releasing its para-wing, which collapsed onto the beach.

The capsule stabilized itself with small, self-deployed legs. An antenna popped out of the capsule's top. It searched for and acquired a signal from the communications satellite high overhead. Then, a door swung open, which had a video screen mounted on it. A video camera with microphones deployed itself.

An image of a man appeared on the video screen. With a broad smile on his face, he said, "Hello! I am Kayleb. I wish to speak to Tawambi."

Tawambi stepped forward, faced the camera and said, "I am Tawambi, I am pleased to meet you."

"Likewise," responded Kayleb. "We have much to talk about. Rex tells me that you just won an election."

"That's true. I've been re-elected governor of this community for another four years."

"How large is your community?"

"We have just over 1000 citizens. Most of us live underground in a network of old bomb shelters connected with tunnels. A few families have built homes on the surface."

"How do you support yourselves?"

"We are farmers and fishermen. The manufacturing industry that thrived here before the war has been mostly destroyed. But we are scavengers, and we've been able to find the things we need to make our lives reasonably comfortable and build a thriving community."

"That's good news. I am hoping to find lots of successful communities like yours that I can tie together with communications equipment. By working together, we can rebuild this once great nation."

"I share your dream for the future, but this is going to be a huge undertaking. Some basic tools and equipment would make the project easier. Do you have any manufacturing capability?"

"I have a large military base that is almost entirely underground. We have a network of machine shops and specialized equipment for making things, but we need to find raw materials like the basic metals. North of my base there is a bombed out mining community that we might be able to get partially back into operation."

"Along with that, there's plenty of scrap metal around here that can be salvaged from the ruins of destroyed factories. Give me a shopping list, and I'm sure we can find whatever you need, but what about transportation?"

"We have some old trucks that are still running, but we might have to do some road repair and road clearing to drive from my base to your community. Fortunately, we have equipment to do that. We can scrounge up a bulldozer and a trailer to haul it with. Throw in a couple dump trucks and a backhoe to load them, and we can make the old highway drivable, if the problems aren't too serious. We'll have to check it out and see what condition it's in."

"We'll help out on this end, but we lack heavy equipment, so we're kind of limited in what we can do. Assuming that we solve the road problem, there are some things that we need. If you'll make them for us, we'll find the raw materials on your shopping list."

"It sounds like we should exchange shopping lists and do some bargaining."

"That just might be the beginning of a relationship that ties our communities together."

"That is my objective," stated Kayleb. "Tying communities together is the first step in putting our once great nation back together."

"You can count me in on that project," responded Tawambi.

"Good! Now, let's trade stories. Tell me what's happened in your community over the years."

"You got it, but first, I'd sure like to know how you managed to get yourself onboard a starship from The Solar System."

Kayleb told Tawambi the complete story and introduced him to the key people onboard the Challenger. Then, Tawambi told the story of his community from the Great War to the present. The stories, plus the questions and answers, lasted well past midnight.

TIME: Day 65, Late Morning

The Challenger had just passed over the community on the west coast, and Rex and Tonya were on the observation deck. "This community baffles me," commented Rex. "Their mood is so fearful and depressed that I decided not to make contact with anyone."

167

"Their mood is puzzling," agreed Tonya. "Why is it so somber? Are those people leading miserable lives? Or is there some other reason?"

"My gut feeling is that we should find out before we tip them off to our presence."

"How are we going to do that?"

"Let's go to the flight deck and talk to Jerry and Kayleb. They've been studying recon data for this community and might know something."

A few minutes later, on the flight deck, Rex gave his thoughts on the situation to Jerry and Kayleb. When he finished his report, Kayleb asked, "Exactly what is it that concerns you so much that you avoided making contact? What I mean is this: making contact is the most direct way to find out what's going on down there."

"If they tell me."

"Why wouldn't they tell you?"

"I don't know, but I detected both anger and fear in the minds of some of the people."

"I did too," added Tonya. "And in the minds of others, I found an attitude of brutality and even sadistic thoughts. It's almost like there's a prison camp down there."

"Prisons disappeared long ago," stated Kayleb. "Most inmates died in the initial phases of the war."

"What kind of community existed there at the time the war started?" Tonya asked.

"It was a military space facility that launched satellites into polar orbit. It would've been equipped with bomb shelters, and that's probably where the present inhabitants are living."

"The only people I detected were men," stated Tonya. "It seems like a community should also have women and children. They were present at Tawambi's beach party."

Facing Kayleb, Rex said, "Tonya makes a good point. The first time we passed over your base, I detected men, women, and children. Why didn't we detect women and children in the Western Community?"

"The obvious answer is that they were all underground," responded Kayleb. "But it seems like some of them should've been outside."

"That's what I think," agreed Tonya. "I guess there's always the possibility that the community is made up only of men."

"That's very unlikely," stated Kayleb. "All of our military bases had both men and women stationed at them."

"So where are the women?" Tonya asked. "Something very strange is going on down there."

"I have a possible explanation," commented Rex. "But it's so sickening that I hope I'm wrong."

"Let's hear it," stated Kayleb.

"My family and I were recently put through a terrible ordeal. The slime-ball in charge kept me under control by holding my wife and daughter hostage at a secret location. What if a similar situation exists down there, but on a much larger scale?"

"Are you suggesting that an entire community is being held hostage?" Kayleb asked.

"It's a possibility that we need to consider. Wars sometimes create power vacuums that evil people might see as opportunities. The Western Community might, in effect, be a brutal prison camp run by an evil dictator with a cadre of supporters, who get special privileges and serve as guards. Women and children are held hostage while the man in each family is forced to go out and work under the watchful eyes of the guards. If any man tries to escape and is successful, his wife and children could be tortured and even executed as an example to others."

"If that's what's going on, it's a heart-wrenching situation," responded Kayleb. "As if the survivors of the war haven't already gone through enough, they now have to live like that."

"We don't know if that's what's happening," stated Rex. "It's just a possibility."

"But it's a possibility that makes sense," argued Tonya. "Look at the evidence. In some of the men, I detected fear and anger. In others, I detected a sense of sadistic cruelty. Most of these also had an arrogant attitude."

Sadness and anger seemed to flood Kayleb's demeanor. He turned to the map of his country that was displayed on a large video screen and asked Jerry for an enlargement of the area between his base and the Western Community. Jerry complied and the area filled the entire screen. Kayleb studied it briefly and said, "It's about 400 miles away, and there's a mountain range to cross, but I still have some very well trained Special Forces people."

Turning to Rex, Kayleb asked, "How good is your telepathic ability? Is there any way you can find out if your theory is correct?"

"I can telepathically listen to their thoughts each time we pass over the area. If any of the men down there have families, sooner or later, I'll catch someone thinking about his family. If they're being held hostage, that should be reflected in his thoughts."

"I'll adjust our orbit to fly over them again," Jerry said.

"Thank you," responded Kayleb. "I need to find out what's going on in that community."

"To find out for sure, you need to get someone inside that community," stated Tonya. "I could do it using the same ruse I used to rescue Rex and Jeff."

"It might not work this time," cautioned Jerry. "You could get yourself killed."

"That's a possibility, but if I can get some of the guards to see me as a possible plaything, they're not likely to kill me. I am capable of presenting myself in a rather alluring way."

"I'm certainly not going to dispute that," responded Jerry while admiring Tonya. "But the problem is that we don't know what you would be getting into. That community might even be some fanatical cult that treats women as little more than slaves and tortures them to death for having sex outside of marriage. Presenting yourself in a seductive way could get you killed in such a cult."

"Jerry's concern is justified," stated Kayleb. "Before the war, one of the religions on this planet had some fanatical offshoots that did treat their women that way. Here in my country, they were never able to get started in any big way. Our government was always quick to prosecute men who violated the civil rights of women. But it's possible that some of those fanatics survived the war and are in control of the Western Community. If that's the case, we have a suicidal enemy. If we try to free those who don't want to be part of the cult, the fanatics will fight us to the death. But if it looks to them like we might defeat them, they will kill all the people that we're trying to rescue before they fight us to the death."

Jerry listened closely to Kayleb; then, he said, "That means we cannot make a rescue attempt unless we have a plan that we're totally convinced will succeed."

"To develop such a plan, we have to have very good intelligence," stated Kayleb. Turning to Tonya, he said, "I appreciate your offer to go into that community, but I can't allow that; it's just too risky."

"I am gifted with special telepathic powers," responded Tonya. "There may be something I can do, so don't rule me out. Also, I want

170

to remind you that Rex did say that I am 'one cool cookie with nerves of steel'."

"There's no doubt about that," stated Rex. "I've seen her in action."

Facing Tonya and displaying obvious admiration for her, Kayleb said, "You are a very special young woman, and I admire you for your courage, but we are going to be careful to not put you into an impossible situation."

"I appreciate your concern," responded Tonya. "I know that being a spy is dangerous work, but if it needs to be done, I will accept the challenge."

"I believe you would be successful," stated Jerry. "But there are other ways to gather intelligence that we should try before we put you or anyone else at risk. We have RPVs, and we can make mechanical bugs with audio and video ability. We should be able to get them into that community, and then back out without attracting attention."

Pleased with Jerry's plan, Kayleb said, "The kind of info we can get that way should make a rescue mission feasible, if one is needed."

"If we can successfully get bugs in and out, we should be able to determine what's going on in that community."

"How do you plan to get them in and out?" Kayleb asked.

"Mechanical bugs don't have very much range, so they'll have to be delivered onsite by an RPV at night. The RPV and bugs will be transported down with a landing capsule. We will have to land it several miles away in an area that the people down there aren't likely to go to."

"What about control? Can you control the mechanical bugs from here?"

"Our control signals will go to the landing capsule and be relayed to the RPV, which will relay the signals to the bugs."

"What happens if you fly the bugs into the bomb shelter, which is deep underground?"

"We could lose the ability to control them."

"So the bugs would be good for outdoor spying, but underground spying is questionable."

"That is correct, but we might be able to learn a lot with up-close spying on their outdoor activities."

"If all else fails, I can go down there," Tonya said.

"That's only a last resort," stated Jerry. "And we would have to have a compelling reason to send you down. I'm not convinced that gathering info is reason enough to put you at risk."

"If it needs to be done, I'll do it."

"I appreciate that, but we're going to try everything else first. You and Rex should go back to the observation deck and put your telepathic skills to use. We'll soon be making another pass over that community."

"You got it," responded Tonya as she and Rex left.

Speaking to Kayleb, Jerry said, "My starship has enormous recon capability, and we're going to put it all to use spying on that community."

"Hopefully, we can get the answers we need," Kayleb said.

Chapter Eight

TIME: Day 65, Early Afternoon

The Challenger was approaching the Western Community from the south. Once again, Rex and Tonya were on the observation deck preparing to telepathically spy on the emotionally distraught people hoping to determine their situation.

"We haven't discovered anything definitive yet," commented Rex. "But I believe there's a ruthless group down there that is subjugating everyone else."

"The evidence we have supports that conclusion," agreed Tonya. "Most of the men fit into two groups: one that is filled with fear and anger, and one that is filled with arrogance and cruelty. I sense profound evil in this second group."

As she finished speaking, Tonya looked at the coastline far below and noticed how serene and inviting it appeared. Then, she looked at the huge storm system currently 150 miles offshore. "I think that storm is moving in," she said. "It seems closer to shore than it was on our last orbit."

"It looks violent," commented Rex. "There are powerful lightening bolts lighting up the clouds."

Tonya watched nature's fireworks in awe; then, she turned her attention to the Western Community and began focusing her telepathic senses on it. Almost immediately, she cringed and cried out in alarm, "A man is being beaten! I feel his intense pain!"

"I feel it too," responded Rex. "Now, I see images in his mind. He is watching his wife being stripped nude by the guards. She is struggling, but they are ripping her clothes off and staking her to the ground in a spread-eagle fashion. One of the guards is getting ready to rape her."

"The man is suffering great anguish!" exclaimed Tonya. "He's threatening the guards, but they're laughing at him, because he's chained to a pole and cannot help his wife. The guards are taunting him and telling him, 'now you know what happens to people who plan escapes'. The man's wife is struggling, but she is securely tied down and cannot fend off her rapist. He is sadistic, and he is deriving great pleasure from forcing himself on her." Boiling over with extreme anger, Tonya coldly said, "I will kill those bastards!"

"I will help you," stated Rex with equally cold determination.

"I want to kill them right now!" Tonya exclaimed.

"I do too, but we can't. I know this is painful for you to watch, but you must tune out your emotions and focus your telepathic powers on everything that's going on down there. Look at the complete picture. We need all the information we can get, so we can plan our mission well. I especially want clear facial images of the guards involved in this. I will try to get the images from the man's mind and the woman's mind."

Tonya listened to Rex, and with total determination to get the information needed to exact revenge, she telepathically focused her mind on other people at the scene. As the minutes passed by, she discovered two mindsets. There were the men, women, and children who were forced to watch the rape and the beating. The dominant feelings in this group were fear, anger, and frustration at not having weapons to kill the guards holding them in check. In the minds of the guards, Tonya found arrogance. They had all the guns and were gloating at the helplessness of those they were bringing suffering to.

The last person Tonya telepathically spied on was one of the guards. He was a young man who was feeling sympathy for the rape victim and the beating victim. This man was wondering if there was some way he could intervene on their behalf, but he decided against it, because he realized that he would fail and then be singled out for punishment. I do not want to continue living the evil ways of my comrades, he thought. I must find a way to free this community and then join them if they'll have me.

A faint smile of hope appeared on Tonya's face. That's a young man I just might be able to work with, she concluded. Tonya focused on the young man ever more deeply. She wanted to be able to identify him from his thought patterns. For a full two minutes, she probed the young man's mind. Then, she lost contact. The Challenger had completed its pass over the scene.

In an icy tone, Rex said, "Let's go talk to Jerry."

Rex and Tonya found Jerry on the flight deck. He and Kayleb

were reviewing reconnaissance data for the area surrounding the Western Community. They were looking for a place to land a capsule containing RPVs and mechanical bugs.

Noticing that Rex and Tonya were very upset, Jerry asked, "What happened?"

In explicit detail, Tonya reported what she and Rex had witnessed. Rex backed up her story by reporting details that he had seen. At the end of the report, Tonya said, "I need to go down there and rescue that man and his wife, and I will kill their tormentors."

"I can't let you go in alone," Jerry said. "It's far too dangerous."

"I will go with her," stated Rex. "Our telepathic powers complement each other. Together, we are a strong team."

"That may be, but there are only two of you," argued Jerry. "We don't yet know how large the enemy force is. When we rescued you and your family, we barely escaped with our lives."

"That's a valid point," acknowledged Rex. "But I believe that an entire society is being subjugated, and there has to be a way to do a rescue mission."

"I have 60 expert Special Forces soldiers," stated Kayleb. "They could make minced meat out of the thugs down there. I just need a quick way to transport them to the action."

"You have an old yellow bus and some old trucks and jeeps that are still running," responded Jerry. "If you could get your soldiers to that bay we took off from three days ago, I could pick them up with my shuttle and land them on the beach a few miles from the scene. They could go the rest of the way on foot, or they could do a parachute landing even closer."

"The soldiers that I'm talking about are a rapid-reaction force with very well maintained weapons and equipment. They have ATVs, jeeps, trucks, and light artillery. They also have two lightly armed scout helicopters, but they don't have the range/payload capability to be of any use on this mission."

"I'm amazed that you could maintain their equipment without an industrial base," commented Jerry.

"It's been a struggle. I used to have a much larger force, but we've had to cannibalize some equipment to keep other equipment working. Also, we have a large machine shop that we've used to make parts. My force may be small, but they are an elite group. Their lack of numbers is made up for by constant training."

"How long would it take them to get to the saltwater bay pick-up point?"

"That's about 240 miles. The old highway should be in fairly good condition. It's desert all the way, so it should not be overrun by vegetation. They might make the drive in five hours, but if the old road is in bad shape, it could just as easily take ten."

"If we get them started right away, there's a good chance we could have them on the beach near the Western Community during tonight's dark period."

"I appreciate your assistance," responded Kayleb. "If you'll let me use your communications equipment, I'll talk to my son, and they'll be on the move in a matter of minutes."

"Your son?" questioned Jerry.

"The officer in charge is my only living son. His name is Torleb. My other son and both of my daughters were killed in the war. They were on a camping trip with other children during the initial nuclear attack. All of them were killed by an off-target nuclear bomb."

"I am sorry that happened," stated Jerry. "That must've been difficult for you and Giselle to deal with."

"It was, and over the years, the memory of their deaths has built a total determination in me and Torleb to defend what we have left. Torleb and his men train relentlessly and intelligently. They are highly motivated and very good with special weapons and tactics. And now, I have a mission for them. They must go to the Western Community and find out what's going on there. If the community is being subjugated by evil-minded thugs, we will deal with them. There is no place for that kind of thing in the nation that I am rebuilding."

Jerry nodded to indicate that he understood. Then, he showed Kayleb how to use the communications equipment. Shortly, Kayleb was discussing the situation with Torleb. When the conversation ended, Kayleb turned to Jerry and said, "They're on the way."

"That was quick," commented Jerry.

"I keep them on full alert," stated Kayleb. "They are our first line of defense. Calling them is like calling the fire department. They respond immediately."

Tonya looked deeply concerned and asked, "What if they don't arrive at the pickup point early enough to be flown to the Western Community tonight?"

"My troops could pull off a daylight raid and win," stated Kayleb.

"But many of the people we want to rescue might be killed by the thugs, and that would defeat the purpose of us going there. We need the element of surprise, which means a nighttime raid, when most of them should be sleeping."

"So what happens if your troops don't arrive early enough to do it tonight?" Tonya persisted.

"Then, we have to go in tomorrow night," responded Kayleb.

"But that man and his wife could be killed by then," argued Tonya. "There has to be another way, a backup plan." Tonya paused a few moments for effect; then, she said, "I have a backup plan that I believe will work."

Being a battle-tested General with an open mind to all possibilities, Kayleb was all ears, and he immediately said, "I'd like to hear the details of your plan."

Looking into his eyes, Tonya said, "You and Jerry have been searching for a place to land a capsule loaded with RPVs and mechanical bugs. Have you found a good location?"

"Yes, we have. It's on the far side of a hill that's about three miles south of the clearing where the rape and beating took place. But what does that have to do with your plan?"

"We need to send down a capsule that's big enough to hold me, along with the RPVs and bugs."

"You've got a lot of guts to be willing to ride one of those things down to the surface."

"Why do you say that? Mike has a reputation for landing them on target every time." Turning to Jerry, Tonya asked, "Do you have a capsule big enough to deliver me to the surface?"

Before Jerry could answer, Rex said, "It has to be big enough for two people because I'm going with her."

"We do have several human-rated capsules," responded Jerry. "They are for emergency use to evacuate this starship, should that ever become necessary when the shuttles aren't available. But before I authorize the use of one of them, I need to know what your plan is, and I need to be convinced that it will work."

Turning to Rex, Jerry said, "I came here from Alcent to rescue you and your family. After everything we did to pull off a successful rescue, I don't want to throw away that success by sending you to your death."

Speaking to Tonya, Jerry said, "You are still young, and you are filled with a zest for life. The best part of your life is still in front of you, and I sure don't want to send you to your death. I need to know what you plan to do if I allow you to go down in a capsule."

"I know my life will be at risk," responded Tonya. "But I know how to use my telepathic ability to stay out of trouble. I felt, and still feel, the pain and helplessness of that man and his wife. It's possible that their tormentors might kill them before the day is done, but I don't think that is their plan. They are sadistic and thrive on making people suffer. For their own sick pleasure, I think they will torment this couple for a few days and give them a slow agonizing death. I have to go down there and find a way to rescue them in the event that Torleb and his men don't arrive on time. I will not feel good about myself if I don't make the attempt."

"It sounds like you don't have a plan other than a deep desire to do the right thing," commented Jerry.

"That's right," Tonya admitted. "We don't yet have enough information to put together a detailed rescue plan, but when we're down there, we'll have RPVs and bugs to gather that info. If Torleb arrives on time, the info we gather will be essential for him to have a successful mission. But if he doesn't arrive on time, Rex and I will find a way to do the rescue. Most likely, we'll do it in the dark of the night, but at this point, we can't even say that for sure."

Jerry looked into Tonya's eyes and sensed a capability far beyond what would be expected of someone so young. Then, he turned to Rex, who said, "I've seen her in action, and she's one cool cookie with nerves of steel. She's just simply not going to make any stupid moves. I am confident we can get the job done."

"My judgment tells me that I should give you and Tonya the opportunity to do this," stated Jerry. "One of my concerns is that we don't have much time to put this together. If we do this, we'll have to send you down in just a few hours, and I don't know if that's possible. So I'm going to convene a meeting of everyone concerned to discuss what we can do. Then, I'll make the final decision."

"Thank you," responded Tonya.

Ten minutes later, Jerry opened the meeting in his office by explaining the situation. Then, he faced Mike and asked, "How soon can you have a three-person capsule ready to send down?"

"Those capsules are for emergency evacuation of this starship, so I keep them ready to go, but why a three-person capsule?"

"Rex and Tonya will go down in a three-person capsule, and we'll remove the third seat, so their weapons and equipment can occupy that space."

"What equipment will they need, and how much time do I have to pack it into the capsule?"

"To start with, they'll need to be fitted with spacesuits to guard against the unlikely event of the capsule springing a leak."

"We have plenty of those. I'm sure we can find suits that will fit. What else do we need?"

"I want the bugs and the gun I had when I rescued Rex and his family," responded Tonya.

"The gun is no problem, but I'll have to give the bugs a quick checkout to make sure they're fully functional."

"We also need some RPVs," stated Tonya.

"We have plenty of those." Turning to Rex, Mike asked, "What's on your list?"

"I want an assault rifle equipped with a telescopic sight, laser range finder, and a fire control computer. I'll also need a pistol."

"Not a problem," stated Mike.

"Also, when you give those bugs a quick checkout, I want to learn how to operate them, so I can give Tonya some backup."

"They're easy to operate. You won't need much training to become proficient."

Facing Rex and Tonya, Kayleb said, "If you can get there undetected, rescuing that man and his wife might turn out to be easy. The guards certainly won't be expecting you."

"I hope it'll turn out that way," responded Tonya. "But we aren't going to take anything for granted. We are going to thoroughly investigate the area before we do anything."

"That's a wise approach," agreed Kayleb. "As I see it, the most difficult part of our mission will be rescuing the subjugated people without getting anyone killed. The intelligence you gather could turn out to be crucial to my son's success."

"We'll learn as much as we can," responded Tonya.

"What we especially need is to find out what's going on inside that bomb shelter. We need to know how many people we're trying to rescue and where they are. Likewise, we need to know how many guards there are and where they're located."

"I think the man who was beaten and the woman who was raped will gladly give us that info," commented Rex.

"That's only true if they're alive and conscious when you arrive," noted Kayleb.

"I expect that they will be," Tonya said. "The sadistic evil ones can only get their sick pleasure by keeping their victims conscious."

Sitting next to Tonya, Jim said, "That's what concerns me about this mission. If you're captured, you'll become one of their victims."

"I'll make sure that doesn't happen."

"No matter how cautious you are, you cannot eliminate the possibility of being captured," Jim argued.

"He's right," warned Trang. "You need to be prepared for that possibility."

"Our capture is possible," acknowledged Rex. "But our telepathic abilities work well together. I believe we can detect them far enough in advance to avoid walking into an ambush."

"Also, I will have my hornets," stated Tonya. "If we're captured by a small number of those thugs, I can put them to sleep before they bring us in."

"What if they're curious about your headband and take it away from you?" Trang asked. "Without that headband, you cannot telepathically control the hornets."

"You're right about that," Tonya admitted.

"I have an idea," stated Connie. "Those control units that convert telepathic signals to electronic signals aren't very big. If you'll come to the medical lab, I will bond them to your temples and cover them with artificial skin. With your hair covering them, no one will even notice the slight bulge on each temple. When you return, I'll remove them."

"Great idea," responded Tonya.

Speaking to Jerry, Rex said, "We need a topographical map of the area."

"We can easily provide that," responded Jerry.

"Have you been able to locate the entrances to the bomb shelter? We could use that info."

"We know where some of them are."

"Many of our bomb shelters followed the same basic design," added Kayleb. "I have a pretty good idea where the entrances are that we haven't been able to spot."

Speaking to Kayleb, Rex asked, "Do you know how they keep fresh air in that bomb shelter? Are there outside ventilation ports?"

"Yes, there are."

"Are they a possible way to get inside undetected?"

"Yes, but it's a dangerous way. The ventilation system has a series of blast proof doors that can be closed during a chemical or nuclear attack. If they discover you in the system, they could close the doors, and you would be trapped between doors with no way out. They could then kill you by injecting a poisonous gas, or they could just leave you there until you starve to death."

"Let's forget that idea. I just thought I had an easy way to get inside and spy on them."

"It's too bad we don't have a colorless, odorless sleeping gas," Mike said. "We could feed that into the ventilation system and knock them out for a while. That would make Torleb's job easy."

"The ventilation system was designed to defeat that kind of attack," stated Kayleb. "The gas would be detected, and doors would close."

"It's been 30 years since the initial nuclear attack," argued Mike. "Is it possible the poison gas detectors are no longer working because of a lack of maintenance?"

"That's possible," admitted Kayleb. "In fact, it's quite likely. I've had a difficult time maintaining basic systems on my base, and I've been able to do so only because I have major underground facilities. The Western Community isn't that well equipped. I suspect that they've devoted whatever resources they have to just staying alive and healthy."

"So an odorless, colorless sleeping gas might work," commented Mike.

"I have a formula for such a gas," stated Geniya. "It's a gaseous version of the hibernation-inducing drug that we're using the mechanical hornets to deliver."

"Is this gas easy to make?" Mike asked. "Or is it a difficult time-consuming process? We only have a few hours."

"I can make it with the equipment and chemicals you have in the medical lab, but I need more than a few hours."

Excited by the possibilities, Kayleb jumped into the conversation and asked, "How much time do you need?"

"Do you know how big that bomb shelter is? What I'm getting at is how much air do I have to treat with the drug to make sure that I've put enough in there to knock everyone out?"

"That base was much smaller than mine. I don't think there were ever more than 500 to 600 people stationed there. Their bomb shelter probably had a shop, a medical center, a power plant, a cafeteria, several bathrooms, and a couple dozen sleeping wards."

"It sounds like there might be 40 to 50 rooms in that underground complex."

"That's a reasonable guess."

"It will take at least a day to make enough gas to get the concentration I need to knock everybody out in that many rooms. And I will have to make an antidote for the soldiers going in, or they will also be knocked out."

"How long will people hit by the gas be out?" Kayleb asked.

"The drug induces hibernation. When people drop into that state, they stay there for at least 24 hours."

"If the ventilation system is operating normally, it should change out the bomb shelter's air in just a few hours. If Torleb waits a few hours before leading his soldiers in, they should not need the antidote."

"That's true, but the ventilation system might not be working as well as it once did. If we decide to make the gas, I will make the antidote too, if I have the time."

"I thought we were planning to go in tonight," commented Tonya. "The gas you're talking about making won't be available before tomorrow night at the earliest."

"It's another backup plan," responded Kayleb. "My son and his soldiers might not arrive at the pickup point on time to be delivered to the scene tonight. If we fly them in tomorrow night, they can go in equipped with the gas."

Speaking to her daughter, Geniya said, "I don't think it's very likely, but it's possible that you and Rex could be captured and imprisoned underground. The gas would be useful in rescuing you."

"What that means is Rex and I should have the antidote with us and take it before we go into action."

"For that to happen, I need to go to the medical lab and start making this stuff," stated Geniya. Turning to Mike, she said, "I need a pressure pump and some high-pressure canisters that I can pump the gas into. Eight one-quart bottles able to withstand 150 psi should be adequate."

"No problem," responded Mike.

"Any chance one or two of those bottles might be ready for us to take along?" Tonya asked.

"I will make sure you have two of them and some antidote," stated Geniya.

Speaking to Mike, Tonya asked, "Can you make me a release valve I can trigger telepathically with the hornet control units that Connie is going to bond to my temples?"

"That's a simple programming task that I will do as soon as I get the bottles and pump for Geniya. The release valves will be easy to make."

"Good! I can envision a scenario where this might come in handy."

"I need to go down there too," stated Jim. "I cannot stay up here while Tonya is down there. If she is captured, I need to be part of the rescue mission."

"My Special Forces soldiers can handle that," stated Kayleb.

"He's right," argued Jerry. "Besides that, you're still recovering from a serious bullet wound."

"I'm well enough to fly our helicopter. If Torleb arrives late at the pickup point, you're not planning to fly his forces in until tomorrow night. But I have an alternate plan that covers their possible late arrival. If I'm along to pilot the helicopter, we could take part of Torleb's forces in during daylight. We just land the shuttle far enough away to not be seen by the enemy. Then, I use low-level flying tech-niques with the chopper to fly them in eight at a time to within a few miles of the action."

"I like it," stated Kayleb. "It gives us added flexibility."

Looking into Jim's eyes, Jerry said, "Before I give the okay, I want Connie to check you out in the medical lab. If she says you're fit to fly, then you can go down."

Jim turned to Connie and said, "You examined me just a few hours ago, and you said I'm almost fully recovered. So I should be able to go on this mission, right?"

Connie thought about the potential risk; then, she said, "I don't have any medical reasons to keep you off the mission."

"Thank you," replied Jim, who then turned to Jerry and said, "The doctor has spoken."

"Okay, you're on the mission," stated Jerry.

Turning away from Jim, Jerry briefly made eye contact with each person in the room. No one said anything, so he said, "It's time to adjourn this meeting. All of you have urgent work to do. We're only nine hours away from our first nighttime opportunity to send down the capsule with Tonya and Rex onboard. The second opportunity will be an hour-and-a-half after that."

After everyone left, Kayleb said to Jerry, "I need to talk to Zeb about the X-plane. I'd like to find a way to use it to support this mission. I know that airplane seems like the wrong system for what we're trying to do, but I have some ideas to kick around with Zeb."

"Let me know if you come up with anything."

"You got it."

TIME: Day 65, Almost Midnight

In the Challenger's hangar bay, Rex and Tonya were sealed inside their landing capsule awaiting release, which was less than a minute away. The cargo shuttle had already departed with Jerry in the pilot's seat and Jim in the copilot's seat. Mike stayed onboard the Challenger to pilot the landing capsule to its destination and to do continued recon of the upcoming battle scene.

Using the Challenger's communications equipment, Mike spoke to Rex and Tonya. "I'm going to release you in 30 seconds," he said. "Are you ready to go? This is your last chance to change your mind and let Torleb do the mission."

"We're going down," Rex and Tonya responded in unison.

"Also, it's not yet clear that Torleb is going to make it on time to do the rescue tonight," added Tonya.

"You're right about that," responded Mike. "He's still a couple hours away from the pickup point."

"And there's a storm offshore that might arrive in three to four hours and make the water too rough for a shuttle landing," commented Tonya.

"OK! You've convinced me," stated Mike as he pressed the release button. "Shortly, your retrorockets will fire, and your descent will begin."

Looking out the view port in front of her, Tonya watched the giant starship appear to drift away, but in reality, it was the capsule that was drifting away. Then, a red warning light started flashing. Rex and Tonya pushed back to make sure they were firmly nested in their seats. The retrorockets fired, and the deceleration hit them hard, effectively gluing them into their seats. In just 20 seconds, the rockets ran out of fuel and were discarded. They would burn up on atmospheric entry.

"We're on our own now," Tonya said.

"It does feel that way," commented Rex. "But Mike is going to make sure that we land on target."

"He does have a reputation for doing that. Hopefully, all will go well, and he'll pull it off one more time."

"You're not worried, are you?" questioned Rex.

"No, but I do feel a bit antsy. This capsule is all there is between us and death. And it does feel pretty small at the moment."

"That's true, but the technology is mature. The earth people have been using these things for 140 years. We really don't have anything to worry about."

"I know that you're right, but I've never done this before, and I do feel a bit nervous about it."

"You're not alone in that, but let's not worry. It's too late to turn back, so let's enjoy the ride."

Mike's voice came through the communication system. "Rex and Tonya, your retrofire was a perfect burn. You're on course."

"Thanks," responded Tonya.

"See what I mean," Rex said. "We have nothing to worry about."

"I'm not worried; I'm just wildly excited. My heart is even racing."

"I'm pretty excited myself. I never dreamed in my wildest imagination that I'd ever do anything like this. But here we are."

"We must be entering the upper atmosphere. I'm starting to feel deceleration."

"I feel it too."

As the capsule dropped deeper into the atmosphere, the deceleration grew intense, and fiery red-hot plasma enveloped the capsule. But the capsule did not burn up despite the high temperature of the plasma. The capsule's heat shield and thermal protection materials did their job.

"I see nothing but fire outside!" exclaimed Tonya. "And I feel extremely heavy."

"This deceleration is pretty harsh," agreed Rex, struggling to get the words out.

The capsule's fiery descent through the upper atmosphere continued without a problem. When most of the capsule's orbital speed had been dissipated and it reached the low end of the hypersonic speed regime, the flaming red plasma that had enveloped the capsule disappeared. The deceleration g-forces were still intense as the capsule continued to lose speed. When the capsule's speed dropped below the speed of sound; a small, rugged, high-speed parachute was deployed, which reduced its speed to less than 300 mph, where a much larger parachute was deployed. At 50 mph, this parachute was discarded, and the capsule's large para-wing popped out. With it, Mike began maneuvering the capsule toward its landing area, which was on the south side of a hill three miles south of the couple that Rex and Tonya hoped to rescue.

"This is maddening," exclaimed Tonya. "It's pitch-black dark out there. I can't see a thing."

"That means our enemy can't see us," stated Rex.

Mike's voice came through the speakers. "You're on course. I'll have you on the ground in a few minutes."

"Thanks Mike," responded Tonya. "I wish I could see where we're going."

"No problem," replied Mike. "Your capsule is equipped with radar, infrared cameras, night-vision cameras, and daylight cameras. I am using that equipment to guide you to a safe landing. I've just turned on your instrument console. You should be getting video of the planet below."

"We are, and I feel better now that I can see where we're going. That looks like ocean down there. I can see the surf pounding the beach. A short distance in from the beach, there are sand dunes with tall grass waving in the breeze. Then, that gives way to what appears to be a rather dense forest."

"It looks like you have us heading north at low altitude above the beach," commented Rex.

"That's right," responded Mike. "The wind is starting to pick up ahead of the incoming storm, but I am going to have you safely down before it gets bad."

"I'm happy to hear that," replied Tonya.

"You're only a minute away from landing."

"We're turning inland," stated Tonya.

"That's right. I need to head inland a bit, so that I can turn back into the breeze."

A few moments later, Tonya said, "We're now turning north."

"You're almost there," responded Mike.

"The terrain looks almost close enough to reach out and touch," exclaimed Tonya. "And we're now turning toward the ocean. We're heading toward the ocean, but we're barely moving."

"That's because your forward velocity is only a bit greater than that of the incoming wind," explained Mike. "You will be on the ground in a few seconds."

Mike hardly finished speaking when the capsule hit the ground with a thud. Shock absorbers under their seats cushioned the impact for Rex and Tonya. The para-wing was released, and it collapsed on the ground a short distance from the capsule.

"You've landed right on target," announced Mike.

"Thanks for doing a great job," stated Tonya. "Now it's time for us to do our job."

Chapter Nine

Rex unlocked the sealed pressure hatch; then, he hit the switch that popped it open. He and Tonya opened the faceplates of their helmets. "That sea breeze sure smells good," commented Rex.

"It has a salty aroma," noted Tonya, "and I like it."

"I have a weather update for you," announced Mike. "The storm that's coming in will be there in an hour to an hour-and-a-half. It contains lots of rain, gusty winds, and plenty of lightning. It's the lightning that's the big problem for the couple that you're hoping to rescue. Kayleb thinks the pole the man is chained to is a lightning arresting tower. If it gets hit, the man will be toast, so you need to get there ahead of the storm. But to keep your own presence a secret, you need to grab that para-wing and stuff it into the capsule. It's big and laid out on top of the sand dune grass. Anyone stumbling into the area will spot it. Your capsule is less likely to be seen. It has a drab sandy color and the grass is taller than it. Good luck and call me if I can help you with anything."

"You got it," responded Rex.

After taking off their spacesuits and stuffing the para-wing into the capsule, Rex and Tonya put on their packs, belted on their pistols, and headed toward their objective. Since time was short, and it was very dark, they decided to hike north on the wet sandy beach where they could make faster progress than plodding their way through the sand dunes. Also, it was low tide, and the incoming high tide would cover their tracks. They wore night-vision goggles that allowed them to see very well, despite the near total darkness.

"Is there any possibility our enemy might have night-vision goggles?" Tonya asked.

"That's very unlikely," replied Rex. "I don't think we have to worry about them seeing us in this darkness, but they could detect us telepathically if any of them are out and about."

189

"They should all be sleeping. But if they aren't, we should be able to discover them telepathically before they discover us."

"Let's maintain silence the rest of the way and stay alert."

"Okay, but first, are you detecting anything?" Tonya asked.

"Only the couple we're here to rescue and two guards, and it appears that they're all sleeping."

"That's the same picture I'm getting. I hope they stay sleeping. That'll make our job easy."

Hoping to beat the incoming storm, Rex and Tonya hiked northward at a brisk pace, even breaking into a slow run at times. Tonya was in the lead while Rex stayed 25 to 30 yards behind her with his rifle ready. Their destination was three miles north of where they landed.

In just over a half-hour, Rex and Tonya reached the outskirts of their objective. Hiding behind bushes, they studied the scene. As expected, the area was deserted except for the guards and their prisoners.

Communicating telepathically, Tonya said, "Those guards must be lazy. Why are they so careless as to be sleeping on the job?"

"I suspect it might be partly due to their arrogant attitude. Apparently, they and their comrades have such complete control over this society that they're just not expecting any trouble."

"Can you tell if they're the rapists we came here to kill?"

"I need a closer look to determine that. But that electrical storm will be here soon, so we need to release the man chained to that pole, which looks like it's made out of steel and is a lightning rod."

"First, we have to deal with the guards," responded Tonya while drawing her pistol, which was equipped with a silencer.

Gripping Tonya's arm, Rex said, "Instead of killing them with bullets, which is something their leader is familiar with; let's hit him with something he knows nothing about. Let's drug those guards into a state of hibernation. This will be something that their leader has never seen before, and he will have to wonder what kind of enemy he has. That mystery gnawing at his mind could turn out to be a big advantage for us."

"I like the possibilities," responded Tonya. "And I have another idea. How would the bad-guy leader react if his guards and prisoners were to mysteriously disappear without a trace?"

"That would be a shocking surprise for him. He would have to wonder if his guards ran away with the prisoners or if all four were taken by an outside force. In the first case he would have to take a good look at his followers and wonder if they're trustworthy. In the second case, he would have to wonder if he's being confronted by an outside military force. That might cause him to send out scouts that we could pick off. Scouts that never return would certainly give him something to think about."

"It sounds like you like my idea," Tonya said.

"I do, but to make all four of these people disappear, we have to take those guards with us without them sounding an alarm. How do we do that?"

"If we drug them into a state of hibernation, we would have to drag them out of here, and they're too big to drag out of the area. So we need to make them walk out of here."

"If we handcuff them and make them leave at gunpoint, they'll be mad as hell. If their leader has any telepathic ability at all, he'll be able to detect that."

"There is another way we can do it, but there is some risk involved. My mother has provided us with a drug that will shut down their ability to resist telepathically induced hypnosis. She uses it when she's treating mental problems."

"So, we just walk up to those guards and inject them? What if they wake up?"

"I did say there's some risk involved. But if we can make these guys disappear, their leader will have a big mystery on his hands. So I think it's a risk we have to take."

Tonya took off her backpack, opened it, and removed a small medical kit. Opening it, she removed two hypodermic needles and handed one to Rex. "Can you telepathically enter the mind of a sleeping individual and keep him sleeping for a few minutes?" she asked.

"Since they're already sleeping, their defenses to telepathic intrusion are shut down, so yes, I can keep one of them sleeping for a while."

"It only takes a minute or two for the drug to shut down their defenses to us. Then, we can telepathically hypnotize them to do whatever we tell them. I'll take the one on the right. Are you ready to do the other one?"

"Where do I stick the needle?"

"A fleshy area is best. Shoulder, buttocks, or upper leg will do just fine."

"Okay, let's do it."

Rex and Tonya did another visual and telepathic search of the area. Not finding anything, they telepathically entered the minds of the sleeping guards and pushed them into a deeper sleep. Then, they left their hiding place and calmly walked into the clearing.

When Rex reached his victim, he dropped to his knees and quickly shoved the needle into the man's shoulder while telepathically keeping him asleep. Slowly depressing the plunger, Rex injected the drug.

Just then, the sky was split by a powerful lightning bolt followed by a booming crack of thunder a few seconds later. This jolted Rex's senses, but he maintained his concentration to telepathically ensure that the man he injected stayed asleep.

However, the man chained to the pole awoke startled, as did his wife, who was still staked out and naked. Another lightning bolt lit up the sky, and the chained man saw Rex and Tonya bent over the guards. He was suddenly filled with hope by what appeared to be happening.

With telepathically induced hypnosis, Rex programmed the sleeping guard to stay asleep until brought out of it. He rolled him over and handcuffed his hands behind his back. Going to Tonya's assistance, Rex helped her handcuff the other guard.

Standing up, Rex walked to the chained man. He removed a high-temperature blowtorch from his belt, pressed the ignition button, grabbed the man's chain, and torched it. The high-temperature flame quickly cut through the chain, freeing the man. Worried about his wife, the man immediately went to her side to comfort her while Tonya finished cutting the cords that secured her to posts driven into the ground.

With muscles that were cold from being naked and stiff from being tied in the same position for many hours, the woman struggled to stand up. Her husband helped her; then, he put his arms around her in a tight embrace. "We will punish those who did this to you," he assured her.

Suddenly, a lightning bolt struck the steel pole. Its energy was conducted harmlessly into the ground, but the booming crack of thunder was deafening. "We need to get out of here!" Rex yelled.

Speaking to the rescued man and woman, Tonya asked, "How serious are your injuries? Can you walk three miles?"

"We will try," responded the man. "Thank you for rescuing us.

We were slated for a slow agonizing death. My name is Rorgust, but people call me Gusty. My wife is Reebee."

"I am Tonya. My partner is Rex."

"Where are you from?" Gusty asked. "How did you happen to come here?"

"That's a long story that'll have to wait 'til later." Speaking to Reebee, Tonya said, "I have something in my pack for you to wear."

"Thank you," she said.

Speaking to Rex, Gusty asked, "What did you do to those guards?"

"We drugged them, and they are under our control."

"What are you going to do with them?"

"We'll decide later. For now, we're just going to take them with us. We want their boss to try to figure out what happened to all of you."

"He'll be wild with rage over this. His name is Mar-ris, and he's an evil man. He is a fanatic who wants total control of my people. He wants to turn my society into a cult with him as the supreme leader. Those who refuse to accept his teachings are branded as infidels and sentenced to be tortured into submission, or even to death."

"Two hostages and two guards disappearing will be a serious blow to his ego," stated Rex. "His claim to be the supreme authority will be in doubt."

"That's true," agreed Gusty. "But Mar-ris will respond, and his response will be brutal. As an example to all others, he will most likely execute my son, who is only nineteen."

"That possibility changes our plans," stated Rex. "We cannot leave. We have to stay here and find a way to prevent that. Let's hide in the bushes and discuss this."

"Why are you putting yourselves at risk for us when you don't even know us? What do you hope to gain? Where are you from?"

"General Kayleb wants to rebuild this once great nation. He wants freedom and democracy to prevail. He is coming here with a military force and wants to develop ties between your community and his. Tonya and I came here to rescue you and your wife and to gain information for Kayleb."

"The first thing you have to tell Kayleb is that Mar-ris is an evil fanatic. If Kayleb attacks, Mar-ris will use my people as hostages. Women and children will be used as human shields."

"Kayleb's soldiers will not do a direct assault. They are superbly trained Special Forces soldiers and will not make their presence

193

known until they are ready to strike with deadly precision. We need to provide them the info they need to plan such a strike."

"I've lived in this bomb shelter for 30 years, and I know every detail. Mar-ris and his gang have only been here three weeks. There is much that they don't know."

"How many are in his gang?" Rex asked.

"There are 34 of them, 18 men and 16 women."

"How many are in your community?"

"Two hundred and thirty."

"How did 34 manage to get control of 230?"

"They came to us playing the role of innocent nomads looking for a place to live. We befriended them and invited them to live with us. Eight days ago, they struck. Our women and children were taken hostage and locked up. They will start killing them if we don't submit to Mar-ris and his fanatical plans. He even passionately talks about expanding across the nation once he indoctrinates us to blindly follow his radical philosophy."

"His vision for putting this nation back together is in direct contrast to the free society Kayleb has planned."

"We have to defeat Mar-ris," stated Gusty. "I just hope we can do it without losing any of our women and children."

"We'll find a way," stated Tonya, who had been listening while giving clothing, food, and water to Reebee. She handed a sandwich to Gusty and said, "You'd better eat this. You're going to need the energy."

"Thanks," he said.

Rex used his communicator to give Jerry and Kayleb the latest information. When he finished his report, he said to his companions, "Torleb and his commandos will not be here until three hours after daybreak. So we have to keep Gusty, Jr., alive if it comes to that."

"I appreciate what you're doing for us," stated Reebee. "But we have a tough problem. Killing some of them to keep my son alive will probably result in some of our women and children being tortured or killed."

"If they bring him out to execute him, we'll have to stop them," stated Tonya.

Speaking to Gusty and Reebee, Rex said, "There is something I don't understand about this. Why would Mar-ris kill your son over your disappearance? His guards could've run off with you, or the four of you could've been captured by an outside force. Either way, this would be beyond your control, so why would Mar-ris kill your son?"

"I know it doesn't make sense," replied Gusty, "but his mindset is to control people by terrorizing them. He will have to punish someone for our escape, and my son will be his choice. Also, if we're unfortunate enough to be captured, we'll be given a painful death, and these guards will be punished for letting us escape."

"We need to jerk Mar-ris around," stated Tonya. "Play with his mind. Throw him off balance."

"What do you have in mind?" Gusty asked.

"First, let's drug these guards into a state of hibernation, so they can't be revived for at least 24 hours. Then, let's strip one of them and tie him down to the same posts Reebee was tied to. Let's chain the other one to the lightning arresting pole."

"He could be killed by a lightning strike," commented Rex.

"That would be a horrible tragedy," quipped Reebee with a laugh.

"But how would Mar-ris react?" questioned Tonya.

"He would blow his top at these guards for letting us escape," responded Gusty.

"Cussing out the guards will give him little satisfaction," stated Tonya. "In fact, it might even aggravate him."

"Why?" Gusty asked.

"Assuming no lightning strike, both guards will be alive, but they'll be in a drug-induced state of hibernation. He'll be unable to revive them to question them or cuss them out. Mar-ris wants total control over everyone, but in this case, he'll be powerless, and that will have to aggravate him."

"I can picture him in my mind," stated Gusty. "He will be mad as hell. But another way to get him bent out of shape would be to take the guards away, so that we all disappear without a trace. That will give him a big mystery to worry about. He will have to send out scouting parties to look for us. He could not just let it go."

"It looks like we have a choice to make," stated Rex. "We can all disappear, or we can leave the guards. Which approach would bring out the most thugs and keep them busy the longest? That is what we need to do, because our objective is to go underground and rescue the women and children. The more bad guys we bring out, the fewer we'll have to deal with down there. Is there any way we can get inside undetected?"

195

"To do that, we need a diversion that grabs Mar-ris and his people and holds their attention for a while," responded Gusty. "Staking out those guards will work for a while."

"Zeb could put on a flying display," suggested Tonya. "The one he did a few days ago held everyone's attention."

"Who is Zeb?" Gusty asked.

"Zeb is one of your interstellar astronauts," replied Tonya. "He also flies a hypersonic X-plane."

"Would he come here?"

"Many years ago, General Kayleb was his C.O.," stated Rex. "Zeb loves to fly, and he would gladly put on an air show here."

"I have an idea," stated Gusty. "Let's leave the guards here, along with a specially written note that will make Mar-ris blow his top. Before he recovers from that, we need Zeb to show up and do the air show."

"That sounds good, but what do we want the note to say?"

"I'm still thinking about the possibilities."

"Why don't we discuss that with Kayleb? He has Special Forces on the way. Our strategy has to work for them."

Rex and Tonya broke out their communicators, and the discussion with Kayleb and Jerry began. When it was over, Rex said, "Now that we have our diversion planned out, is there any way we can get inside undetected?"

"There are three entrances and they're all watched by armed guards," responded Gusty.

"How many?" Rex asked.

"There are two guards at each entrance during daylight hours. At night, the doors are locked and checked on periodically by a pair of patrolling guards."

"How many are guarding the imprisoned women and children?"

"They are being held 200 feet underground in a section of the bomb shelter that has rooms connected by a long hallway. This hallway has a guard station at the east end and also at the west end. There are two guards at each station around the clock."

"During the day, 10 people are doing guard duty," noted Rex. "And two guards are already out of action. That leaves 22 that we need to draw outside with some sort of diversion. While they're outside, we would only have to deal with two guards at a time to rescue the women and children. Is there a way in that's not guarded?"

"All entrances are guarded."

"But is there another way in? You have to circulate air in and out. Are the ventilation shafts big enough to crawl through?"

"There are four ventilation shafts, and they are big enough, but you wouldn't be crawling through. There is a drop of 200 feet down to the living quarters. The 200 feet is divided into 40-foot segments with a landing and blast protection doors at the bottom of each segment. Steel ladders are mounted in the ventilation shafts, so they could be used as emergency exits. All blast protection doors have been locked open for many years."

"So if we're willing to climb down 200 feet of ladders, we can gain entry through one of these shafts?"

"The outside vents are secured with steel grate doors covered with wire mesh and screens. These doors haven't been opened in years and are probably rusted shut."

"I have a blowtorch that will cut an opening for us."

"Wouldn't it be easier to just use my hornets to put a couple guards to sleep?" questioned Tonya. "Then, we can just walk in and down the stairs. Plus, we'll have two fewer guards to worry about."

"What hornets are you talking about?" Gusty asked.

"I have six mechanical hornets that look like the real thing. I use them to sting people with a potent drug that induces hibernation."

"Wow! I'm starting to like our chances. Let's forget the ventilation shafts and go in through the backdoor."

"There is something I've been wondering about," Tonya said. "What happens to the men after they've been brought in from a day of work?"

"Those that cause problems are locked up alone. Those that behave and work hard are allowed to spend the night with their families."

"So what did you do that got you chained to a lightning rod while your wife was raped?"

"I discussed escape possibilities with her. Mar-ris was nearby, and he telepathically overheard us."

"How many of his people have telepathic ability?" Rex asked.

"Mar-ris is the only one that I know about. He uses that ability to keep tabs on his people. They fear him. He is ruthless. He actually gets into their minds and uses psychological techniques to control them."

"It sounds like he's a very dangerous man who needs to be eliminated," stated Rex.

"There are two others that need to die along with him," stated Reebee with cold determination.

"That kind of justice is appropriate," agreed Gusty. "But our most important goal is to rescue our people without getting any of them killed. Once we've achieved that, we can administer justice."

"What would the thugs who follow Mar-ris do if we were to assassinate him?" Rex asked.

"Some of his followers are fully indoctrinated and are fanatics. They would try to avenge his death."

"What you're telling me is that killing him on sight would not help us."

"We have to rescue everyone before we kill him, but he must die. He is far too dangerous to let live. His telepathic powers are so good that he could even use them to escape from prison. It's possible that he could telepathically hypnotize a guard and get that guard to unlock his cell."

"In that case, here is what we need to do," stated Rex. "You and Reebee and Tonya will go underground to do the rescue. I will stay here to deal with Mar-ris and keep Kayleb and Jerry informed."

"You'll have the most dangerous mission," stated Gusty. "Don't underestimate Mar-ris. You're going to have a very capable and ruthless opponent."

"I understand that, but I also have some very special telepathic powers. I am capable of building a mental shield around my thoughts that will make it difficult for Mar-ris to discover me. Along with that, I am going to move out of this area and find a hill or boulder to get behind. I don't believe he will detect me."

"How will you watch this area?"

"I'll leave behind two small RPVs and use their eyes and ears. I also have hornets with stingers and dragonflies with eyes and ears."

"The thunderstorm seems to have passed," Tonya said. "Let's chain this guard to that pole and stake that one out."

A few minutes later, the job was done. Tonya then injected them to drop them into hibernation. Turning to Gusty, she said, "Lead the way to the back entrance. First light isn't that far away."

The trio departed with Gusty and Reebee armed with guns taken away from the guards. Rex attached a note to the steel pole; then, he parked RPVs, hornets, and dragonflies in key locations. Now I need to find a good hiding place, he thought, as he wandered into the forest.

After walking a hundred yards, he found a large boulder. This will do just fine, he decided. With the boulder between him and the subdued guards, Rex made himself comfortable, put on a headset, and checked the sound and images coming from the mechanical insects and RPVs. Everything is in good working order, he concluded. Now, I have to wait.

Rex had one of the RPVs focused on the overall scene with the subdued guards at the center of the picture. The other RPV was focused on the doorway where Gusty said Mar-ris and some followers would come from.

A half-hour later, the bulk of the storm clouds had passed by, and the first light of early dawn was starting to appear. It sure is quiet and peaceful, noted Rex, but this is probably the calm before the storm. Soon, Mar-ris and I will be locked in a life-and-death struggle, but I will win.

The sky gradually brightened. Expecting Mar-ris to appear on the scene at any moment, Rex mentally prepared himself for combat. He looked at images from both RPVs and noted that everything was still peaceful. He looked at the doorway that he expected Mar-ris to emerge from. It was built into a heavily reinforced concrete structure that was covered over with soil several yards deep. A jungle of plant life was growing in the soil. They've made that entrance look like the local landscape, thought Rex.

Rex got on his communicator and called Zeb. With Jerry, Trang, Mike, and Kayleb listening in, Rex said, "Hello Zeb! Are you in the area?"

"I'm circling about two minutes away."

"Good! It's starting to get light here, and I'm going to need an over-flight soon."

"Let me know when."

Rex's conversation was interrupted when the bomb shelter door opened. A big, husky man with thick brown hair emerged. Noticing the fire-belching dragon tattoo on his forehead, Rex concluded, that's Mar-ris.

"Hey Zeb, I'm going to need an ear-shattering, low-level pass in a couple minutes."

"I'm on the way," responded Zeb, while banking the X-plane into a tight turn and pushing the engines up to full power.

The first thing Mar-ris did was look toward the site where Gusty and Reebee were supposed to be secured. He was visibly shaken by what he saw. Quickly stomping his way to the naked guard tied to the posts where Reebee had been tied down, Mar-ris kicked the man and screamed at him. But all to no avail. He could not rouse him. Mar-ris screamed at the man chained to the lightning rod. But even with kicking him, he could not revive him either.

"What the hell happened here?" Mar-ris screamed. "Where are my prisoners? Why won't these guys wake up?"

Mar-ris was surrounded by his cronies, but fearing his wrath, no one volunteered an answer. So filled with rage was Mar-ris that he had failed to notice the piece of paper that was taped to the lightning arresting pole. But one of his followers saw it and pointed at it. Mar-ris ran to the pole, grabbed the note, and read it. It said:

Mar-ris,

Did you happen to notice what I did to your guards? They are in a deep sleep and will stay there until I revive them. Within this hour, you will join them. You do not have the power to stop me, so do not even try.

Your enemy,
Gusty

Mar-ris boiled over. He faced the forest and yelled, "Gusty! You son-of-a-bitch! You have no power over me! I will find you and cut off your hands and feet!"

Screaming at his followers, Mar-ris said, "Spread out and find him! He can't be far away!"

Turning to the bomb shelter entrance, Mar-ris yelled at the people guarding it. "Get into the forest and find Gusty. I don't need that entrance guarded. All of Gusty's people are locked up."

At that moment, everyone was jolted by the sudden sharp crack of a powerful sonic boom, followed immediately by the thunderous roar of jet engines, as Zeb made a low-altitude supersonic pass over the area. The sonic boom compression wave was intense and severely rattled Mar-ris's already agitated nerves. Badly shaken, Mar-ris and his cronies looked up and spotted the X-plane rapidly flying away out over the ocean. They saw it pitch up into a vertical climb, loop over, and roll into a dive back down to low altitude, where it leveled off and headed back toward them.

"What the hell is that?" screamed Mar-ris. "Where did it come from? What's it doing here?"

Rex was prepared for Zeb's arrival. It was the distraction he needed. Using a joystick control unit, Rex launched one of his mechanical hornets and flew it toward Mar-ris, approaching him from behind. Mar-ris was so focused on the X-plane and so filled with rage that he never felt the minor sting to the back of his neck.

Just as the sonic boom from Zeb's second flyby hit Mar-ris and his followers, Rex spotted the man who had raped Reebee. He quickly launched a second hornet and stung him in the back of his neck. The man felt the sting and cussed at the hornet while swatting at it.

Getting back on his communicator, Rex said to Zeb, "Mission accomplished, see you later."

Mar-ris yelled at his cronies, "That was just an airplane! It's gone now! Get into the forest and find Gusty! After I torture him, I will hang him."

As the last of his henchmen disappeared into the forest, heading in different directions, Mar-ris concentrated on clearing his mind. Determined to find Gusty, he focused his telepathic powers into the forest directly in front of him. After a few moments, he broadened his search. But it was a futile effort, because the hibernation drug was starting to take effect. Feeling weak, Mar-ris sat down on a bench to rest. Momentarily, he slumped and fell off the bench, hitting the ground with a thud. His descent into a state of hibernation was well underway.

While watching imagery of the scene, Rex thought, so much for my ruthless opponent. Now, I have to get ready to use my other two hornets on the two men heading this way.

Meanwhile, at the back entrance on the east end of the bomb shelter, Tonya had also taken advantage of Zeb's two flybys. She had stung both guards with the two hornets that she had. The guards were now out cold. To Gusty and Reebee, the flight of the hornets looked almost magical, because Tonya did not use a joystick control box. Instead, she controlled them telepathically. Doctor Connie had attached small control units to Tonya's temples and covered them with artificial skin. These control units converted Tonya's telepathic signals to electronic signals that directed the activities of the hornets. To Reebee and Gusty, it looked like the hornets had accomplished their mission totally on their own.

Obviously impressed by what he had just seen, Gusty said, "Wow! Those things really do work. Can you reload them?"

"I sure can," replied Tonya.

"That's going to make it possible to rescue my people without losing anyone. But we're going to need some luck. The first thing we have to do is walk down 20 flights of stairs undetected. The greatest danger is that we'll meet enemies coming up the stairs."

"I can check out the stairs," stated Tonya.

"How?" Gusty asked.

After removing a mechanical dragonfly from her pack, Tonya said, "This little bug has eyes and ears, plus antennae to broadcast signals with. While we go down the stairs, I'll keep him a few flights of stairs ahead of us, so we don't encounter any surprises. We'll wear headsets, so we can see and hear what he sees and hears."

Tonya only had two headsets. She gave one to Gusty and showed him how to use it. The headset looked very much like a pair of reading glasses with a small speaker next to each ear. The half-lens shape of the video screens allowed the wearer to view the video from the dragonfly and also look over the top of the screens to view the surroundings.

While making eye contact with Gusty and Reebee, Tonya asked, "Are you ready to check out the situation down there?"

"The sooner we do this, the better it'll be for my people," responded Gusty.

"Before we head down the stairs, I need to make sure we don't lose contact with Rex," Tonya said, while reaching into her pack. She removed a radio transmitter/receiver and placed it under a bush above the entrance. Removing a small spool of fiber-optic filament from her pack, she plugged one end into the radio device and said, "We need to string this to the bottom of the stairway and connect it to another radio transmitter/receiver. We're going to be 200 feet down and under a lot of steel-reinforced concrete. This fiber-optic line will give us good communication with the rest of the rescue team."

Satisfied with the placement of the radio device, Tonya said, "Okay, I'm ready to go." Using her telepathic ability, she flew the dragonfly down four flights of stairs while she and Gusty viewed video from it. "All clear so far," stated Gusty as he turned around and picked up the guns from the fallen guards. "My people can use these," he said. "Let's go down there."

Alertly and quietly, the trio descended all 20 flights of stairs without incident. At the bottom, they came to a closed door. "What's on the other side of that door?" Tonya asked.

"There's a long hallway with side rooms. The first ten rooms on each side of the hall are sleeping wards equipped with bathrooms. I believe the first two rooms are being used by the guards as living quarters. My people are locked up in the next 14 rooms. After that, the rooms are being used by Mar-ris's followers, with Mar-ris having a complete ward all to himself. Beyond the sleeping wards, there is a cafeteria and a medical center. At the west end, there are two more rooms that are being used as guard stations. Those rooms are also furnished with beds and have bathrooms."

"So we're faced with the possibility that there are guards in four different rooms and maybe in the hallway," Tonya said.

"That's true. Unfortunately, we have to open that door to find out how many there are and their exact locations, and opening the door will alert them that we are here."

"Not necessarily," argued Tonya. "If they hear the door open, their first reaction might be that one of the other guards is coming in for something. If one of our enemies is standing in the hallway, he or she will certainly look toward the doorway to see who is coming in. But since all of your people are locked up, the first reaction should be that one of the guards opened the door."

"That's a good possibility. So how do you want to take advantage of that first reaction?"

"I need to get one of my dragonflies in there, so I can look around. Here's how I think we can do that: Reebee, you will open the door while staying behind it, so you can't be seen. Do it slowly, so it looks like an unlatched door that swung open a few inches on its own. Gusty, you will stand over here with your gun ready. I will park this dragonfly right here, so I can fly it down the hallway when the door is open. Does anyone see anything wrong with this plan?"

"I think we should do it," responded Gusty. "We have to find out what's happening in there, so we can make our plans."

"That's how I see it," stated Tonya. "But first let me make sure that we have communications with the outside world."

With a bit of sticky gunk, Tonya stuck a radio device on the wall in a dark corner where its small size and dull color made it barely noticeable. Then, she plugged the fiber-optic line into it.

Tonya pressed a button on her communicator. Within seconds, a green light on her communicator blinked twice. "That's Rex," she said. Then, the green light blinked three times. "And that's our starship. We now have contact, so let's open the door."

Reebee slowly turned the doorknob and popped the door open a few inches. Tonya marched the dragonfly forward far enough to see down the hallway. Twenty yards away, a young man emerged from a side room, closely followed by two women who were holding guns on him.

"What do you make of that?" Tonya asked Gusty in a soft whisper.

"That's my son, and it looks like he's in trouble."

Tonya flew the dragonfly down the hallway, keeping it near the ceiling. She landed it on a light fixture above the trio, where it could pick up the conversation. One of the female guards said, "Later today, you are going to join your parents topside. But first, we are going to have some fun with you."

"I'm not interested in gratifying women such as you."

"That's a bad attitude. You should pour your heart and soul into pleasing us. We could speak to Mar-ris on your behalf, and maybe even keep you alive."

"You want to keep me alive, so I can be your plaything."

"Why would that be so bad? We are good-looking women, and you are a hunk. Plus, you are young and in your prime."

"And what happens after you grow tired of me?"

"Let's just say that you have an incentive to make sure that we don't grow tired of you."

"And how are you going to convince Mar-ris to let me live? He is an evil man."

"That's true. He is evil, but he is our father, and he still thinks of us as his little girls. And he will let us keep you as our personal slave. So let me tell you again: you have an incentive to please us."

As the trio steadily approached them; Tonya, Reebee, and Gusty stood very still, barely breathing, and with their guns ready. But so intent were the female guards on pursuing pleasure that they showed no concern over the door that was open only a few inches. They entered one of the rooms used by the guards and closed the door, which was only ten feet away from Gusty, Reebee, and Tonya.

Gusty breathed out a sigh of relief and said, "That was close. Had we been discovered, we would've had to shoot those women, and Rory might've been killed in the crossfire. As it is, I think he will be busy for a while."

"Do you think he'll submit to having sex with those women?" Reebee asked.

"What choice does he have?" responded Gusty. "He does want to avoid being tortured, and he wants to stay alive."

"I was raped yesterday. And now our son is being used."

"That's unfortunate," stated Tonya. "But this situation does give us an opportunity. While they're preoccupied with sex, we can take them out. Let's give them a few minutes to get started, and then, let's make our move."

"We can't just rush in with guns, ready to open fire," stated Gusty. "One of them might be holding a gun on Rory while watching the action."

Tonya reached into her pack and pulled out a pressurized canister full of sleeping gas. "If I can find a way to empty this bottle into that room, they will all go to sleep."

"That might work," commented Gusty. "It's quite likely that those women are the guards responsible for this end of the hallway."

"If that's the case, why aren't they doing their job?" questioned Reebee.

"It could be over-confidence," responded Gusty. "After all, they do have all of our people locked up, and there are supposed to be two guards on duty at the top of the stairs."

"What if we're wrong?" Reebee asked. "What I mean is there are two rooms on the other side of this door that are being used by guards."

"We could gas both rooms," suggested Gusty.

"I only have two bottles of gas," stated Tonya. "And I want to save one, in case we need it."

"Okay, let's gas my son and his guards; then, we'll go into the other room with guns ready."

Using imagery from her dragonfly, Tonya noted that the long hallway was still clear, so she flew the dragonfly to the closed door that Rory had been taken through. She carefully inspected the door. "Look at this image," she said to Gusty.

He did as requested and said, "Part of the rubber seal is missing at the bottom of the door. And that doesn't surprise me. Much of what we have is worn out and in a state of disrepair."

"We now have a choice to make," Tonya said. "I can slip a tube under that door and empty this bottle of sleeping gas into the room, or I can have two of my hornets crawl under the door and into the room. Then, I can sting the two guards into submission."

"The sleeping gas might be the safest way to go," Gusty said.

"But if I can do the job with the hornets, I can save the gas for later, just in case we need it."

"Good point. If only we could see what's happening in there, we could make the best decision. Will your dragonfly fit under the door?"

"I'm not sure. Let's find out." Tonya removed a second dragonfly from her pack and landed it on a light fixture near the ceiling. "Now we can keep an eye on the hallway while we try to get the other dragonfly into the room," she said.

Tonya marched the dragonfly along the bottom of the door, looking for the largest open space. When she found it, she had the bug crawl under the door. It was a tight fit, but the bug was able to crawl into the room, which was a sleeping ward with enough beds for 30 people.

Looking at images from the dragonfly's cameras, Tonya noted that the first bed was unoccupied. So she flew the dragonfly onto the top of a bookcase at the head of the bed. From there, she could see the entire room.

One of the women was sitting on the second bed with her back toward the door. Obviously excited, she was watching the activity on the third bed, where Rory was naked and flat on his back with the other woman naked and on top of him.

Ignoring the activity, Tonya looked around and said, "The room is empty except for Rory and the two women."

"And one of the women is busy satisfying herself," stated Gusty.

"I want to see what's going on," demanded Reebee.

Gusty handed her his headset. Reebee put it on and said, "That bitch is using our son."

"I saw that, but our son doesn't seem to be feeling any pain."

"Rape is rape," stated Reebee. "She will pay for this."

"That will have to wait until later," stated Tonya. "We have a rescue to complete, and I believe I can use my hornets in this situation. The woman watching the action has both guns, and they're on the bed next to her, so she won't reflexively shoot anyone when I sting her."

Tonya had already recharged her hornets. Now, she removed them from her pack and sent them under the door and into the room. Very quickly, Tonya stung the spectator female in the back of the neck.

206

"Ouch!" She exclaimed and swatted at the hornet. However, the other female ignored the ouch-exclamation, because she was doing some exclaiming of her own, but it was for a different reason. Just as her orgasm reached a delightful conclusion, she also felt a sting to the back of her neck. Tonya flew the hornet past the woman's eyes, so she could see what had just stung her. "Nothing like a damn bee to ruin good sex!" she exclaimed.

"Does that mean I get to live?" Rory asked.

"Okay kid, you keep performing like this, and we'll make sure you stay alive."

The other woman said to her sister, "You've had your fun, now it's my turn."

"I need some time to recover," stated Rory. "I'm not Superman."

"That's okay, kid. We'll lie down with you and help you recover."

The woman on top of Rory stretched out next to him on his right. Her sister took off her clothes and stretched out on Rory's left. Shortly, both women became very drowsy and drifted into a deep sleep, well on their way to a state of hibernation.

Pleased by her success, Tonya smiled and said, "Some women sleep very well after sex, while others fall asleep at the very thought of sex. I guess we have one of each in bed with Rory."

After laughing softly at Tonya's remark, Gusty said, "We're on a dangerous mission, and you are actually enjoying yourself."

"I am a jungle girl, and I grew up flirting with danger. Coming out on top has always given me a natural high like none other."

"Well, so far, we're definitely coming out on top," stated Gusty.

"That's true, but we're now facing the most dangerous part of our mission. If there are guards at the other end of the hallway, like you say there are, then we have a problem. If they're doing their job, then they are watching the hallway. And that means we have to take them out before we can release your people."

"The problem is bigger than that," stated Gusty. "We still have a room on this end to check out. We've taken care of the guards who are in bed with Rory, but the room directly across the hall from that room is also used by the guards."

"That brings up a dangerous possibility," commented Tonya. "What if Rory discovers that the women in bed with him are out cold? Will he take their guns and go after the remaining guards down here and try to rescue your people?"

"He probably will, but he is blessed with good judgment, and he will think before he acts."

"We need to tell him that we're here and that he should stay put until we figure out what to do. We don't want him to do anything that would ruin our strategy."

"How do you plan to talk to him? We can't go into that room. The guards have to be watching the hallway, and they would certainly see us."

"I have another high-tech trick in my bag that just might work." Tonya removed another dragonfly from her backpack and said, "This one's only purpose is communication. Its face is a tiny speaker. One side of its head is a microphone. Fine metal fibers in its wings function as antennae for broadcasting and receiving radio waves."

"Wow, what a bag of tricks you're carrying. You seem to come up with something for every problem we face."

"Advanced technology is a huge advantage when it comes to defeating an enemy. Are you ready to talk to your son?"

"Yes."

Tonya marched the dragonfly to the door, and it crawled under it and into the room. She flew it to the bed Rory was in and landed it on the forehead of the woman who had taken advantage of him.

Rory was motionless and quietly looking at the ceiling. He saw the dragonfly pass over him and land on the woman next to him. He wondered why she didn't swat at it. The answer wasn't long in coming. Much to Rory's surprise, the dragonfly started talking: "Hello Rory! This is your Dad. Don't move, just listen. The women next to you are out cold. We drugged them using the stingers on mechanical hornets. We are being rescued. You can get out of bed and pick up the guns, but don't leave the room until we tell you to. I will answer all your questions later. Okay?"

"Dad, you're safe! Is Mom with you?"

"Yes, and she's also just fine."

"Thanks for the great news. I'll do as you asked, and I have a ton of questions, but I guess they have to wait."

"Keep the dragonfly close to you as you move around the room. It is the only way I can talk to you."

"You got it."

"Now, we have to figure out how to complete the rescue," stated Tonya.

"That would be a lot easier if we knew exactly where the guards are and if we could watch them," stated Gusty.

"I still have two dragonflies with a full charge on their batteries, but if the door seals are in place, I can't get them into any of the guardrooms."

"The room across the hall from Rory is our most immediate problem," stated Gusty.

Tonya removed one of the remaining dragonflies from her pack and marched it through the door that was still open only a few inches. Once into the hallway, she headed it toward the room in question. After inspecting the door, she said, "The rubber seal is intact all the way around the door."

After a bit of thought, Tonya asked, "How do you know that the guards are using two rooms at this end and two rooms at the other end?"

"Back during the war, those rooms were used by our security forces. They have some special features. For example, the doors and walls are bulletproof to small arms fire. In each door, there is a bulletproof window that allows them to see out, but no one can see in. When you try to look in, all you see is a reflection of yourself. Those rooms once had video systems for monitoring our entire underground complex, but those systems broke down years ago."

"So how can they see down the hallway?"

"There are mirrors mounted outside the doors. They use them to watch the hallway and the entry doors. If we walk through this door, they will see us, if they're doing their job."

"We must not reveal our presence," stated Reebee. "If they find out we're here, they might start killing our people to make us surrender. It's even possible that some of our people might be hostages in one of the guardrooms."

"You could be right about that," acknowledged Gusty.

"We need to see what's going on inside the rest of the guardrooms," stated Tonya. "Otherwise, we're stuck right here."

Tonya flew one of her dragonflies to the far end of the hallway to examine the door seals. After inspecting both doors, she said, "The seals are intact. There must be some way to find out what's going on inside those guardrooms."

"All of these rooms are connected by a ventilation duct," Gusty said. "You could send one of your bugs into the room Rory is in and have it crawl through the vent grate and into the duct. From there, you could go to the guardrooms."

"That's a great idea, but when the bug enters the metal duct, it will be cut off from my control signals. And I will be cut off from the signals it will be broadcasting."

"I guess we can scratch that idea, but somehow we have to take out those guards without them knowing that they're under attack. I don't want to lose any of my people if we can possibly avoid it."

"Let's consider another angle," suggested Tonya. "Since we can't get into the rooms, maybe we can draw them out. Once they're in the hallway, I can sting them with my hornets. Also, I can fly dragonflies into their rooms once they open the doors. That way, we can see if there are any hostages or guards still in the rooms."

"As a last resort, we could just shoot them, but the gunfire will certainly announce our presence. And if we don't get them all, some of my people might die, or we could get hit by return fire."

"You're right," agreed Tonya. "Our guns have to be an emergency last resort."

"So how do you plan to draw them out?"

"It has to be something that does not make them suspect our presence, but what?"

"One possibility is to just wait until they come out on their own. Sooner or later, they'll have to make a trip to the cafeteria, or go harass some of my people, or something else."

"How far would this door have to be open before they would investigate it or come out to close it? Would they even care if this door were open all the way?"

"That is something I don't know. We could try it and find out."

"Before we do anything, I need to reload my hornets and charge their batteries. I only have two of them. Rex has the other four."

"While you do that, Reebee and I will watch the hallway and stairway."

Tonya's communicator vibrated, indicating an incoming call. It was Rex. "Mar-ris and Reebee's rapist are both out cold," he reported. "I also stung the two guards who were approaching me through the forest, and they're now in dreamland."

"We're at the east end of the hallway where Gusty's people are locked up," Tonya said. "And we've put four guards out of action."

"That makes it ten down and 24 to go," noted Rex. "Also, I believe those that are up here are effectively out of play for a while."

210

"Why?"

"They're out in the forest looking for Gusty. Fearing the wrath of Mar-ris, they might not want to come back empty-handed, so I'm guessing they're going to search for a few hours before returning."

"By then, Kayleb's Special Forces should be here."

"What we need to do until then is take out targets of opportunity while staying concealed."

"And we need to defend the people who are locked up, if it comes to that," stated Tonya.

"You're right, but let's hope we aren't forced into that situation, because it will be a bloody shootout. I have an idea how to keep the guards up here away from you, if any of them come back early, so let me do that, and I will call you back."

The conversation between Rex and Tonya was picked up by communications equipment on their landing capsule and transmitted to the Challenger and to the shuttle. This kept everyone informed on their mission progress.

Rex slipped his communicator into a pocket. He had already reloaded and recharged two of his hornets. The other two were still in the clearing by the bomb shelter entrance. Rex telepathically searched his vicinity. Finding no one nearby, he quietly headed toward the clearing.

When he reached the edge of the forest, he searched the clearing visually and the surrounding forest telepathically. Not finding any enemies, he put down his rifle and took off his pack. Reaching into it, he removed a pen and a pad of paper. In large bold print, he wrote a note. Then, he removed handcuffs from his pack.

After one more inspection of the area, Rex walked quickly up to Mar-ris. Grabbing Mar-is by the hands, he dragged him to the lightning pole. Pulling his hands past the pole on two sides, he handcuffed them together. The handcuffs were connected by a short chain.

Rex picked up the original note signed by Gusty and taped it to Mar-ris's forehead. He taped a second note to Mar-ris's chin. It said:

To the Doomed Followers of Mar-ris,
        You can leave this area, or you can stick around and join your leader. It's your choice!

                                        Your enemy,
                                        Gusty

Rex stood up, smiled, and thought, that should give them something to think about. But to make this message more effective, I should drag the rest of my victims into the clearing and place them in side-by-side arrangement. First, I need to reload and recharge my other two hornets.

While constantly checking out his vicinity to make sure he was alone, Rex readied his hornets for more action. Then, he dragged the nearest body into the clearing and placed him next to Mar-ris. This was the man who had raped Reebee. Then, he dragged the other two into the clearing and also placed them near Mar-ris. Satisfied with the arrangement of his victims, Rex went back into the forest to hide behind the boulder he had originally selected.

Rex had left two RPVs and two hornets on the edge of the clearing. Using a headset and the RPV's cameras, he observed the clearing. With his telepathic powers, he constantly searched his vicinity for enemy personnel.

Nearly an hour passed by with no activity. Then, a young woman, followed by a young man, emerged from the forest on the east side of the clearing. Both were carrying rifles. When they spotted Mar-ris and five of their comrades sprawled out next to the lightning arresting pole, they stopped dead in their tracks. They quickly looked around, and then, hastily retreated into the forest.

While watching them with video from an RPV, Rex thought, they must think that an attack has taken place and that the attackers are still around. I wonder what they're going to do now. Maybe I can find out. Using care to keep it inside the forest, Rex flew one of his RPVs to the vicinity of the young couple. Approaching them from behind, Rex landed the RPV on a tree branch where he could see and hear them. Since the RPV was designed for silent flight, they did not hear its approach and were unaware of its presence.

Video from the RPV gave Rex a good view of the young couple. They were hiding behind some bushes at the edge of the forest and were silently staring into the clearing. Eventually, the young man broke the silence. "I wonder what happened here," he said, speaking not much louder than a whisper. "It looks like Gusty did to Mar-ris what the note said, but how did he do it?"

"I don't know," responded the young woman, "but I don't like this. We could be next."

"You're right, but we need to investigate the scene. Then, we'll decide what to do."

"I don't want to just walk over there. We might be attacked if we're out in the open."

"Let's get as close as we can while staying in the forest," stated the young man, as he began stealthily making his way toward the lightning pole with the young woman quietly and alertly following.

I wonder how they're going to react when they get there, thought Rex while following them with the RPV. They are being very cautious.

In just a few minutes, the young couple reached a point that was as close to the scene as they could get without leaving the concealment of the forest. They studied the scene while hiding behind some bushes.

"They look dead," commented the young woman. "Gusty not only got Mar-ris, but he also got Reebee's rapist."

"That brutal bastard should be punished," stated the young man. "I'll never forget the day he was after you. If I hadn't been there to threaten him, you would've been his victim."

"I know, and I don't feel safe in this group. I think we should leave. With Mar-ris and his top lieutenants out cold, this might be a good time to take off."

"I agree, but where do we go?"

"Anywhere that gets us as far away from Mar-ris and his thugs as possible."

"This won't be easy for us, because to avoid suspicion, we'll have to leave almost empty-handed. We'll have to live off the land until we find a group of people to join. And I'm worried about that. Joining this group was sure a big mistake."

"That's true, but we lived alone for a long time before joining this group, and we can do it again. Maybe we can help our situation by misleading the guards down at the room we live in."

"How?" questioned the young man.

"We'll tell them that Gusty escaped and that we need supplies, because it might take us a few days to track him down."

"That might work."

"You seem reluctant," stated the young woman.

"We are the least-trusted members of the group. We're still treated as outsiders. I think Mar-ris has even instructed others to spy on us. The only reason we were allowed to go into the forest together was because Mar-ris was in such a rage that he forgot about us. What

I'm getting at is the guards in our sleeping ward might be very suspicious when we start loading up with supplies."

"No problem. I'll hold my gun on them, and you can tie them up. There are only two of them."

"They won't be expecting us to do that, so we should be able to pull it off. But that's only half of our problem. Mar-ris's daughters are at the other end."

Believing that he was observing defectors, Rex decided to recruit them. He turned on the RPV's speaker and said, "You don't need to worry about Mar-ris's daughters. They're out cold."

Already on edge, the young couple was so startled to hear a voice coming out of a tree that they froze in their tracks. To put them at ease, Rex said, "Relax! I'm not going to hurt you. I can help you, but in return, I want you to help me free Gusty's people."

Looking up into the tree and not being able to see anyone or the small, dark-colored RPV on top of a branch, the young man asked, "Who are you? Where are you?"

"I will answer all of your questions later, but if you want to escape from Mar-ris's gang and join our side, you need to act now, because more of the gang will be returning from the forest soon."

"Let's join them," stated the young woman.

"What do you want us to do?" the young man asked.

"Stay out of sight for a few minutes," stated Rex. "Two gang members are arriving from the west."

The man and woman coming in from the west boldly walked right up to Rex's victims. "What the hell happened here?" exclaimed the woman. Noticing the messages taped to Mar-ris's face, she dropped down to her knees and read them aloud.

While she was reading, Rex launched a hornet and stung her male companion in the back of his neck. He cussed at it and swatted at it, but it flew straight up and out of reach.

The woman looked up and laughed. "You make such a big deal out of a little bee sting," she said. Then, she stood up and said, "Mar-ris is really out. He's barely breathing. Where the hell is Gusty, and how did he do this?"

She looked at Reebee's rapist and said, "Look at this bastard. He's out cold too." Then, she kicked the man in the groin and said, "I owe you that."

Turning to her companion, she said, "I don't like this. Let's get out of here. We don't know what we're dealing with."

At that moment, a hornet stung her in the back of the neck. "Where are these damn bees coming from?" she exclaimed. "Is there a nest around here?"

"I don't know," replied her companion, "but I feel tired. Let's rest for a few minutes." He sat down on a bench and his head drooped. Leaving the bench, he stretched out on the ground. "I'm going to take a nap. Wake me up in 20 minutes, and we'll leave."

The woman dropped to her knees next to the man and asked, "Why are you so tired? We had a good night of sleep."

Getting no response, she sat down on the bench and said, "I guess I'll relax until you wake up." Little did she know that she was about to become very relaxed. Soon, she fell off the bench with her body totally limp and partly draped on top of her companion.

"My victims are starting to pile up," announced Rex through the RPV's speaker.

"I'm impressed," responded the young man. "Where did you get hornets that can knock people out like that? How do you control them? Are the victims going to die?"

"They'll wake up in a day or two; unless, we decide to keep them out longer. I'll answer the rest of your questions later. We have a rescue to complete. My name is Rex."

"My name is Abel. My wife's name is Jessie. What do you want us to do?"

"Here's the situation. The guards at the eastern entrance and Marris's daughters are out cold. We need to put the guards at the west end of the hallway to sleep. I have hornets in position. I need you to open the door, so they can fly in. Keep the door open and engage the guards in a way that will distract them for a few minutes."

"We can do that," responded Abel.

"Also, I need to know if there are any additional guards down there. So I need you to look into the rooms used by the guards."

"We'll check them out," responded Jessie. Speaking to her husband, she said, "If we can pull this off, maybe Gusty's people will accept us into their society. I don't want for us to have to live alone and off-the-land anymore. It would be nice to have some children and be a family that's part of a stable society."

"We will accomplish our mission," stated Abel. "And then, we'll talk to Gusty about joining his society."

Jessie and Abel visually inspected the clearing before stepping out of the forest. In case one of Mar-ris's cronies had already returned and was watching from a hiding place, they decided to act surprised by all the guards laid out before them.

"How did this happen?" exclaimed Jessie in a loud voice that sounded shocked.

"I don't know, but we'd better go below and report this," responded Abel in a loud voice that sounded filled with alarm.

With that comment, they rapidly walked to the unguarded entrance directly across the clearing. They stepped in and headed down the stairs. There were 20 flights of stairs to descend to the living quarters 200 feet below ground.

Rex's conversation with Abel and Jessie was picked up by the communications equipment on the landing capsule and transmitted to the Challenger. This gave the mission commanders real time intelligence about the ongoing activity on the ground.

Also, Tonya, Gusty, and Reebee listened to the conversation and knew that Abel and Jessie were on the way. But Rex had no way to know that they were listening, so he called Tonya and asked, "Did you hear my conversation with Jessie and Abel, and do you know that they're on the way?"

"Yes!"

"That's good, because I believe Jessie and Abel are for real. If they are successful, we should be able to free Gusty's people."

"Gusty is one happy camper," stated Tonya. "He believes Jessie and Abel will be successful, and we're ready to support them. My hornets are ready to go, and if need be, we'll use our guns."

"Hopefully, there won't be any gunfire until Kayleb's Special Forces arrive. They have lots of firepower, and they know how to use it. We need to stay out of sight and let them do the shooting."

"That's our objective, but we'll support Jessie and Abel with our guns if we need to. Speaking of them, they've just arrived."

At the other end of the hallway, the door opened, and Abel walked through, followed by Jessie. Abel approached the door to the guardroom, stood in front of the window, and knocked on the door.

One of the guards opened the door. "What are you doing here?" he asked. "You're not supposed to be back until this afternoon."

"I know, but I have some bad news to report. Gusty and Reebee have escaped, and Mar-ris is unconscious. He needs medical help."

"No way!" exclaimed the guard. "That's just not possible."

"Jessie and I will stand guard if you want to go topside and see for yourself."

"I don't trust you. I think you're lying. If I go topside, I will take your wife with me."

"My wife's not going anywhere with you."

"That's right," stated Jessie while pointing her rifle at the guard. "Put your hands above your head and turn around slowly. And tell your partner to drop her gun, or you're both dead meat."

The big burly guard cussed at Jessie and Abel; then, he said, "You won't get away with this. When we report this to Mar-ris, you two will wish that you never messed with us."

Tonya was watching the confrontation with video from her dragonfly. She had already flown one of her hornets into the guardroom. With it, she stung the female guard. Launching the other one, she stung the big burly guard that Jessie was threatening. Both guards were so enraged by the confrontation that they ignored the minor pain from the stings. But Jessie and Abel saw the hornets sting their opponents. They knew they only had to keep them under control for a minute or two.

Abel jabbed the big guard in the back with his rifle and said, "You and your girlfriend are going to get facedown on the floor."

Grudgingly, they complied. "You can't win," stated the woman. "If you kill us, Mar-ris will get you. If you don't kill us, we'll get you."

"That's not going to happen," responded Jessie.

"Why?"

"Because both of you are tired. You're starting to feel sleepy, so-o-o-o very sleepy. You're having trouble keeping your eyes open. You're falling asleep. When you wake up, you'll be in jail."

"I'm not going to fall asleep," responded the woman.

"Yes, you will," stated Jessie.

The woman on the floor was determined to stay awake. She struggled to keep her eyes open, but the hibernation drug was potent and starting to work. Slowly, her eyes drifted shut. Then, her body went limp as she began her descent into a state of hibernation. Her male companion followed her into dreamland.

Abel reached down and grabbed the set of keys attached to the burly man's belt. "Let's check out the other guardrooms," he said.

"They have to be empty," stated Jessie. "If there were any guards in them, they would've kept us from doing what we just did."

217

"I hope you're right, but they could be sleeping on the job, so we need to be careful."

"How do we be careful? If we open those doors, and they're waiting for us, we could be instantly shot."

"You're right, so let's put them in that situation."

"How?" questioned Jessie.

"Let's make it impossible for them to see what's going on in this hallway. Then, they'll have to open the doors and come out; then, we'll ambush them."

"I see what you're getting at," Jessie said. "And all we have to do to blind them is hang a curtain over the windows in the doors."

"That sounds easy, but these are metal doors, and there's nothing to hang a curtain from. And we don't have any tape."

"So let's put your muscles to work. Pull a mattress off one of these beds and lean that against the door. I will keep my rifle ready for use while you're doing that."

Abel quickly propped a mattress up against the door, completely covering the window. "That takes care of that," he said. "Now, we need to wait a few minutes to see if the door opens."

A couple minutes later, Abel said, "It looks like this room is empty. I doubt that on-duty guards would allow themselves to be blinded without reacting."

"What if they're sleeping on the job?"

In answer to Jessie's question, Abel slid the butt of his rifle past the mattress and banged on the door three times. Then, he stepped back, pointed his rifle at the door, and waited. After about a minute he said, "I think the room is empty."

"I doubt that there are any guards at the other end of this hallway either. They certainly would've challenged us by now."

"That sounds good, but just in case we're wrong, let's recruit some help. Stand here with your rifle ready. Watch this door and the other end of the hall."

Abel walked to the first room where Gusty's people were locked up and stuck a key into the lock. He opened the door and looked at the people in the room. A mood of somber depression hung over them. Looking over the group, Abel felt their anxiety. "Cheer up!" he said. "You're being rescued. Mar-ris and his daughters are unconscious, but most of his followers are still at large, so there's still much danger. I am working with the rescuers, and I need your help. I need two men who are good with guns."

218

An air of stunned disbelief pervaded the people. But one of the men stepped forward and asked, "Is this some kind of trick?"

"It's not a trick. You are being rescued."

"By whom?"

"That I don't know, but they do have some marvelous technology."

At that moment, a small RPV that came from Tonya's backpack flew into the room. From its speaker came an announcement, "This is Gusty speaking. I am outside the door at the east end of the hallway. We are being rescued. Abel and Jessie are helping us. Do whatever Abel is asking."

The sight of the hovering RPV along with Gusty's message had an electrifying effect on the people in the room. Their gloomy mood suddenly changed to a mood of excited optimism filled with hope.

Abel now had their full attention, and he said, "I need to station two armed men at the west end of this hallway, while Jessie and I check out the guardrooms at the east end."

Six men stepped forward. "I only have two guns," Abel said.

"That's okay," one of the men said. "The rest of us will be there if needed."

The men followed Abel to the unconscious guards. Two of them picked up their guns. One of them stood at the bottom of the stairway to listen for anyone coming down the stairs. The other armed man watched the door behind the mattress. The unarmed men used their eyes and ears to support the armed men and would pick up and use their guns if they were shot.

Speaking to Jessie, Abel said, "Let's go meet Gusty and check out those other guardrooms." With their rifles ready, Abel and Jessie briskly walked to the east end of the hallway.

When they arrived, Gusty spoke through the partly open door, "There are three of us here, and we're friends, so relax your trigger fingers. I am going to open the door."

When the door was open, Gusty looked at Jessie and Abel and said, "Thanks for your help. When this is over, you're welcome to join my society."

"Thank you!" responded Jessie and Abel in unison.

Gusty introduced them to Tonya. After greetings were exchanged, Gusty said, "Tonya and Rex are the covert part of the rescue team. The heavy hitters will be here shortly. We have to protect my people until then. We have four additional guns; two from Mar-ris's daughters and two from the guards at the topside entrance."

"There are several guns in the topside clearing," stated Abel. "Let's make sure these guardrooms are empty, and then, let's go get those guns."

Gusty was starting to feel good about the situation, and his elevated mood was obvious. He pointed at the door on his left and said, "Rory is in there with Mar-ris's daughters. I guess he was too much for them. They're both out cold."

Gusty knocked on the door. Rory opened it and came out.

"It looks like you survived their vicious attack quite well," commented Gusty.

"I did, but they wanted to make me their personal slave." Turning to Tonya, Rory said, "Thanks for rescuing me."

Tonya smiled and said, "You're welcome, but we're not out of this yet. I would like to secure the topside clearing if possible. Then, Jim can land the first group of soldiers right where we need them."

Pointing at the door on his right, Gusty said, "First, let's check out that guardroom. It must be empty, but let's make sure."

Gusty boldly stepped in front of the one-way window to show his face. Then, he knocked on the door with a crisp, hard knock. There was no response, so Abel unlocked the door and pushed it open a few inches. This allowed Tonya to fly a dragonfly into the room. What she saw shocked her. There were two guards in the room. A man was standing behind a woman holding a gun to her head. Behind him, a female guard was pointing a gun at six children.

The man could see Gusty through the window in the door. "I don't know how the hell you escaped," he yelled. "But as you can see, I have a gun against your sister's head. You and your pals are going to come in here and drop your guns, or your sister will die."

While staying on the outside of the bulletproof door, Gusty asked, "What assurances do I have that you won't kill all of us anyway?"

"You don't have any guarantee."

"In that case, I want you to drop your gun, because if you kill my sister, I will kill you."

"If I surrender, you might kill me anyway."

"I promise that I will grant you and your wife safe passage into the forest. You will have to leave this area and never return."

"I don't trust you," replied the guard.

Tonya stepped in front of the window, and said, "You can take me along as a hostage."

"Who are you?"

"I am Tonya. I came here with an outside military force. We've captured Mar-ris, and as you can see, Gusty is free. Your only chance at freedom is to use me as a hostage and leave."

"I don't trust any of you."

"I understand, but whether you like it or not, I am your only chance for freedom. If you kill Gusty's sister, you and your wife will both die. Is that what you want?"

"We're ready to die for our leader."

"That makes no sense. Your leader has been captured. It's time for you to think of your own future."

"You're right. We should think about our future. You want to be our hostage. Okay! You can come in! But everyone else must stay outside. You will come in slowly, with your hands out in front where I can see them."

Tonya slowly squeezed through the partly open door with her hands leading the way. Once through the door, the guard ordered her to close it. Then, he said, "You wanted to be my hostage; well now you are! So here's what's going to happen! Your leader will free Mar-ris, or you will die, along with Gusty's sister and these children. Is that what you want?"

"No! That's not what I want. But I guarantee you that if you kill any of us in this room, you and your wife will both die." Looking past the man, Tonya made eye contact with his wife and asked, "Is that what you want?"

Before the woman could respond, the man coldly said, "My wife wants what I want."

"I would like to stay alive," the woman said, timidly.

"Don't you turn on me now!" the man bellowed at his wife.

Using telepathically-induced hypnosis, Tonya planted a message in the woman's mind. She told her, killing children is a terrible thing to do. You must not do this. Your trigger finger is frozen. You cannot move it. You love children, and you wish that you had children of your own. You cannot kill these children. Your trigger finger is paralyzed. It will not move.

Using the control units glued to her temples that converted her telepathic signals to electronic signals, Tonya telepathically triggered the release valves on the two bottles of sleeping gas in her backpack. The bottles had silencers on them, so the escaping gas could not be heard.

Speaking to the man, Tonya said, "I think your wife loves you and wants to stay alive, so you can raise a family and have a long happy life."

"That might be, but we are going to live our lives in accordance with the doctrine preached by Mar-ris. He has a vision for a strong society."

"Mar-ris has been captured. He will go to jail. His vision is dead. You need to forget about him. I can lead you and your wife away from here, and you can build your own life."

"No! Your leader will free Mar-ris. You will contact him and relay my demands."

"My communicator is in my backpack. I will have to reach in and get it."

"I don't trust you. You might have a gun in there. Turn around and back toward me. I will get your communicator for you."

Tonya did as requested. While she was backing toward the man, she began telepathically searching his mind. She wanted to control his trigger finger to prevent him from shooting anyone while passing out. When Tonya had backed all the way to the man, he asked, "Where in your pack is your communicator?"

"Lift the top flap and look in. It's a small dark object."

"I don't see any small dark object in here," he said. "All I see are these propane bottles and a small camp stove. I can use these. They are now mine."

While looking in the pack, the man inhaled the colorless, odorless, sleeping gas coming out of the bottles. Like a drunk passing out, he slowly crumpled to the floor.

Seeing her husband fall like a limp sack of potatoes, the woman immediately suspected a heart attack and went to his aid. While pointing her gun at Tonya, she dropped to her knees to assist her husband. Telepathically in control of the woman's trigger finger, Tonya slowly turned around, and reached out to take the woman's handgun while she passed out. She stuck the gun into her belt and reached down to retrieve the man's pistol.

Looking around the room, Tonya noted that everyone was groggy and starting to pass out. She telepathically closed the valves on the gas bottles.

Walking to the door, Tonya looked through the one way glass. She noted that her cohorts looked worried, but they were very alert with their guns ready. Slowly, Tonya opened the bulletproof door a crack while staying behind it. Speaking through the crack, she said, "I am coming out. Lower your guns, please."

They did, and Tonya quickly stepped out, closing the door behind her. "Everyone is sound asleep in there," she said. "You can't go in there, or you'll pass out too."

Reaching into a side pocket in her pack, she pulled out a small bottle of pills. "These are an antidote to the gas," she said. "Take one of these and wait 15 minutes before you go in. Or you can wait until the ventilation system replaces the air in there."

"It'll take an hour for a complete air exchange," Gusty said. "I don't want to walk away from here without tying up those guards."

"Everyone in that room is dropping into a state of hibernation," Tonya said. "They'll be out for at least 24 hours."

"That works," responded Gusty. "Now let's do a head count for Mar-ris's gang. Eight are out cold in the topside clearing. Eight bomb shelter guards are out of action. Abel and Jessie have joined us. That's 18, so there are only 16 left. Two of them are at the freight entrance, which is on the north side. So they probably don't know what has happened in the south side clearing or down here."

"That means they're not on edge and looking for trouble," stated Tonya. "So we should be able to easily take them out."

"Or we can convince them to leave," stated Gusty.

"How?"

"I believe the freight elevator is at the bottom of its shaft. So let's take Mar-ris's daughters and the other four guards down here, lay them side-by-side on the elevator floor, and send them up to the two topside guards."

"That should freak them out," commented Abel.

"Let's do it," stated Tonya.

"Mar-ris's daughters are naked," Rory said. "Should we dress them?"

"Leave them naked!" exclaimed Reebee.

Gusty unlocked the rooms his people were imprisoned in, but directed them to stay put, except for some of the men. To them, he said, "I need you to go to the medical lab and get six gurneys. We need to haul the unconscious guards to the freight elevator."

Soon, the hibernating guards were loaded up, and everyone was going west. At the end of the hallway, they turned right to head down the industrial wing of the bomb shelter. Halfway down this hallway, Gusty stopped the group. Pointing at a door, he said, "Our electrical power plant is in there. If I'm not mistaken, two of my technicians are locked up here to keep the plant running."

With a gun in one hand and a key in the other, Gusty unlocked the door and cautiously entered. He quickly spotted the technicians, who were busy monitoring equipment and were surprised to see him. "More than half of Mar-ris's people are out of action," Gusty told them. "We'll get the rest of them before this day is over."

The men were overjoyed with the good news. "How can we help?" they asked.

"Just keep the generators running."

"You got it," they responded.

Electricity was essential for survival in the bomb shelter, and Gusty's technicians had always kept the electrical power plant healthy. Before the war, a vast inventory of parts was placed in the shelter's warehouse, which even included spare generators and turbines. The turbines were fueled with natural gas from a pair of wells that tapped into a vast underground field.

Continuing on their way, Gusty's party came to the elevator. They laid the unconscious guards on the floor. Tonya placed a small RPV on top of a stool in the back of the elevator. "Now, we'll be able to see their reaction when they open the door," she said.

Gusty pressed a button, and the old elevator started creaking as it headed upward. "The guards up there have to be able to hear this thing," he said. "They must be wondering why it's coming up and who might be on it."

A few minutes later, the slow-moving elevator reached the top, and its doors opened. Wearing headsets, Gusty and Tonya watched the guards. They reacted with stunned disbelief and muttered to each other, trying to figure out what happened. The female guard looked very worried. Her male companion appeared to be in a cool analytical frame of mind, but the possibilities he suggested were ominous and made the female even more worried.

Gusty let their minds and emotions work for a couple minutes; then, he turned on the RPV's speaker and said, "Hello! This is Gusty! We're having a party in the cafeteria to celebrate my freedom and the release of my people. If you're in a party mood, you might come down and join us. If you're not up for a party, you might want to head into the forest and escape from here. It's your choice. When our party is over, we're going to come looking for you. We'll be the hunters, and you'll be the prey. That should be great sport, don't you think?"

"I don't want to be hunted down like a wild animal," responded the woman.

"You should've thought about that before you helped Mar-ris imprison me and my people. Yesterday, I was beaten, and my wife was raped."

"That was brutal," admitted the woman. "We were appalled by that brutality, but we were powerless to stop it. If we had tried to intervene, we would've been severely disciplined. Mar-ris is a barbarian."

"Mar-ris has been captured. He is chained to the same pole I was chained to."

Speaking to her male companion, the woman said, "That means we are free of this evil man."

"That is good news," he responded. "It's definitely something to celebrate." Facing the RPV, the man said, "It seems that we have something in common. You are free, and we've gained our freedom with the capture of Mar-ris. Was that party invitation serious, or were you just jacking us around?"

"I was playing with your minds, but when this is over, there will be a party."

"So, are we invited, or do you want us to run, so you can hunt us down?"

Before Gusty could respond, the man's female companion said, "We are not going to run; we are going to surrender."

The man looked at the woman and said, "I am not going to run without you." Facing the RPV, he said, "I agree with my wife. We surrender."

"That's a wise decision," responded Gusty. "Lay your guns on the elevator floor and step aboard. I will bring you down."

"Before we do that, I would like to know what happened to the people on the elevator. Are they dead?"

"They are alive, but they've been drugged. We'll revive them in a day or two."

"Are you going to drug us?" the woman asked.

"Can you behave without being drugged?"

"We won't give you any trouble. We are happy to be free of Mar-ris and his insanity. We now have a chance to begin a new life. Maybe we could join your society. I am pregnant, and I need a place to settle down."

The announcement surprised the man who looked at his wife with a pleased expression and said, "Honey! You never told me!"

"I had to wait until I was sure. And I really do not want to raise a child in a society where Mar-ris is the self-appointed supreme leader."

"I don't either," responded the man. Facing the RPV, he asked, "Can we come to the party? We have one more thing to celebrate."

"Come on down, and we'll talk about it."

Shortly, the elevator arrived. The man and the woman stepped off without their weapons, which were on the floor. "My name is Kellic," stated the man. "My wife's name is Kaylee."

Gusty shook hands with them and said, "The two of you present me with a problem. Do I trust you or not?"

"My wife needs a place to settle down. Give us an opportunity to earn your trust, and we won't let you down."

Intervening on their behalf, Abel said, "Kellic and Kaylee are the only people in Mar-ris's gang to give genuine friendship to Jessie and me. They are good people who do not accept Mar-ris's extreme views. I think we can trust them."

From the moment the elevator arrived, Tonya telepathically looked into the minds of the new arrivals, trying to discover deceit. Finding only honesty, she said to Gusty, "I agree with Abel. I believe we can trust Kellic and Kaylee."

"My instinct is telling me the same thing," stated Gusty. "We still have 14 gang members to contend with. Maybe they can help us."

"My wife is pregnant," stated Kellic. "I'd like her to stay out of harm's way, but I will do whatever needs to be done."

"Very well! Kaylee and Jessie will stay down here. Reebee, you will stay with them. Abel and Kellic will come topside with the rest of us. We need to secure the perimeter."

Several minutes later, Gusty and Tonya arrived topside. Kellic, Abel, and 12 men from Gusty's society were with them. They were inside the south entrance, which was the doorway used by Mar-ris earlier in the day.

Tonya stopped the group and said, "Before we go outside and reveal our presence, we need an update from Rex." With her communicator, she called Rex and reported, "Twenty have been dealt with; 14 are still at large."

"Four of them are in the clearing," Rex said. "Put on a headset and take a look."

Tonya and Gusty put on headsets and tuned in to sound and video from Rex's RPV, which was focused on the four guards. They had read the notes taped to Mar-ris's face and were arguing about what to do. "We need to get out of here," stated one of the men.

"No! We need to stay and fight," argued another man.

"Who are you going to fight? Look around you. There's nobody here."

"Gusty is here somewhere. Maybe we should go below and bring some of his people up here and kill one every 15 minutes until he shows himself. Then, we'll force him to revive our people."

"I don't like that plan. He might be down there with his people. They might be free and waiting to ambush us."

"Do you have a better idea?"

"Yeah! We get the hell out of here while we can!"

"We're not going to run! We're going to stay and win this fight!"

Speaking into her communicator, Tonya said to Rex, "I've heard enough. Let's sting them and put them to sleep."

"I can't," responded Rex. "I haven't had the opportunity to reload the two hornets that I've stationed by the clearing."

"Mine are ready, but I only have two."

"Sting the guy who wants to stay and fight, and let's see how the other three react."

"I have a hornet on the way," stated Tonya.

While piloting the hornet, Tonya continued to observe and listen to the men. "We don't know what we're fighting," argued one of the men. "Take a look at Mar-ris and the rest of these people. They're not dead, but their pulses are very slow, and they're barely breathing. There's not a mark on any of them. How did Gusty do this, and which one of us is next?"

The belligerent man yelled, "You are a coward who wants to run! We are going below to drag some women and children up here. We'll force Gusty to show himself; then, we'll get to the bottom of this." So enraged was the man that he didn't even feel the hornet sting to the back of his neck, and no one paid any attention to the little bee as it flew away.

"You call me a coward, and then, in the next breath, you talk of dragging women and children into the fight. Maybe you are the coward. I am not following you."

The belligerent man lost all patience. He pointed his rifle at his verbal opponent and said, "You're right. You're not going to follow me below. You're going to lead the way. Then, if there's an ambush, it will be you who gets shot."

"You really are a coward, aren't you?"

"Say what you want, but you're going to lead the way, and I am going to get Gusty."

"Very well! But when this is over, you and I have a score to settle."

"Let's go!" yelled the belligerent man. Then, it happened. He started to feel weak on his feet. He struggled to remain standing, but the hibernation drug was too powerful to resist. "I will rest for a minute," he said, while slumping down to a sitting position on a block of wood. "Then, we're going below to get some hostages."

His determination was all for naught. A few moments after sitting down, he fell off the block of wood and passed into dreamland.

The other three men looked at him, then at each other. They were obviously freaked out. "What the hell is happening here?" one of them asked.

The man who wanted to leave said, "I don't know, but it's obvious that we're dealing with forces we know nothing about."

"You most definitely are!" exclaimed Rex, using his RPV's speaker. "Drop your guns, kick them away from you, lie facedown on the ground, and I will let you live!"

The men stared into the tree where the voice came from and saw nothing, but they heard a new command, "Drop your guns now, before I change my mind!"

The men took one more look at their fallen comrades. Then, they dropped their guns, kicked them away, and sprawled out facedown on the ground.

Gusty and Tonya rapidly crossed the clearing with their followers. The unarmed members of the group armed themselves with the guns of the hibernating thugs and the three facedown newcomers. In a matter of minutes, they searched the forest around the clearing.

Tonya's communicator beeped. It was Jim. "I'm on the way," he said. "I have eight heavily armed soldiers onboard. Do you have the clearing under control?"

"We sure do."

"Are you okay?"

"Yes!"

"That's great. I'll be there in less than ten minutes. We landed the shuttle in a sheltered bay 25 miles south of you, so it's only a short hop away."

"There are only ten bad guys left to track down."

"Torleb and his troops will take care of them. You and Rex did your part of the mission very well. You are to be commended."

"Thank you."

A few minutes later, Jim arrived, flying low over the treetops. He landed the helicopter a short distance east of the lightning arresting pole. Torleb and seven soldiers hopped out. Gusty met them and paired them with his people, who had intimate familiarity with the local terrain. These two-person teams took up positions in the forest to await the return of the remaining thugs.

Jim took off immediately to ferry in additional troops. Twenty-five minutes later, he returned with eight more soldiers.

Tonya greeted him and said, "During your absence, Torleb's men captured two more of Mar-ris's henchmen. There are only eight still at large."

"They will be captured or killed when they return," stated Torleb. "It will be their choice. They can fight us and die, or they can surrender and live."

"Do you want me to bring in more of your troops?" Jim asked.

"Let's leave eight on the shuttle to perform security duty and bring the other 16 here. If some of the thugs still at large don't come back, I will send out patrols to track them down. The more people I have looking for them; the more likely it is that we'll be successful."

"What about the 20 that are back at the pickup point? Do we need to fly the shuttle back there and bring them here?"

"I don't think that will be necessary. Besides, I would like to leave them there to guard my equipment."

"Okay. Two more trips and I'll have 16 more soldiers here."

"Good!"

As the day wore on, the remaining fugitives returned from the forest one and two at a time. When confronted by professional soldiers ready to kill them, they all made the wise choice and surrendered.

After capturing the last two, Torleb met with Gusty, Rex and Tonya. "We have them all in custody," Torleb reported. "Now, we have to decide what to do with them."

"That's a tough decision," responded Gusty. "If we put them in prison, I'll be stuck with having to feed them and provide for all of their needs. We're planning to move to the surface and build homes. That's going to keep us busy enough, without having a bunch of prisoners to care for."

"Some kind of exile might be better," suggested Rex. "An uninhabited island out in the middle of the ocean would be perfect."

"How do I get them there?"

"Jerry can drop them off anywhere. If you want to exile your prisoners, I will talk to him about that."

"Exile is worth considering, but I'd like to discuss this with General Kayleb. He might have a better idea."

"When it comes to meting out justice, my father is very fair-minded," stated Torleb. "He'll know what to do."

"Good! I'll discuss this with him later, but right now, it's party time. My people have just regained their freedom, and we have some celebrating to do."

"It's a beautiful day for an outdoor party," commented Tonya.

"You're right about that," responded Gusty. "You, Rex, Torleb, and his troops are all invited. I'm going below to tell everyone that they are free. They'll be up here shortly."

To his people already in the clearing, Gusty said, "Get the barbecue pits going. Steak, sausage, and seafood will be here shortly, and I am starving. My best cooks will prepare side dishes in the cafeteria, and they'll be brought up."

Gusty turned and headed for the south entrance to the bomb shelter. When he arrived below and delivered the good news, his people reacted boisterously, releasing pent-up emotions. In short order, people and food began arriving in the clearing. Tonya and Rex were treated as heroine and hero. They, along with Torleb and his troops, were special guests of honor.

When the party was well underway, Tonya's communicator beeped. It was Trang and Geniya. "How are you feeling?" Geniya asked.

"Mother! It's great to hear from you. Right now, I'm flying high. Our mission is over, and we achieved all objectives."

"I know. Your Dad and I are sitting here with Connie in the shuttle's portable medical lab, and we have nothing to do."

"That almost sounds like a complaint."

"It's actually a backdoor compliment. We are proud of you and Rex for accomplishing your mission with no fatalities or serious injuries for Connie and me to treat."

"I'm very happy about that too. Last time, I almost lost Jim, and I sure don't want to go through that again."

"Speaking about Jim, he's on the way. He heard there's a party going on, some sort of victory celebration. He wants to go to that with you."

"I'll give him a warm welcome."

A few minutes later, Jim landed the helicopter on the nearby ocean beach, where it was guarded by Torleb's troops on a rotating basis. Jim joined the party, and Tonya never left his side. Both were happy that the dangerous mission was essentially over. They were hopelessly in love and had a wedding to plan, but that would wait until they were back on Alcent.

The afternoon gave way to nightfall, and the party continued. However, Tonya and Rex had no sleep the previous night and were running purely on adrenaline. A half-hour after sunset, their exhaustion caught up with them, and Jim flew them back to the shuttle, where they collapsed into a long sound sleep, superbly happy with the outcome of their mission.

Chapter Ten

TIME: Day 67, One Hour After Sunrise

Like a jungle creature, Tonya awoke suddenly. Instantly fully alert, she recalled the events of the previous day and smiled that the mission had gone so well. Gusty and his people were freed without losing anyone, and Mar-ris and his gang were captured without firing a shot. Now, they had to be dealt with.

I need to be there, Tonya decided. I want to see what Kayleb decides to do with that gang. I know what I would do with Mar-ris and his top lieutenants. Their crimes illustrate their evil minds. They masterminded the enslavement of Gusty and his people. Then, there was the brutal way they raped Reebee, and tormented and beat Gusty. Those three men are so evil that they do not deserve to live. I would like to drop them unarmed into the midst of a pack of hungry lupusaurs and let the law of the jungle prevail.

Deciding she wanted to enjoy some early-morning fresh air, Tonya left the cargo shuttle's small passenger section and went to the helicopter operations deck. There, she found Trang, Rex, Jerry, Jim, and Kayleb. Jim stepped forward and greeted Tonya with a big hug that she eagerly returned.

"How do you feel this morning?" Jim asked.

"I'm happy that our mission went so well, but I feel grubby. A hot shower would be great."

"Unfortunately, our shuttle isn't equipped with a shower stall."

"I know, so I guess I'll have to settle for a quick dip in the ocean."

"That could be dangerous. We know nothing about this ocean. This could be a shark-infested area."

"I'm not sensing the presence of any dangerous creatures."

Using his communicator, Jim logged onto the shuttle's main computer and called up sonar data. After reviewing it, he said, "There aren't any large sea creatures in this area." Then, Jim checked water temperature and said, "The water is 71 degrees."

"That's good enough for me," responded Tonya. Wearing only shorts and a tank top, she slid down onto the shuttle's starboard wing, walked to the leading edge, and dove in. She swam vigorously for a few minutes; then, she approached the wing's trailing edge. Jim was there waiting for her. He reached down, grasped her right hand, and pulled her out.

"That was refreshing!" exclaimed Tonya. "Now, I need some breakfast. I'm starving."

"I'll join you. Then, I'm flying Rex and Kayleb to Gusty's base."

"I'm coming with."

"I wouldn't dream of leaving you here. Gusty and his people will be very disappointed if you don't show up there today."

Forty-five minutes later, Jim flew the helicopter over Gusty's base. He circled low to let everyone on the ground know that he had arrived, so he could land without accidentally killing or injuring anyone.

"Everything looks peaceful down there," noted Tonya. "Mar-ris and his top two lieutenants are still out cold, and they're chained to the lightning arresting pole."

"Torleb and three of his troops are standing there guarding them," stated Kayleb. "And Gusty is talking with Torleb."

"Guess I'll set us down on the beach," Jim said.

Immediately after landing, Jim met with Gusty and Torleb. Then, he called Jerry and reported, "Everything is still under control here and all is peaceful."

"Good!" responded Jerry. "For the sake of convenience, I am going to fly the shuttle closer to the base. If the water is deep enough, I'll taxi into the bay and drop anchor a hundred yards offshore from where you landed the chopper."

"That will be convenient," agreed Jim. "This is just a suggestion, but when you arrive, you should be prepared for a warm welcome. Gusty and Reebee are eager to meet you."

"I am looking forward to that. See you shortly."

Wondering how Gusty and Kayleb would resolve the big problem they now had, Jim turned his attention to them and heard Gusty ask Kayleb, "What are we going to do with Mar-ris and his gang?"

"To start with, we can't look at the gang as a unit; we have to look at each member as an individual." While pointing at Mar-ris and his two most brutal thugs, Kayleb said, "Those three are especially bad, but there are others who might want a better life than the evil ways of Mar-ris."

"You're right about that," acknowledged Gusty. "In fact, there are two that I plan to welcome into my society. Their names are Abel and Jessie. I'm also thinking about bringing in Kellic and Kaylee, but they haven't yet proven themselves as fully as Abel and Jessie have."

"I have something for you to consider," stated Tonya. "Two days ago, when Reebee was being raped, I was on the Challenger, and we passed over your base. I was looking for information by telepathically probing the minds of the people in the clearing. I didn't have time to get into everyone's mind, but I did get into Kellic's mind, and he was appalled by what was happening to you and Reebee. He realized that he could not stop it without falling victim to Mar-ris. But he was thinking about finding a way to rescue you and Reebee and free your people. I believe Kellic and Kaylee would be a good addition to your society."

Seeing Tonya as a heroine and respecting her judgment, Gusty listened attentively and considered Tonya's remarks; then, he said, "I am going to trust your opinion and welcome them."

"I don't think you'll be disappointed."

"That takes care of the four easy decisions," stated Kayleb. "Now, we have to decide what to do with the other 30." Turning to Gusty, Kayleb asked, "What do you want to do with Mar-ris?"

"He is a very dangerous man," responded Gusty. "His telepathic powers are the best I've ever seen. He uses that ability to control and indoctrinate people. His political and religious philosophy is one of intolerance. Anyone who does not accept his teachings is considered to be an enemy who must be converted or killed. I do not even want him here as a prisoner in solitary confinement. I believe he would find a way to use his powers to get someone to release him. I will execute him rather than keep him here."

"I have a maximum security prison ward on my base where he could be kept," stated Kayleb. "But I don't know if there's any point in keeping him alive. His radical philosophy has no place in the nation I'm trying to rebuild. I want my people to have freedom, and I'm not willing to grant freedom to a man who would seek to destroy our freedom, which means Mar-ris would have to be locked up for life. But that presents me with a big problem; in that, I don't want to be responsible for taking care of his needs for the rest of his life. My people have better things to do."

"We could take him and his top lieutenants back to Alcent and feed them to a pack of lupusaurs," suggested Tonya.

"That's the kind of justice I could live with," stated Gusty with a smile.

"I'm not sure Jerry would want to pollute Alcent with this vermin," commented Kayleb. "Realistically, I think we only have two choices with Mar-ris: execution or exile."

"If we decide in favor of execution, we'll have to carry out the sentence without waking him up," stated Gusty. "His telepathic powers are so strong that he could probably stop the execution by taking control of the minds of the executioners."

"That makes this a tough decision," stated Kayleb. "I have a problem with executing a man without first explaining the charges to him and giving him a chance to defend himself."

"It would be very dangerous to do that in this case," argued Gusty. "He has an awesome telepathic ability to control those around him. We must not revive him."

"My telepathic powers are also very good," stated Rex. "I'm not recommending that we revive Mar-ris, but if the need arises, I believe I can control him."

"I have great respect for your ability," Gusty said. "But I do not even want to give Mar-ris the opportunity to inflict more harm."

"With that in mind, let's discuss exile," suggested Kayleb. "For that to work, we have to find an uninhabited island in a remote part of one of our oceans. We need to make certain that Mar-ris has no opportunity to come back here, and we don't want him to be a problem for anyone else either."

"The only sure way to guarantee that he'll never be a problem is to execute him," argued Gusty.

"I know, but this planet does have numerous isolated islands. If Jerry would be willing to drop Mar-ris and his worst followers on one of them, I don't think we would ever again have to worry about them."

"Jerry will be here shortly," Jim said. "We can ask him."

"We need to make sure these three stay conked out," stated Tonya, as she removed a hypodermic needle from her pack and proceeded to inject a few drops of the hibernation drug into Mar-ris and his top two lieutenants.

At that moment, Rory arrived on the scene and asked, "Have you decided what to do with Mar-ris's daughters?"

"Not yet," responded Gusty. "Do you have any suggestions?"

"If we could get Mar-ris and his most evil followers out of the picture, I believe the girls could be motivated to become useful members of our society."

"After what they did to you, I'm surprised you could feel that way," commented Gusty. "How do you propose to motivate them to reform their lives?"

"I'd like you to sentence them to two years of community service and appoint me to be their parole officer. I'll develop a daily work schedule for them that they'll have to accomplish to my satisfaction. At the end of two years, they'll be accepted into our society, or they'll be exiled. It'll be up to them to prove themselves."

Gusty smiled at his son's proposal and said, "This wouldn't have anything to do with their demand that you satisfy them in order for you to stay alive, would it?"

Rory grinned and said, "To me, it seems like a fair turnabout of events."

"Do you really think you can reform those girls?" Gusty asked. "Take a look at how evil their father is."

"That's my point. When you consider how evil Mar-ris is, the girls didn't turn out all that bad. Their only real crime is that they found me sexually arousing and decided to use me. In all honesty, I didn't find the experience all that painful, and I haven't suffered any damage. If we get Mar-ris out of here, I believe those girls could learn proper behavior and become productive members of our society."

"I get the feeling that you actually like them, despite what they did to you."

"Yeah, I guess maybe I do."

"In spite of their nasty behavior, you like them anyway."

"Maybe I'm deluding myself, but when I look past the behavior that they learned from their father, I see the potential for them to become likeable, socially responsible women. Also, they had a tough childhood in that they lost their mother at an early age. A good mother would've given them a role model to counter Mar-ris, but they didn't have that."

"You seem to know a lot about these women," noted Gusty.

"When the gang arrived here, I spent some time visiting with them, but that came to an end when Mar-ris decided to enslave us."

"So now, you think you can reform them."

"I can't reform them. They have to reform themselves. I just think we should give them the opportunity."

"Have you considered the possibility that they might hate us after we get rid of their father?"

"Yes and here's how I'd like to handle that. Assuming that we exile Mar-ris to an isolated island, we just explain that to the girls. Then, we give them a choice. They can go into exile with him, or they can stay here and do two years of community service with me as their parole officer."

"How will the girls react if we execute Mar-ris?"

"They will probably hate us, and we'll have a difficult time turning them into productive members of our society. The way I see it, our nation has lost so many people because of the war that we really can't afford to lose any more. If at all possible, those that are left need to become responsible members of our society. I believe the best way to give the girls a chance is to avoid executing their father. If Jerry is willing, we need to exile Mar-ris and those followers that are so thoroughly indoctrinated that we can't do anything with them. Those that we think we can work with, we offer a choice: stay here and do community service for two years or go into exile with Mar-ris."

"Community service isn't much of a punishment," argued Gusty.

"It can be, if we subject them to a heavy workload doing distasteful jobs. Anyway, if we lock them up, we have to take care of them. With community service, we can make them earn their keep."

Facing Gusty, Kayleb said, "Your son has wisdom beyond his young age. What he's saying makes sense. We need to talk to Jerry and find out if he's willing to transport some of our prisoners into exile."

"He's on the way," stated Jim. "He'll be here shortly."

The words were barely out of Jim's mouth when the cargo shuttle made a low pass over the clearing, heading north. Jerry banked the shuttle into a left turn and headed out to sea. A few miles offshore, he banked into a 180-degree left turn and headed back toward the clearing. A mile offshore, the shuttle's hydrofoils entered the water. The hydro-drogues deployed, rapidly slowing the shuttle to less than 40 mph, causing it to settle onto the water and ride on its hull. A hundred yards offshore, Jerry brought the shuttle to a stop and dropped anchor.

Jerry opened a door in the side of the shuttle's fuselage and dropped a folded-up boat into the water, which immediately self-inflated. He and Trang stepped into the boat, followed by Connie and Geniya. The men rowed the short distance to the beach, where everyone stepped ashore.

Gusty and his people were thrilled by the shuttle's arrival. Everyone went to the beach to welcome the interstellar visitors, and Tonya introduced them to Gusty and Reebee.

Speaking to Jerry, Gusty said, "Thank you for bringing people here to rescue us."

"You and Reebee, and the rest of your people, were being subjected to a huge injustice, and we could not let that stand."

"We are very fortunate that you discovered our plight, because Reebee and I were slated for a slow, agonizing death caused by dehydration and starvation. Thank you for saving us from that fate. I don't know how we can ever repay you."

"Payment isn't necessary. Some things just need to be done, because they are the right thing to do."

"That's a principle I've believed in for as long as I can remember," stated Gusty with a warm smile. "It was taught to me by my parents."

"That means we have something in common," responded Jerry. "I think it's amazing that men growing up on planets light-years apart could have the same principle taught to them by their parents."

While smiling at her parents, Tonya said, "I can remember a time or two when my parents told me that some things need to be done just simply because they are the right thing to do."

Speaking to Trang and Geniya, Gusty said, "I don't know everything you taught her, but you do have a terrific daughter. She and Rex were instrumental in the rescue of my people. They accomplished their mission like a pair of seasoned professionals."

"We are proud of her," responded Trang, "and we are greatly relieved that the mission is over. One of our biggest concerns was that she was heading into an unknown situation. There just wasn't any way to make detailed plans in advance. She and Rex were left with having to deal with whatever surprises they encountered here."

"Well, they did such a great job that no one was killed or injured, and that leaves us with 30 healthy prisoners that we have to do something with. Some of them are so dangerous that they have to be executed or banished from our society."

"Banishment can only work if we put them some place where they can never come back," stated Trang.

"An isolated, uninhabited island would work, but unfortunately, I don't have any way to get them there."

"I do," stated Jerry. "It's anchored right out there."

Gusty's eyes lit up upon hearing Jerry's remark. "That almost sounds like an offer to transport my prisoners," he said to Jerry.

"It was," responded Jerry.

"I appreciate that. I don't know yet how many there'll be, but I at least have to get rid of Mar-ris and his top two lieutenants."

"There are lots of islands in this planet's oceans," Jerry said. "Do you have any particular one in mind?"

"There's an island 3000 miles south of here that might work. Before the war, that island had a tracking station on it to track military satellites launched into polar orbit from here. I had three launch pads a mile south of here. They were hit by a small nuclear bomb, as was the island with the tracking equipment. A submarine picked up all survivors on the tracking island, and it was abandoned. The nearest land to that island is 1500 miles to the east."

"Fifteen hundred miles should be enough distance to make that island serve as a prison," stated Kayleb. "It would be very hazardous to attempt such a voyage with the kind of raft or boat that Mar-ris will be able to build."

"Even so, the voyage would be possible," argued Jerry. "Back on Alcent, the traitors who abandoned Zeb built a raft and sailed 1600 miles south. Their objective was a stranded space shuttle. They wanted the technology for the war about to start here."

"Zeb told me about that," stated Kayleb. "Unfortunately, no matter what island we put Mar-ris on, there's always the possibility for escape. To the best of my knowledge, the old tracking station is the most isolated island on this planet that is also uninhabited. We either put these people there, or we have to execute them."

"I agree that escape is possible," acknowledged Gusty, "but how likely is it? Consider the difficulties Mar-ris and his henchmen will face. They're going to be unconscious when we deliver them to the island. When they wake up, they won't even know where they are. If they are able to build a raft or boat, what direction would they sail?

If they set sail without a definite destination, they could run out of food and water and perish at sea. They could encounter a fierce storm and be killed."

"If they know how to do it, they could probably guess their location using the stars," stated Kayleb. "However, I doubt that any of them ever had that kind of specialized training."

"I do have a recon satellite in polar orbit," commented Jerry. "We can keep an eye on that island. Any kind of boat or raft big enough to sail on the ocean would take a while to build and would be big enough to easily spot."

"That satellite is a great piece of equipment," acknowledged Kayleb. "I've studied some of the images from it. We'll definitely get plenty of warning if Mar-ris attempts an escape."

"How big is that island?" Rory asked. "Is it big enough so that the people we send there will be able to eke out a living? Or will exile be nothing more than a death sentence caused by dehydration and starvation?"

"I've been to that island," responded Gusty. "It's roughly three miles long by two miles wide. It has several high hills and small lakes. It rains frequently, and fresh water won't be a problem. The climate is tropical. There are trees and shrubs that produce fruit and nuts. Also, there is ocean fishing. The people we put there won't have any problem staying alive. We'll give them the basic tools and utensils they need, plus seeds for a variety of foods they can grow. The rest will be up to them."

"That island doesn't sound like much of a prison," commented Tonya. "It sounds more like Paradise Island."

"That could work to our advantage," responded Gusty.

"How?" Tonya asked.

"If life is easy for them, they could grow fat and lazy and have no incentive to attempt an escape. A harsh life would make them want to leave. All we want to do is get them permanently out of our hair. It's either execution or put them somewhere where they'll stay."

"Too bad there aren't any lupusaurs living on that island," commented Tonya. "They could deliver justice in a hurry."

"I can't argue with that," responded Gusty with a grin.

"All things considered, I believe that island will serve our needs," stated Kayleb while making eye contact with Gusty. "Unless someone has a serious objection for us to consider, I am going to sentence Mar-ris and his top lieutenants to permanent exile on that island."

Kayleb patiently waited, but no objection was raised, so he turned to Jerry and asked, "Is the transportation offer still open?"

"You bet it is," responded Jerry.

"Thank you," Kayleb said to Jerry.

"There is at least one more person that we should consider banishing to that island," stated Gusty. "And that is the man who held a gun to my sister's head."

"That man has a wife," noted Tonya. "In my brief encounter with them, I sensed that she might be in an abusive relationship. If we send her to that island with her husband, she will be at the mercy of four brutal men."

"You bring up a valid point," responded Gusty. "When she wakes up, you should talk to her in private. If she is in an abusive relationship and wants out, she might be a good candidate for community service, or maybe she might just want to join our society. I'll trust your judgment in regard to her."

Speaking to Tonya, Geniya said, "I can wake her up when you're ready to talk to her."

"Let's go do that now. And while we're there, let's make sure that her husband stays conked out for another day or two."

"Except for these three devils, all of our prisoners are locked up down below," stated Gusty. "Torleb's troops are guarding them. They will give you access to the woman you want to talk to."

"We'll report back," responded Tonya, as she turned and left, followed by Geniya and Connie.

After the women left, Kayleb said, "Tonya's concern for one woman needs to be extended to all of our female prisoners. I don't think we should send any of them into exile with Mar-ris."

"Why not?" questioned Gusty. "Some of them are just as bad as the men."

"I am concerned about them having children. I don't want innocent children marooned on an island where Mar-ris is in charge."

"What you're saying is that you don't want to punish innocent children for his crimes."

"That's right."

"So what do you propose to do with the worst of the female prisoners?" questioned Gusty.

"If you don't want to be responsible for them, I can take them off your hands. We'll lock them up at night and put them to work during the day. I like Rory's idea. After two years, they will be offered membership in my society, or they will be kicked out. It will depend on their behavior."

"Thank you for the offer. My community just isn't big enough to be burdened with lots of prisoners to keep under control."

"I appreciate that, but I also have another objective in mind. I believe that our prisoners will be less likely to plan a revolt if we split the gang. Dividing them reduces their ability to cause trouble, and there will be fewer of them to deal with if they do act up."

"I agree, and now I think it's time to go below and interrogate our prisoners," stated Gusty. "We can awaken them one at a time and question them individually."

"While you're doing that, I can telepathically probe their minds," offered Rex. "I will be able to determine if they're telling the truth or being deceitful."

"That info will make it easier for me to decide what to do with each one," commented Kayleb.

"What kinds of questions do you plan to ask?" questioned Jerry.

"First, I will explain that Mar-ris and his lieutenants are being permanently exiled to a small isolated island. Then, I will ask if they want to be exiled with Mar-ris or stay here and do a combination of jail time and community service, with the possibility of eventually joining my community or Gusty's. With Rex acting as our truth detector, it should be easy to determine where their minds are at and then decide on the appropriate sentence."

"I will look at their mental reactions to your questions and compare those reactions to what they say," stated Rex. "If I'm not sure about the mindset of any particular individual, I will throw in a few key questions of my own."

"I appreciate your help," responded Kayleb. "When it comes to punishing people, I want to do everything I can to avoid making mistakes, and your telepathic ability will be a big help."

"My telepathic skills are very good, but so are Tonya's. We should also have her present. That way, we can compare notes."

"I like that idea," stated Gusty. "Let's go below and get started."

Gusty led the small group down to the guardrooms, where the prisoners were being held. One at a time, they were restored to consciousness and interrogated. Then, judgment was rendered. It was early evening when the last prisoner was dealt with.

Three of the men were sentenced into exile with Mar-ris and his lieutenants. The man who had held a gun to the head of Gusty's sister was in this group. When this man's wife was offered an opportunity to go into exile with her husband, she exclaimed, "Absolutely not! I'd rather stay here and spend the rest of my life in prison. I haven't been his wife anyway. I've been his slave. Going to prison would give me freedom from him."

"If you stay here, you might not have to go to prison," stated Tonya. "You could ask Gusty for permission to join his society."

"Would he let me do that after what we did?"

"It looks to me like you were an unwilling participant in what happened."

"That's right. Mar-ris is a brutal man, and my husband is just as bad. I had to cooperate."

"Under the circumstances, I believe Gusty's people would accept you. I will make that recommendation."

"Thank you!"

When the situation was explained to Mar-ris's daughters, they said, "We'd rather go into exile with our father than stick around here and do shit-work disguised as community service." However, they changed their minds when Rory told them that he would be their parole officer if they stayed. "Are you going to be hard on us?" one of them asked.

"You'll be on a tough schedule, and you'll have to satisfy me every day."

Both women beamed naughty grins at Rory and said, "We'll do our best to make you happy."

None of the women in the gang were sentenced into exile with Mar-ris. They faced a combination of jail time and community service with the opportunity to earn their way back into society. The men not sent into exile were given the same opportunity.

Speaking to Jerry, Kayleb said, "I'd like to get the exiled ones out of here as soon as possible, so we can be rid of them."

"We still have a couple hours of daylight left, so we could do that yet today, but I think we should wait until tomorrow."

"I guess we should make sure that island is uninhabited before we take Mar-ris there."

"As you know, Mike and Moose are on the Challenger. I talked to them this morning and asked them to do a detailed recon of the tracking island."

Jerry grabbed his communicator, punched in Moose's number, and received an immediate response, "Hello! Moose here!"

"This is Jerry. What can you tell me about the island?"

"It's deserted."

"Is that a guarantee?"

"Let's just say that we've found absolutely no evidence to indicate that anyone has lived there in a long time."

"In the morning, we're going to move some evil men to that island. We need to be sure that there's no one living there for them to victimize."

"The only way to be positive would be to search the island on foot. Even then, you might not find people who want to stay hidden."

"We could fly back and forth over the island with our chopper, while Rex and Tonya telepathically search for people."

"That's a great idea. We've done everything we can from up here, and we've found nothing."

"Thank you. Talk to you later."

TIME: Day 68, Two Hours After Sunrise

Jerry landed the shuttle on the east side of the tracking island, taxied to 200 yards offshore, and dropped anchor. Speaking to Jim, he said, "Let's get the chopper in the air and search the island."

"You got it," replied Jim.

A short time later, the helicopter was airborne with Jim in the pilot's seat. He flew the chopper low and slow over the island's sandy beaches. Cameras beamed a steady stream of video to the shuttle's main computer. It analyzed the video, looking for patterns of depressions in the sand that might indicate recent footprints. Rex and Tonya telepathically searched the forest for human life. In the event unexpected trouble was encountered, four of Torleb's soldiers sat in open doors with automatic weapons ready for use.

After circling the island twice, without finding anything, Jim flew a crisscross pattern over the island. Once again, the search came up empty. "I'm convinced there's no one here," stated Rex.

"I disagree," countered Tonya. "I sense that there is someone here."

"I'm not detecting anyone," responded Rex.

"I'm not either, but I have a strong feeling that there is someone here."

"Any idea where?" Jim asked.

"Let's fly back to the small lake at the south end of the island."

A minute later, the chopper arrived over the lake. "Would you mind landing on the water?" Tonya asked.

Jim inflated the helicopter's pontoons and made a gentle landing on the lake. "Now what?" he asked.

"Take us over there," responded Tonya, while pointing at a large boulder on the eastern shore.

After deploying the helicopter's marine propeller, Jim piloted it to the water's edge. With her mind telepathically focused, Tonya stepped into the shallow water and waded ashore. She walked around the large boulder, and behind it, she found a cave entrance near the bottom of a rock cliff. Tonya noticed a small stream of clear sparkling water trickling out of the cave and thought, how convenient is that, a cave dwelling with fresh running water.

Speaking to Rex, who was at her side, Tonya said, "There is someone in there."

"I sense that too," responded Rex.

Two of Torleb's soldiers were standing behind Rex and Tonya. "Let's check it out," one of them said.

Carrying flashlights and handguns, the soldiers cautiously entered the cave. Two minutes later, they emerged, escorting a sleepy-eyed, middle-aged man. "We found him sound asleep," one of the soldiers said.

Facing the man, Rex asked, "Who are you?"

"My name is Awegust. I've been alone since I was fifteen. Back then, people called me Awegy."

"How did you end up alone on this island?"

"There used to be many people here to operate a satellite tracking station. Then, a nuclear bomb hit us and destroyed all of that. That was a long time ago. I've been alone for so many years that I've come to believe that I might be the only person alive on this planet."

"A devastating nuclear, chemical, and biological war was fought. Ninety-nine percent of our people were killed. How did you survive?"

"I was exploring this cave when the bomb exploded. I felt the shockwaves in the rock, but I didn't know it was a bomb. I thought it was an earthquake. Also, violent thunderstorms with strong winds and heavy rainfall were passing through this area at that time. I guess I mistook the bomb blast for a loud crack of thunder. I stayed camped out in this cave for a couple days until the nasty weather passed. When I came out, I discovered the horrible truth. The buildings and

246

tracking equipment were gone. I looked for survivors in our bomb shelter, but it was deserted. I searched the island, but I found no one. The realization that I was alone filled me with despair, but I overcame that. And as you can see, I've survived."

"That nasty weather is probably the reason you survived," commented Rex. "The wind carried away what would've been radioactive fallout, and the heavy rain probably washed what fallout there was into the ocean."

"I guess I was very lucky. But there must've been other survivors. We had a pretty good bomb shelter."

"Gusty told me that all survivors were picked up by a submarine. I guess they missed you because you were in the cave."

A puzzled expression appeared on Awegy's face. He appeared to be searching his memory. After a few moments, he said, "I need to talk to Gusty. He might be my uncle. My father had a brother named Rorgust."

"Gusty is a nickname; his full name is Rorgust."

Awegy's spirits were suddenly lifted. He became cheerful and said, "I've been alone for as long as I can remember, and now, I find out that a close family member might still be alive."

"If you'll come with us, you can meet him and find out if he's your uncle."

"That would be great, but who are you? Where are you from? What are you doing here?"

"That's a lot of questions all at once."

"I haven't had anyone to talk to in a very long time, and now, you show up. I have enough questions to keep us busy all day."

"For now, let's start with what you just asked. My name is Rex, and I am from the eastern region of our once great nation."

"My name is Tonya, and I am from the dinosaur planet that orbits Alpha Centauri A."

"You are here from another planet!" exclaimed Awegy in disbelief.

"That's right."

"Wow! That's incredible! I've been a hermit for many years, and now, I have an interstellar visitor. What brings you to this planet?"

"I came here with a group of people to rescue Rex and his family. But one thing led to another, and a couple days ago, Rex and I arrived at Gusty's base. We were the scouts for a military mission to rescue Gusty and his people. Now we have six evil men to get rid of. Instead of executing them, we decided to put them someplace where they could

247

not escape and could not victimize anyone. We selected this island for that purpose, but we first had to make sure that no one was living here. We need you to come with us and maybe join Gusty's community."

"Are you proposing to rescue me from the intense loneliness I've had to deal with here?"

"Yes."

"When do we leave?"

"As soon as you're ready."

"I'm ready now."

"Good, follow me."

Everyone stepped aboard, and a few minutes later, the helicopter landed on the shuttle. Awegy was already wildly excited by the day's events, but seeing the shuttle really grabbed his imagination. "I'm going to ride that to Gusty's base!" he exclaimed.

"That's right," affirmed Rex. "But first, we have some prisoners to dispose of, and I think the best place to put them is in the cave where we found you."

"Everything that I used to stay alive over the years is in that cave."

"I'll recommend that cave to Kayleb and Gusty, and the decision will be theirs to make."

"Gusty is here?" asked Awegy.

"He's standing right there," responded Rex while pointing at Gusty. Rex stepped out of the helicopter, closely followed by Awegy.

Noticing the heavily bearded man following Rex, Gusty stepped forward and asked, "Where did you find him?"

"He was sleeping in a cave on the shore of the southern lake. His name is Awegust."

A surprised expression lit up Gusty's face, and he said, "My oldest brother and his wife were killed in the nuclear attack. They had a son named Awegust."

Gusty shook hands with Awegust and asked, "What was your father's name?"

"Joegust."

"That was my brother's name. What was your mother's name?"

"Margust."

"That was his wife's name, and that means you are my nephew. Welcome to my community."

"Thank you, but where is your community?"

"Three thousand miles north of here."

"That's a long way off."

"I know, but this shuttle will get us there in 45 minutes."

An expression of amazement covered Awegy's face, and he exclaimed, "Wow! That's fast!"

"Much of our flight will be above the atmosphere, and you'll see our planet from a new perspective."

"A short time ago, I was a hermit, sound asleep in my cave. Now, I'm part of a family, part of a community, and I'm going into space. This is a thrilling cultural shock to say the least."

"If it's too much for you to deal with, we can leave you here."

"No way! I'm coming along."

"I don't mean to interrupt your family reunion," Rex said. "But I think we should dump our prisoners and get out of here."

"I second that motion," stated Kayleb.

An hour later, all six convicts were in Awegy's cave, along with their survival gear. "When they wake up later today, they won't have a clue where they are," commented Gusty.

"And they won't have a clue how they got here," stated Kayleb. "That double mystery will give them something to think about for a long time."

"Once Mar-ris figures out that he's on an island, I believe he'll start building a boat or a raft," commented Gusty.

"They're going to have a hard time building anything with the survival gear we gave them," stated Kayleb. "I believe they're stuck here for the rest of their lives. But if they try anything, we'll know about it. We do have a very capable recon satellite to watch them with."

Speaking to Jerry, Kayleb said, "We are done here."

"Good," responded Jerry. "Let's get everyone in their seats. Jim and I'll close up, and we'll return to Gusty's base."

Chapter Eleven

TIME: Day 72, Early Evening

Captain's Log

"With Mar-ris and his gang out of action, and with the era of poison rain over, Gusty and his people have started building homes above ground. They are eager to get out of their bomb shelter and have a normal life on the surface.

"Two married couples from Mar-ris's gang have been accepted into Gusty's community. Mar-ris's daughters and four other gang members are doing community service on Gusty's base. The rest of the gang members are on Kayleb's base, where they have been placed on construction crews that are building homes on the surface. Torleb's troops are supervising the former gang members, who have been told that some of the new homes will be theirs, if they work hard and live responsible lives for two years. If not, they will continue to live in jail when not working.

"Kayleb is now in contact with 15 communities located in various parts of his devastated nation. These communities were discovered through the combined efforts of Rex and Tonya using their telepathic abilities and by Mike and Moose using our recon instruments. We've dropped communications equipment to those communities. Good communication between Kayleb and these widely-scattered communities enables them to work together to begin rebuilding their nation.

"As for us, we have one more thing to do before we depart for Alcent. There are ancient man-made caves here that we need to explore. One of the rooms in this ancient cave dwelling has script carved into its stone walls. This script appears to be in the same language as the writing on cave walls discovered by Tonya on Alcent. Where did these ancient people come from? Are the people currently living on Zebron their descendants? What happened to the people who lived in the cave dwellings on Alcent? Does a similar fate await us? Tomorrow morning, we'll begin looking for answers."

After making his log entries, Jerry went to the apartment that he and Connie lived in. He looked at her and noted her appearance. "You look every bit as beautiful as the day we married," he said.

"Thank you! I'm pleased that you like my new outfit."

"I do, but it's the person in the outfit that I'm in love with."

Connie flashed her husband a radiant smile and gave him a big hug. "Are you ready for dinner?" she asked.

"I am hungry," responded Jerry.

"I am too, but this dinner is much more than just satisfying hunger. Since we're leaving tomorrow, you could call this a farewell dinner, or you could even call it a state dinner."

"You're sure putting a lot into having dinner with friends."

"I know, but heads of state will be present. You are Captain of this starship and the leader of our community. Trang is a starship Captain and the leader of his community. General Kayleb is the leader of a shattered nation that he is trying to rebuild."

"Something tells me that you planned this dinner with all of that in mind."

"I thought it would be a good way to spend our last evening here. You and Trang and General Kayleb are nation builders in our interstellar community. It seems to me that the dinner table is a good setting in which to discuss the future."

Jerry beamed Connie a smile of approval and said, "I can go along with that. Thanks for putting it together."

"You're welcome. Also, we have some guests of honor. Tonya and Jim will be there, along with Rex and Shannon. Your old buddy Moose agreed to be the master chef."

"That means the food will be great. Let's go."

A few minutes later, Connie and Jerry arrived in the Challenger's cafeteria. The other guests were already seated at the table and were having a lively conversation, which wound down as everyone stood up to welcome Jerry and Connie.

Everyone sat down except Kayleb. He remained standing and said, "Soon, all of you will be gone, and I am going to miss you. Thank you for coming here. You've been a fantastic help to us, a real Godsend. I hate to see you leave."

"We won't be that far away," responded Jerry. "We can always come back, if the need arises."

"I greatly appreciate your willingness to do that, especially in view of the fact that coming here takes time away from building your community on Alcent."

"Establishing a viable community on Alcent is our primary mission, but we're also on a mission of scientific discovery."

"But you didn't come here for science; you came here to rescue Rex and his family. Then, you went out of your way to rescue Gusty's community and help me. And I appreciate all of that."

"We had to do those things," responded Jerry.

"Why?"

"Because they were the right thing to do."

"I like that approach to life," stated Kayleb.

"It has worked well for me, and it sometimes leads to unexpected benefits. When we came here to rescue Rex and his family, we never dreamed that we'd find cave dwellings similar to those on Alcent. I'd really like to know where those Ancient Ones came from and what happened to those that lived on Alcent. Maybe we'll discover some clues tomorrow morning that will help us solve that mystery."

"I've always been curious about the local caves," admitted Kayleb. "But exploring them has not been a very high priority in recent years. I am looking forward to tomorrow morning."

In a booming voice from the kitchen, Moose called out, "Are you people going to be talking all night, or are you ready for some delicious food?"

"I've been starving for hours," Jerry yelled back in a lighthearted jovial tone. "What's been taking you so long?"

"Culinary artwork cannot be accomplished in mere moments," responded Moose while delivering the first of his entrees. "It takes the master chef time to create these kinds of delicious delicacies."

Everyone looked up at Moose, who was obviously enjoying the attention. "Everything smells good," commented Connie. "My mouth is watering."

"You are in for an exquisitely pleasurable dining experience," stated Moose. "So eat slowly and savor it."

Jerry and his dinner guests grinned at Moose. Speaking to his guests, Jerry said, "You've just been exposed to the flamboyant side of Moose's personality."

"If the food is as good as it smells, he deserves to boast a bit," commented Giselle.

A half-hour later, Moose brought several dessert dishes to the table and received an enthusiastic round of compliments. "I could easily become addicted to this alien food," commented Kayleb to Moose. "I might have to talk you into staying here to be our cook for special occasions, not to mention your engineering skills."

Speaking to Jerry, Moose said, "My many skills and talents have now gained recognition on three planets. If the demand for my services continues to grow, I might have to hit you up for a pay raise."

Turning to Kayleb, Jerry said, "If his ego continues to expand, I might find him increasingly difficult to work with. What kind of job were you planning to offer him?"

"Wait a minute guys!" protested Moose. "I'm not available for a job change. I'm happy right where I am."

"I guess I reached the wrong conclusion," responded Jerry. "I thought you needed a pay raise to keep you from jumping ship."

"You shouldn't be taking me seriously when I'm just kidding."

"Now that we've settled that, we can get on with the rest of the evening," Jerry said while grinning.

"This is my last night on your ship," Kayleb said to Jerry. "If you don't mind showing me around, I would like one last tour."

"You got it."

"I'd like to tag along," stated Giselle.

"In that case, I'm coming too," Connie insisted.

The tour ended on the observation deck, where Kayleb and Giselle spent several hours soaking up the ever-changing views of their planet. Finally, they retired for the night.

TIME: Day 73, Sunrise

Moose and Jerry landed the shuttle in the ocean bay 110 miles south of the cave complex. After preparing the helicopter for flight, Jerry and Jim boarded it and sat in the pilot's seat and copilot's seat. Their passengers were Kayleb, Giselle, Connie, Trang, Geniya, Tonya, and Rex. Before taking off, Jerry said to Moose, "Take good care of this shuttle while we're gone."

"You can count on that," responded Moose.

The 40-minute flight to the cave complex was uneventful. Jerry landed near three jeeps that were parked a short distance from the caves. Two of Torleb's soldiers were sitting in one of the jeeps while two others were alertly standing guard.

One of the jeeps had a trailer hitched to it. The load on the trailer grabbed Connie's attention. She stared at it and said, "It looks like that trailer is loaded with chicken crates filled with chickens."

"You did say you needed a few roosters and some laying hens," commented Kayleb. "I remember the story you told about crawling around out in the brush to rob a few eggs from a goose nest."

"That little escapade seemed like it would be easy, but it got pretty exciting when a big, mean-tempered bear showed up."

"That bear was the most entertaining part of your story. I still laugh when I think about the ingenuous way you mislead that bear, and the way Zeb brought him to a screeching halt was especially funny."

Connie laughed and said, "You're right. It was funny, but I really don't need that kind of entertainment every time I need a few eggs for the dinner table. You can't imagine how much I appreciate the hens. Thank you."

"You're welcome. There are also 200 pounds of apples and five young apple trees in the backseat of that jeep."

"Thank you," stated Jerry. "You grow the best apples I've ever eaten."

"All of this is a small token of appreciation for what you've done for us," responded Kayleb. "Do you want us to truck everything to your shuttle, or can your chopper haul it?"

"How many chickens are there?"

"One hundred twenty and they average seven pounds each."

"We can take everything on our return flight."

"Good, let's go cave exploring."

When Kayleb and Jerry arrived at the caves, they found Rex talking to Zack who had just emerged from one of the caves. "I am more convinced than ever that there is a sealed room in there," stated Zack.

"Why?" Rex asked.

Zack laid out his drawing of the cave complex and said, "Look at this hallway. It has a half-circle shape. This entrance is right here behind us. If you enter here and follow the hallway, you will exit the cave complex over there." Zack pointed at the opening, which was 50 yards away. "Twenty minutes ago, I entered that entrance and walked the hallway to this entrance. I walked into and out of all 15 rooms shown on this drawing. Every room has a room directly across the hallway from it, except this one right here in the middle. This whole project has perfect symmetry except for the missing room. The room directly across from where the missing room should be has words carved into its rock walls."

"Let's go to that room first," stated Jerry. "I'd like to see how the writing compares with what Tonya found back on Alcent."

"Torleb, Zeb, and Zonya are probably still in that room," commented Zack. "At least that's where I left them. They were trying to make sense out of the writing."

"That's a tough problem," stated Jerry. "Our people have been trying to translate the writing Tonya found, but we haven't had any luck. We need some clues to start with, and there aren't any."

Zack led the way into the cave complex with everyone else following. Shortly after entering the complex, Connie said, "I sure get a strange feeling in this hallway."

"Strange in what way?" Jerry asked.

"I am walking where people lived a very long time ago. It's possible that a woman my age lived here. What kind of person was she? What was her daily life like? What kinds of problems did she face? What if I were transported back in time and had to live that woman's life, would I be able to do it?"

"It seems like you're making this cave exploration very personal."

"That's my way of trying to gain some insight into the people who lived here. Imagine the kinds of problems they must've faced in everyday life."

"Zeb could shed some light on that. He lived in a cave for 30 years, and just a few days ago, we rescued a man who also lived in a cave for 30 years."

"They managed quite well, given their circumstances. But I'm having a hard time seeing myself as a cave dweller."

"I definitely like our situation better," stated Jerry. "But these early humans did have secure homes that were built to last for an eternity."

"I can understand the need for this kind of home on Alcent because of the dinosaurs, but why on this planet?"

"There are other dangers besides dinosaurs. For example, the most powerful hurricanes and tornadoes ever recorded back on Earth could do nothing to these caves."

"This is the room," announced Zack as he stopped and pointed at the entrance.

Once inside the room, Jerry looked at all the walls in turn. Then, he scanned the walls with his digital camera and loaded the file into his portable computer, which compared the writing to that found by

Tonya in a cave on Alcent. The computer reported: the language in both caves is identical.

"That confirms what we suspected," commented Jerry. "I just wish that we could understand what it says."

"Why would they've written all of this and not leave some clues, so we could figure it out?" questioned Connie.

"What makes you think they wrote it for us?" Jerry asked.

"They carved it in granite. It was meant to last through the ages; if not for us, then for some other race in their distant future."

"That makes sense, so where is the info we need to figure out what this says?"

"There has to be a sealed room containing that info," stated Zack.

"You might be right," responded Jerry. "I think it's time to find out if there is a secret room."

Jerry and Jim went into the rooms adjacent to the suspected sealed chamber and attached microphones to selected points on the rock walls. They also attached microphones to selected points on the hallway wall of the suspected sealed room. When all instruments were in place, they hit selected points on all three walls with concussion-type impact sound, as well as, high-intensity sound over a broad range frequencies. Data from the various microphones went into Jerry's portable computer as it was generated.

Jerry and Zack were watching a video screen connected to the computer. Everyone else was looking over their shoulders. When a 3-D image of the secret room appeared on the screen, Zack exclaimed, "I was right! I just knew it was there!"

"I'd sure like to know what's in that room," stated Jerry. "We need to find a way in."

"I've been over every inch of those walls," declared Zack. "There isn't any way in that I could find."

"There has to be a way in," stated Connie. "They would not have left a sealed room full of information without there being a way in to access the info."

"How do you know there's information in there?" Jerry asked.

"I don't. That's just an assumption on my part. But that room could be a sealed time capsule filled with information about the Ancient Ones. They would not have left the info without a way in."

"That makes sense," agreed Zack. "But the walls are solid granite."

"They appear to be solid granite," stated Jerry, "but they might not be. Take a look at this image of the front wall. There's a section in the middle that conducts sound differently from the granite that surrounds it."

"If it's not granite, what is it?" Zack asked.

"I don't know," replied Jerry. "But it could be some type of resin filled with an aggregate composed of crushed granite. The Ancient Ones might've used such a material to seal the chamber, and to all outward appearances, it would look like granite." Jerry pointed at the wall and said, "As you can see, it does look like seamless granite."

"You're right," Zack said. "It's impossible to see where the granite stops and the filler starts, but why would they put so much effort into making it look like there isn't a room here?"

"One obvious answer is the room contains something of great value that they didn't want plundered by treasure hunters."

"But we figured out that there's a room here," argued Zack. "We could be treasure hunters."

"But we have technology," countered Jerry. "Maybe they sealed the room the way they did, so that only people with technology could discover it. Maybe their thinking was that people with the technology to discover the room and get inside it would have the knowledge to appreciate whatever it is that's in the room."

"What technology are we going to use to get into the room?" Zack asked.

"We can drill a hole through one of the walls and put some camera carrying bugs in the room. It won't take long to find out what's in there."

"Drilling a hole through a wall would be kind of like breaking in," stated Tonya.

"Not really," argued Jerry. "We're not going to damage or steal anything."

"I know that our intentions are good," acknowledged Tonya. "But we don't know what we're getting into. What if the room is filled with an inert gas to preserve the contents of the room? Drilling a hole will let oxygen in."

"Good point," admitted Jerry. "How do you propose to investigate the room?"

"The people who sealed the chamber obviously had some pretty good technology. If it was their intention to preserve the contents of the room for a future generation, then it seems logical that they would've provided a way for the future generation to get in without breaking in."

"That makes sense, but how do we get in? These walls are solid."

"They are granite except for the filler material, and we don't know what it is, but the answer to getting in has to lie in that material," stated Tonya while pointing at it.

"It's rock solid," argued Jerry, "and it looks like plain old granite. How are you going to gain entry through that?"

"I don't know, but I think it contains the secret to getting in."

"Tonya might be right," stated Trang. "Back before I left Proteus on our interstellar mission, we had a large group of scientists working hard to develop exotic materials with phenomenal characteristics. Some of those materials even had artificial intelligence built in."

"How did your scientists do that?" Jerry asked.

"The concept behind making an intelligent material is actually quite simple. All you have to do is develop a material with the desired characteristics and load it up with tens of thousands of nano-processors. The material has to be designed to support the nano-processors in that it has to enable communication between them, as well as, conduct energy to them. Lots of redundancy can be built into such a system, so that loss of individual processors does not degrade the performance of the system."

Wearing a skeptical expression, Jerry stared at what looked like a plain old granite wall. Then, he turned to Trang and said, "It sounds like you're suggesting that we might be standing in front of an intelligent wall."

"I know it sounds like a pipe dream, but the Ancient Ones evidently had some awesome technology."

"But a rock-hard wall possessing intelligence is hard to believe. To start with, we think the Ancient Ones came here 120,000 years ago. What kind of processors could you build into a material that could last that long? And where does the power come from? Artificial intelligence has to get energy from somewhere."

"I could give you a list of possibilities," replied Trang. "But I can't give you definite answers, because I don't know."

"That's fair," commented Jerry. "We think the Ancient Ones came here from a star 60 light-years away. If that's true, then their technology could've been far more advanced than ours."

"For the sake of discussion, let's assume that they did seal the room with an exotic material that has artificial intelligence built in. The question we need to answer is: what did they program that intelligence to do?"

"The obvious answer is that it would be programmed to keep undesirable intruders out of the room."

"Assuming that you're correct, what will it do to us if it doesn't like us?" questioned Trang.

"We have no way to answer that question, but it sure looks like the Ancient Ones wanted to keep out undesirables, so there should be some kind of defensive mechanism in place."

"Drilling a hole through the wall would be one way to find out if there are defensive systems in place," suggested Tonya while grinning at Jerry.

"Are you volunteering to drill the hole?" questioned Jerry with an even bigger grin.

"I'll pass on that, but I do have an idea that might work."

"What do you have in mind?"

"I'd like to telepathically probe that wall. The Ancient Ones may've had telepathic ability, and if this wall does have artificial intelligence, it may be programmed to respond to telepathic communication."

"It's worth a try, but if there are defensive systems in place, I hope you don't provoke a response."

"If the Ancient Ones were as smart as we think they were, they should've been able to program this thing to tell the difference between us and plundering treasure hunters."

"You're assuming that everything is still in good working order after 120,000 years," stated Jim. "You could be placing yourself in grave danger by attempting to communicate with a malfunctioning system."

"There is some risk involved," admitted Tonya. "But the Ancient Ones are a mystery that is starting to intrigue me to no end. This is something I must do."

Stepping forward, Tonya put her hands on the wall, and focused her mental powers into telepathically transmitting images into the wall. Almost immediately, she said, "I'm getting a response. This wall is getting warm."

Before Tonya could say anything more, tentacles of blue light emanated from the wall and touched her in a searching manner. In just a few seconds, Tonya was enclosed in a shimmering shroud of blue light. The shroud contained numerous small tentacles of intense blue light that seemed to be dancing all over her body.

"What's happening to you?" Jim yelled, sounding very alarmed. But Tonya did not respond.

Jim reached out to rescue Tonya from the shroud, but additional tentacles of blue light erupted from the wall and pushed him back. "I don't like this!" he exclaimed. "What's going on here?"

The answer wasn't long in coming. The wall became very warm, so much so, that Tonya's friends could feel the heat. A small hole appeared in the wall that quickly expanded into a door-sized opening that Tonya stepped through. In just a few seconds, the opening contracted down to a small hole, which closed entirely, followed by the complete disappearance of the blue light.

Jim stepped forward and pounded on the wall with clenched fists, but received no response. "How do I get her back?" he yelled out.

"Calm down," advised Jerry while putting a hand on Jim's right shoulder. "I know you're worried, but I don't think there's anything we can do except wait."

"I can't just wait! She could be in serious trouble!"

"That's possible, but I think we have to wait."

"That's not going to be easy."

"I know, but I don't think we have any choice. Trang was right. That wall is an exotic material with intelligence built into it. Apparently, it was designed to perform the role of gatekeeper."

"Why did it drag Tonya in?"

"I don't think it dragged her in. It looked like she walked in of her own free will."

"But she may've been controlled by whatever that is!" exclaimed Jim while pointing at the wall. "Who knows what's happening to her now that she's in there?"

"Unfortunately, we don't know; we can only speculate."

At that moment, one of Torleb's soldiers came running in filled with excitement. "Something weird is happening on top of this rock!" he exclaimed. "You need to come out and see this!"

Everyone followed the man as he ran back out. Pointing at the cliff top, he exclaimed, "Look at that!" Looking up, everyone saw an intense beam of blue light that stretched upward as far as the eye could see.

Jerry grabbed his communicator and called Mike. "Where are you at?" he asked.

"We're approaching your position from the west."

"Things are happening down here. There's a brilliant beam of blue light emanating from the cliff top. I need an analysis of it."

"I'll get back to you shortly," responded Mike.

"Thanks."

Jerry turned to Trang, who was staring at the beam. "Do you have an opinion?" Jerry asked.

"It looks like the equipment in that sealed room is transmitting a report."

"But who is it going to? We believe the Ancient Ones were here 120,000 years ago. The civilization that sent them here might not even exist anymore."

"That might be," acknowledged Trang, "but they evidently had the technology to build equipment that would stay functional for 120,000 years. That seems unimaginable, but we are watching it operate. My youngest daughter has been captured, and it looks like a report is being transmitted."

Jerry's communicator beeped with a call from Mike, who reported, "That blue beam is some kind of energy field that I'm not able to define. The blue color is not the color of the beam. The bluish hue is generated by the beam's interaction with the atmosphere. The color disappears above the atmosphere, but the beam is still there. I don't know what it is, but it seems to have punched a hole through space."

"What do you mean by 'a hole through space'?"

"We're not able to observe background stars through the beam. All radiation from them is completely blotted out. Whatever this energy field is, it has the effect of changing space as we know it."

"What do you think its purpose is?"

"I don't know. What were you doing before the energy beam appeared?"

"We discovered a sealed room in the cave complex, and one of its walls captured Tonya."

"Are you serious? Tonya was captured by a wall."

Jerry quickly gave Mike the details of Tonya's capture along with Trang's thoughts on the nature of the exotic material making up the wall. "That makes the purpose of the beam quite obvious," commented Mike. "It has to be for communication. Equipment left behind by the Ancient Ones is reporting back to them."

"We think they came from a star 60 light-years from here.

Communication traveling at the speed of light will take 60 years to arrive there."

"They might not be communicating at light-speed. This energy beam appears to have punched a hole through space. It's possible that the Ancient Ones have instantaneous communication inside that tunnel, and the tunnel is pointed toward the star we think they came from. So what is there about Tonya that would cause the equipment in the cave to phone home?"

"Her telepathic ability triggered the wall to open up," responded Jerry.

"But what message did she transmit into the wall to provoke that response?"

"That we don't know."

"Apparently, she put forward the kind of information that the Ancient Ones programmed their equipment to react to."

"That brings up an ominous possibility," commented Jerry. "If this equipment is capable of instantaneous communication across 60 light-years of space, then it might be looking for a response from the people it is sending the information to. What if that civilization no longer exists? Then, there will be no response. What if the equipment hangs onto Tonya indefinitely while waiting for a response that never comes?"

"We aren't going to wait indefinitely," stated Jim, who had been listening in on his communicator. "If Tonya isn't released soon, we're going to figure out how to rescue her."

"That will require great caution," stated Jerry. "We're dealing with technology far beyond what we have. I saw how easily you were repelled when you tried to prevent Tonya from entering that room."

"We have to do something," Jim insisted.

Looking into Jim's eyes, Trang said, "I know how you feel. That's my daughter in there. I want her back as much as you do. Waiting is difficult, but I think that's what we have to do."

"How long do you think we should wait?"

"I don't know, but it's possible the Ancient Ones only want information. If that's the case, it seems like they would release Tonya when they get the info they want."

"So, you think Tonya is being interviewed and nothing bad is happening to her?"

"That's a strong possibility. Let's try to think about it from their point of view. Let's assume that they did plant human colonies on several life-friendly planets. If you were them, wouldn't you want to know what happened to those colonies?"

"I would, but for me, it's a moot question, because 120,000 years have gone by, and I'd be dead."

"But they might not be dead," argued Trang. "We have an age control drug. I am 145 years old and look like I'm only 45. The Ancient Ones might have better age control drugs than ours. They might have very long life spans. We just don't know."

"You don't seriously believe that the people who sent a starship here 120,000 years ago might still be alive."

"Why not? If they have drugs that stimulate their bodies to regenerate tissue as it breaks down, then they could live a very long time. Death might come only from disease or fatal injury."

"It sounds farfetched to me," stated Jim. "If they had those life-extension drugs, why didn't they give them to the colonists they planted here? Why aren't these colonists and the ones they planted on Alcent still around?"

"The colonists may've been given those drugs to increase their probability of being successful. But for whatever reason, they may've lost the ability to make those drugs."

"I guess you could be right," admitted Jim. "But to me, it's just unimaginable that the Ancient Ones could still be alive after 120,000 years. But if they are, what kind of info are they trying to get from Tonya?"

"I don't know, but if they invested a lot of time, money, and energy into starting human colonies on life-friendly planets, their number one interest should be to find out if their investment bore fruit. So they're probably going to qualify Tonya as an information source. They'll want to know who she is, where she came from, and what she's done. Then, they'll pump her brain for whatever information they think she's qualified to give."

"I hope they don't damage her mind when they're pumping information out of it."

"Why would they want to injure a descendant of one of the colonies they planted?" questioned Trang.

"A lot can happen in 120,000 years," stated Jim. "We have to face the possibility that we're not dealing with the same people that started the colonies. We might be dealing with their descendants, and they might be evil."

"That's definitely possible," admitted Trang. "But unless we're willing to break into that room, we still have to wait."

"Maybe not," stated Rex. "My telepathic ability is almost as good as Tonya's, and I am very good at transmitting images. I could try communicating with the intelligence built into that wall. Maybe it will tell me what's happening to Tonya."

"That's a great idea," stated Jim.

"It might be a great idea, but there is some risk involved," Jerry warned. "You could get drawn through the wall. Then, I'll be missing you and Tonya."

"That is possible, but Tonya rescued me and my family, so I owe it to her to try to find out if she's in danger. This is something I must do."

Rex stared at the energy beam heading into space and wondered what the Ancient Ones wanted from Tonya. Then, he headed for the cave entrance at a brisk pace.

When Rex arrived at the wall, he put his hands on it and focused his mental power. He formed a mental image of Tonya and telepathically projected it into the wall. Rex held the image for ten seconds; then, he projected an image of Jim with a worried expression. After ten seconds passed by, he telepathically projected an image of Jim and Tonya together and smiling. Rex received no response, so he repeated the sequence of images, again, no response.

Rex turned to Jerry and said, "I don't know what kind of intelligence we're dealing with, but it apparently has not been programmed to respond to our concerns."

"What makes you say that?" Jerry asked.

"I tried to tell it that Jim is worried about Tonya and would like to have her back. I got no response. They could at least have told us if she's okay."

"We may be dealing with an unemotional computer that just doesn't care about Tonya," stated Jim, sounding worried.

Looking into Jim's eyes, Jerry said, "If there's something they want from Tonya, they're not going to harm her."

"What do they want?" Jim asked.

"I don't know," responded Jerry. "But Tonya provoked an immediate reaction when she contacted the wall. She must've presented an image of something that was of great interest to the Ancient Ones. But what was it?"

Turning to Trang and Geniya, Jerry said, "She's your daughter, and you know her better than anyone here. What message do you think she communicated?"

"Tonya was pretty excited about the caves she discovered back on Alcent," responded Geniya. "Maybe she projected images of them."

"Why would this artificial intelligence react to that?" Jerry asked.

"I don't know," responded Trang. "But what if Tonya projected images of some of the words on the walls in that cave complex? What if this artificial intelligence recognized that those words came from a cave on Alcent that was built by the same people who built this cave complex?"

"That could get a reaction," stated Jerry. "Especially, if there is something about that cave that the Ancient Ones are interested in."

"Also, that message would've told the Ancient Ones that Tonya and her people are capable of interstellar travel," commented Trang. "And that capability might be of interest to them."

"Why do you think that?" Jerry asked.

"There might be something in those caves that is crucial to them, and they might want to use us to go there for them."

"What could possibly be in a cave built 120,000 years ago that would be crucial to them today?" questioned Jerry.

"I could try to find out," stated Rex. "I'll need to borrow your computer and call up that ancient script. I'll telepathically project it into the wall. Maybe I can gain entry."

"You got it, but if you're successful, you'll be trapped in there with Tonya, and I'll have two people to rescue."

"Not necessarily, if that energy tunnel through space does provide near-instantaneous communication with the Ancient Ones, I might be able to negotiate with them for Tonya's release and mine."

"How are you going to do that?" Jerry asked.

"I'll have to find out what they want and figure out if we can do that."

"As evidenced by that energy tunnel, their technology is far superior to ours. What could they possibly want from us?"

"I'm going to try to find out."

Jerry turned on his computer and called up the script from the cave dwelling on Alcent. Rex focused on it word-by-word. When he reached the end, he scrolled back to the beginning. Holding the computer in one hand, he stepped up to the wall and placed his other hand on the wall. He focused on the script display and began telepathically transmitting the image into the wall. In just a few seconds, streamers of blue light began emanating from the wall and connecting to him. The streamers danced all over him, and he was soon enclosed in a shroud of blue light. The wall became very warm, and a small hole appeared that grew into a door-sized opening. The blue shroud enclosing Rex lifted him off his feet and carried him through the wall. The opening in the wall immediately flowed shut.

"Two of our people are now imprisoned," stated Jerry.

"And we have little choice except to wait for Rex to accomplish his objective," commented Trang.

"I wish I knew what's going on in there," Jim said.

"Judging from how quickly Rex gained entry, it looks like they want info about those caves back on Alcent," commented Jerry.

"But what are they looking for?" questioned Jim. "Why did they so quickly grab Tonya and Rex? What's so urgent?"

"We'll find out when Rex and Tonya are released," responded Jerry.

"How can you be so sure they'll be released?" questioned Jim. "We're dealing with aliens we know very little about."

"That's true, but there are some things we do know. To start with, we are here and they aren't. I think they need us to investigate those caves back on Alcent. Rex will make it clear to them that we aren't going to do that unless he and Tonya are released."

"It's great to demand that, but they could release Rex and hold Tonya hostage until they get what they want."

"Nothing doing!" exclaimed Jerry. "We aren't leaving here without Rex and Tonya."

Time dragged on slowly. Finally, after a half-hour passed by, the wall opened, and Rex stepped out. Speaking to Jim, he said, "Tonya is fine."

"Thank God for that!" Jim exclaimed.

Turning to Jerry, Rex said, "They want to talk to you before they release Tonya."

"I don't have telepathic ability," stated Jerry.

"That's not a problem. They quickly pulled an understanding of English out of Tonya's brain."

"I am amazed that they could do that so fast."

"Their technology is incredible, but they need help."

"What do they want us to do?"

"Come with me," responded Rex. "They'll explain everything to you."

Jerry did not immediately respond to Rex. Instead, he considered the possibility that Rex may have been hypnotized by the Ancient Ones and be under their control.

Noticing that Jerry was reluctant to follow him, Rex said, "Don't worry; we'll be fine."

"Okay, I'll join you, but I'll need a couple minutes to prepare for the meeting. Would you mind telling the Ancient Ones that I'll be there shortly?"

"You got it," responded Rex as he turned and stepped through the opening in the wall. Shimmering blue light filled the opening and prevented Jerry from seeing into the room.

Reaching for his communicator, Jerry called Mike and said, "I'm going into the concealed room. If anything happens to me, you are in command of the Challenger."

"Will do," responded Mike. "But what do you think might happen?"

"We are dealing with an advanced race that we know little about, so anything could happen. I want you to be prepared for all possibilities."

"Understood, but what are you most concerned about?"

"Rex said that they quickly pulled an understanding of English out of Tonya's mind. That means that they have a phenomenal ability to get into people's heads, which means that they might be able to program my mind, so that I will, in effect, be one of them."

"I see what you're getting at. They aren't here, but we are. So if they could take over your mind, they would have the Challenger at their disposal."

"That's what I'm worried about, so I want you in command."

"Understood."

Turning to his wife, Jerry said, "Keep an eye on me when I come out of there. If I do anything that is the least little bit out of character, I want you to give me a complete mental evaluation. You should enlist Geniya's help with this. She and Akeyco have been in my mind before."

Connie gave her husband a big hug and said, "I want you back with a sound mind, so that medical procedures won't be necessary."

"I expect the real me to come back, but we need to be prepared for the worst." Jerry hugged Connie a little longer than usual. Then, he faced the opening in the wall and stepped through the shimmering blue light. In just a few seconds, the opening closed, and the blue light disappeared.

Connie stared at the wall. It looked so hard, so cold, and so impenetrable. "I feel helpless," she said. "My husband could just as well be a million miles away, because he's not coming back unless the Ancient Ones allow him to."

"All of our people will be released," stated Trang. "The Ancient Ones need our help with something, and they aren't going to get it until after they release our people."

"But they might no longer be our people," stated Geniya. "Jerry's concern is justified. The Ancient Ones might be able to take control of people's minds. We'll have to watch Tonya, Rex, and Jerry for any little thing that is out of character."

"But what could the Ancient Ones possibly gain by taking control of only three of our people?" questioned Trang. "Surely, the rest of us could overpower three people."

"Knowing that, the Ancient Ones would not program them to do anything physical. It would have to be something else. And I don't know what, but we do have to think about the possibilities and be alert for them."

A half-hour later, the wall opened and Tonya stepped out, followed by Rex and Jerry. The wall closed and the shimmering blue light disappeared. One of Torleb's men came running in and announced, "The blue energy beam coming out of the cliff top is no longer there."

Jim stared at Tonya, wondering if she was still the same woman that he was in love with. Seeing Jim's worried expression, Tonya went to him, and he welcomed her with a tight embrace. "Are you okay?" Jim asked. "I was worried about you."

"I'm just fine, and I'm sorry that I caused you so much worry, but I had to go in there. We had an ancient mystery to solve."

"It sounds like you think you've solved that mystery."

"I just talked to our ancestors; at least, that's who they claimed to be."

"I find that hard to believe. You're telling me that the people you talked to claim to be 120,000 years old."

"They said they are 124,000 years old."

"I just can't imagine becoming that old. How did they do it?"

"They developed drugs that cause their bodies to regenerate tissue as it breaks down. As the centuries rolled on, they learned how to genetically alter their bodies, so that they no longer needed the drugs. Best of all, they've promised to give us that information if we solve a couple mysteries for them."

"What mysteries do they want solved?"

"During a 1000-year time period that started 123,000 years ago, they sent out several starships to explore and colonize life-friendly planets. The people on one of those starships discovered Zebron and Alcent. Soon after they planted colonies on these planets, the Ancient Ones lost contact with them. They think the starship never left the Alpha Centauri system, and they want us to search for it"

"Finding a wrecked starship from 123,000 years ago is a pretty tall order," stated Trang who was listening to Tonya with great interest "If it's even here, it could be buried under hundreds of feet of volcanic ash that is now overgrown with jungle. It could be buried in the muck at the bottom of an ocean. And which planet is it on?"

"Finding their starship is only part of the problem," stated Jerry. "They also want us to figure out what happened to the colonists they planted on Alcent."

"Do they also want us to walk on water?" questioned Trang.

"It does sound like they want us to work miracles," Jerry admitted. "So I did not make any guarantees. I told them only that we would try."

"That starship came here 123,000 years ago. That's a very long time. What is there about that ship that could possibly be relevant-to them today?"

"I just talked to an ancient one named Tabor. He was alive back then, and his oldest son Bule was the Captain of that starship."

"So it's not the starship he's interested in. What he really wants is to find out about his son."

"That's what Tabor wants, but the rest of them want to know what happened to the colonists they put on Alcent."

"Why haven't they sent an expedition here to investigate this?"

"Tabor said their home planet was involved in a brutal interstellar war a few years after Bule arrived here. They destroyed their enemy, but their home planet was left in ruins. Much of their technology was lost. What they had left was poured into rebuilding their planet and turning it into a comfortable place to live. The war and its aftermath changed their priorities, and they never again sent out starships, but they are now considering going back to the stars."

"How does finding an ancient starship help them do that?"

"It doesn't, but Tabor thinks finding that starship is our best chance to find out what happened to Bule."

"But that starship might not exist anymore. It might've been destroyed by their enemy in the interstellar war, or some tragic accident might've resulted in its destruction, killing Bule and his crew. My starship was only a few weeks away from destruction when you came along and prevented that. Had our antimatter fuel exploded, there would now be no trace of my starship. All that would remain is a large new crater on Aphrodite."

"Bule's starship was fueled by antimatter, so an accidental explosion would've resulted in total annihilation."

"What else did Tabor tell you about that starship?"

"It was unable to travel faster than light. It took 80 years for Bule to make the 60-lightyear journey to here. The starship's life support system used genetically engineered organisms to recycle all waste generated on the ship to produce food, water, and oxygen. Everyone on the ship was genetically altered to keep them from ageing."

"That means the people who started colonies here had lots of time to be successful," commented Trang. "Death could only have come from disease or fatal injury."

"Since I am a descendant of Bule and his people, how come I don't live forever?" questioned Zack.

"The genetic alteration was a complex procedure that could only be done to adults," responded Tonya. "And it did not pass on to their children. At some point, the colonists must have lost the ability to do the procedure."

"I am an adult," stated Zack. "I want that genetic alteration done to me. Imagine living 100,000 years. Imagine all the things I could see and do. We need to solve the mysteries Tabor wants us to solve, and I think the best place to start is in the caves back on Alcent."

"We've been in those caves," responded Jerry. "And except for the writing on the walls, we didn't find anything. It looks like the people who lived there packed up everything and left."

"Any indication where they went?"

"None."

"Have you looked for concealed rooms in those caves?"

"We never considered that possibility, but in view of what just happened here, looking for concealed rooms is our first order of business."

"How long will it take us to get there?" Zack asked.

"It sounds like you've decided to go with us," replied Jerry.

"I can't miss out on this. Besides, you're taking my brother and his family along, and they're the only family I have. So I'm hoping you'll allow me to board your starship and join your society."

"I believe we can find a spot for you," responded Jerry with a big smile.

"Thank you! And I can assure you that you won't regret this decision. So how long will it take to get to those caves on Alcent?"

"You sure are eager to get there."

"That's because I sense that we're going to make a discovery that's going to just blow us away."

"What do you think that's going to be?"

"I don't know, but it's going to be a shocking surprise, and I am eager to start the investigation."

"You were right about this secret room, so I have to give some credence to your intuition."

"So when will we arrive there?"

"We're leaving later today. The interstellar voyage will take 15 days. But when we arrive home, I'll need a couple days to get reacquainted with my daughter. Then, we'll go cave exploring."

"I hope you'll keep me informed as to what you find in those caves," stated Kayleb.

"You can count on that," responded Jerry. "It looks like our planets share some common history. Maybe there's something there that will influence our future."

"Knowing the past is always helpful in planning the future," stated Kayleb, "especially if mistakes were made that we can learn from."

"You're right about that," agreed Jerry. "But I don't think we're going to learn anything more in these caves today, so it's time to pack up and go home."

It was with heavy hearts that the people said goodbye to each other. Kayleb and Giselle wanted their newfound friends to stay longer, and the feeling was mutual. But it was time for Jerry and his colleagues to leave. The helicopter was loaded, and there was a hearty round of handshakes and hugs.

After everyone boarded the helicopter and waved goodbye, Jim started the turbine and took off. Feeling a sense of loss, Kayleb and his people watched the departing helicopter until it was out of sight.

Chapter Twelve

TIME: Day 73, Late Afternoon

With Jerry and Moose in the pilot's seat and copilot's seat, the large cargo shuttle was ready for takeoff. The helicopter was onboard and tied down. The apples, apple trees, and crated chickens were secured. All passengers were seated.

Having never been in space, Zack was given a window seat. He was so filled with anticipation that he was unable to settle down. "I'm going into space!" He exclaimed to his brother Rex who was sitting next to him.

"Fasten your seatbelt and hang on," stated Rex. "Shuttle takeoff and climb is a wild ride you'll never forget."

Rex had hardly finished speaking when the muffled whine of a turbine caught everyone's attention. Zack looked out the window and noted that the shuttle was in motion. Shortly, the water appeared to be rushing by at ever greater speed. Then, the shuttle rose up and rode on its hydrofoils. Suddenly, the powerful nuclear thermal rocket roared into action with the acceleration pushing everyone firmly back into their seats. Within ten seconds, the shuttle lifted off the water and pitched into a steep climb.

Zack managed to keep his nose glued to the window until the NTR shut down. In sharp contrast to the roar and acceleration, all was now silent, and Zack felt weightless. Turning to Rex, he said, "You were right. Takeoff and climb is a thrilling ride, and the awesome view is out of this world."

"We are out of that world," stated Rex. "And I don't know if we'll be back."

"That's true, but I don't feel bad about leaving, because we're going to a planet where dinosaurs reign supreme. Plus, we have a big mystery to solve."

"What happens if we don't find the answers the Ancient Ones want?"

"I predict that we will and that we'll be surprised by what we discover."

"But what happens if you're wrong and we disappoint the Ancient Ones?"

"Why would anything happen?" questioned Zack. "We're doing them a big favor by investigating an ancient mystery for them. If we fail, why wouldn't they just thank us for our efforts?"

"I expect that they will."

"So why are you suspicious?"

"I'm bothered by the same thing that concerns Jerry," stated Rex. "Namely, the Ancient Ones have a phenomenal ability to get into people's heads. Who knows what they've planted in my mind?"

"I think you're being needlessly distrustful. We should just take them at their word, solve the mystery, and report back to them. Then, they'll give us the age control information, and we can enjoy very long lives."

"I hope you're right, but it's possible the ancient mystery thing is just part of the story. They might also have some other agenda that's planted in my mind, Tonya's mind, and Jerry's mind. I am going to constantly critique my thoughts, looking for clues as to what that might be."

"I think you should set your worries aside and enjoy this flight. We have an awesome view out this window."

"You're right about that, but I want you to be aware of my concerns."

"You're my big brother, and you've always been a worrier, but if it'll make you feel more at ease, I'll keep an eye on you in search of unusual behavior."

"That's what I want."

"So can we forget about this for a while and just enjoy this flight?"

Rex looked past Zack through the window at the planet far below and said, "It has been our lifelong home, and despite the horrible war, I am going to miss it."

Twenty minutes later, the shuttle caught up to the Challenger. Taking advantage of his window seat, Zack stared at the starship right up to entering the hangar bay. "This starship is huge," he exclaimed.

"You'll be given a tour," stated Rex, "and you'll be impressed."

Zack continued staring out the window while entering the hangar bay. "Our pilots are really good," commented Zack. "It's amazing how they can so deftly guide this big shuttle into its berth without crashing into anything."

"All of our new friends are very good at the things they do," commented Rex.

"I'm hoping to learn some advanced technical skills from them."

"All of Earth's knowledge is in their computer library, but it's all in English."

"That's no problem. You can teach me English, and the earth people can show me how to use the computer library."

"I admire your ambition."

"I expect to live 100,000 years, so I want a solid foundation of knowledge on which to build my life."

"You've just given new meaning to long-term planning, but you're getting ahead of the curve, because we haven't yet solved the ancient mystery."

"No, but we will. Then, we'll have to adjust our thinking to living a little longer."

"That's quite an understatement."

Speaking through the shuttle's sound system, Jerry announced, "The hangar bay doors have been closed, and the hangar bay has been pressurized, so you're free to exit this shuttle. We will be leaving Zebron in two hours."

Rex turned to Zack and said, "We need to go to the observation deck, so we can view our home planet for our last two hours here."

"I am definitely ready for some space-age sightseeing. You lead the way, brother, I'm following."

Having overheard the conversation, Jim said to Tonya, "We need to go to the observation deck too. We faced some difficult challenges on B-2, and we were victorious. Now we need to enjoy the scenic beauty of the planet to cap off our memories of the place."

"Those memories will be with me for the rest of my life. I am happy with what we accomplished here. But most of all, I'm happy that I didn't lose you when you got shot. That bullet was only inches away from your heart."

"I know, but thanks to immediate medical attention, I survived. Now, I want to celebrate our successful mission, so let's go to the observation deck where we can act like tourists and enjoy the spectacular view."

"What a great way to begin our two-week vacation."

"What vacation are you talking about?" questioned Jim.

"Our return voyage should be a vacation for us, and I'm ready for some quiet, peaceful relaxation with you."

Jim smiled warmly and gave Tonya a big hug; then, they headed for the observation deck, closely followed by Rex and Zack. When the foursome arrived, they were joined almost immediately by Zeb, Zonya, Trang, and Geniya. Within a few minutes, all off-duty personnel were on the observation deck to get their final view of Zebron before departing.

Everyone felt a sense of relief that their mission was brought to a successful conclusion. The intense stress that people felt during parts of the mission was gone, and a party atmosphere developed. Lighthearted conversation and laughter soon pervaded the group.

Time flew by and the party was interrupted by Mike who announced over the intercom, "Prepare for acceleration! We've started the 15-minute countdown to engine ignition."

Speaking to Zack, Rex said, "You have 15 minutes to enjoy floating around in zero gravity; then, it'll be 1g for the return flight, which will take nearly 15 days."

Wanting to take advantage of the final minutes of weightlessness, Rex's children, Jeff and Kristy, joined Zack for some zero-g antics. The time went by fast and engine ignition happened on schedule. Acceleration started out at a gentle .05g and gradually built up to 1g, allowing everyone time to find a deck to use as a floor.

Being on their first interstellar voyage, Rex and his family and Zack decided to watch their home planet recede in the distance. After three hours, Zebron was 350,000 miles away and appeared only a little larger than a full moon.

Turning to Rex, Zack said, "I could become addicted to space travel. How do I get a tour of this starship?"

"We're going to the cafeteria to eat dinner, so that's where we'll start your tour."

"Now that you've mentioned food, I am hungry."

An hour later, after leisurely completing his first starship dinner, Zack was given a tour of the Challenger by Jim and Tonya. The tour ended on the observation deck, where Zebron now looked like a tiny bright disk set in a spectacular background of colorful stars contrasted against the stark blackness of space.

"Zebron sure looks small," commented Zack. "I am amazed that we've traveled so far in just a few hours."

After logging onto his personal computer, which he wore on his wrist, Jim said, "Engine ignition was five hours ago. Our present speed is 110 miles per second, and we are nearly one million miles from Zebron."

"Traveling a million miles in just five hours is incredible!" exclaimed Zack.

"We have 2,450,000,000 miles to go, and we'll reach a speed of 3863 miles per second before we start slowing down. The trip will take almost 15 days."

"So I have two weeks of interstellar flight to enjoy; then, we're going to get some answers for the Ancient Ones. After that, we're going to have very long lives to live."

"As jacked up as you are, I'm wondering how you're going to get any sleep tonight," commented Jim.

"If I could get myself a portable lounge chair or an air mattress, I'd like to make myself comfortable right here on the observation deck and view the universe until I drift into sleep."

"I think that can be arranged," responded Jim. "Anything else you need?"

Switching his gaze from Jim to Tonya, Zack asked, "You wouldn't happen to have a twin sister who could stay here with me? This is a romantic setting."

Recognizing the gaze and the question as a compliment, Tonya smiled warmly and said, "I don't have a twin sister, but I do have a sister."

"Is she on this ship?"

"I'm afraid not. She's on Alcent."

"I'd like to meet her. Is she single?"

"Yes."

"Promise me you'll introduce us and put in a good word for me."

"That I can do," responded Tonya.

"Is there anything else we can do for you tonight?" Jim asked.

Returning his gaze to the universe, Zack said, "Earphones and some space-age music from Earth would be nice."

"That's an easy request to fulfill."

An hour later, Zack was set for the night, and Jim and Tonya were in their stateroom. "I am happy to be going home," Tonya said. "It seems like we've been away forever."

"It sounds like you're homesick."

"I've lived my entire life on Alcent, and it's my home."

"I sense that there's more to it than that."

Tonya stepped into Jim's open arms, snuggled up to him, and

said, "I'm ready to get married and build a home with you. Can you imagine having a home of our own and some children?"

"Yes, I can. I've been thinking about that a lot, and there's no one I'd rather spend the rest of my life with than you."

Tonya snuggled up to Jim even tighter and said, "I love you, and I'm tired of standing. I think we should lie down and continue this conversation in bed."

"That's a great idea," Jim eagerly responded.

TIME: Day 84

Jerry and Connie were in the cafeteria enjoying breakfast. "Do you know what day this is?" Connie asked Jerry.

"I hope I haven't forgotten our wedding anniversary," replied Jerry, while looking concerned.

"No, it's not that. Today is Denise's birthday. Our lovely daughter is six years old today, and we aren't there for her."

"Let's finish breakfast and send her a Happy Birthday wish, along with a promise to give her a big party when we get home."

"That will make her happy. I wish we could talk to her, but we're still so far away that it takes too long for messages to travel back and forth. How long will it take for a message to get to her?"

Jerry consulted his wrist computer and said, "We are 387 million miles from Alcent, and communication traveling at light-speed takes 34 minutes and 40 seconds to get there."

"So the best we can do is send her a birthday wish and wait for a response that will be at least an hour and ten minutes later."

"That's the best we can do with our technology. We could have near instantaneous communication if we had the technology of the Ancient Ones, but we don't."

"Maybe someday we will, but in the meantime, let's send Denise a birthday wish when we get back to our apartment."

TIME: Day 88, Lunch time

With the two-week return voyage almost over, the Challenger was approaching Alcent and would soon be orbiting the planet. Once again, all off-duty personnel and guests were on the observation deck.

"How far away are we?" Zack asked Jim.

After consulting his computer, Jim said, "Our altitude is 525 miles. We'll soon be in orbit at 250 miles."

"Alcent looks so peaceful and inviting," commented Zack. "It's hard to believe that it's teeming with dinosaurs."

"Well it is," affirmed Jim. "We even have pterodactyls with wingspans measuring 52 feet."

"I have trouble visualizing a flying creature that big. I need to see them."

"You will, because we have a pterodactyl family living next door to us, and they frequently fly over Pioneer Island."

"They come that close! Aren't they dangerous?"

"This pair seems to like us."

"It's hard for me to picture living so close to such big predators."

"You'll get used to it."

"My life is going to be exciting," stated Zack. "Dinosaurs and pterodactyls to see up close, and there's the ancient mystery to solve." Turning to Tonya, Zack said, "Plus, you promised to introduce me to your sister."

"I'm not sure that I should," responded Tonya while displaying a devilish grin.

"Why not?"

"You just put my sister dead last on your list of exciting possibilities."

Feeling uncomfortable while enduring Tonya's piercing eye contact, Zack quickly admitted, "Yeah, I guess I did, but that was unintentional. I haven't yet met your sister, but if she's anything like you, she will definitely be at the top of my list."

"That was a pretty good comeback," responded Tonya while displaying a smile of satisfaction.

"So do I get to meet your sister?"

"I'll introduce you."

"Thank you. How long before we arrive on Pioneer Island?"

"About three hours."

"Will your sister have time to give me a tour of the island?"

"I don't know. You'll have to talk to her about that."

At that moment, Tonya became aware that Rex's children, who thought of her as a heroine, were impatiently trying to get her attention. Turning to Jeff and Kristy, Tonya heard Jeff ask, "Are you going to show us the dinosaurs?"

"Yes."

"When?"

"It might be a few weeks, because we have a big mystery to investigate for the Ancient Ones."

"But we want to see the dinosaurs right away," protested Jeff while looking disappointed.

"That might be possible," Jim said. "Jerry did say he needed a day or two to spend with Denise before going back to the caves."

"Does that mean we can see the dinosaurs tomorrow morning?" Jeff asked, sounding hopeful.

"I will see if I can make that happen," Jim promised.

"That's great!" exclaimed Jeff.

"Will you come with us?" Kristy asked Tonya.

"I wouldn't miss this for anything. Besides, I need to find out if I can telepathically influence the big dinos."

"I thought you could telepathically get into the heads of all animals," commented Jim.

"I've never had an opportunity to test my telepathic skills on the big dinos, so I don't know about them."

"It would open up some exciting possibilities if you could convince them that we are friends and also influence their behavior."

"That would be wonderful. I might even be able to wander around in dinosaur-land the same way I roam the jungle where I grew up."

"I don't think I want you doing that. I think we should live the safest lives we can."

"You were the one who mentioned the exciting possibilities."

"Maybe I spoke too quickly."

TIME: Day 88, 7:00 PM

The cargo shuttle was heading north, one mile west of Pioneer Island, at an altitude of 29,000 feet. Alcent's people were almost home and were looking down on Pioneer Island in anticipation of being there soon. Zack and Rex were impressed by the immense size of Clear Lake and noted how isolated Pioneer Island was.

Still traveling at supersonic speed, the shuttle created a sonic boom that jolted the senses of the people on Pioneer Island who were eagerly awaiting the arrival of their loved ones. "Mom and Dad are almost home!" exclaimed Denise, right after she was hit by the sonic boom. With binoculars, she watched the shuttle bank into a 180-degree turn a couple miles north of Pioneer Island. During the turn, the shuttle's speed dropped to subsonic. Upon completion of the turn, its altitude was less than 10,000 feet. "It's now coming toward us!" exclaimed Denise.

The shuttle steadily lost altitude and appeared to grow larger in Denise's binoculars. "The hydrofoils are down!" she exclaimed. "It's ready to land."

A half-minute later, the hydrofoils hit the water with the shuttle traveling 200 mph. The hydro-drogues deployed, rapidly slowing the shuttle to less than 40 mph, causing it to settle into the water and float on it hull. With its marine propeller churning the water under its tail, Jerry piloted the big cargo shuttle into South Bay and pulled up to a new dock that had been constructed during his absence.

Looking out the cockpit window, Jerry saw Denise standing on the dock wearing a huge smile. Jerry waved at Denise who waved back and became very animated. She cheered while jumping up and down. "My daughter's giving me a hero's welcome," Jerry said to Mike who was in the copilot's seat.

"I'll bet Matthew and Michelle are right there with her," responded Mike.

"They are, and I think they'd like to see you."

"I want to see them too," stated Mike as he stood up and headed for the exit.

Mike opened the shuttle's forward side door, stepped out, and received a big hug from Michelle and Matthew. Denise ran past them to greet Jerry and Connie with a tight embrace. "I'm glad you're here!" she exclaimed. "I missed both of you! And I have a big surprise for you!"

"What is it?" Connie asked.

"We have a house to live in! Do you want to see it?"

"Sure," replied Connie.

Walking on the rough wood planks of the new dock, Denise headed for shore with Jerry and Connie following her. When the trio reached the sandy beach, they walked across it to the open cage elevator. While riding it to the cliff top, Jerry looked down on South Bay and said, "It sure is great to be home."

At the top of the cliff, Jerry stepped off the elevator and surveyed the plateau. It looked different from what he remembered before going to Zebron. All of the small prefabricated homes had been assembled. Landscaping was in progress, and vegetable gardens had been planted. "This place looks like we've been gone for quite some time," commented Jerry.

"It's starting to look like a spacious village," noted Connie.

"I like it. Maybe we should go away more often."

"I'd rather stay here and do our share of the village building."

"I'd love to get into that, but I can't until I get this ancient mystery solved. However, we are taking a two-day vacation before we go back to cave exploring."

"We have a new home to live in," stated Denise. Sounding impatient, she said, "Let's go see it. We can use this ATV."

While driving north in the ATV, Jerry asked Denise, "Where is our new home?"

"Keep going, I'll tell you when to stop."

Jerry drove slowly, so he and Connie could look at all the development that was done during their absence. After several minutes passed by, Denise said, "Stop! There it is."

"I like its location," Connie said. "It's just a short walk from the medical lab."

"I like the landscaping," stated Jerry. "They've transplanted a nice selection of local plants into an attractive arrangement of rocks and driftwood. It looks natural, like it belongs here."

Pointing at a wood sculpture attached to the exterior wall next to the front door, Connie said, "Look at that pterodactyl carving. It looks so life-like. Someone put a lot of thought into making our prefab home look unique, rather than a product of mass production."

"I helped build it," stated Denise. "Do you like it?"

"It's beautiful," responded Connie. "Would you like to show us the inside?"

Denise proudly stepped up to the front door, but before opening it, she said, "Guess what's on the dining table."

"I don't know," Jerry said. "I think you should show us."

Denise opened the front door and pointed at the dinner table. Prominently displayed in the middle of it was a birthday cake with six candles. "Michelle baked it for my birthday. Do you like it?"

"It looks good," Connie said while putting her hands on Denise's shoulders. "We're sorry we missed your birthday, but don't worry, we'll have a party for you in a couple days. We just need to get settled down first."

"That's okay mom. You had to go rescue Rex and his family. Do you want to see my bedroom?"

"Sure!"

Denise went to a tiny room and said, "This is my room. It isn't very big, but it's mine, and I like it." Taking her parents to the other bedroom, Denise said, "This is your bedroom. Do you like the flowers on the dresser top?"

"They're beautiful," responded Connie.

"I helped pick them."

"Thank you, I like flowers."

Then, Denise showed her parents the bathroom and kitchen. "Our house is small, but I love it. I hope you both like it too."

Jerry and Connie enjoyed their daughter's enthusiasm. She was obviously thrilled by the new home. "I'm happy you like our home," Connie said to Denise. "We like it too; even though, it is small."

"We'll be adding some rooms after we get this ancient mystery solved," Jerry promised.

"That'll be fun," stated Denise. "Can I help build them?"

"We'll find something for you to do, and it sure looks like you've been a busy girl while we were gone."

"Yeah, I was, but I missed you. You were gone too long."

"We missed you too," stated Jerry. "I hope we don't have to leave again for a long time."

"Good! I want you home. Can we go swimming? Our new dock is fun to jump off of."

"After being in space a couple weeks, a good swim will be refreshing," commented Jerry.

"I'm coming with," Connie insisted, "but I'll need a couple minutes to change."

"We all need to change," Denise said.

A few minutes later, the Jerontis family was on its way back to South Bay. This time, Jerry drove the ATV as fast as was safe. The open cage elevator delivered them to the sandy beach of South Bay. With Denise leading the way, they ran across the sand and out to the end of the dock where Denise dove in, followed immediately by her parents. Denise surfaced and swam with graceful skill.

"You swim really well," stated Connie. "It looks like you've been taking lesions."

"Michelle's been teaching me and Matthew how to swim."

"She must be a great teacher, because you are good."

After 15 minutes in the water, Denise said, "I'm hungry. Can we go to your welcome-home party and get something to eat?"

"Sounds good," responded Jerry.

Wanting Denise to feel like she was welcoming them home, Jerry and Connie allowed her to lead the way to a banquet table on the beach. After filling their food trays, they sat on a log facing a large bonfire, which was only a few yards from the water.

"It sure feels good to be home," stated Connie. "I'm glad we're taking a couple days off before we go dashing off in pursuit of that ancient mystery. All I want to do is putt around the house. Maybe I can find a flowering plant or two to transplant, so I can add my own personal touch to our yard."

"That sounds relaxing," commented Jerry. "You can start by helping me decide where to plant our apple tree."

"We have five apple trees."

"We're going to give four of them away. Who gets them will be decided by a lottery."

"Make sure Dianne gets one. She can use her skills to stimulate twigs to set roots. Then, anyone who wants an apple tree can have one."

"In a few years, we might end up with more apples than we know what to do with."

"I don't think so. There are just too many things you can do with good apples, but I'm wondering about all those chickens we brought back. What are we going to do with our share?"

"Somewhere on our property, we'll have to build a small chicken coop to protect them from the elements."

"It seems like they would be healthier if we could let them spend some time outdoors."

"That will require a fenced enclosure with a fenced top, so they don't fly out. Also, chickens will be tempting prey for the hawks and owls that live on this island. The fenced top will keep them out."

"It sounds like you're going to be busy during our short vacation."

"We're giving most of the chickens away. We're only going to have eight, so the shelter will be small and won't take long to make. I already have the light-weight wire mesh. I made it in the Challenger's shop a couple days ago."

"What are we going to feed them?"

"While we were gone, our people have been busy harvesting wild rice. We have an abundant supply. The chickens will do just fine eating this natural grain as a mainstay, and of course, we can supplement that with other things."

"It sounds like you have it all figured out."

"I have put some thought into it."

"That's great, because I'm looking forward to having a constant supply of fresh eggs."

"Mom! Who is that girl over there?" Denise asked.

"Her name is Kristy, and she's twelve years old. The boy next to her is Jeff, and he's ten years old. Rex and Shannon are their parents. They are the family we went to Zebron to rescue."

"Jeff and Kristy look like nice kids. I'm happy you rescued them."

"They seem to have made friends with Zonya's grandchildren. They sure are busy talking."

"Joeby and Tara are my friends too. Maybe I could join them and meet Jeff and Kristy."

"Okay, let's walk over there, and I'll introduce you."

Eager to meet the new kids, Denise tugged her mother's hand, towing her along. Seeing them coming, Kristy turned to greet them. Kristy liked Connie and was eager to meet her daughter. After the introduction, Kristy faced Denise and said, "I am so happy that your father came to Zebron to rescue us."

"My Dad is the greatest," stated Denise. "I missed him when he was gone, but I'm happy he brought you here. You're going to have fun living with us."

"I want to see the dinosaurs. Have you seen them?"

"Yes!"

"Was that fun?"

"It was scary."

"I want to see the dinosaurs too," stated Jeff. "Can you ask your father?"

"Sure," responded Denise, while sensing that being the Captain's daughter might have some advantages with her new friends, even though, they were older.

"Can we see them tomorrow?"

"Let's go ask my Dad." Feeling like she was the center of attention, Denise proudly led the way to where her father was sitting.

With the four older children standing behind her, Denise faced her father and smiled ear-to-ear. "Uh oh, I can tell you want something," he responded.

"We would like to go see the dinosaurs tomorrow. Can we?"

"There are some things I need to do around home tomorrow."

"Jim and Tonya could take us," suggested Kristy.

"Have you talked to them about that?" Jerry asked.

"I have," stated Jeff, "and Jim said he would take us if he could use the submarine."

"Okay, if the sub's available, you can go"

"Wow!" exclaimed Jeff. "That's great!"

"Don't get too excited just yet. I have to find out if the sub is available."

"When will you know?" Denise asked.

Jerry reached for his communicator, contacted Pioneer Island's central computer, and asked for the submarine's schedule. It instantly appeared on his communicator's small screen. Jerry scrolled through the schedule. Looking at the children gathered before him, he said, "The sub's schedule is open for the next couple days, so you can go if Jim and Tonya will take you."

A loud cheer erupted from the children. "Let's go talk to Jim and Tonya," stated Jeff.

"They're over there," Kristy said while pointing at them.

Filled with excitement, the children quickly bounded over the sand, surprising Jim and Tonya with their sudden appearance. "What's up?" Jim asked them.

"Jerry said we could use the sub tomorrow," responded Jeff. "Will you take us to see the dinosaurs?"

Turning to Tonya, Jim asked, "Do we have anything planned for tomorrow?"

"We've been gone for such a long time, I thought it would be fun to stay home and relax, maybe do some sunbathing on the beach."

"You could sunbathe on the deck of our boat," suggested Denise.

"But that's not the same as the sandy beach."

"It's better than the beach," Denise insisted. "Out on the lake, you have the waves and the wind. Sailing is fun."

"Well, okay, if you insist, I guess we can go."

"I think you're funning with me. I think you want to see the dinosaurs too."

Tonya smiled at Denise. The smile was worth a thousand words. It told Denise that her thinking was correct.

Speaking to the rambunctious group of children, Jim said, "We'll set sail at lunchtime."

"Wow! That's great!" exclaimed Jeff. "We're going to see the dinosaurs!"

Chapter Thirteen

TIME: Day 89, 11:00 AM

Jim and Tonya were onboard the research submarine awaiting the arrival of their passengers. Second only to the helicopter, the submarine was Jim's favorite toy. With an overall length of 36 feet and a maximum internal diameter of seven feet six inches, the little submarine could accommodate four people on an extended voyage of exploration. Additional people could be carried on shorter voyages.

Most of the submarine's ballast and batteries were contained in its keel, which had a maximum width of 54 inches and a depth of 46 inches. The electric motors, essential equipment, facilities, and instrumentation occupied about half the space inside the main hull, leaving the other half for human occupants.

The most appealing feature for users of the submarine was its transparent plastic hull. Advanced plastics technology made it possible to have a strong, tough hull that was as clear as high quality window glass.

For sailing on the surface, the little submarine was easily converted into a sailboat. One feature that helped make sailing on the surface enjoyable was the submarine's spacious deck. Mounted just above the hull, the deck was eight feet wide by 28 feet long.

On each side of the submarine, a plastic storage tube was mounted just below deck. Each tube extended nearly the entire length of the submarine and contained a deflated pontoon. These tubes were attached to telescoping booms that could be extended 21 feet out from the submarine's hull. When the pontoons were deployed and inflated, the submarine's telescoping mast could be extended upward and its main sail deployed, thereby converting the submarine into an outrigger-type sailboat.

However, if there was insufficient wind to operate a sailboat and if the sky was clear and sunny, the submarine's solar sails could be used. These were rolled up inside tubes mounted on each side of the submarine. Deploying the solar sails was easy. They were simply unrolled and laid out horizontally along the tops of the booms supporting the outrigger pontoons. During midday, the energy radiating down on the solar sails from Alpha Centauri A would produce 40 to 45 kilowatts of electrical power.

To control the boat while sailing on the surface, a control console was mounted on the aft end of the deck on the starboard side. A second control console was mounted on the starboard side at the forward end of the deck. The hatch for entering the submarine was centered in the forward deck.

Stretched out on a lounge chair on the forward deck, Tonya yawned and said, "This warm weather makes me feel lazy."

"Good! That means you're in the mood to relax and enjoy an afternoon of sailing."

"I feel more like taking a nap than going sailing."

"How can you be sleepy? We slept in this morning."

"It's the weather. It's warm, and I'm looking at a blue sky filled with fluffy white clouds that are lazily drifting along."

Jim gazed at the sky for a few moments. "That is a relaxing scene, but your nap is going to be cut short. I see the elevator descending, and our passengers are on it."

"Those people are sure fired up about seeing the dinosaurs. Especially the children, they can hardly contain themselves. I'm not sure they have the patience for a two-hour sailing voyage."

"We'll just have to figure out a way to entertain them."

"That might be difficult; they want to see the dinosaurs now."

"The big sauropods usually don't arrive at the lake until late afternoon, so the kids will have to wait several hours."

"There must be other dinosaurs we can see while we wait for the sauropods," Tonya said.

"Okay, let's not sail directly to Sauropod Meadow. Let's sail to a point that's about four miles south of the meadow. Then, we'll cruise north along the shoreline and see what we might discover."

"I like that plan."

A few minutes later, all passengers were onboard. Zack, Rex, Shannon, Jeff, and Kristy had never seen dinosaurs and were thrilled to be going on a voyage in search of them. Denise, Tara, and Joeby had already seen the big dinos, but they did not want to be left out, so they pleaded their way onto the voyage.

Using the boat's electric motor, Jim pulled away from the dock and headed south toward the mouth of South Bay. Standing next to Jim, Jeff exclaimed, "We're on our way! We're going to see the dinosaurs! How long will it take to get there?"

"A couple hours," replied Jim.

"That's a long time. Can we go faster?"

"The big sauropods don't come to the lake until late afternoon. So you'll have to have fun sailing until then. Want to help me drive the boat?"

"Can I? I mean, you'll let me do that?"

While holding the wheel, Jim backed up a bit and motioned Jeff to where he had been standing. Jeff stepped into position behind the wheel and grasped it with both hands. "This steering wheel is called a helm," Jim said. "Just hold it steady. When we get out of South Bay, I want you to make a slow left turn. Can you do that?"

"Sure can," responded Jeff while feeling seven feet tall. A moderate southerly wind blew small waves into South Bay and whipped Jeff's bushy hair around.

Jim backed a few feet away from Jeff to give him the feeling that he was the man in control of the helm. Rex walked by Jeff to the forward handrail and looked straight ahead, but the southern shore of Clear Lake was 20 miles away, and he could not see it. His distant gaze was interrupted by Jeff, who yelled, "Hey Dad! Look at me! I'm driving the boat."

Rex turned, looked at Jeff, and quickly noted the pride his son was feeling. Rex switched his gaze to Jim and smiled in approval.

Jim felt a tap on his left shoulder. It was Zack, who said, "I'm impressed by how quiet this boat is. I can't hear your motor or your propeller, and I don't feel any vibration. It's like I'm just standing on a big log that's quietly floating along."

"This is a research vessel. It was designed for silent operation. We don't want the boat to scare away the creatures we're trying to study."

"This is great. I've never liked a lot of noise. I enjoy the peaceful sounds of nature."

"Nature's not always peaceful. The sound from a couple T-Rexes facing off will just about make your blood curdle."

"You've seen that?"

"Yes! They were fighting over a female in heat."

"I can only imagine what that battle must've been like."

289

"They didn't actually come to blows. It was more like an argument. They were trying to intimidate each other with their ferocious roaring. Eventually, one of them backed away."

"I'd like to see a T-Rex confrontation."

"You will, if you spend much time sailing along the eastern shore of this lake. There are lots of them over there."

"Sounds like a dangerous place, where it would be impossible to live a peaceful life."

"It is."

"What about Pioneer Island?"

"Bears and pterodactyls are the biggest creatures we've seen on the island. We have radar to warn us when pterodactyls are in the area, and we've set up surveillance cameras to monitor our beaches. When bears come ashore, we tag them with radio transmitters, so we always know where they are."

"The island sure is quiet at present. All I hear is the wind rustling through the trees and waves splashing against the bow."

"We like living here. It's peaceful most of the time."

"I haven't even been here 24 hours, and I can tell you without a doubt that I am going to enjoy living here. There's unlimited opportunity for adventure. Also, Akeyco promised to show me around the island tomorrow."

"So, you talked her into it. Was it a tough sell?"

"Well, I did have to turn on a little charm."

"She's a great gal. Be sure to treat her well."

"You can count on that."

"We're out of South Bay!" Jeff yelled. "Is it time to start turning?"

"Anytime you're ready," replied Jim.

Jeff slowly turned the helm counterclockwise, and the boat immediately began turning left. When the boat was heading eastward, Jim said, "Okay, straighten her out." Jeff did as requested.

With Rex and Zack listening, Jim said to Jeff, "We're now going to deploy our sail."

"How do we do that?"

"First, we have to deploy the outriggers, and that's easy. All you have to do is flick this switch."

Jeff did as directed, and telescoping booms began to extend outward from each side of the boat. When they were fully extended, the pontoons at their outer ends inflated.

"That was neat!" exclaimed Jeff with wide eyes. "We can't tip over now."

"That's right, and it's time for us to go to the aft helm. You hold this one until I get there; then, you can come and join me."

A minute later, Jim, Jeff, Rex, and Zack were on the aft end. Kristy and Joeby were below deck viewing the underwater world through the boat's transparent hull. Everyone else was up front.

Speaking to Jeff, Jim said, "Now you can press this switch." Jeff did so, and a narrow deck panel extending from the aft helm to mid-deck popped open. A sail was stored in the open compartment. Jim grabbed the control ropes, threaded them through the proper pulleys, and secured them.

"Now you can flick this switch," Jim said to Jeff. He did and the telescoping mast began extending upward, pulling the sail with it. When the mast was fully extended, the sail flowed to the north, flapping loosely in the wind.

Turning a crank, Jim hauled in the control rope to set the sail. It soon snapped taut. Jim continued cranking in the control rope until the sail was properly set.

To Jeff, Jim said, "Now you can turn this knob all the way off. That shuts down the electric motor."

Jeff did so, and Jim said, "We're now a sailboat, and we have enough wind to easily get to the east coast in a couple hours."

"Sailing is fun!" exclaimed Jeff as he was hit by spray from a breaking wave.

"Our moderate wind seems to have developed into a pretty stiff breeze," commented Zack. "Just how seaworthy is this boat?"

"We can handle any kind of weather. If a storm develops, we'll retract everything, go below deck, and dive. It'll be crowded, but we can manage for a few hours. But this wind is far from dangerous; it's just strong enough for some darn good sailing."

"This lake is huge," stated Zack. "I can't even see the north end or the south end. I imagine it can get pretty rough out here during a windstorm."

"The rougher it gets; the more fun it is."

"I'm game for some of that fun."

"First, you have to become an expert in how to handle this boat."

"I'm ready to learn."

"It's going to take a couple hours to sail to the east coast, so let's get started with your training."

"Count me in on that training," Rex said. "I don't know that I want the wild adventure you guys are talking about, but I do want to learn how to operate this boat."

"You got it," responded Jim. "I'll start by showing you how everything works."

Meanwhile, at the front end of the boat, Denise and Tara were hanging on to the deck rail and looking down at the water. Wearing swimsuits and lifejackets, they squealed with delight every time a crashing wave broke against the front of the boat and showered them with spray.

"This is fun!" exclaimed Denise. "I'd like to dive in and go swimming."

"The lake is too deep here," warned Tara. "You could drown."

"No, I wouldn't. I know how to swim, and I'm wearing a life-jacket."

"There might be a monster in this deep water that could eat you."

"We haven't found any monsters in this lake."

"There might be some that you haven't found. They might be hid-ing, just waiting for something to eat."

"I think you're afraid to jump in."

"I'm not afraid. I just want to be careful. I used to live on an island near a jungle where lupusaurs lived. They would sometimes hide, waiting for something to eat. We had to be very careful."

"That must've been scary."

"It was, and I'm happy I don't live there anymore. I like living with you on Pioneer Island."

"I'm glad you live with us. You're fun."

Another breaking wave showered the girls with spray, and they again squealed with delight. "We don't have to go swimming to get wet," stated Tara. "We can get wet right here and be safe."

An hour-and-a-half later, with the eastern shore only a half-mile away, Tonya was scanning the countryside with binoculars looking for dinosaurs. The children were gathered around her. "Do you see any?" Jeff asked.

"Yes, but they're not on the shore. They're inland a couple hun-dred yards."

"Can I use the binoculars?" Jeff asked.

"Yes, but you have to share them with everyone."

Jeff quickly spotted the dinosaurs. "They sure have lots of horns!" he exclaimed. "And they look mean!"

"I want to see them," Kristy said while reaching for the binoculars. Jeff continued looking through the binoculars for as long as he thought he could get away with. Then, he reluctantly handed them to his sister.

"Some of them have a strange-looking plate behind their heads," Kristy said. "And it has horns on it too."

"That plate is a neck shield," stated Tonya. "All those horns help them fight the T-Rexes who want to eat them."

"Will we see T-Rexes?" Jeff asked Tonya.

"I don't know."

"What is the name of these dinosaurs?"

"They are styracosaurs."

"We're going to pull in the sail and outriggers," Jim announced. "We want to make the boat look small, so we can get close to these dinos without alarming them."

Twenty minutes later, the boat was anchored 50 yards offshore in 40 feet of water. Everyone was watching the styracosaurus herd as it steadily marched toward the water.

"They look mean," stated Kristy.

"They really look big," Jeff said. "I don't want to go ashore. I could be killed."

"Moose had a ride on one of them," Jim said.

"No way!" exclaimed Jeff. "He could never get on one. They're too big, and they look mean. They could kill Moose."

"The animal was in the water when Moose crawled on top of him, and Moose didn't know that it was the biggest bull in the herd. Then, the T-Rexes came, and the big bull went to fight them."

"That's too wild to be true. You're telling me a story."

"Will you believe me, if I show you the video?"

"You have pictures of that."

"We sure do."

"Show me later. I want to look at the dinos now. They're here, and some are walking into the lake."

While pointing at one of the brutes in the water, Jim said, "See that one with the L-shaped scar on his shield. His name is L-Scar. He's the one Moose rode." Jeff stared at the animal; still not sure that Jim was telling him the truth and not just a story.

Tonya was also staring at L-Scar. She wondered if she could tele-pathically influence this animal. Focusing her mental powers, she began probing L-Scar's brain. She projected an image of Moose into L-Scar's consciousness and got an immediate reaction. L-Scar looked around and sniffed the breeze. He seems to be looking for Moose, Tonya concluded, but I need to know for sure. Tonya stopped pro-jecting Moose's image and focused on telepathically reading L-Scar's mind. Almost immediately, she picked up an image of Moose approaching L-Scar in an open meadow. Wow! I can get into his brain, and he has pleasant memories of Moose. I wonder if he would also like me. I need to find out. Without a word to anyone, Tonya dove in and started swimming toward L-Scar.

"What are you doing?" Jim yelled, not believing what he was seeing.

While treading water, Tonya turned and said, "You needn't be so upset. All I want to do is find out if L-Scar will treat me like Moose."

"Have you lost your mind? That's a wild, dangerous animal!"

"You're overreacting. L-Scar never threatened Moose."

"You're not Moose. He might attack you."

"I've already gotten into his mind, and I believe I can convince him to be friendly toward me."

"We have a great future ahead of us, and you're taking an unnec-essary risk."

"This is something I need to do."

"Knowing you as well as I do, I know there's nothing I can say to change your mind. So I'm going to keep my rifle ready, just in case L-Scar decides to be aggressive."

"Thanks, but you're not going to need your rifle. If I thought you would, I wouldn't be doing this."

"You're probably right, but I'm going to have the gun ready any-way." Jim quickly dropped below deck and emerged with his rifle and a video camera that he handed to Rex. "We need to film everything L-Scar does in reaction to Tonya."

"Is Tonya going to be killed?" Kristy asked, sounding worried.

"No, she's not," responded Jim.

"Is she going to ride him?" Jeff asked, sounding excited.

"I sure hope not, but I don't know. She has a mind of her own."

L-Scar had waded so far into the water that only the top two feet of his body was above the water. He was using the bony growth at the end of his tail to pound the water next to his body. This effectively washed water over his back.

Tonya resumed swimming toward L-Scar, stopping about 20 feet away from him. Focusing her mental energy, she telepathically entered his mind where she saw an image of herself. I guess I have his attention, and he's not the least bit alarmed. But why should he be? He's a ten-ton brute, and I'm just a 135-pound woman. But one swipe with that tail could kill me, so I need to stay away from it.

An image of Moose appeared in L-Scar's mind. After several seconds, Moose's image disappeared, and Tonya's image came back. Is this animal actually thinking? Tonya wondered. It looks like he just compared me to Moose. I wonder if he would accept my presence the same way he accepted Moose. Why did he tolerate Moose's presence? What could such a big animal possibly want or need from humans? Maybe nothing, maybe these dinos are just mild-mannered creatures who are only belligerent toward their enemies.

He sure is curious about me. He's trying to get my scent, but this cross-breeze is making that difficult. I think it's time to move closer.

While staying telepathically tuned to L-Scar's mind, Tonya slowly swam closer. He is calm, noted Tonya. I'm not sensing any alarm at all. Tonya swam to the south to get upwind from L-Scar. She stopped when she was about ten feet south of L-Scar's face. He visually followed her movement, flared his nostrils, and smelled the air.

Tonya saw her image in L-Scar's mind, then an image of Moose, then an image of herself. It sure looks like he's comparing me to Moose, Tonya surmised. What does he think of us? On what level is he able to think? He's demonstrating the ability to recall the memory of Moose and compare him to me. What happens next? What do I do now?

A new memory appeared in L-Scar's mind. It was an image of Moose in the water reaching out and scratching L-Scar's nose. A pleasant aura pervaded L-Scar's mind. It seems L-Scar enjoyed contact with Moose. I sure hope he doesn't expect me to scratch his nose. Those horns just look too deadly to get close to.

A new image formed in L-Scar's mind. It was Tonya scratching his nose. Uh oh, it looks like I am expected to scratch his nose. Is that what he thinks humans are good for? Why can't he just go ashore and rub his nose against a tree?

Maybe I'm not being very smart, but I'm not detecting any belligerence in this animal's mind, so I'm going closer. While staying tuned to his brain, Tonya slowly moved closer to L-Scar. She stopped just out of reach of his horns and reached toward his nose. "If you want your nose scratched, you need to step forward."

L-Scar lifted his nose and stretched toward Tonya, but he could not quite reach her outstretched fingers. So he stepped closer to her and made contact, rubbing a sensitive part of his nose against her fingers. Tonya obliged him with a gentle scratching motion. Tonya detected a sense of pleasure in the big dinosaur's brain and concluded; he really is enjoying this.

Standing on the boat with his rifle ready, Jim said, "I can't believe she's doing this. She's scratching a ten-ton dinosaur's nose."

"And she's making it look like it's no big deal," noted Rex.

"She might be relaxed, but I'm worried, and I wish she'd get out of there. How long is she going to hang around scratching his nose?"

"Maybe not much longer, L-Scar just turned his nose away from her."

Tonya was now facing the animal's left shoulder and noticed an area where the hide was twitching. Looking at the area, she saw two sty-tics that were gorged with blood. "So that's why you were splashing water on your back. You were trying to drown those tics."

Tonya drew her knife, reached up, and slid the blade under the nearest tic. With a twisting motion, she pried the tic loose and noted its inch-long blood suction tube. After removing the second tic, she crawled onto L-Scar's back and removed three more tics. He doesn't mind my presence at all, Tonya noted. Maybe he thinks people are good for removing tics.

I managed to get on his back the same way Moose did. It was at this point that the T-Rexes arrived, and L-Scar went to fight them, taking Moose along for the ride. I sure don't need that wild ride, but I do need to find out if I can get this animal to do what I want. Hypnotists do very well with the power of suggestion. This animal is totally relaxed and at peace with the world. I wonder if he'll respond to my suggestions. Let's see if I can turn him around.

Focusing the powers of her mind, Tonya telepathically placed an image in L-Scar's mind of him turning to his left. She held the image until it was the only thought in L-Scar's mind, and he turned left until he was facing inland. Using a new image, Tonya suggested to L-Scar that he walk ashore, and he did.

"She's riding him!" Jeff exclaimed.

"She got him to go ashore," Jim said. "But he may've wanted to go there anyway. I'm concerned that she won't get him back into the water. Then, she'll be stuck in the middle of a herd of dinosaurs."

"Is Tonya going to die?" Kristy asked Jim, sounding dreadfully worried.

"She's perfectly safe at the moment."

"That girl has a lot of nerve," commented Rex.

"More than enough to get her in trouble someday," stated Jim.

"I don't think that's going to be today," Rex said. "It looks to me like that animal is doing what she wants him to do."

"She sure looks at home on that dinosaur's back," commented Shannon. "What I mean is, she looks so natural, like she belongs there."

"She is a jungle girl," stated Jim. "As a teenager, she drove her parents nuts by disappearing into the jungle for days and weeks at a time."

"It's obvious that she survived all of that in good shape," stated Shannon. "So why are you worried about what she's doing now?"

"Those are wild animals, and we don't know what they're going to do. They have awesome fighting ability. They can successfully defend themselves against T-Rexes, which means they could easily kill humans."

"But if they don't see humans as a threat, why would they attack?" questioned Shannon.

"I don't know," responded Jim. "The problem is we just don't know enough about these animals."

"It looks like Tonya's trying to increase our knowledge about them."

"I can't deny that. I just don't like it when she puts herself at risk."

"She doesn't seem to be at much risk. L-Scar is willingly doing her bidding. He's carried her inland to the other side of his herd. He's just standing there, and Tonya's viewing the countryside. What kind of animal is going to attack her when she's sitting on that brute?"

"Only T-Rexes, and there aren't any around at present."

"So what are you worried about?"

Turning to Rex, Jim asked, "Is your wife always so difficult to argue with?"

"She keeps me on my toes."

A few minutes later, L-Scar started walking. He circled around the south side of his herd and returned to the water's edge. Then, he headed north until he was opposite the submarine, where he entered the water and waded toward the sub. When he stopped, Tonya waved at everyone and asked, "Anyone want to go for a ride?"

"I do!" exclaimed Jeff.

"I don't know if I want you doing that," Shannon quickly said.

Grinning from ear-to-ear, Jim asked, "What are you worried about?"

Shannon faced Jim and said, "Okay, you got me."

Looking at his parents, Jeff pleaded, "Can I go ride him with Tonya?"

Speaking to Tonya, Rex asked, "Do you have enough control over L-Scar for this to be safe?"

"So far, he's done everything I've suggested, but he is a wild animal."

"Why do you think he's doing what you want?"

"I don't know why, but he seems to enjoy human contact."

"He's accepted you and Moose, but we don't know that he would accept my son."

"I can ask him."

"Are you telling me that he's actually going to answer a question that you ask with telepathic images?"

"If you will allow Jeff to swim to about 20 feet away, so L-Scar can plainly see him, I will present L-Scar with an image of Jeff on his back with me, and we'll see how he reacts."

"I don't know. This all seems kind of dangerous for my son."

"Dad, I know how to swim, and I have a lifejacket on."

"That's true enough, but there are other dangers besides drowning." Turning to Jim, Rex asked, "Have you ever seen predators in this lake that might attack a human in the water?"

"We haven't found any. Also, Zeb lived on an island for 30 years and frequently took a dip in the lake. He was never bothered by anything."

"I am an excellent swimmer," stated Zack. "If I had a spear gun, I could look around underwater and deal with anything that looks threatening."

"Hang on a minute," stated Jim while disappearing below deck. Shortly, he was back on deck. While presenting a spear gun to Zack, he asked, "Will this fit the bill?"

Zack inspected the gun and admired it. He was obviously impressed. "This thing really looks lethal," he said.

"It's even more lethal than it looks at first glance. Take a good look at this spearhead. It has a double explosive charge. When the spear hits an attacking predator, the first explosion drives this projectile deep into its flesh. Then, the projectile explodes, and that should instantly disable any predator."

"I will dive in and look around," Zack said, after Jim showed him how to operate the gun.

Zack slipped into the underwater world. A minute later, he surfaced and said, "There's nothing down there except for a few fish that look like they might be good to eat."

"Now can I go ride L-Scar with Tonya?" Jeff asked.

Shannon looked at Rex for the answer, and he reluctantly said to Jeff, "Okay son, you can go, but do exactly what Tonya tells you."

While Zack went back underwater for another look around, Jeff slid into the water and started swimming toward L-Scar. Pointing upwind, Tonya said, "Swim over to there, so L-Scar can get your scent."

Jeff did as directed, and L-Scar followed his movement. Tonya telepathically tuned into L-Scar's mind and saw an image of Jeff in the water. "You have his attention," Tonya said. "You can come a little closer."

L-Scar flared his nostrils and sniffed the air. "He has your scent, and he's not alarmed." With Jeff only 15 feet away, Tonya said, "Stay put while I show him an image with both of us on his back."

Tonya presented L-Scar with an image of her pulling Jeff onto his back and sitting in front of him. "Still no alarm." Tonya stopped projecting the image, so she could read L-Scar's mind. "He seems puzzled, and I think he's searching his memory."

Gradually an image formed in L-Scar's mind. The image was fuzzy, and Tonya had a difficult time seeing detail in it. What memory is he trying to recall? Tonya wondered. It seems like L-Scar is struggling to recall more detail. Could it be that he's had contact with humans years ago? It looks like I'm seeing an image of two humans in his mind. I wish I could make them out a little better, but this does look like a man and a woman. Yes, one is definitely a man with long brown hair and a brown beard. The other is blonde and looks female. Who are those people? How long ago did L-Scar encounter them? Where are they now? They must've treated L-Scar very well, because there is a pleasant aura surrounding his memory of them. Maybe his past experience with people is the reason he likes us. I wonder what those people did to earn his trust.

The image in L-Scar's mind changed to one in which the shadowy figures were walking in a meadow. They climbed on top of a large boulder. L-Scar stopped next to the boulder, and the humans climbed onto his back.

The image disappeared, and a new image formed showing Jeff and Tonya on his back. A pleasant aura surrounded the image.

Turning her attention to Jeff, Tonya said, "It's going to be okay. You can swim toward me."

Jeff was hesitant. "He looks pretty fierce, now that I'm close to him."

"You don't have to ride him if you're afraid to come over here."

"But I want to ride him. How come you're not afraid?"

"Sometimes things happen that do make me afraid. A healthy amount of fear is good, because it inspires caution, and being cautious can keep you alive."

"Are you afraid of L-Scar?"

"I respect the fact that he's a wild animal, but I believe he trusts us, so I don't fear him. I just respect his capability, and I don't want to ever make him mad at me."

Jeff thought about what Tonya said. "I don't want him mad at me either. I am going to use caution and approach him slowly." Swimming in slow motion, Jeff headed for L-Scar's left shoulder while Tonya tuned into his mind looking for a danger signal. But L-Scar stayed calm. Jeff arrived at L-Scar's side, and Tonya reached down, grabbed one of his hands, and pulled him aboard.

Jeff sat down in front of Tonya and proudly waved at his parents. "I'm sitting on a dinosaur!" he exclaimed.

Tonya guided L-Scar to the far side of his herd, so she and Jeff could survey the countryside. Using her telepathic powers, Tonya searched the area for T-Rexes and saber-toothed cats. Jeff stared at everything that caught his attention, still not sure that he was riding a dinosaur or just dreaming the whole thing. Tonya hit him with reality when she said, "Look over there! There's a pack of T-Rexes."

"Are they going to attack?" Jeff asked, sounding deathly afraid.

"I don't think so. L-Scar sees them too, and he hasn't bellowed out a warning, so he must think that they're not hungry at the moment. Besides that, they're still a quarter-mile away."

"What are we going to do?"

"I want you to relax and just watch them. I need to test my telepathic powers on T-Rexes, so don't talk to me for a while. I need to focus my mind."

"How close are they going to come?"

"I don't know. Let me see if I can telepathically get into their heads and find out what their intentions are."

At that moment, L-Scar slammed the bony blob at the end of his tail into the ground three times, making a loud boom, boom, boom sound. Four adult males joined him, and the herd came to full alert.

"I guess L-Scar does sense that they might be hungry," commented Tonya. "Or maybe he's just being cautious and wants to be prepared, if an attack does come."

Remembering what Tonya said a few minutes earlier, Jeff's lesson about being cautious was now reinforced. "Even big, fierce animals have to use caution to stay alive," he said.

"In this case, it's justified. T-Rexes are ferocious predators."

"Is L-Scar afraid?"

"I don't sense fear in his mind. I sense confidence. He knows how to fight, and he's big and well equipped. Look at all those horns. Plus, he has a muscular tail with a heavy bony blob near its end. He could easily break a T-Rex's leg with that tail and then finish him off when he's down."

Trying to sound brave, Jeff said, "If L-Scar isn't afraid, I won't be afraid either."

"That's the spirit. Now, let me see if I can get into the T-Rex pack leader's head."

Tonya stared at the big T-Rex in front of the pack and focused her mental powers. Sinking ever more deeply into a trance, she tuned out her surroundings and focused on the big T-Rex. She mentally searched for the energy field surrounding his mind and for the wavelength of his brain waves. Several seconds ticked by before she found it. Tonya telepathically tuned in to the animal's brain and immediately sensed an aura of deception. That pack leader does have an attack plan, noted Tonya. I wonder what it is. It seems like part of the plan is deception. They're acting disinterested in L-Scar's herd. They're marching northward, acting like they're just passing through, but the images in that leader's mind tell a different story. When they're out of sight, they're going to circle back and approach this herd against the wind. Then, they're going to charge over that little hill to the north. Now, I see an image of them isolating a styracosaurus from the rest of the herd. They quickly kill it by overwhelming it with an attack from all directions. These animals definitely have the ability to think when it comes to planning a hunting strategy. But will it work?

I get the feeling L-Scar has been around for a long time. He could not be as old as he seems to be without being savvy to T-Rex hunting tactics.

Tonya proved to be correct. When the T-Rexes disappeared into a forest a half-mile to the north, L-Scar barked out an order, and two of the big bulls next to him walked to the top of the low-lying hill north of his herd. There they alertly watched the forest the T-Rexes had just entered.

"We need to get back to the boat before those T-Rexes come back," Tonya said. "If there is a battle, I don't want to be in the middle of it."

"Will L-Scar take us back to the water when he's worried about T-Rexes?"

"I don't see why not. He has two big bulls on alert. Anyway, T-Rexes live here, and an attack is always possible, so they always have to be alert."

"But can you get him to take us back?"

"Let's find out." Tonya focused her mind and telepathically sent L-Scar an image of him returning to the water. She held the image for several seconds. Eventually, the suggestion had its intended effect. L-Scar looked around for danger and saw none, so he started ambling toward the lake.

"He's taking us back!" Jeff happily exclaimed.

The words were barely out of Jeff's mouth when one of the sentries bellowed out a warning. L-Scar immediately turned to the right and charged to the hilltop, where he was joined by other large bulls.

"The T-Rexes are coming back!" Jeff exclaimed. "And they're running fast. I'm scared. Can Jim shoot them with his rifle?"

"I don't think so. Those low hills along the beach are keeping him from having a shot. Let me try something else."

While the large males formed a defensive line with additional males behind the line, Tonya focused her telepathic powers on the lead T-Rex. She sent him an image of him being cut off from his pack and surrounded by angry styracosaurs that attacked from every direction at once. Tonya poured her total mental energy into the image, and it worked. The T-Rex pack leader became confused. He stopped his charge and that of his pack, coming to a dead stop barely 30 yards away. He defensively spun around checking his surroundings. That's it big guy; you are surrounded, thought Tonya while maintaining the telepathic image. That's the stick, now for the carrot, thought Tonya, while adding an image of a large dead sauropod to the T-Rex's mind. The dead sauropod instantly got the T-Rex's attention. He looked around trying to spot the dead sauropod. Tonya looked east and spotted a rock formation a couple miles away. She added its image to the sauropod image. Within seconds, the big T-Rex spotted the rock formation, and Tonya reinforced the image of a dead sauropod next to it. The big T-Rex roared out a command and headed for the rocks with his pack following.

"The thought of an easy meal was too much for him to resist," Tonya said.

"What do you mean?" Jeff asked.

Tonya explained to Jeff what she had done, and he said, "That's really neat the way you tricked him."

"I enjoyed it."

L-Scar, Tonya, and Jeff watched the T-Rexes rapidly leave the area. Telepathically, Tonya entered L-Scar's mind to see what she might learn. She saw an image of the fleeing T-Rexes, then an image of herself and Jeff. Next, an indistinct image appeared, showing the blonde woman and the bearded man with brown hair, along with an image of fleeing T-Rexes.

Once again, he's comparing me to those people in his past. Apparently, one or both of them had a telepathic ability like mine and were able to mislead T-Rexes and send them on their way. That would be reason enough for L-Scar to like people.

Who was that bearded man and blonde woman? Are they still alive? If so, where are they? Where did they come from? Are they descendants of the ancient cave dwellers?

Growing tired of the silence, Jeff asked, "What are you thinking about?"

"L-Scar remembers a man and a woman, and I don't know who they are, so we have a mystery to solve. We need to get back to the boat, so I can tell everyone about this."

A few minutes later, L-Scar was back in the lake, where Jeff and Tonya slid off his back. Jeff headed for the boat, but Tonya decided to leave a last impression in L-Scar's mind. She telepathically indicated that she was leaving and swam in front of him, where she reached out and scratched his nose. Then, she backed away and started swimming toward the boat. Reading L-Scar's mind, she sensed that he was sad to see her leave.

Jeff arrived at the boat ahead of Tonya, and Rex helped him climb aboard. "I rode a dinosaur!" Jeff exclaimed. "And T-Rexes came, and Tonya tricked them and sent them away, and the T-Rexes were scary, but everything was fun. I want to ride L-Scar again."

303

"Well, I don't know about that," responded Rex. "You might not be so lucky next time."

"What do you mean?"

"What if Tonya wasn't able to trick the T-Rexes into leaving, and they attacked L-Scar's herd?"

"L-Scar and all those big bulls have lots of horns to fight with, and they have tail clubs. I would've been safe."

"The battle would've been a life-and-death struggle, and you might've fallen off and been trampled."

"Maybe I could ride him when there aren't any T-Rexes around."

"Son, you have a lot of determination."

"Is that bad?"

"No, it's good. We just have to channel it in the right direction, so you don't get into situations you're not prepared for."

"You and Mom and Tonya can help me."

"You can count on that."

When Tonya arrived at the boat, Jim reached down, grasped one of her hands, pulled her aboard, and said, "I'm glad to have you back in one piece. You sure have a knack for getting into touchy situations."

Displaying the cocky demeanor of one who had just gotten away with a daring escapade, Tonya flashed Jim a mischievous smile, and said, "I've heard similar words from my father more than once."

"I hope you don't see me as a father figure just because I'm concerned about your safety."

"I'd be disappointed if you weren't concerned, and you can rest assured that I don't see you in fatherly terms." Tonya backed up her words with subtle but unmistakably suggestive body language.

Jim smiled and said, "I like where your mind is at. Hold that thought for later."

"Don't worry, I will. Days like this excite me to no end. I love to face danger and prevail over it."

"I know. You're a jungle girl."

"You'll be surprised by what I learned today."

"I'm not surprised that you got into the heads of the big dinos. I was pretty sure that you would."

"I was pretty sure that I would too, but I made a surprising discovery when I was in L-Scar's mind. There are other people here. At least there were people here not too many years ago."

"What makes you think that?"

"L-Scar compared me to people in his past. I saw an image of Moose in his mind. Also, there was an image of a man with a brown beard and a woman with blonde hair. Moose's image was sharp. The man and woman were indistinct, so I'm assuming that L-Scar encountered them several years ago and had trouble remembering exactly how they looked."

"Either that or he encountered them recently and has a bad memory."

"I don't think he has a bad memory. His mental image of Moose was sharp."

"If you're correct, and L-Scar has a good memory, then he probably encountered those humans early in his life. If we could figure out how old L-Scar is, we could get a pretty good idea when those humans were here."

"I don't know how we're going to determine L-Scar's age. We just don't have much to go on. We know only that he's an adult male still in prime condition."

Turning to Rex, Jim said, "You're a veterinarian. How old do you think L-Scar is?"

"I have no experience with dinosaurs, but on Zebron, we have ten-ton mammals that look like your elephants, and they can live 50 to 60 years. They are prime adults when they are 10 to 30 years old."

"Okay, let's assume L-Scar is 20 to 25 years old. If he encountered those humans early in his adult life, he might be trying to recall an event that happened 10 to 15 years ago."

"That could easily make it a fuzzy memory," commented Tonya. "If they were here ten years ago, where are they now?"

"That's impossible to know," responded Jim. "If they're nomads, they'd only have to hike a mile a day to now be over 3000 miles from here. Four miles a day could put them on the other side of this planet."

"It sounds like you're trying to tell me that finding them will be difficult."

"They could be anywhere. But why do we need to find them?"

"They might be descendants of the people who came here 123,000 years ago on Bule's starship. And Tabor made it quite clear that he wants us to find out what happened to those people."

"Do you seriously think that the bearded man and blonde woman could shed light on such an old mystery?"

"I don't know. We don't even know if they are descendants of the Ancient Ones, but if they are, they might know something.

Legends do sometimes get passed down through the ages. It's called folklore."

"It's going to be hard to find two people, who could be anywhere on this planet."

"How do you know there are only two people?" Tonya asked. "They could be members of a large group."

"We did a thorough recon of Alcent before landing, and we found no evidence of large groups of people."

"That doesn't mean there aren't any. My people were here, and you didn't find us."

"That's because you're a small group, and you were living underground."

"That's my point. There could be people living in caves all over this planet."

"They would have to be widely scattered small groups, or we would've seen some evidence of their existence."

"That's a valid argument, but it doesn't seem likely that the bearded man and blonde woman are alone on this planet. It seems like they must, at least, belong to a small group, and I think we need to locate them."

"How do you propose to do that?"

"Rex and I could do a telepathic search from the Challenger. If there are cave dwellers here, they'll have to come out of their caves to hunt for food, and that's when we'll find them."

"Searching this whole planet for what could be a small group of people sounds more difficult than looking for a needle in a haystack."

"Have you forgotten about all the war survivors that Rex and I found on Zebron?"

"You and Rex do have amazing telepathic powers, but it's a very big planet to be looking for a bearded man and blonde woman."

"I know, but we must find them. I have a strong feeling that they are the key to solving the ancient mystery."

"I respect your intuition, but it's hard to believe that two people living in the present time could know anything about such an old mystery."

"First, we have to find them; then, we'll know if my intuition is correct."

"Where do you want to start looking?"

"I want to try to get into the heads of the big sauropods and see if they have any memories of people. If they do, we'll see what we can learn from them."

"Sauropod Meadow is just a few miles up the coast. That's where the sauropods bed down for the night after coming to the lake to drink. It's late afternoon, so let's head that way."

"Are we going to see more dinosaurs?" Jeff asked.

"We sure are," responded Jim. "And the sauropods are a whole lot bigger than the styracosaurs and T-Rexes."

"Even bigger than L-Scar!" exclaimed Jeff, in disbelief.

"The biggest one is ten times heavier than L-Scar."

"Wow! That's big. Can Tonya and I ride him?"

"Absolutely not! He's so big that you could easily break your neck just falling off of him."

"How long will it take to get there?"

"About a half-hour," responded Jim while hauling in the anchor.

"Sailing is fun. Are we going to use our sail?"

"We're going to use our electric motors. We'll hoist the sail for our return voyage."

"Do you have any pictures of the sauropods?"

Jim handed Jeff a video headset and said, "Put this on, and I'll show you a video of them coming to the lake to drink water."

After watching the video for a couple minutes, Jeff said, "Wow! This is neat. I think they'd be fun to ride."

"You can't do that, but I can give you a pretend ride."

"How are you going to do that?"

"When the herd leader was sleeping, we used an RPV to attach a camera pack to his middle horn. It has three cameras and three microphones. Video and sound are combined in the computer to give you a 3-D illusion that is very realistic. You need to sit down before I show you this, because that big sauropod swings his head around a lot, and you're going to feel like you're sitting on his head. You might get dizzy watching this."

Jeff sat down and said, "I'm ready."

Jim fed video and sound from the computer into Jeff's headset. Jeff immediately experienced the illusion of sitting on the big sauropod's head and started swaying from side to side with the sauropod's head movements. "I feel like I'm riding him!" Jeff exclaimed. "This is wild!"

"What do you see?" Jim asked.

"I see an open meadow and other animals, and the lake is straight ahead. I feel like I'm heading toward the lake."

"Good, that means the sauropods are on the way, because you are watching real-time video. You are looking at what the big sauropod is looking at, and you are hearing what he hears."

"This is fun!" exclaimed Jeff.

Jim handed out additional headsets, so others could enjoy the illusion of sitting on the big sauropod's head. Jeff continued to chatter about what he was seeing and hearing, and everyone wearing a headset joined in.

As the minutes ticked by, Jim piloted the boat northward, staying about 50 yards offshore. When the big sauropods were in view, Jim steered the boat closer to shore.

Still wearing his headset, Jeff exclaimed, "The lake is really close. We're on the beach. I see our boat a little offshore. I see me, and that means the big sauropod is looking at us."

Jeff removed his headset and stared at the big sauropods, totally blown away by their size. "Wow! They are big, they're huge!"

Jeff slipped his headset back on and said, "Now, I see us the way the big guy sees us."

Dropping into a telepathic trance, Tonya searched for the sauropod herd leader's mind and quickly found it. Feeling satisfaction at the achievement, Tonya thought, this is great, now I can probe his memory, but how do I stimulate him to bring memories into his conscious mind where I can see them? I need to find out if he has seen the bearded man and blonde woman. Do I need to go ashore, so he can see me as an individual? Would that stimulate him to recall any memories of humans that he might have? I need to find out.

Tonya stepped to the edge of the deck and prepared to dive in, when Jim grabbed her left arm and said, "I hope you're not planning to go ashore."

"As a matter of fact, I am."

"Do you know how dangerous that is?"

"Yes, I do, but I need to go ashore, so the sauropods can see me as an individual. Hopefully, I can stimulate their memories of people."

"Connie was almost killed by a saber-toothed cat when she and Jerry went ashore here."

"Saber-toothed cats are easy to find telepathically. I've already searched the area, and there aren't any here."

"There might be other predators lurking in those bushes," stated Jim while pointing at them.

"I'm not sensing anything except the sauropods."

"What if one of them decides to attack you?"

"They're not predators."

"An animal doesn't have to be a predator to attack. It merely has to feel threatened."

"That sauropod herd leader might weigh 100 tons. How could such a giant creature possibly feel threatened by me?"

"You make a good point, but we know very little about these animals and how they'll behave toward people."

"Jerry walked under that big herd leader, reached up, and touched his belly. And there was no reaction. The big guy just kept on drinking."

"That's just one encounter. We don't know that there'll be no reaction next time."

"You're right, but I have to try to get him to remember that encounter. Then, I have to see what kind of aura surrounds the memory. If I am successful with that, I will project an image of the bearded man and blonde woman into his mind and see what kind of reaction I get."

"Why can't you do that from here?"

"I will have a better chance to succeed if he can see me as an individual."

"I can see that you're determined to go ashore, so I'm going with you, and we're taking rifles and pistols along."

"Good, two people walking side-by-side on the beach, rather than just me, might be more likely to stimulate a memory of the bearded man and blonde woman."

Jim dropped a tightly packaged inflatable boat into the water and triggered its self-inflation cartridge. In a matter of seconds, the boat fully inflated. Tonya stepped into it, and Jim handed her the rifles and paddles. Jim joined her in the boat, and they rowed it to the beach, landing about 30 yards south of the sauropods.

Alert for danger, Jim got out of the boat and stood on the beach. Holding his rifle in a quick reaction position, he stared at everything in his vicinity. Even though Tonya had told him there weren't any predators in the area, Jim suspected that there were and didn't want to be taken by surprise. What kind of predator could escape discovery by Tonya's keen telepathic powers? Jim wondered. She is good, but I just know danger lurks here. But where is it? And what is it?

Sensing Jim's concern, Tonya asked, "What are you worried about?"

"There is unseen danger here. I can feel it."

"What kind of danger?"

"I don't know. I just feel that we're at grave risk."

"I've telepathically searched this area, and there's nothing here except for the big sauropods."

"I respect your ability, but I sense danger."

"I can see that you really are worried."

"You got that right!"

"Let me see if I can discover anything at all." Years of living in the jungle gave Tonya a finely tuned sense of perception that she now put to use. While firmly gripping her rifle, she visually searched the surrounding area, looking for the slightest unnatural movement in the grasses and bushes. Tonya listened to the sounds coming from her vicinity. She intently searched the area telepathically. After several minutes of fruitless searching, she said, "I'm not finding anything."

"I don't know what it is," stated Jim. "But there is something here. We're in grave danger. We need to do what we came here to do and get out of here."

"Okay, let's walk toward that big sauropod and see if we can stimulate some memories of people in his mind."

Jim looked toward the boat and noted that Rex and Zack were holding rifles and were alertly watching the area. Shannon was filming everything with a video camera. Satisfied that everyone was ready, Jim started walking toward the big sauropod. It stopped drinking and looked toward him.

Tonya telepathically entered the big dinosaur's mind and saw Jim's image there. This is good, noted Tonya. Jim has his attention and I'm not detecting any sense of alarm, only curiosity. Now, how do I get him to remember other people?

"Stop and let me join you," Tonya said to Jim.

Walking quickly, Tonya caught up to Jim, who was swatting at an insect that was buzzing around his face. "You look kind of funny swinging away at a helpless little insect," commented Tonya with a bit of laughter."

"That wasn't a harmless little insect! That was some sort of hornet, and I don't like being stung. I had to chase it away."

Still giggling, Tonya said, "I see some humor in that."

"How so?"

"Here we are, facing a 100-ton dinosaur, and you were just flailing away at a little bug."

"It wasn't little! It was the biggest bee I've ever seen!"

"Hopefully, Shannon has it all on video, so we can take another look at your narrow escape."

Jim silently glared at Tonya while she said, "Your antics did get the full attention of the big sauropod. I see a clear image of both of us in his mind. But he's not comparing us to remembered people like L-Scar did."

"Can you stimulate his memory?"

"I'll try." Tonya telepathically projected an image of Jerry into the big sauropod's mind. Holding it as intensely as she could, she managed to displace the image of her and Jim. After a few moments, she broke off the telepathic transmission and noted that the image of her and Jim reappeared in the big dinosaur's mind.

Tonya telepathically fed the big sauropod an image of the blonde woman and bearded man. She held it until it was the only thing in the sauropod's mind; then, she released it. Again, the image of her and Jim reappeared.

"I'm not getting anywhere," Tonya said. "He's just not recalling any people memories. His mind keeps returning to us."

"What would his mind switch to if we weren't standing here?"

"I can find out on the way home. When we're a mile or two off-shore, I'll hit him with some images of people and see what response I get."

"Let's head for home and try that."

"Are you in a hurry to get out of here?"

"Yes I am. This is a dangerous place to be."

While looking around, Tonya said, "The area seems quite peaceful. Oh! I know what you're worried about. You're afraid that little bug might come back."

Jim ignored Tonya's remark and pointed inland to his right. "That swarm of something just appeared," he said. "It rose up out of the bushes and is coming this way."

"It looks like a very large flock of tiny birds."

"Or large hornets who think they're killer bees!" exclaimed Jim. "We need to get out of here right now!"

Not waiting for her to argue, Jim grabbed one of Tonya's hands and took off running toward the boat. Pushing the boat into the water, he and Tonya hopped in and furiously paddled the boat toward the submarine. While en route, Jim yelled, "Everyone below deck right now!"

Rex wasn't sure what the urgency was all about, but he immediately started hustling the children through the hatch and into the sub's interior. When he finished getting them to safety, he grabbed the binoculars and focused on the approaching swarm, which was only 50 yards away. "They are large hornets," he exclaimed to Jim and Tonya, who had just arrived.

While tying the boat to the sub, Jim felt a sting on his neck. "Ouch!" he exclaimed. "Some are already here, and their sting hurts like hell!"

Everyone quickly dropped into the sub's interior. Unfortunately, several of the hornets joined them before Jim could get the hatch closed. All of the hornets attacked Jim, but his friends quickly slapped them senseless. Jim suffered nine stings before all of the hornets could be killed. "Their venom is very painful," he said. "It leaves a hot burning sensation."

Being a veterinarian, Rex decided to treat Jim as a poison victim. He opened the sub's medical cabinet and grabbed a scalpel. "This is going to hurt," he said to Jim, "but you're going to have to grit your teeth and bear it. I have to get as much of the poison out of you as I can, because we don't know what it is, and it could be lethal."

Rex quickly made a small X-shaped incision through each sting, and Tonya suctioned each wound with a suction device. Before they finished, Jim said, "I'm feeling lightheaded, almost like I'm drunk."

Rex called Doctor Connie and explained the situation. "There's a bee sting antidote in the medicine cabinet that you can administer," she said. "Unfortunately, we don't know if it'll work, because it was developed to counter the venom made by bees on Earth, and we don't know what kind of poison these hornets make."

"We need to try it. Tell me where in the cabinet it is and how much to inject."

Connie gave Rex explicit instructions on how to treat Jim, concluding with, "You need to get him back here as quickly as possible, so I can check him out in the medical lab."

Having overheard Connie's request, Jim hoisted the anchor and plotted the return voyage in the sub's navigation computer. He put the sub on autopilot so its navigation computer would return it to South

Bay. With the electric motors running at full power, the return voyage would take less than an hour.

Rex stayed in communication with Connie, while continuing his treatment of Jim, who was steadily weakening. "I don't like the way his condition is deteriorating," Connie said. "I need him back here sooner than the boat can get him here. Jerry and Mike are on the way with the helicopter. Jerry will bring Jim back, and Mike will stay with the sub."

"Thanks," replied Jim who overheard the message. "I'm starting to feel pretty woozy. I might be losing consciousness."

"Rex and I'll pull you through this, and Jerry will be there shortly. Just hang on."

Speaking to Rex, Connie said, "If you have any dead hornets lying around, I need them. Hopefully, I can get enough venom out of them for the automated lab to analyze. I need to find out what kind of poisons are in that venom, so I can determine the best treatment."

"We killed several that we can send you. Also, there are thousands outside. If it weren't so dangerous, we could try to capture some of them."

"No, don't do that."

"When the chopper arrives, the rotor downwash is going to blow them away," stated Jim. "Some will be in the lake trying to avoid drowning. We could pick up some of them."

"Great idea, I can get ample venom out of them."

"It sounds like the chopper's here," stated Jim. "And I feel like I'm going to pass out."

"Hang on," Connie said. "You'll be here in a few minutes, and I will pull you through this."

"We're here," announced Jerry through the communicator. "It's safe to come out. We've blown away your hornets."

Jim stopped the electric motors and opened the hatch. With a boost from Zack and Rex, he weakly climbed out. Zack and Rex helped Jim into the inflated boat. Deeply worried about Jim, Tonya also stepped into the boat. While Zack rowed it to the helicopter, which had landed on its pontoons, Tonya picked several hornets out of the water, put them in a jar, and closed the lid. Mike pulled Jim aboard the helicopter, and then stepped into the boat. Tonya quickly scrambled aboard. Mike rowed away from the helicopter. When he was at a safe distance, Jerry took off.

A few minutes later, Jerry landed near the medical lab on Pioneer Island. Jim was unconscious and had to be carried into the lab. Connie immediately started intensive care procedures while Dianne milked venom from several dead hornets and entered it into the automated lab.

Tonya telepathically entered Jim's mind, so she could feed mental energy into his brain. What she found was totally unexpected. It was a shocking surprise. Jim was hallucinating, or so it seemed. It wasn't the fact that Jim seemed to be hallucinating that shocked Tonya; rather, it was the clear image in the hallucination that blew her away. The scene was a sandy beach, where a bearded man and blonde woman were talking to each other. The dialog was in the language of the Ancient Ones and Tonya understood it clearly. I guess Tabor dumped an understanding of that language into my brain Tonya concluded. But where is this scene coming from? Is it real or is Jim just dreaming? It has to be real because Jim doesn't know the Ancient One's language and cannot dream in that language. But Jim doesn't have telepathic powers, so how can he be picking this up? The hornet venom must contain a powerful drug that has triggered a latent telepathic ability in Jim's brain. If this scene is real, then the bearded man and blonde woman have to be nearby, because telepathic communication is a line-of-sight thing. But how come I'm not picking this up? My telepathic powers are very good. What would that hornet venom do to my powers? I might have to try it. Apparently, it's not lethal to humans in the amount that's in Jim. Except for being in a deep state of unconsciousness, his physical well-being seems to be normal. I wonder how long he'll be unconscious. When he regains consciousness, will he still be able to detect the bearded man and blonde woman? Will he remember any of this? Maybe not, so I need to see if there's anything about that beach that will help us identify it in the Challenger's data base.

After studying the images in Jim's mind for a few minutes, Tonya concluded: There's nothing unique about that beach. It's just sand backed by forest. That beach could be anywhere. There must be something in these images that would narrow down our search. This is late afternoon, and Alpha Centauri A is low in the western sky. There is a bright glare off the water, which means this beach could be on the west side of an island or on the eastern shore of this lake. Also, the beach is not next to a grassy meadow; it's next to a forest.

Tonya's intense scrutiny of the scene was interrupted by the blonde woman who turned to the man and asked, "How long are we going to stay out of sight?"

"What do you mean?" he asked.

"There are interstellar travelers here. We should meet them."

"How do you know we can trust them to not take advantage of us?"

"We don't know, but we've been alone for a very long time, and I would enjoy having some company."

"How are we going to visit with people who don't understand our language?"

"It would take time, but we could teach them our language, or we could learn theirs."

"I think we need to observe them longer to make sure we can trust them."

"They might discover us while we're watching them. I think it would be better to just reveal our presence at a time and place of our choosing."

"If we're careful, they won't spot us. We're never out in the open when they're around, and we've been shielding our thoughts, so they can't telepathically discover us."

So that's it! Tonya silently exclaimed to herself. I can't telepathically detect them because of a mental shield they've built around their thoughts. But some kind of drug has apparently triggered a latent telepathic ability in Jim's brain and has also made his brain hypersensitive to the telepathic medium, so that their shield isn't working as far as Jim is concerned.

That bearded man's suspicions toward us might be the opening I need to find them. If they're watching us and are trying to learn about us, that means they have to be nearby, maybe on the next island north of us or on the next island south of us. What if I were to go to those islands and wander the western beaches? What if my thoughts were in their language and they telepathically detected my thoughts? Wouldn't that get their attention? If I go there alone, they could hardly feel threatened. Maybe they'll reveal themselves.

The problem is they might not be on one of those islands. They could just as easily be on the eastern shore of Clear Lake. From there, they could see our shuttles come and go, and they could telepathically spy on us. They couldn't understand the language our thoughts are in, but they could pick up our moods and see the images in our minds.

Tonya returned to studying the beach images in Jim's mind, which were coming from the minds of the blonde woman and bearded man. In frustration, Tonya silently exclaimed to herself: Darn it! I wish I could tell where that beach is. Maybe I can get them to tell me.

Facing in the direction of the next island north of Pioneer Island, Tonya telepathically directed a message toward it in the language of the ancient one's: Who are you? Where are you? Talk to me! Looking at the images of the bearded man and blonde woman in Jim's mind, Tonya saw no reaction. Facing in the direction of the next island south of Pioneer Island, Tonya repeated her message and received no reaction.

There is a stretch of beach a couple miles south of L-Scar's herd that looks like this, noted Tonya, and there was an image in L-Scar's brain indicating he has seen these people. Maybe they're living over there. Facing in that direction, Tonya repeated her telepathic message with as much mental power as she could muster. Looking at the images of the bearded man and blonde woman in Jim's mind, Tonya saw an immediate reaction. "Did you hear that?" the man asked the woman.

"Yes! Where did it come from? It was in our language. But how could it be? We are alone."

Aha! Tonya silently exclaimed to herself. I now know where you are.

Tonya decided to quickly hit them with another message, "I will be on your beach tomorrow morning. You can come out of the forest and talk to me, or you can stay hidden. It's your choice."

"Somehow, we've been discovered," the bearded man said to the blonde woman.

"We have a decision to make," she responded. "I say we meet them."

"Let's talk about this and think it over," responded the man as the couple disappeared into the forest.

Before breaking telepathic contact with Jim, Tonya hypnotically planted a suggestion into his mind: you are going to regain consciousness, and you are going to remember these people and the setting. Tonya repeated the message several times until she was sure that it was firmly imbedded in Jim's mind; then, she broke telepathic contact.

Speaking to Connie, Tonya asked, "How long is he going to be out?"

"I don't know, but I'm guessing he'll wake up in a couple hours."

"How much danger is he in?"

"That hornet venom is a potent hallucinogenic drug, and it looks like Jim received enough stings to be fatal. But you and Rex quickly removed much of the venom, so Jim should fully recover."

"That means Rex's quick action saved Jim's life."

"I believe so."

"How will I ever thank him for that?"

"Maybe he just found a way to thank you for rescuing him and his family."

"That might be, but I'm going to thank him anyway."

Jerry had been silently watching the women work on Jim, but with Connie's prognosis that Jim would come out of it, Jerry faced Tonya and said, "Tell me about the hornets."

Tonya told Jerry how the attack happened. Then, Jerry asked Dianne, "What can you tell me about these things?"

While displaying a dead hornet on a plate, Dianne said, "These things are capable of being very nasty. Notice how big it is. The wingspan is nearly three inches. The venom is deadly, and they're big enough to deliver a large dose in just one sting, let alone hundreds of stings."

Handing Jerry a magnifying glass, Dianne said, "Take a look at its mouth. It looks like it was designed to bite a piece of flesh out of its victim."

"Are you suggesting that these things are carnivorous?" Jerry asked.

"It sure looks that way."

"Jim is missing a tiny piece of flesh next to each one of the stings," stated Connie.

"This is frightening!" exclaimed Tonya. "The swarm that came after us was huge. We barely escaped with our lives, and I'm sorry to say that I did tease Jim about his narrow escape from the little bug that he was swatting at."

"You were very fortunate," stated Dianne. "An attack by a swarm of these things would be similar to an attack by a school of piranhas. Maybe even worse, these things could sting you to death, and then eat you at their leisure. Bite-by-bite, they could even carry you back to their nest."

Tonya shuddered and said, "That approaching swarm was like a scene out of a horror movie. How do we defend against such an attack?"

"Firing smoke bombs into an approaching swarm might deter them," commented Jerry. "If we could come up with a chemical

317

smoke that would be toxic to them, it would be even better. We might also design a smoke bomb that releases lots of heat."

"We have to perfect a defense," stated Tonya. "I felt helpless when that swarm was approaching. All we could do was run."

"It's fortunate that you had the sub to retreat to," Jerry said.

"Most of the time, we're not going to have a place to retreat to," Tonya said. "So how do we avoid being attacked? It's important to note that Jim was the only one who was attacked. Did that happen because the hornet he swatted at identified him as an enemy? But how could one little insect arouse an entire swarm to come out and attack Jim? Are these things always that aggressive toward a perceived enemy?"

"Killer bees are," stated Dianne.

"How did the swarm know who to attack? Why didn't they attack me?"

"Scent is a big thing in the animal world," responded Dianne. "The hornet Jim swatted at could've picked up Jim's unique scent and communicated that to the swarm."

"What you're saying is we shouldn't swat at one of these things unless we're going to kill it," stated Tonya.

"That's right," agreed Dianne. "But most of the time, their scouts are probably out looking for food, rather than enemies. So if one of these hornets is showing a lot of interest in you, you'd better not let it fly back to its nest. You could end up on their dinner plate."

"These things are worse than Earth's killer bees," stated Connie. "They're bigger, carry deadlier venom, and are capable of eating their victims. If a colony of them ever takes up residence here on Pioneer Island, we'll have no choice but to exterminate them."

"You're right about that," agreed Jerry while looking at the hornet's mouth. "A large swarm of these things could strip a child down to its skeleton in a few minutes. We need an ironclad way to prevent that from ever happening."

"Prevention starts with education," Dianne said. "We have enough dead hornets, so that we can show everyone what they look like, and I will get that done."

"Thank you," Jerry said.

"There's something else we need to talk about," Tonya said, while making eye contact with everyone. To build their anticipation, Tonya paused for a few moments; then, she said, "There's a bearded man and a blonde woman living on the eastern shore of Clear Lake, and they speak the language of the Ancient Ones."

Everyone reacted to Tonya's announcement with a wide-eyed expression of surprise. Jerry was the first to speak. "How do you know that?" he asked. "Have you seen them?"

"Only indirectly."

"What do you mean by that?"

Starting with the memories in L-Scar's mind and ending with the images in Jim's mind, Tonya told the entire story about the blonde woman and the bearded man. When she finished, Jerry said, "This planet sure is full of surprises. I wonder what's coming next. What makes your story so incredible is that you believe these people are living where there are T-Rexes, saber-toothed cats, killer hornets, and who knows what else. How do they stay alive? What's their secret? We have to meet them and find out how they do it."

"Does that mean you're taking me over there tomorrow morning?" Tonya asked.

"Most definitely! Rex will come with us. If Jim is awake and feeling good, he will also make the trip."

"You need a doctor on the crew," suggested Connie. "It's always possible something will happen that will require immediate medical attention."

"Are you volunteering for the job?"

"Yes!"

"Good! We'll set sail at 8:30 AM.

Chapter Fourteen

TIME: Day 90, 7:45 AM

Jerry and Connie were alone onboard the submarine, which was anchored in South Bay. They had awoken early and wanted to enjoy some early morning solitude.

"What a quiet, peaceful morning," commented Connie after letting her gaze meander around South Bay. "I remember how noisy it was in the city I grew up in. Here, I have the sound of waves washing the beach, the breeze rustling through the forest, and the chirping of birds."

"You forgot to mention the seagulls," stated Jerry while two of them flew over and let out their wailing cries.

"Their loud screeches can sure disrupt a peaceful morning."

"That's true, but I enjoy having them around."

At that moment, King and Queen passed over at an altitude of 300 feet. "Those pterodactyls still amaze me," Connie said. "I love to watch them fly. It's amazing that such large creatures can be so graceful in flight."

"They are big. King's wingspan is 52 feet, and Queen's only a little smaller. Every time I see them fly over, I'm reminded that we live on a dinosaur planet."

"As if we need a reminder," Connie said.

"Sometimes I do. I tend to get caught up in the peaceful life we have here on the island. The dinosaurs are out-of-sight and out-of-mind. But pterodactyls soaring around bring me back to reality."

"Not to change the subject, but I wonder how Jim is feeling this morning."

"You're the doctor. Would you care to throw out an opinion?"

"When Jim regained consciousness last night, he was fully alert. It seems like the hornet venom sharpened his senses. I wanted to keep him in the lab, but he insisted on going home. I couldn't find any medical reason to keep him, so I let him go."

"I'll bet Tonya was happy with his recovery."

"She was elated and promised that she would never again rib him about having a narrow escape from a little bug. They were hanging onto each other when they left, so I think they had a good night celebrating Jim's recovery."

"That means Jim might be feeling pretty good this morning," commented Jerry while smiling.

While radiating a romantic glow, Connie said, "You might be right about that. There's nothing like a little bedroom activity to lift one's spirits."

"Is that a medical opinion?"

"No, it's an opinion based on our love life."

"Does that mean you agree with me that Jim might be feeling pretty good this morning?"

"I think so; unless the drug in the venom has a delayed hung-over effect, which is possible."

"Jim should be here shortly, so we'll find out if he's back to normal."

"Even if he's not, there's no way we could keep him off this voyage. When he came to last night, he just simply would not stop talking about his vivid dreams. He's convinced that the bearded man and blonde woman exist, and he wants to meet them."

"We aren't going to meet them; unless, they want to meet us. The forest is evidently their home, and we would have a hard time finding them on their turf."

"Tonya thinks they'll come to the beach to meet us."

"Why?"

"The blonde woman wants to meet us. The man is hesitant, but Tonya thinks the woman will convince him to meet us."

"If she's right, this could prove to be a very interesting meeting. It's the kind of thing Zack is interested in. I wonder why he doesn't want to go with us."

"As if you don't know," commented Connie. "He's excited about Akeyco driving him around the island."

Grinning from ear-to-ear, Jerry said, "So you're telling me that he's going to let a little romance get in the way of meeting the forest people. What's wrong with his priorities?"

"There's nothing wrong with his priorities, and you know it, but they're not going to be alone today. Shannon, Kristy, and Jeff want to tour our island too. Since they're family, Zack could hardly object."

"Extra people in the ATV should not keep a budding romance from growing," commented Jerry.

"You're right about that; if there's chemistry between them, it will catch fire. Love always finds a way."

"I think I'll keep an eye on them this evening," Jerry said. "Maybe I'll be able to pick up some clues as to how their day went."

"You're not planning to spy on them are you?"

"I'm not going to be obvious about it, but we're giving Denise a birthday party on the beach, and they'll be there. It should be interesting to see how they behave toward each other."

"Okay, I'm game for that."

"I thought you didn't want to spy on them."

"This won't be spying," argued Connie. "We'll all be at the same party. Besides, I love a good romance. I hope there is chemistry between them that catches fire."

"You're just a hopeless romantic."

"Judging from the way you're talking, I'll have to guess that you are too."

"Romance has been good to us."

"It's been great," whispered Connie while giving Jerry a hug.

After the hug, Jerry and Connie soaked up the sights and sounds of South Bay, each lost in thought while enjoying the peaceful setting. Several minutes passed by before the solitude was broken by the arrival of Rex, Jim, and Tonya.

"How are you feeling this morning?" Connie asked Jim.

"I have some sore spots that are slightly swollen. Otherwise, I feel great. I'm actually in a state of euphoria. First, the dreams, and now this unnatural high; am I still under the influence of the hornet venom?"

"Apparently, you are."

"What am I going to feel like after it wears off?"

"I don't know. What are you worried about?"

"This stuff is really powerful. I just hope it's not like an addictive drug. I don't want to suffer withdrawal symptoms and an intense craving for more."

"If that happens, I'll help you deal with it."

"Thanks, I appreciate that."

"We need an effective antidote for that venom," stated Jerry.

"Dianne and Geniya are working on that," responded Connie.

"This planet is sure full of surprises," Jerry said. "Yesterday, we discovered a small, but very dangerous enemy. And that enemy led to the discovery of evidence that there might be people living in the countryside. And that's almost unbelievable. How could they possibly survive over there?"

"Let's go meet them and find out," suggested Jim while untying one of the ropes securing the sub to the dock.

"You sound convinced that they want to meet us," responded Jerry while untying the other rope.

"I believe they do."

"Why?"

"Just a feeling I have."

"In a couple hours, we'll find out how valid your feeling is."

Using battery power, Jerry pulled away from the dock and piloted the boat out of South Bay. Turning the boat to the east, he said, "We're going to sail to L-Scar's stomping grounds and then turn south. Hopefully, you'll recognize the scene that was in your vision last night. Then, we can use RPVs to search the area for bearded men and blonde women."

"I only saw one of each," responded Jim.

"I know, but it's highly unlikely that there are only two people living over there. The people you saw have to be part of a group."

"I don't think so," stated Tonya. "I heard the blonde say, 'we've been alone for a long time'. She also said she would enjoy some company."

Sounding skeptical, Jerry asked, "How do you know that's what she said? They're aliens. How could you possibly understand their language?"

"They spoke in the language of the Ancient Ones."

"We don't know that language. How were you able to understand it?"

"My understanding of that language must've come from Tabor when I was in the secret cave room back on Zebron."

"I was there too, but my conversation with him was in English."

"He must've pulled an understanding of English out of my brain and put an understanding of his language into my brain."

"It's really scary that they have the technology to do that at all, let alone, across 60 light-years of space. Who knows what else they've programmed into your mind, or my mind, or Rex's mind."

After a few moments of silence, Jerry asked Tonya, "When did you first become aware that you could understand the language of the Ancient Ones?"

"When I heard it being used by the bearded man and blonde woman."

"And that conversation was going on in Jim's mind?"

"I telepathically tuned in to Jim's mind, and his mind telepathically detected the bearded man and blonde woman talking to each other. I recognized their language as that of the Ancient Ones, and I understood it clearly."

"Prior to that time, you had no clue that you could understand that language?"

"That's right."

"So it was hearing that language that triggered your brain to make you aware that you could understand it?"

"That's what it looks like."

"What worries me about this is I'm wondering what other things Tabor put in your mind and what will trigger them into awareness. We could end up being his robots if he has programmed our brains to react to certain things in certain ways."

"You were concerned about that possibility shortly after coming out of that secret cave room back on Zebron," noted Tonya.

"And now we have an example that validates my concerns, and it's no small thing. If Tabor could instill an understanding of a language into your brain, which is a major feat, it seems he could've put just about anything into our minds."

Facing Jerry, Connie said, "It sounds like you're worried that Tabor might have some sinister plan to do us harm."

"That's right, and since we don't know what it is, it's going to be hard to defend against."

"But he's 60 light-years away. Why would he want to harm us? What could he possibly gain?"

"I don't know, but the possibilities are ominous, and we can't take them lightly."

"So far, the only thing we have is Tonya's understanding of the Ancient Ones' language, and that's a good thing that might help us solve the ancient mystery. As far as we know, that's all Tabor wants."

"I have no evidence that he has some other objective; I'm just suspicious."

"When dealing with the unknown, being suspicious is healthy, but I think we should take a break from being suspicious and enjoy this day."

"Is that medical advice or wifely advice?"

"Maybe a little of both."

"Okay, let's do some sailing."

In just a few minutes, Jerry and Jim had the outriggers and sails deployed and the electric motor turned off. A gentle breeze out of the north filled the sails and propelled the boat at only three mph.

"This wind isn't strong enough to give us much speed," Jerry said. "So let's lay out our solar sails and make some electricity."

After the solar sails were deployed, Jerry said, "Even though Alpha Centauri A is still low in the sky, we're getting enough electricity to more than double our speed without using the batteries."

"Good," stated Jim. "We'll be there in just over an hour."

While looking at the distant countryside on the east side of Clear Lake, Connie said, "That means I have an hour to enjoy the lake before we start searching for the mystery couple."

"We won't have to search for them," Tonya said. "They're going to come out of the forest to meet us."

"You don't think they're going to check us out first?" questioned Jerry.

"I suspect that they're already watching us."

"How?"

"There's a seagull perched on top of the mast that seems very interested in us. I believe that bird is being telepathically controlled by the mystery couple and that they're using its eyes to observe us."

"Can their telepathic powers possibly be that good?"

"I think so. I don't know how else they could survive in the countryside other than to use the eyes and ears of animals to scout their surroundings. I've sometimes done that."

"But that doesn't mean that this gull is under the control of the blonde or the man. I've seen gulls on our mast before, and they're always curious about us."

"Maybe that bearded man and his companion have been using gulls to keep an eye on you from day one. If so, they know you quite well by now. And that's why we aren't going to have to search for them. They know you well enough to trust you, and they are going to come out of the forest to meet us."

Jerry thought about Tonya's remarks and tried to recall all the times that a curious gull had been hanging around. Finally, he said, "You could be right. And to think, I never suspected that we were being spied on."

"Will our lives ever stop being full of surprises?" Connie asked.

"I hope not," replied Jerry. "Surprises keep our lives interesting."

"I know, but some day, I'd like to think that we have a good understanding of our new home here on Alcent."

"A good understanding will come, but surprising new discoveries will always be part of our lives. Jim's telepathic ability while under the influence of a drug in the hornet venom is an even bigger surprise than the forest people." Turning to Jim, Jerry asked, "Do you still have that telepathic ability?"

"It seems to have gone away."

"It sounds like you're not sure."

"I'm not telepathically detecting anything, but it's possible that I still have telepathic ability and just don't know how to use it. A drug in the venom may've been nothing more than a switching device that just turned on an ability that I've had all my life."

"Or there might be a chemical in the hornet venom that the brain needs to engage in telepathic activity," stated Rex. "For those of us who have telepathic ability, our bodies may be making that chemical naturally. People who don't have telepathic ability might just be lacking the ability to make the required chemical."

"We might have here an opportunity to discover why some people have telepathic ability and some don't," Jerry said. "And we may discover how to give telepathic ability to all of us."

"It's amazing that all of this might happen simply because I got stung by a few hornets," commented Jim.

"That would not be unusual," stated Connie. "Over the ages, many scientific discoveries have happened by chance or accident. You getting stung just might turn out to be a key event in our history. Dianne and Geniya are doing a detailed study of that venom. We'll find out exactly what it is and go from there."

"There's another possibility we need to think about," commented Rex. "Let's assume that the hornet venom does contain a chemical that makes telepathic communication possible. Since the hornets are making the chemical, they might be in telepathic communication with each other. That would enable thousands of them to act as a single entity, which would explain why only Jim was attacked. They weren't acting as individual insects; they were acting as a single creature with many parts."

"That's a scary possibility," stated Jerry. "Tens of thousands of these things acting as a single creature would make them a giant enemy far more dangerous than a pack of T-Rexes, which can be killed with rifles. But how do you fight these things?"

"I think I have the answer," responded Tonya. "If telepathic communication enables them to act as a single creature, then we might be able to use telepathic signals against them. It should be possible to confuse them, scatter them, and maybe even make them retreat in fear."

"If that works, it could be a very effective defense," stated Connie. "I watched Zeb bring a charging bear to a dead stop by telepathically making the animal think it was charging a T-Rex. But what kind of telepathic signal would you transmit into a swarm of hornets to make them retreat in fear?"

"I don't know," replied Tonya. "I'll have to experiment with that to find out if I can make them flee."

"I don't like that idea," stated Jim. "You could end up getting killed."

"We should be able to set up an experiment; wherein, I am protected while I hit them with a range of telepathic signals."

"We're getting ahead of ourselves," commented Connie. "First, we have to identify the chemicals in the venom, and then determine if one of them makes telepathic communication possible."

"I don't think it's necessary to do that research first," countered Tonya. "Because no matter how it turns out, I need to find out if I can telepathically influence those hornets. If I am successful, we'll have a potent defense against them."

Speaking to Connie, Jerry said, "Sorry honey, but Tonya's right on this one. We can do her experiment and the lab work at the same time. We need to discover a defense as quickly as possible."

Connie nodded and said, "I will call Dianne and bring her up to date."

Speaking to Rex, Tonya said, "Let's discuss telepathic techniques and see if we can figure out what might work against these hornets."

Turning to Jim, Jerry said, "Everyone else is busy, so I guess we're stuck with the responsibility of sailing this boat."

"That's a tough break," responded Jim with a broad grin. "We'll just have to deal with it as best we can."

"I'll keep the helm for a while, so you can rest up."

"Okay, but if it gets too stressful for you, just let me know, and I'll take over. I want to make sure that I shoulder my share of the responsibility."

"You got it, but whatever you do, just make sure you conduct yourself in a professional manner, so we can impress that seagull up there, just in case the forest people are using it to spy on us."

"How do you impress a seagull?" Jim asked. "Or I guess I should say, how do we impress the forest people?"

"I don't know, but we need to convince them that we aren't a threat to them, so they'll come out of the forest to meet us."

"How do we do that when all they can do is observe our behavior through the eyes of that seagull? It won't do them any good to listen to us with that gull's ears because they can't possibly understand English."

"Tonya understands the Ancient Ones' language," stated Jerry. "She could try reaching them by speaking to that gull in their language, or she could try direct telepathic contact."

"If anyone could talk to a gull, Tonya could," Jim said. "I've seen her call wild parrots down out of a tree and have them land on her outstretched arm."

"It comes down to a question of timing. When do we have Tonya attempt contact? Do we do that now? Or do we wait until we're sailing south along the east coast?"

"I think we should wait until the forest people can see us and size us up. It'll be easier for them to judge that we are trustworthy."

"Thanks to that seagull, they might already be watching us."

"Or they might not. When sailing along the coast, they could watch us while hiding in the forest. And I think that's the best time for us to attempt contact."

"I think you're right," stated Jerry, "so we'll wait until then. Who knows, they might contact us first."

An hour later, as the boat approached the east coast; Tonya pointed inland and said, "There's L-Scar's herd."

"That was quite a stunt you pulled off yesterday when you climbed on L-Scar's back and rode him," commented Jim.

"Yeah, I know, but it was fun. And it was in L-Scar's mind that I discovered images of a bearded man and a blonde woman. And now we have reason to believe that they might be living in that forest to the south, so let's go find them."

"That almost sounds like a direct command," stated Jim, who was on the helm.

"I'm a little jacked up at the moment," responded Tonya with a smile. "I'm excited about finding these people. I sense that they're going to have a major effect on our lives."

"That means it's time to be on guard."

"Why?" Tonya asked.

"Because what you sense usually happens, and it could be bad news."

"You're not innocent either," stated Tonya. "Yesterday, you sensed great danger, even when I couldn't find any. And the danger showed up in the form of a little bug."

"I've learned to pay attention when my inner voice is screaming at me, and you do too. So what kind of impact do you think these forest people are going to have on us?" Jim asked.

"I don't know. I just sense that they're going to hit us with some unbelievable news, and that they're going to have a major impact on our lives. We need to find them."

"As you can see, we're sailing south, and we're close to shore. Now, we have to find that rather indistinct piece of forest that was in my vision yesterday."

"I'll help you look for it. Maybe I can spot it. There has to be something about it that we can recognize."

Speaking to Tonya and Jim, Jerry said, "While you two are doing that, I'll fly an RPV down the beach. Maybe I can find a human footprint or some other evidence of their presence."

Handing Rex an RPV, Jerry said, "I want you to look around in the forest."

"That will be interesting," responded Rex. "I can compare what I see to life back on Zebron. Who knows, I might even find some human life."

"That's the objective," stated Jerry as he turned to Connie to assign her a task. But she beat him to the punch by saying, "I'm having fun exploring the countryside with these binoculars."

"Let me know if you find anything that might indicate a human presence."

"You can count on it."

The sailboat headed south along the east coast of Clear Lake at a steady speed of five mph. An hour passed by with nothing of consequence discovered. While approaching the mouth of a river, Rex said to Jerry, "That's a fairly large river. Have you ever explored it?"

"Not yet, but it's on our list of things to do. There's a huge countryside surrounding Clear Lake that we need to explore. But we've only been here three months, and we're just getting started with exploring the place."

"If we could find a safe way to do it, I'd love to lead an exploration party up that river," Rex said.

"We have detailed images of this entire area that were taken from the Challenger. Those images might be helpful in planning an exploration trip."

"I'll take a look at them, and see what kind of trip I can put together. When it comes to getting acquainted with life, you just can't beat an on-foot exploration party."

"It's going to be a long hike. This river originates in the mountains 50 miles to the east and is fed by snowmelt in the summertime."

"It might be a long hike, but it will be interesting. Just think of the variation in life from the lowlands around this lake to the alpine meadows in the mountains."

"We need to find the bearded man and blonde woman," stated Tonya. "They may've already explored this river. They could be your guides and keep you out of trouble."

"That would be great," responded Rex.

"I have a feeling we're going to find them in this area," stated Jim. "This river just looks like a place where forest people might like to live."

While looking up the river with binoculars, Connie said, "I see a pair of pterodactyls coming this way. They're just gliding along, gradually losing altitude as they get closer to the river."

Jerry grabbed a rifle and said, "I hope they're not planning to attack us."

"I don't think so. It looks like there are people on their backs. They're still too far away to be sure, but it looks like a human is lying facedown on the back of each pterodactyl. One of them appears to have blonde hair and the other appears to have brown hair. They might be the people we came here to meet."

Connie handed the binoculars to Jerry and said, "You should put down your rifle. If these people are using that seagull to watch us, they're probably not going to come within rifle range if they feel threatened."

Jerry put the gun back in its case but left it unlatched, so he could get to it quickly. With the binoculars, he looked at the pterodactyls, which were now much closer because they were approaching at 60 mph. "You're right," he said. "There is a blonde on one and a bearded man on the other."

Turning to Tonya, Jerry said, "Try making contact."

Tonya focused her telepathic energy on the incoming pterodactyls. In the language of the Ancient Ones, she said, "I am Tonya. Who are you? What do you want with us?"

"I am Bule," responded the bearded man. "My wife's name is Selene. We wish to visit with you."

"We'll meet you on the beach."

"Let us check it out first. Many dangerous animals live in this area."

"Okay, contact us when you're ready."

Speaking to everyone on the boat, Tonya said, "The man's name is Bule. His wife's name is Selene. They want to meet with us, but they want to check out the area before we go ashore."

"We also need to check out that forest with our RPVs," stated Jerry.

While Rex and Jerry snooped around in the forest with RPVs, Bule and Selene made several passes with their well trained pterodactyls. Bule and Selene telepathically searched the forest for predators while their pterodactyls searched with their sharp eyesight and sense of smell.

When Bule and Selene were satisfied that there were no predators present, their pterodactyls glided to a landing on the beach. They quickly released the straps that secured them to the backs of their pterodactyls and slid off of them.

Standing straight and tall between their pterodactyls, Bule and Selene faced the sailboat anchored a short distance offshore. They watched Jerry, Rex, and Tonya step into a small inflated boat and row it to shore.

Tonya stepped out of the boat and approached Bule and Selene with Rex and Jerry on either side of her. The trio stopped a couple yards short of Bule and Selene. Everyone made eye contact to size each other up. Tonya was first to speak. She smiled and in the language of the Ancient Ones, she said, "I am Tonya." Motioning toward Jerry, she said, "This is Jerry Jerontis, Captain of the Starship Challenger, which has come here from Earth." Motioning toward Rex, she said, "This is Rex. He is from Zebron."

Bule and Selene made eye contact with each person as they were introduced. Then, Bule said, "I am Bule, and this is my wife Selene. We've been alone for a long time, and we are happy to meet you."

Even though Bule spoke in the language of the Ancient Ones, Rex and Jerry understood him clearly. Both surmised that Tabor programmed their minds to understand the ancient language. Jerry was totally surprised to find himself speaking to Bule in this language. "We're having a beach party tonight on Pioneer Island. You're welcome to join us."

Before Bule could say anything, Selene said, "We accept your invitation."

"Would you like us to fly in?" Bule asked.

"You're welcome to do that, or you can sail back with us on our boat. It's your choice."

Speaking to Bule, Selene said, "Let's join them on the boat, so we can visit with them."

"I guess that decides it," Bule said to Jerry.

"We'll set sail as soon as you're ready," responded Jerry.

"We need to release our pterodactyls," stated Bule as he turned to his bird and removed his saddle. Selene did the same. Both spoke to their birds, which then ran down the beach, spread their wings, and took off.

"How do you get them to come back when you need them?" Rex asked.

"We contact them telepathically," responded Bule.

"I suspected as much, but do they always do your bidding?"

"We have a good working relationship with them. They are as devoted to us as a well trained dog is to its master."

"I can see some big benefits to such a relationship."

"We depend on them for many things. As you can see, they are circling this area watching for dangerous animals."

As if to back up Bule's claim, one of the pterodactyls passed by at low altitude and let out a couple screeching cries. "They've spotted a pair of saber-toothed cats," stated Bule. "The cats are south of us, so they do have our scent."

"How did you determine all of that from his warning screeches?" Jerry asked.

"The loud cries were meant to get my attention. After that, I telepathically read his mind. We need to leave, because the cats are coming this way."

A couple minutes later, the cats arrived, but everyone was onboard the sailboat and heading away from shore. However, the cats were hungry and did not give up. They charged toward the water, leapt far out into the lake, and began swimming toward the boat. But it was a futile effort, because Jim fed more power to the electric motors and pulled away from them.

"They sure are determined predators," commented Rex.

"We make it a point to avoid them, but despite our best efforts, we've had a few run-ins with them over the years. They are cunning hunters and are very dangerous. It looks like this pair has figured out that they can't catch us. They're returning to shore."

Bule's eyes roamed all over the sailboat. Speaking to Jerry, he said, "I like your boat. Would you mind telling me about it?"

Jerry explained the salient features of the boat to Bule and Selene. Then, he took them below deck, so they could see the underwater world through the transparent hull. Amazed by the abundant variety of aquatic life, Selene said, "This is fascinating. I'd like to see more."

"We can convert this boat into a submarine," Jerry said. "Then, we can take it down to the bottom for part of the return voyage."

"That would be interesting and fun," responded Selene while glowing with excitement.

"The wind has picked up some since this morning," stated Bule. "Maybe we could enjoy sailing for a while before we take it down."

"Sounds like a plan," Jerry said. "Let's go topside and do some sailing."

Shortly, everyone was above deck enjoying the wind and the waves against the backdrop of a blue sky sprinkled with a few large billowing cumulus clouds. This provided the perfect setting for getting acquainted. Tonya was visiting with Selene while Rex and Jerry were visiting with Bule. Not having an understanding of the Ancient Ones' language, Jim and Connie were left out of the conversation.

Noticing this, Bule asked, "How did it happen that only three of you understand my language?"

Rex and Jerry told Bule the story of what happened in the caves on Zebron. They relayed their belief that Tabor instilled the language into their brains. They also voiced their concern that something sinister might have been programmed into their minds. Jerry concluded with, "Tabor wants us to solve the mystery of what happened to the people who came here 123,000 years ago in a starship commanded by his son Bule. You have that same name and speak the language. Therefore, you must be a descendant of those people. Maybe you can help us solve this ancient mystery."

"We might be able to shed some light on that mystery, but first, I have a couple questions for you."

"That's fair, fire away."

"Tonya introduced you as the Captain of a starship from Earth. Where is Earth?"

"It is the third planet of the Sun, which is one of the brightest stars in our nighttime sky. It is 4.35 light-years from here."

"I know where it is, and we long ago suspected that the Sun might have a life-filled planet."

"Well, your suspicions were correct. Earth is overflowing with life, and some of it ended up here."

"So why did it take you so long to get here?"

"What do you mean? We reached 70 percent of light speed, and it only took 6.5 years to get here."

"By my way of thinking, it took you 123,000 years to get here, and I'm wondering why it took you so long. What I mean is where have you been?"

"I am confused. How do you figure it took 123,000 years to get here when it only took 6.5 years?"

"I will explain, but first take a good look at my face and imagine what I'd look like without my beard."

Jerry studied Bule's face and mentally removed his beard. A surprised expression appeared on Jerry's face as he said, "Without the beard, you'd look a lot like what I see when I look in the mirror."

"That's the first thing I noticed about you," stated Bule. "Selene noticed it too. What I'm trying to say is that you have a striking resemblance to our son. We've been watching you since you arrived, wondering if it could possibly be true that our son has finally returned."

"I don't mean to disappoint you, but I can assure you that I'm not your son."

"We've already concluded that, but you could very well be a descendant of our son and therefore, a descendant of us."

"You can't possibly be serious," reacted Jerry in shocked surprise.

"To the contrary, I am serious."

"How could that possibly be?"

"This is going to be hard for you to believe, but I was once a starship captain. We came here 123,000 years ago. After settling down and doing a good many years of research, we came to believe that there might be a life-filled planet orbiting the Sun. I sent my starship there with my son in command. They were supposed to investigate the Solar System and return, but they never did. In the last report I received from my son, he said that they discovered a planet with vast oceans and a nitrogen/oxygen atmosphere. I've often wondered what happened to my son and the rest of the people on my starship. Our communications equipment broke down and we had no way to repair it, so we've been totally cut off. It's possible that my son and the others on the starship landed on Earth and thrived. And now, after 123,000 years, you've come here, and you could be a descendant of my son. So what took you so long?"

"You sound serious, but I think you're asking that question in jest."

"Maybe a little of both."

"To address your question seriously, I have to make several assumptions, and the first one I have to make is almost impossible to believe."

"What's that?"

"I'm having trouble believing that you and Selene are 123,000 years old. Both of you look to be 30 to 35."

"I'll take that as a compliment," stated Selene who was visiting with Tonya but overheard Jerry's remark.

"You should take it that way," Jerry said while noting how good Selene looked. "Your youthful beauty makes it extremely difficult to believe that you and Bule are as old as he says you are."

"Thank you for another compliment. I know this is hard for you to believe, but we have been here for 123,000 years."

"How is that possible?"

"Before we left home on our interstellar voyage, we were genetically altered to stop the ageing process."

"That's all well and good, but this is a rather savage planet. How did you avoid becoming a meal for a predator during all those years?"

"We have very special telepathic powers. There's not an animal on this planet that we can't mislead, and believe me, we've been all over this planet."

"Okay, that's my next question. How could you travel the planet for tens of thousands of years and not have a fatal accident somewhere along the way?"

"We never took any stupid risks. We've had accidental injuries, but never anything serious."

"Are you saying that riding pterodactyls isn't risky?"

"It's safer than hiking through the jungle."

"That, I'll have to agree with."

"Do you have any more questions?"

"Yes! How could you possibly avoid contracting a fatal disease or fatal infection for 123,000 years?"

"We are blessed with very good immune systems. We just don't get sick. When was the last time you were sick?"

"It's been so long that I can't remember."

"You just made my point. I can't remember the last time one of us was sick either."

"We've answered all your questions," stated Bule. "And I'm still wondering what took you so long?"

"I think you know the answer," responded Jerry.

"I've done my share of speculation, but there's no way to know for sure. That's why I'm looking for your opinion."

"I'll give you my opinion, but first I have to say that I'm still skeptical about your claim to have come here 123,000 years ago. It's not because I disbelieve you; rather, it's because I'm having trouble conceiving the possibility that anyone could stay alive that long on this savage planet without guns and medical technology."

Before Bule could respond to Jerry, Tonya said, "I do very well in the jungle without guns. In fact, I've never shot an animal in self-defense. I've done very well by understanding nature and using my telepathic powers to deceive predators."

"It sounds like we have something in common," Selene said to Tonya.

"We need to visit the jungle I grew up in," stated Tonya. "I'll show you an old cave complex I discovered. One of the rooms even has writing on its walls."

"Do you have video of that writing?" Bule asked.

"We sure do," replied Tonya. "Would you like to see it?"

"Yes!"

Jerry handed Bule a video headset and accessed the cave video in the computer. Soon, Bule was silently reading the writing on the cave walls. When he finished, he said, "I built those caves, or I should say we built them. We had a similar cave complex not too far from here. It's near the beginning of the river that flows into Mystery Lagoon. We were a research colony. After completing our primary research objectives, we decided to move on to the Sun to see what we might discover there, but Selene and I decided to remain here because we enjoyed living here. We expected our son and the rest of our people to return in 25 to 30 years, but they didn't. It's been 123,000 years, and now a man who appears to be a descendant of my son has returned with a starship. What took you so long?"

"Apparently, your starship was lost in a tragic accident," responded Jerry. "It's possible that your son and your people safely landed on Earth before the accident. With the loss of your starship most of your technology was lost. Your people would've resorted to living off the land. If they landed in an area that was lush with life, living off the land would've been easy. As the centuries passed by, all of your advanced technology would've disappeared. I guess it took a very long time to reinvent the starship, but here we are, better late than never."

While grinning broadly, Bule said, "It's taken long enough to get an answer out of you as to why it took you so long to get here, but since you just might be my many times-removed great-grandson, I guess I'll have to cut you a little slack."

Jerry intently stared into Bule's eyes and said, "You are serious, aren't you?"

"The possibility does exist. When we get to Pioneer Island, I'll remove this beard if you'll lend me your shaving equipment. Then, we'll pose for a family portrait."

"We need more evidence than just a side-by-side portrait showing that we look alike. We need to do some genetic work on you and Selene and me. If there's something in me that's unique to you and Selene, then, I'll start calling you Grandpa."

"Okay, son, I can live with that."

"How about me?" questioned Rex. "Are you also going to claim me as one of your kin?"

"We did plant a colony on Zebron, but none of them were my relatives, so you and I aren't related."

"If you guys are done with your family reunion, I have a question," piped up Tonya.

When the men turned to Tonya, she faced Bule and asked, "Can you read to me the writing on the walls in that cave room, or maybe just tell me what it means?"

"My name and the name of my starship are written on that wall, along with the date that we arrived here and the date that my son departed for the Sun. Also, where we are from and our purpose for coming here is written on that wall. Our basic research objectives are outlined. Also, there are instructions telling you how to enter the sealed room behind the back wall, along with a brief list of what's in the room."

"What is in that room?" Tonya asked.

"Our communications equipment and our archives are in that room. All of the most advanced knowledge from my home planet and the knowledge gained on my research mission is stored in those archives."

"That explains why Tabor was so interested in me," commented Rex.

"What do you mean?" Bule asked.

"I gained immediate entry into the secret room in the caves on Zebron when I telepathically transmitted images of the writing you put on the cave walls here. Tabor was obviously hoping to find out what happened to you."

"If I could repair my communications equipment, I could let him know, and I could also introduce him to his many times-removed great-grandson."

"We haven't yet established that," stated Jerry.

"No, but I'm willing to bet that Tabor is your many times-removed great-grandfather."

"I think we should do the lab work before we tell your father that I am one of his descendants."

"Okay, there's no hurry. I don't have any functioning communications equipment anyway."

"Maybe we can repair it," suggested Jerry.

"To do that, we must first figure out how to get into the sealed room. The intelligent material that makes up the entry wall is no longer functional."

"We could cut our way through one of the other walls."

"That could be fatal, because the room has defenses to guard against unwanted treasure hunters, sometimes known as plundering thieves."

"Maybe those defenses are no longer functioning."

"That's a possibility."

"Let's visit those caves tomorrow and figure out what we need to do."

"Okay, son, that's a good plan."

Speaking to Jerry, Selene said, "We've been everywhere on this planet except the underwater world. If we could dive into the depths of this lake, I'd sure like to see what's down there."

"We can sure do that."

While displaying a warm smile, Selene said, "Thank you son."

"You're not going to start calling me that too, are you?"

"Why not, there's no doubt in my mind that you are a descendant of my son."

"Why are you so convinced?"

"It's a matter of a great-grandmother's instinct. Besides that, you look like our son, and you act like him."

"I think we'd better get the genetic research done, so we can prove this one way or the other."

"I already know which way that's going to go."

"I guess I'll have to start calling you Mom then, but that's going to take some getting used to, because you look so much younger than me."

"Thank you for another compliment, but if you can get us into our archives, we can make you look younger and stop your ageing."

"I can see some advantages in that. We'll start working that problem tomorrow."

Speaking to Jim in English, Jerry said, "Our guests would like to see the underwater world, so we're going to dive."

"You've sure been busy visiting with them," responded Jim. "I wish I could understand what was said."

"Don't worry," Tonya said. "I'll fill you in."

"Thanks," responded Jim as he began hauling in the sail under Bule's watchful eyes. The telescoping mast was retracted. The solar sails were rolled up and stowed. The outriggers were deflated, and the telescoping booms were retracted.

"We are now a submarine," Jerry said to Bule.

"Good work, son, let's dive."

"I guess there's no way I'm going to avoid that label."

"Not unless you can prove that we're not family."

"I'll get that lab work started when we get home."

Everyone dropped into the submarine's interior. Being the last one in, Jim closed the hatch. Jerry put the submarine into a dive and was soon cruising ten feet off the bottom at a depth of 285 feet.

"It's a fascinating world down here," commented Selene. "The water's so clear, and there's so much diversity in life."

Echoing his wife's comment, Bule said, "You're right, it is fascinating. I could stay down here all day."

While Jerry and Rex entertained their guests, Tonya relayed the high points of the previous conversation to Jim and Connie. "What a surprise for my husband," Connie said. "There's no way, even in his wildest dreams, that he could ever have imagined that he'd find people on this dinosaur planet who would claim to be his ancestors."

"What are the chances that it's true?" Tonya asked.

"I don't know, but I am going to get the lab work started as soon as I can. Just the possibility of it being true could make tonight's beach party feel like a family reunion for Bule and Selene."

"They haven't had any family or friends around for a very long time. They could end up mentally and emotionally adopting Jerry as family whether he is or not."

"Since he reminds them of their son, that will be easy for them to do," commented Connie.

"That means they'll look upon you as their daughter-in-law."

"That's going to take some getting used to, but they seem to be nice people, so everything could work out very well."

After a bit of silence, Connie noticed that Tonya seemed lost in thought. "What are you thinking about?" she asked.

"I was just thinking about the intimate knowledge I have about the jungle I grew up in. If Bule and Selene have wandered this entire planet for 123,000 years like they claim, then they must have an intimate knowledge of the entire planet. What is there about it that they don't know?"

"So why don't we test them?" Jim asked. "Let's put together a list of questions that we know the answers to and that they should know the answers to, and let's see how they do."

"Why do you want to do that?" Tonya asked. "What I mean is, why do you disbelieve them?"

"It's their age claim that's not believable. How could anyone live that long?"

"That's a legitimate question, but why would they claim that great age if they aren't that old? What could they possibly gain by pulling off the greatest old-age hoax of all time?"

"I don't know. I'm just suspicious, and the test I have in mind isn't that difficult to put together."

"How will they react if they suspect that we don't believe them and that we are testing them?" questioned Tonya.

"Why would they react adversely? Their story is incredible to the point of being unbelievable. They should expect us to be skeptical."

"My only concern is that our relationship with them seems to be off to a good start, and I don't want to throw cold water on it."

"If we ask the right questions, they won't get suspicious," argued Jim. "They claim to have been here for a long time; where-as, we are new here. They should expect us to want to tap into their knowledge about this planet. We'll tell them what it is we're trying to learn and see what they have to offer. Then, we'll check out what they tell us."

"When you put it that way, it sounds perfectly reasonable."

"It sounds like you approve of my plan."

"Yeah, I do, and I have a ton of questions to ask them, but they probably won't mind. They haven't had anyone to talk to in a very long time."

"That remains to be determined."

"Well, I'm betting that they are for real," stated Tonya.

"I'm willing to be convinced," Jim said.

An hour later, Jerry brought the submarine to the surface, and everyone went to the upper deck. "Our next stop is Pioneer Island," Jerry announced while pointing at it.

"You sure have a scenic location for your home," Selene said.

"We like it," stated Jerry.

"I might fall in love with it and not want to leave."

"You and Bule are welcome to stay with us as long as you like."

"Thank you, son."

A short time later, Jerry piloted the boat into South Bay. The first thing Bule noticed were the space shuttles anchored there. He looked at them with admiration and a sense of longing. "It's been a long time since I've been in space," he said.

"Tomorrow, we're going to investigate the caves Tonya discovered," responded Jerry. "We're going to fly there in the cargo shuttle."

Bule's face lit up. "That's going to bring back some memories," he said.

"What will, the caves or the space flight?"

"Both! I'm really looking forward to going into space and going back to those caves. Let's get up early and get an early start."

"I'm already planning an early start, but that's tomorrow. What would you like to do for the rest of today?"

"Relax, have fun, get acquainted."

"That's a tough request to deal with," commented Jerry with a broad smile. "Let's start with a tour of my space shuttles."

"I'm all for that. I'd love to compare your technology to what I had when I landed here so long ago. In addition to being the starship captain, I was also a shuttle pilot."

"It's obvious that you never lost your desire to be a pilot. A couple hours ago, I watched you pilot a pterodactyl."

"And tomorrow morning, I will once again fly in a space shuttle. Going from a pterodactyl to a space shuttle is quite a jump in technology."

"That just might be the understatement of the century," commented Jerry with a laugh. "You'll have to let me know which level of technology makes flying the most fun."

"Why would you want to take my word for that?"

"What do you mean?"

"I think you should check it out for yourself."

"Are you suggesting that I should go flying on the back of a pterodactyl?"

"Why not?"

"I don't have a pterodactyl to go flying on, and if I did, I don't know how I would control it."

"It sounds like you're just afraid to experience a daring new adventure."

"I never let fear govern my life, but I do have to admit that I'm not comfortable entrusting my life to a pterodactyl. They are wild creatures."

"That's true. They are wild, and they enjoy their freedom. But, over the years, we've found them to be a safe, reliable means of transportation. Some pterodactyls actually like people. Others will try to eat you."

"We've seen both kinds. A couple weeks after we arrived here, King killed a pterodactyl that was intent on eating either Dianne or Connie. I could almost believe that he was watching over us."

"I know about that incident, and he was watching over you."

Jerry looked into Bule's eyes and said, "You could not know about that unless you were telepathically in communication with King."

"We were."

"Did you have anything to do with him defending us, or did he do that on his own?"

"Yes to both questions."

"I don't understand your answer. Either he defended us on his own, or he didn't."

"He defended you on his own, but we've had a good working relationship with King and Queen over the years. They developed a loyalty toward us and apparently, a fondness for people, because when you arrived, they decided to check you out. After you befriended them by cutting down that huge tree that was leaning against their cliff top home, they became firmly in your camp."

343

"There was a marauding bear that was after them. We had to drop that tree because it gave the bear access to the cliff top where they had a nest."

"Through King's eyes, I telepathically watched you drop that tree. When that tree fell, I sensed a huge sense of relief in King's mind. Dropping that tree made King and Queen loyal to you."

"I'm starting to get the feeling that you've been watching us for quite some time. You seem to know everything about us. And I must say that I'm really surprised, because I never in a million years suspected that people were spying on us."

"We had to spy on you to find out if we could trust you. Put yourself in our position. You would've done the same thing."

"When did you start watching us?"

"A few hours after you arrived here, King and Queen flew over you. That was our first look."

"I guess you've seen enough to trust us, or you wouldn't be here, and you wouldn't be telling me about your spying program."

"That's true, but trust goes both ways. How much do you trust me?"

"It's obvious that I trust you, or I wouldn't have brought you here."

"But do you trust me enough to go flying with me?"

"We are flying to the caves tomorrow morning."

"But that has you in control. I'm talking about going flying this afternoon on the backs of pterodactyls. Do you trust me to control the bird that you'll be riding?"

"My good judgment tells me that you're trustworthy, but I think flying a pterodactyl for nothing more than the thrill of flying amounts to taking an unnecessary life-and-death risk."

"There's not much risk involved. They are strong flyers, and you'll be riding King who is extra big and strong and loyal to you."

"It sounds like fun, but I want to think about this first."

"Take your time, son, and think it over. But just don't let the word get out that this old, old man has more guts than his many times-removed great-grandson."

"Okay! You've convinced me! We'll go flying this afternoon."

Bule smiled and said, "It sure didn't take you long to think it over and make up your mind."

"Well you are kind of persuasive," stated Jerry, while nudging the boat into its berth at the dock, where he and Jim tied it up.

"I am hungry," Jerry said to Bule. "Let's eat lunch before we tour the shuttles."

"Now that you've mentioned it, I feel hungry too, and I'd like to sample some of the smoked fish and smoked meat that Moose has made."

"You even know about that! Is there anything about us that you don't know?"

"Plenty, but you'll have to admit that it doesn't take much of a spying program to pick up on Moose's preoccupation with making and eating good food."

"You're right about that," responded Jerry with a grin.

With Jim and Tonya leading the way, everyone stepped onto the dock and walked to the elevator. After looking at it critically, Bule asked, "Is this contraption safe to ride, or should I call in some pterodactyls to fly us to the top?"

"Of course it's safe to ride," stated Jerry. "I was in on its design and construction."

"I know you were. I watched you build it. You made some of the hardware on your starship. It was brought down in a capsule that made its final landing approach suspended from a para-wing. King and Queen were very curious about that para-wing and watched it closely."

"I remember that, but I never dreamed anyone was using their eyes to watch us."

Bule closely inspected the open-air elevator cage, turned to Jerry, and said, "Nice work." Then, he motioned to Selene to step aboard. She was followed by Connie, Rex, Jerry, and Bule. To give their guests more space, Tonya and Jim elected to wait for the elevator to come back down.

As the open-air elevator ascended the face of the cliff, Bule and Selene looked down at South Bay, its beaches, and the forest. They listened to the peaceful sounds of nature, punctuated by the distant cries of a seagull. When the elevator reached Stellar Plateau, Bule and Selene were the first to step off. They looked in all directions to take in the breathtaking scenic views. Then, they looked at the tents and small homes scattered around the plateau. "This is beautiful," Selene said to Bule. "I'm tired of us wandering this planet alone. I think we should stay here and live with these people."

"Will they allow us to do that?"

"Jerry said we could stay as long as we like."

Speaking to Bule and Selene, Jerry said, "As you can see, we have plenty of space here on the plateau. We should be able to find a place to build you a home."

"We appreciate that," responded Selene.

When Jim and Tonya arrived on the plateau, everyone began walking toward Connie and Jerry's home. Along the way, Jerry introduced Bule and Selene to whomever they encountered. All of Jerry's fellow pioneers were intrigued by Bule and Selene's fantastic story of which Jerry provided only the most essential details. So many questions were asked that the half-mile hike to Jerry's home took nearly an hour.

All were famished when they finally arrived, so Connie went to the refrigerator and began bringing out food. Fortunately, she had a good supply of Moose's smoked fish and smoked ostri-dino meat. Bread, rice, salad, and fruit made up the rest of the quickly improvised meal, which was served at an outdoor table in the front yard. Even though she was only six years old, Denise eagerly helped set the table. She was fascinated by Bule, who looked like a bearded version of her father.

When everyone was seated at the table eating lunch, Denise found out that Bule and Selene flew on pterodactyls and that made her even more fascinated by them. Speaking to her father, she asked, "Will they teach me to fly on Queen's back?"

"That will have to wait until you are a little older," responded Jerry.

"But I'm already six. How old do I have to be?"

"I'll have to think about that."

"Will Bule and Selene come to my birthday party tonight?"

"I will ask them." Speaking to Bule and Selene in their language, Jerry relayed Denise's question. They smiled at Denise and nodded.

"Does that mean they're coming?" Denise asked.

"Yes, they are."

"How come Bule looks like you?"

"He doesn't look like me. He has a beard, and I don't."

"But he could shave his beard; then, he would look like you."

"Yes, he would."

"How come?"

"He thinks we are family."

"How can he be family? He's from here, and we're from Earth."

"His son flew a starship to Earth long ago. He thinks I am a descendant of his son."

"Is that true?"

"We are going to run some tests to find out."

"How long will the tests take?"

Jerry looked at Connie with an expression that seemed to say, it's your turn to answer questions. Picking up on the handoff, Connie said to Denise, "It shouldn't take more than a few days."

Denise was lost in thought because there was something going on here that was difficult for her young mind to deal with. It was confusing, so she asked another question, "If their son flew to Earth long ago, how come they look so young?"

"Bule and Selene came from a planet far away from here, where the doctors know how to keep people from getting old."

"Are you going to learn how to do that?"

"I think so."

"But I want to get older, so I can grow tall like you."

"Don't worry honey; we won't stop you from growing up."

Content with the answer, Denise looked at Bule and Selene with an expression loaded with curiosity. Then, she turned to Connie and said, "I hope they are family. Then, I will have some grandparents." With that comment, she returned to eating.

Speaking to Jerry, Selene said, "I don't understand English, but it looked like your daughter asked a lot of questions about us."

"Your guess is correct. Denise has a very active curiosity."

"That's good. It's a sign of intelligence."

"We think she's very smart for her age."

"It's been a long time since I last had the pleasure of responding to a child's curiosity. I need to learn English, so I can interact with the children here."

"There are three of us who know your language, and all of us will help you."

"Good! I want to learn English as quickly as possible."

Grinning at Jerry, Bule said, "Are you worn out by your daughter's questions, or can I ask a few?"

"Do I look tired?"

"No, but I saw you hand off your daughter to your wife."

"You're very observant, but I'm not wary of answering questions, so go ahead and fire some at me."

"There's something I'm curious about. I'm wondering how you discovered us. We're very good at shielding our thoughts from telepathic detection, yet we received a strong message from Tonya last night telling us that she would be on our beach this morning. How did she know where we were?"

"Tonya discovered you through Jim's mind."

Turning to Tonya, Bule asked, "How did you do that?"

"It happened by accident. Jim was stung several times by large hornets yesterday. A chemical in the venom gave him a temporary hypersensitive telepathic ability. He was unconscious at the time, but I was telepathically tuned in to his mind, and I saw a clear image of you and Selene walking on the beach. You were talking, and that conversation was also in Jim's mind."

"So that's how you found us. One of you had a supersensitive telepathic ability."

"That's what happened, and because it happened, we found you. But now, we're left with three very big questions: Is there a chemical in the hornet venom that would give telepathic ability to people who don't have it? Do the hornets have telepathic communication that enables the swarm to act as a single creature with many parts? And can their tiny brains act as one to form a collective intelligence with far more capability than their individual brains have?"

"I can only answer the second question. We know that they do have telepathic communication with each other. It's done at a high frequency that I can't detect, but Selene can."

"Those hornets have the potential to be extremely dangerous," stated Tonya. "They could easily kill and devour a human. We need an effective defense. Can we use their telepathic ability against them?"

"Yes," responded Selene. "On several occasions, I've telepathically deterred them from attacking us. But you have to be able to telepathically operate at their frequency."

"We need to go to their territory," Tonya said. "I want to find out if I can telepathically detect them. If I can, I'd like you to teach me how to deter them."

"I will gladly do that, and it's not difficult. They are small creatures and aren't able to generate much power behind their telepathic signals. Their range is limited, but it's adequate for the short-range telepathic communication that enables them to act as a single entity. If you can telepathically operate at their frequency, then you can easily overpower their communication, causing them to scatter in a state of confusion."

"I need to find out if I can do that. If I can, then the next step will be to find out if I can control them and make them attack an enemy. If I were being pursued by a pack of lupusaurs, could I use the hornets to give the lupusaurs something else to think about?"

"That can sometimes be done, but usually it's easier to just telepathically mislead the pursuing predators."

"But if I could control the hornets and be surrounded by a swarm of them, it seems like I could go for a walk in the countryside and be safe from most predators."

"That's a valid strategy," stated Selene. "We've done it."

"I'll bet you and Bule have all kinds of tricks for survival in the countryside."

"We wouldn't be alive if we didn't."

"You must have a wealth of knowledge that you can teach us about this planet."

"You can't imagine how much we've learned about this planet," stated Selene while smiling broadly. "We have the accumulated knowledge of a lifetime, and it's been a very long life. We've seen three ice ages come and go in the time we've been here."

"How did you cope with them?" Jerry asked.

"We migrated toward the equator, as did most animals."

"How long did each ice age last?"

"About 20,000 years."

"How long ago was the last one?"

"About 5,000 years."

"How long is the warm period between ice ages?"

"About 20,000 years."

"How warm does this planet get between ice ages?"

"During the last warm period, we lost both polar icecaps, and it was unbearably hot at the equator. We went from that to global cooling and a new ice age."

"So what's happening to our climate at present?"

"We are in a warming period. The polar icecaps are shrinking, and sea level is rising. In 5,000 years, it's going to be a whole lot warmer here on your island. If we can get into our archives in those caves we built long ago, we might be able to keep you from ageing, so that you'll still be alive then."

Selene's remarks had quite an impact on Jerry. He was silent for a few moments while thinking about them. Finally, he said, "I can't imagine living long enough to see ice ages come and go."

"I know that it's possible for you to do that, because Bule and I've done it."

"You and Bule have had truly phenomenal lives. Is there anything about this planet that you don't know?"

"It's impossible to know everything," responded Selene. "But I believe we have enough knowledge to share with you to earn a prominent position in your society."

"There's no doubt in my mind that you can help us immensely."

"This afternoon, I'm going to help you discover the thrill of flying," Bule said to Jerry.

"That's not the kind of help I had in mind," responded Jerry while staring at Bule.

"What did you have in mind?" Bule asked.

"You have a lot of knowledge about this planet that we'd like to tap into."

"Pterodactyls are part of this planet, and I can teach you how to fly one. Besides that, there are some benefits that come from having a good working relationship with pterodactyls. King is already loyal to you. Going flying with him will strengthen that bond."

"Okay, let's finish eating, and then, let's go flying."

"You're on."

Speaking to Jerry, Connie said, "I wish I understood their language, so I could be part of the conversation. Just now, I sensed that Bule was trying to convince you of something. What was that all about?"

"He's insisting that we go flying this afternoon, and I'm not sure that I'm up for that."

"Why wouldn't you be up for that? You're an excellent pilot, and you keep telling me that our shuttles are easy to fly."

"That they are. The flight control computer is capable of doing everything."

"Bule was once a starship captain, and he hasn't been up in a long time. I can understand why he would be so insistent on going flying. I think you should go along with his wishes."

"Thanks honey. I'm glad that you approve. I was concerned that you might object to us going flying."

"Why would I object? Is there something that you're not telling me?"

"You made the assumption that we're going up in one of the shuttles."

"Are you taking him flying with our helicopter?"

"No, that's not what he wants to do."

All of a sudden, an expression of alarm spread across Connie's face, and she said, "You didn't let him talk you into going flying on pterodactyls, did you?"

"You need to understand that Bule is very persuasive."

"That means you did let him talk you into it. Are you crazy? You could be killed. I could lose you forever. Do you really need to do this?"

"I don't need to, but I believe I should."

"Why?"

"I'll be riding on King's back, and he's been loyal to us. In fact, he saved either your life or Dianne's life when he killed a pterodactyl bent on eating one of you. Do you remember that?"

"Of course, how could I forget?"

"Bule said going flying on a pterodactyl strengthens their loyalty. He said that a pterodactyl can be every bit as loyal to a human as a dog is to its master."

"That all sounds great, but I'll still be worried. What if King has a heart attack when you're at 2,000 feet?"

"I'm planning to wear a parachute."

"I can see that you're going to do this, despite my concerns."

"I have to, just to save face."

"Now, I'm starting to see the real reason. This is a male ego thing. You can't let him outdo you."

"That is part of it."

"Please be careful. We might have a very long life ahead of us, and I sure don't want to lose you when the future is so filled with promise."

"Pterodactyls are part of our future, and I can see many benefits to having a working relationship with King and Queen."

"I can see that too, but I'll still be worried. Please be careful."

"Don't worry honey, I'll be okay. Bule and Selene have been flying pterodactyls for a very long time, and they don't even have parachutes."

A short time later, when all were finished eating, Connie said, to Jerry, "I'd like you to ask Bule and Selene if they would mind coming to the medical lab for a few minutes. I want to draw blood, so I can blood-type them, do their blood chemistry, and get started with doing their genetic blueprint. We need to find out if they are your ancestors."

Jerry relayed the request to Bule and Selene. "I am a medical doctor," responded Selene. "But I haven't had any equipment to work with in a very long time. I'd love to see your medical facilities. Also, we haven't eaten out in a very long time. Please thank Connie for so quickly preparing a delicious lunch for us."

Jerry relayed the compliment to Connie. In response, she flashed an appreciative smile at Bule and Selene.

Speaking to Bule, Jerry said, "Before we go to the medical lab, there's something I need to show you." Jerry quickly stepped into his home. When he came back out, he handed Bule the knife and belt buckle emblem that he had recovered from the bottom of Mystery Lagoon.

Bule reacted with shocked surprise. "I lost these a hundred years ago!" he exclaimed. "Where did you find them?"

"We found them inside a space capsule that we recovered from the bottom of Mystery Lagoon."

Bule looked puzzled. "How did they get inside a space capsule?" he asked.

Jerry told Bule the story of Trang's people, how their space capsule ended up at the bottom of the lagoon, and how the octopus-like creatures living at the bottom of the lagoon used the capsule as a repository for shiny objects. At the conclusion of the story, Jerry asked, "How did you lose you knife and belt buckle?"

"I was flying a pterodactyl over the lagoon when a mishap occurred."

Bule's comment shocked Jerry. "You've just convinced me that it's safe to go flying on pterodactyls, and now you're telling me a mishap occurred. I need to hear the rest of the story."

"There's really not much to it. I was flying a pterodactyl low over the lagoon when one of his enemies showed up. My bird would've been at a serious disadvantage fighting an enemy with me on his back, so I slid off of him and dropped into the water. We were only about a hundred feet above the water, but I hit the water with enough speed to rip off my belt and knife."

"You're lucky you survived."

"I hit the water feet first with my arms extended above my head. I made my body straight as an arrow. I've watched how pterodactyls shape their bodies when they dive into the water at great speed. All I did was mimic them; except, I went feet first instead of head first."

"Did you have any injuries at all?"

"None, but my clothing was ripped off, and I lost it."

"What happened to your pterodactyl?"

"He fought off his enemy and chased him away; then, he landed in the water and picked me up."

"The story has a happy ending, and now you even have your knife and belt buckle back."

"They've been in the family a long time. They were given to me by Tabor to bring to whatever new world we decided to settle down on." While handing the knife and belt buckle to Jerry, Bule said, "Since you are family, I am giving these to you."

"Thank you, but we don't know for sure that I am family. Let's go to the medical lab and get the tests started."

In addition to drawing blood, Connie gave Bule and Selene a brief medical exam. Neither one had any complaints, nor did Connie find any problems. Automated equipment quickly did blood type and chemistry. Blood was also entered into a machine that was used to determine the genetic blueprint of Alcent's creatures. The machine would compare Bule and Selene's complete genetic blueprint to Jerry's.

"How long will it take to find out if I am a descendant of theirs?" Jerry asked Connie.

"It might take a few days. We have to find something in you that could only have come from them. The problem is complicated by the fact that there's more than 100,000 years separating you from them. A lot can happen to a gene pool in that much time."

"Promise me that you'll tell me as soon as you know anything."

"You can count on that."

"How about Bule and Selene's health? Did you see anything in the numbers that would even give a hint as to how old they are?"

"Not a thing, they have the health of people who are about thirty, and you might tell them that."

Jerry did as requested, and Bule said to Jerry, "Now that I've been pronounced to be as medically fit as a thirty-year old, I'm ready to go flying."

"I need to stop by the cargo shuttle and pick up my parachute," stated Jerry. "Then, I'll be ready to trust my life to King's flying ability."

"Parachute, what's that for? We never wear parachutes."

"That's because we don't have any," stated Selene. "But if Jerry has an extra one, I think you should wear it."

Looking at Selene, Bule started to object, but sensing where her mind was at, he quickly decided that objecting to her reasonable request wasn't in his best interest. He turned to Jerry with a questioning expression.

"I can fit you with a parachute," responded Jerry. "And I see that there's an ATV available, so let's hop in and ride it to South Bay."

Bule, Selene, Denise, Connie, and Jerry stepped into the ATV with Jerry in the driver's seat. Shortly, they arrived at the elevator and rode it down to the beach. Moving at a leisurely pace, they walked across the sandy beach and out to the end of the dock where the shuttle was tied up.

"What a powerful-looking machine," commented Bule.

"We're happy with it," responded Jerry. "Would you like a tour while we're here?"

"That will bring back memories of the days when I had a shuttle. I'd like to start by sitting down in the cockpit."

"Tomorrow morning, we'll fly this bird in a sub-orbital flight to visit your caves."

"I'm ready to go up right now."

"I thought we were going up on pterodactyls. Now, you're telling me you'd rather go up in this bird."

"I would, but you need to experience the wild freedom of flying on a pterodactyl, so let's go do that."

Jerry walked his guests through the rest of the shuttle. Then, he went to a cabinet and removed two parachutes. While handing one to Bule, he said, "This one should fit you just fine."

"Let's go back to the plateau, and I'll see if I can summon King and Queen."

"What if they're not interested in flying?"

"Pterodactyls enjoy flying, and these two enjoy being around people, so they're not likely to ignore my call."

"Do you have a parachute that will fit me?" Selene asked Jerry.

Jerry reached into the cabinet, selected one, handed it to Selene, and said, "This one should do just fine."

"I need two of them," Selene said.

"Why two?"

"One for me, and one for Connie."

Caught off guard by the remark, Jerry's eyes opened wide, and his mouth dropped open. "I don't know if I want her going up," he said. "It's just too dangerous."

"You and Bule are going up, and we can't let you guys have all the fun."

Jerry brought out a second parachute and said, "I'm not worried. She won't go up anyway."

"I think she will," stated Selene.

"I don't think so."

"Would you like to bet a home-cooked fish dinner on that?"

"You're on," stated Jerry while handing Connie the parachute.

"What's this for?" she asked.

"It's yours to wear when you and Selene go flying with King and Queen."

"Are you crazy? I'm not going up."

Jerry confidently turned to Selene and asked, "When do I get my dinner?"

"You haven't won the bet yet. You have to at least give me a couple hours to persuade her."

"Okay, I'll give you until first sunset. But it won't matter, she won't go up anyway."

"Would you like to up the ante?"

"No, I'm happy with having you cook dinner for me."

"You're the one who'll be cooking dinner," stated Selene.

"Wait a minute now; I don't want you using any of your telepathic trickery to convince her."

"I promise I won't do that."

"Well then, how are you going to persuade her? You don't speak English."

Selene smiled smugly and said, "You don't know pterodactyls as well as I do. I have more than 100,000 years of experience with them."

"I'm not sure what that has to do with Connie."

"You'll find out when you see Queen take Connie for a ride."

Speaking to Jerry, Connie said, "I wish I understood their language, so I could know what you two were talking about."

"Selene thinks you're going to go flying with Queen."

"Well, I'm not."

"That's what I told her. I even bet her a home-cooked dinner that you won't."

"You did."

"Yes."

"That throws a different light on the subject. I might go up for a very brief flight, just so I can watch you cook dinner for Selene."

"The flight has to be at least 15 minutes."

"Now, you're setting conditions."

"I have to. I sense you women are conniving against me."

"How can we do that when we can't even talk to each other?"

"I don't know, but when it comes to scheming against men, women always seem to find a way."

Connie grinned and was silent for a few moments to let Jerry's mind work; then, she said, "Don't worry honey. I'm not going up, and I wish I could talk you out of it."

"King's a big bird. He's a strong flyer, and I'll be wearing a parachute. I'll be just fine."

"I'll feel better about it after you land."

Handing Connie a parachute, Jerry asked, "Would you mind carrying this? I have a feeling that Tonya will want to use it."

"You're probably right about that. She's a jungle girl who thrives on being wild and free."

A short time later, the group was back on top the plateau. The first thing they noticed were all the people milling around. Word had spread that Bule and Jerry were going flying on King and Queen, and everyone wanted to watch.

Speaking to Jerry, Bule said, "We need everyone to move to either side. King and Queen need room to land."

Jerry spoke to his people, and everyone shifted either to the west or to the east, leaving an open north/south lane down the center of the plateau. "That should give them plenty of room," Jerry said.

Bule nodded in agreement; then, he faced the Western Island home of King and Queen. Telepathically, he reached out and established contact with King who was busy pruning his feathers. Using signals that he had trained King to recognize, Bule indicated that he wanted to go flying. King reacted favorably. He and Queen were soon airborne. They circled low over the south end of Stellar Plateau. Recognizing Bule, Selene, Jerry, and Connie; King and Queen glided to a landing a few yards away. They gazed intently at the small group of humans, making eye contact with each one.

Connie was galvanized when Queen made eye contact with her. She definitely recognizes me, Connie concluded. And I think she remembers that I carried her infant into the medical lab and saved its life. I wonder how intelligent these creatures are. On what level are they able to think?

Connie's eye contact with Queen was broken when Bule and Selene held out in front of them the saddles they needed to put on King and Queen to make riding on their backs possible. Bule and Selene took two steps forward, stopped, and waited. The final decision was up to King and Queen, since they were wild creatures acting on their own free will. Their decision wasn't long in coming. Almost immediately, they stepped up to Bule and Selene and turned their left sides toward them. Bule and Selene began putting their saddles on the pterodactyls.

Connie watched Queen and marveled at how docile this fierce wild pterodactyl was in Selene's presence. Selene put a wide belt around the base of Queen's neck and another wide belt around the base of her tail. The belts were connected by a pair of straps that passed between Queen's legs and another pair of straps over her back. Connie noted a pair of stirrups near Queen's tail where Selene could secure her legs. There was a pair of hand stirrups near Queen's neck where Selene could secure her arms while wrapping them around Queen's neck. Selene would lie prone on Queen's back while flying. There was a belt in the middle to wrap around her waist.

When the saddle was secure, Selene stepped in front of Queen and briefly wrapped her arms around Queen's neck. Then, she backed away a couple steps. It was then that Queen made a decision. She looked at Selene; then, she looked at Connie. Her eye contact with Connie was unwavering. Those eyes seem to be filled with admiration, Connie concluded as Queen slowly approached her. Queen's beak went past Connie and she rubbed her neck against Connie. Queen came to a stop with her left side against Connie.

Speaking to Jerry, Connie said, "It looks like Queen wants to take me for a ride. What happens if I don't go?"

Jerry relayed the question to Selene, who said, "Queen will be offended. Connie needs to accept that invitation." Jerry passed the message to Connie.

"I really don't want to do this. It's going to scare the daylights out of me."

"I think Queen wants to take you flying to reward you for saving the life of her infant. I think you need to do this."

Connie thought about it for a few moments. Sounding very reluctant, she said, "Okay, help me with my parachute, and I'll do it. But I want to stay in contact with you." Connie attached a communicator to her head with a speaker in her right ear. Jerry did the same with his communicator.

Jerry helped Connie with her parachute. When it was securely in place, Selene helped her mount Queen. Jerry watched with great interest, but his gaze was interrupted when King's head slid over his right shoulder from behind his back. Jerry was startled by the unexpected pterodactyl head brushing against his neck. King stepped forward until his left side was rubbing against Jerry. Noticing this, Connie said, "I guess it's going to be you and me all alone in the wild blue yonder."

"Our flight adds new meaning to that old cliché. It's definitely wild because these creatures are wild and free, and I have no clue as to how to control them."

"I know how you like to be in control, so you're not going to chicken out on me, are you?"

"No way! I would forever lose face with Bule if you go up and I don't."

"That means we're going flying wherever these birds decide to take us."

"I'm assuming that Bule and Selene can telepathically influence them."

"That's true, but King and Queen are wild and free. They don't have to respond to telepathic signals."

"You're right about," admitted Jerry while securing himself to King's back.

Bule faced King and Selene faced Queen. They gently patted the sides of the pterodactyls' heads and stepped back away from them. King and Queen walked to the edge of the cliff overlooking South Bay. They paused for a few seconds, looking down on the bay.

Without warning, Queen jumped off the cliff, spread her wings and became airborne. At first, she soared like a glider, but then, she began flapping her wings to gain altitude, while Connie held on for dear life.

A few seconds behind Queen, King jumped off the cliff, spread his wings, and followed her. "This is wild!" exclaimed Jerry. "I've done this many times with our hang glider, but I could only go down. This guy can flap his wings and climb."

"I'm glad you're having fun," stated Connie. "I'm terrified. I've never feared height in our flying machines, but on this bird, I feel exposed to danger. I'm very aware of how high I am."

"Don't worry honey. These birds are powerful fliers, and they enjoy flying. They are in their element, and they're sharing it with us. I suspect they are going to show us what they enjoy most."

"What do you think they're going to do?" Connie asked, sounding alarmed.

"I suspect they're going to do some aerobatics."

"I was afraid you'd say that."

"Just relax and enjoy it. Take a look at the awesome view we have from up here."

"How high are they going to take us?"

As if in answer to Connie's question, King and Queen banked into a tight 180-degree turn and dropped into a dive back toward Stellar Plateau. They leveled off and made a low-altitude, high-speed pass over the plateau. Quick to react, Jerry freed his right hand and waved at the spectators who responded with loud cheers. Meanwhile, Connie hung on for dear life.

"Just as I suspected," Jerry said. "These birds are going to showoff a bit."

"I hope they don't showoff too much," Connie said. "This is thrilling enough without aerobatics."

"Try to relax. This might be the wildest ride of your life. Try to enjoy it."

"I'm trying."

King and Queen continued northward over the western shore of Pioneer Island. Looking down on the beach, which was 100 yards below, Jerry spotted an ATV. Akeyco was driving, and Zack was sitting next to her. Shannon, Kristy, and Jeff were sitting in the back. Jerry scratched King on the neck and pointed down. King sensed what Jerry wanted, so he let out a loud screeching call.

Everyone in the ATV looked up, and they were shocked to see Jerry waving at them from the back of a pterodactyl. No one had bothered to call them and tell them about the flight.

Upon seeing the pterodactyl with Jerry on its back, Jeff became very animated. He jumped up and pointed at it; then, he lost his balance and tumbled out of the ATV, landing on the sandy beach. Akeyco brought the slow-moving ATV to a stop. Jeff ran up to it while pointing skyward and exclaiming, "Jerry never told me he flies on pterodactyls!"

"He's never done this before," stated Akeyco. "I wonder what's going on."

"Connie's up there too!" exclaimed Kristy while pointing at her.

King and Queen circled the people below one time and then continued on their northward journey. "Where are they taking us?" Connie asked Jerry.

"I don't know, but I'm enjoying the ride."

A few minutes later, King and Queen circled over the north end of Pioneer Island. They flapped their wings with graceful power, steadily climbing. "I suspect we're going to gain a few thousand feet of altitude," commented Jerry. "We're circling under a large cumulus cloud. I believe King and Queen came here to take advantage of the strong updraft under this cloud."

Jerry proved to be correct. Several minutes later, King and Queen were ducking in and out of the billowing mist along the cloud's bottom. Then, they spread their wings to their full span and soared like gliders in broad circles under the cloud.

"We are riding the updraft," Jerry said to Connie.

"I'm finally starting to relax," responded Connie. "These birds know what they're doing. This is fun."

"I'm happy that you are enjoying yourself. This is real flying. It's a wild primitive expression of freedom. Best of all, these birds are sharing their world with us."

"How long are they going to keep us up here?"

"I don't know. They're not working very hard at the moment. Their wings are almost motionless. They're just riding this thermal, and they make it look effortless. Despite the extra weight they're carrying, they could probably do this all day."

"We aren't going to be up here all the rest of the day, are we?"

"I don't know," responded Jerry. "These birds have minds of their own. We're just going along for the ride."

"In other words, we're trapped on the backs of pterodactyls, lazily soaring at 3,000 feet or whatever our altitude is."

"We aren't trapped. We could slide off these birds and pop open our para-wings. From this altitude, we could easily glide all the way back to Stellar Plateau."

"I think we should stay put and let this play out," Connie said. "Since King and Queen are free to take us where they will, we can learn something about them by staying put and finding out what they decide to do with us."

"Are you comfortable with that?"

"What do you mean?"

"Less than an hour ago, you insinuated that we'd have to be

crazy to go flying on these pterodactyls; now, you want to stay up here for as long as it takes for this whole thing to play out, why the change of heart?"

"I feel a sense of freedom up here."

"A couple minutes ago, you said you felt trapped."

"Except for my para-wing, I am trapped on Queen's back, but Queen's free to go where she pleases, so I feel free too."

"It sounds to me like you've bonded with Queen."

"Considering where we are, it's hard to not feel oneness with her."

"Good point," Jerry said.

"When we came here three months ago, I never dreamed that someday, I'd see our island from the back of a pterodactyl."

"I didn't either, but we're now doing that, and our relationship with King and Queen is forever changed. Too bad we don't have tele-pathic powers, so we could communicate with them."

"We need to experiment with that hornet venom," stated Connie. "Maybe we can give ourselves telepathic powers."

"That would be great," Jerry said.

After riding the updraft for 20 minutes, King and Queen headed south. "It looks like we're returning to Stellar Plateau," commented Jerry.

King and Queen glided southward, steadily losing altitude. "It looks like we'll be home shortly," Connie said.

When King and Queen were over West Bay, they turned right. "I guess we're not going home just yet," Jerry said.

"Maybe they're taking us to their home. We're headed toward Western Island."

A minute later, King and Queen glided to a landing on their cliff top home. "Why have they brought us here?" Connie asked.

"I don't know. Let's dismount and take a load off their backs and see what happens."

The answer to Connie's question wasn't long in coming. Queen stepped up to the dome-shaped shelter that she and King had built for their infant. With her right foot, she moved the rock blocking the entrance. She made a soft cooing call, and almost immediately, the head of an infant pterodactyl poked out of the entrance. When the chick was all the way out, Queen pushed it toward Connie. Queen's eyes met Connie's eyes. "What are you trying to tell me?" Connie asked. "I know you don't understand me, but what's on your mind?"

Queen pushed the chick closer to Connie. "It looks like you're trying to show me that my medical treatment worked well and that your chick is healthy. Let's take a look."

Connie dropped to her knees, reached out, and grabbed the chick, which showed no fear, just lots of curiosity. After picking it up, Connie said, "You've grown a lot. I'll bet you already weigh 30 pounds. Let's take a look at that infected leg I treated."

Jerry dropped to his knees, so he could help Connie control the active chick. With King and Queen alertly watching, he held it while Connie examined its right thigh. "It's completely healed," she said. "All that's left from that nasty infection is a small scar where there was once an open, festering gash."

"You do good work," Jerry said, while releasing the chick.

Standing up and facing Queen, Connie said, "I don't know how to tell you this, but your chick is fully healed."

"She seems satisfied," commented Jerry. "I think she can sense your positive mood."

"I think you're right, so what do we do now?"

"Well, thanks to you, I have to go home and cook a fish dinner for Selene."

"Make sure you cook enough for me and Bule," stated Connie with a broad grin.

"I still think you women did some conniving on this. I don't know how, but I just feel that you did."

"I'll never tell. We do need to keep some secrets."

Using arm signals, Jerry and Connie indicated that they were ready to go home. King and Queen understood. After pushing her infant back into its protective shelter, Queen pushed the rock back against the entrance. The infant was thus protected from attack by birds of prey.

Shortly, Jerry and Connie were back on top of King and Queen and airborne for the short flight home. Coming in from the north, King and Queen glided to perfect landings on Stellar Plateau. There was much cheering, and King and Queen seemed to enjoy all the fanfare. They strutted around like sports heroes who had just won the big game. It was obvious that they enjoyed contact with humans. While King and Queen were reveling in all the attention they were getting, Selene walked up to Jerry and said, "I'm sure hungry for a fresh fish dinner."

"I don't know if we have any fresh fish," responded Jerry.

"That's an easy problem to fix," stated Selene, as she turned to King and Queen and did some telepathic communicating. The pterodactyls took off, heading out over Clear Lake. A few minutes later, they returned, marched up to Jerry, and dropped two large salmon at his feet.

Facing Jerry, Selene said, "I'm sure hungry for a home cooked fish dinner."

Jerry looked at the fish; then, he looked at the pterodactyls and said, "This is too much. Even you guys are supporting the conniving against me."

"It almost sounds like you feel you're up against a stacked deck," commented Selene.

"It sure looks that way. I think you knew in advance that there was no way for you to lose our bet."

"Queen has been firmly in my camp for several years. I was pretty sure she could coax Connie into going flying."

"I'm glad she did. It was a thrilling flight for both of us, not to mention what this flight holds for our future. The reality of being able to go flying on the backs of pterodactyls adds a whole new dimension to our lives."

"Pterodactyls have played a major role in our lives. In fact, they're one of the big reasons we're still alive."

At that moment, Moose walked up to Jerry and said, "I have to hand it to you. That was a very daring thing you and Connie just did. I'll need a full report with no details left out."

"That report comes for a price."

"What's the price?"

"I lost a bet, and as a result, I have to cook a fish dinner for our new guests. You can help me with that, and I'll tell you all about flying on King and Queen."

"That's a tough price. You know I enjoy cooking. Let's take the fish down to the beach and grill them for tonight's party." While appraising the fish, Moose said, "They're easily 50 pounds each. That should be more than enough for everybody."

Moose and Jerry each picked up one of the fish and headed for the elevator. "Our barbecue pit and a touch of all the right spices will turn these fish into a delicacy," stated Moose.

Chapter Fifteen

TIME: Day 90, 7:00 PM

Denise's birthday party was in full swing. Being a popular child, everyone attended. Even though it was Denise's party, she had to share guest-of-honor status with Bule and Selene, who were the talk of the island. Denise, Bule, and Selene were seated at a large, rustic table made out of heavy wood planks. Coming from the barbecue pit, Jerry walked up to the table carrying a large plate full of fish fillets. He smiled at Selene when he set the fish down in front of her. "I hope this meets your expectations," he said.

Selene selected a fillet and put it on her plate. Breaking away a bite-sized piece with her fork, she placed it in her mouth and savored it in a prolonged taste test. Holding Jerry in suspense as long as she could, she eventually smiled at him and said, "This is delicious."

"Thank you, I'm glad you like it. I guess this pays off my losing bet."

"You're paid in full. Now that we have that out of the way, let's eat. I'm ready to sample all of the delicious-looking food you have on the table. Do you people always eat so well?"

"We try to."

"Bule and I've lived off the land for the most part. We've often gone for days at a time without a prepared meal, just eating nuts, berries, fruit, tubers, whatever. Our prepared meals have almost always consisted of meat or fish supplied to us by our pterodactyls."

"You've certainly stayed healthy living that way."

"Yes, but it sure is nice to sit down to a full meal prepared by others. We haven't had that luxury in well over 100,000 years."

Speaking to her father, Denise said, "Dad, what are you and Selene talking about?"

Jerry translated the conversation to Denise. Then, Denise said, "I wish I understood their language, so I could talk to them. They're nice."

"Be patient, we're going to teach them English."

"But I have questions for Selene."

"What do you want to know?"

"We get our clothes from our starship, but they don't have a starship, so where do they get their clothes?"

Jerry relayed the question to Selene. She smiled at Denise and said, "There are plants growing here that produce soft fibers. Other plants produce strong, durable fibers. I make yarn from plant fibers; then, I knit it into clothing."

Jerry translated Selene's answer to Denise, who stared at Selene's outfit with an obvious sense of curiosity. When finished with her appraisal, Denise said, "She makes neat clothing. Will she teach me how to make something I could wear?"

Jerry relayed the question and comments to Selene. "Your daughter is ambitious for such a young child," responded Selene.

"Denise is blessed with a creative imagination. She likes to make things."

"I haven't had the opportunity to work with a child in a very long time, so I will gladly help Denise make something she can wear. This will be fun for me."

Upon hearing her father's translation of Selene's comments, Denise smiled at her, got up, walked around the table, and gave her a big hug. Selene returned the hug and said to Jerry, "I haven't been hugged by a child in a long time. You have a sweet daughter." It was obvious that Selene was emotionally moved by the hug, because a joyful tear rolled down her right cheek.

"It looks like your motherly instincts are still alive," Jerry said.

"Yes, they are," responded Selene. "Despite my age, I still function like a young woman, and I would like to have some children, but for some reason, I haven't been able to get pregnant. Maybe your wife could check us out in the medical lab and determine what the problem is."

"She will be happy to."

"We would appreciate that," stated Bule. "Selene and I have had extensive medical training, but we don't have any equipment, so what we can do is very limited."

"You've kept yourselves healthy for a very long time, so your training did pay off, despite the lack of equipment."

"My people lived here a good many years before I sent them to Earth. During that time, we did extensive research on plant life and

366

animal life. We discovered many plants that produce natural remedies for some illnesses, as well as, plants that help keep the immune system healthy. Also, Selene and I are lucky to be blessed with good immune systems to start with. We just don't get sick."

"We are fortunate you decided to join us. There is much we can learn from you. How much do you know about space medicine?"

"What do you mean?"

"You came here on a starship. Did you have any drugs that would help astronauts recover from long-term exposure to low gravity?"

"We used centrifugal force to create artificial gravity on my starship. We had to, because it took us 80 years to get here, and we didn't have any drugs to prevent damage from that long of an exposure to weightlessness."

"We didn't either, so on our flight here from Earth, we used centrifugal force to create artificial gravity equal to normal earth gravity of 1g. But how would you help people recover from exposure to .1g for 30 years?"

"I would bring them back gradually, over a long period of time."

"That's what we're doing, but progress is painfully slow."

"You must be talking about Trang's people, those who were stranded on Aphrodite for 30 years."

"That's right. There are 14 of them, and they are in a very weakened state. Aphrodite's gravity is only .1g. These people are currently living on Trang's shuttle, which is tethered to his wrecked starship. We are spinning that combination to create artificial gravity with centrifugal force. We started at .1g and increased it by .01g per day, but we ran into problems at .4g. The people are very tired, and tissue in some of their vital organs just doesn't seem to be strengthening in response to the slowly increasing artificial gravity. Trang's wife Geniya is the doctor in charge, and she's at wit's end trying to figure out what to do next."

"I don't know if we can help her with that problem. Early in our space age, experiments were run by exposing plants, animals, and humans to prolonged periods of weightlessness. But I doubt that any of those experiments were run for 30 years, and I don't know if any drugs were developed to help the recovery process. We need to get into the sealed room in my cave complex, so I can search our medical archives. There might be something there. I just don't know. What is Geniya doing now?"

"They've reduced the artificial gravity to .3g. That was 17 days ago. Her patients seem to have stabilized at that level of gravity. She's ready to slowly begin increasing it again. It would be nice if there were a drug to speed up the recovery, and at this point, we don't know if she'll be able to move them past .4g."

"If we can get into my archives, my top priority will be to search our low gravity research results for such a drug."

"I'll tell Geniya that."

After the conversation between Jerry and Bule ran its course, Connie nudged Jerry's arm and said, "Zack and Akeyco are going for a stroll on the beach, and they're not taking anyone with."

Jerry looked at the young couple and said, "They seem to be quite comfortable with each other. I sense there's a romance brewing there."

Zack and Akeyco walked in silence for a while. When they were a short distance away from the beach party, they stopped and looked back at it. "What a great scene," commented Zack. "Imagine people from so many different worlds congregating on a beach for a party, and I am part of the group. I never dreamed that I would someday leave Zebron, but here I am."

"You're one up on me," responded Akeyco. "I was born here. This planet is my home."

"But your parents are from Delta Pavonis, and that's a long way from here."

"I know, but I feel very much at home here. I like living on this island."

Zack put his right arm around Akeyco and said, "Thanks for showing me around. I enjoyed today very much."

"I enjoyed it too. It was fun."

"Seeing the island was interesting, but I enjoyed being with you. That's what made the day so special." With his right arm around Akeyco, Zack pulled her a little closer, and he turned to embrace her.

But she stopped him and said, "Zack, you're a wonderful man, but there's something about me that you need to know before you get involved with me."

"What could be so awful that it would turn off my feelings for you? When you meet someone, either sparks fly or they don't, and you've set me on fire."

"But you don't know me."

"So what's going on in your life that's going to turn me off?"

Because of her attraction to Zack, Akeyco did not want to tell him what was on her mind for fear of turning him away, but personal integrity compelled her to tell him. Hesitantly, she said, "I like you, and I don't want to lose you, but relationships must be built on honesty, so I have to take the risk and tell you."

"Tell me what?"

Facing Zack and looking into his eyes, Akeyco said, "I'm pregnant."

The news hit Zack hard. His elated mood instantly changed to being downhearted. "Are you trying to tell me that there's no chance for me, because you're already involved with another man?"

"No, I'm not."

"Then, how did you get pregnant?"

"I'm carrying a test-tube baby."

Zack's elated mood came back. "Does this mean that there's room for me in your life?" he asked.

"Your question implies that my pregnancy isn't a problem for you."

"I'm sure you had a good reason for getting pregnant with a test-tube baby. Would you like to tell me about it?"

"Sure, but first, let's sit down. I'm tired of standing. There's a log over there. We can sit on the sand and lean back against it."

A minute later, Zack and Akeyco were sitting next to each other. Zack's right arm was wrapped around her.

"The story about my pregnancy is kind of complicated, so I'm going to start at the beginning. Just bear with me for a few minutes."

"I'm not in any hurry, so just take your time."

"My people arrived here 30 years ago. After landing here, my father sent our Chief Engineer Kon and 13 others to Aphrodite to manufacture antimatter fuel for our starship. Then, tragedy struck. Our starship was nearly cut in half by a meteor impact. Actually, it was a double tragedy. We lost our starship, and fourteen of our people were stranded on Aphrodite.

"Three months ago, people arrived here from Earth. We believed they could help us, but we didn't know if we could trust them, so we kidnapped Jerry. We drugged him, and my mother telepathically probed his mind. We learned that we could trust the earth people.

"Before we released Jerry, we wanted to give him a special gift to make amends for capturing him. We have a drug that speeds up the healing of injuries, and it has two really neat side effects. It makes a middle-aged adult function like a young adult, and it slows down the ageing process. We wanted to give this gift to Jerry, but the drug is tricky and dangerous. It could only be used on earth people if they are genetically compatible with us. Since we come from planets that are 20 light-years apart, we could not assume genetic compatibility. We needed proof, but we lacked the lab equipment to do the tests, so we had to find another way. I was ovulating at the time, and my mother assumed that fertilization could only occur if we are genetically compatible with earth people. So she harvested Jerry's sperm and my egg and put them in a test tube. Fertilization did take place. When I looked at that test tube, I saw the beginning of a human life that came from me. I did not want it to die, so I asked my Mom to implant it in my uterus. She did, and I'm now two months pregnant. Also, we did inject Jerry with the age-control drug before releasing him, and it did make him function like a much younger man."

"So Captain Jerry Jerontis is the father of your baby?"

"That's true, but he was never sexually involved with me. He was unconscious at the time. It was purely a medical procedure."

"How does he feel about this?"

"He is supportive of my decision to give my fertilized egg a chance at life. We are friends."

"How does his wife feel about this?"

"Connie is a doctor, and she knows the difference between romance and medical procedures. She also supports my decision, and we are friends."

"You also have my support. I admire you for deciding to give life a chance."

Now it was Akeyco's turn to become emotional. She turned to Zack and gave him a big kiss. "Thank you for understanding me," she said. "Now we can have a romantic relationship without me having to guard a big secret, which wouldn't have been a secret much longer anyway."

"What happens if our romance grows, and we get married some day?"

"What do you mean?"

"With your people coming from Proteus, Jerry coming from Earth, and me coming from Zebron, we could end up with an interstellar family."

"What would be wrong with that?"

"Not a thing! I think it would be great. Our marriage might tie together people of three different interstellar origins."

"Before we get involved in interstellar politics, I think we should just have a romantic relationship and see how it works out."

"That's an idea I can live with."

TIME: Day 91, 8:30 AM

The big cargo shuttle was taxiing out of South Bay with Jerry in the pilot's seat. Bule was given an honorary position in the copilot's seat. Everyone else involved in the cave exploration mission was seated in the shuttle's passenger compartment.

Chief Engineer Mike Johnson was included in the crew because he had a habit of making difficult problems look easy to solve. Trang and Geniya were part of the crew because they wanted to visit the Crater Lake area where they had lived for 30 years. The remaining crew members were Moose, Zack, Selene, Rex, Jim, and Tonya.

Immediately after clearing South Bay, Jerry brought the shuttle up to hydrofoil speed and ignited its nuclear thermal rocket. When Bule felt the sudden acceleration, he exclaimed, "Wow! This is great! After all these years, I'm heading for space once again."

Shortly, the shuttle reached 200 mph, and Jerry pitched it into a steep climb. In just a few minutes, the shuttle climbed through the atmosphere and entered the vacuum of space. Shortly thereafter, the shuttle reached the required velocity for its ballistic trajectory to Crater Lake, which was 1600 miles to the south. Jerry shut down the NTR, and suddenly, everyone was weightless. Looking down on the receding planet, Bule exclaimed, "This is awesome! I'd forgotten what a thrill it is to fly into space!"

"Is it more exciting than flying on pterodactyls?"

"It's a different kind of thrill. When you fly on a pterodactyl, you have to put your faith in a creature made out of flesh and blood, a creature with a mind of its own."

"This shuttle also has a mind of its own. It's called a flight control computer."

"That's true, but you get to program that computer. It does exactly what you want it to do."

"Are you implying that pterodactyls don't always do what you want them to do?"

"I've had a few mishaps, but for the most part, they are reliable."

"For some reason, you forgot to mention those mishaps before Connie and I went up."

"I didn't want to scare you out of flying. Besides that, I survived all of my mishaps, and King and Queen are reliable."

"Okay, you're forgiven, but I want you to tell me about those mishaps sometime."

"That will make good campfire conversation. Right now, I need to enjoy a view I haven't seen in a very long time."

Ten minutes later, the shuttle re-entered the atmosphere in a steep dive. At 75,000 feet, Jerry began a gentle pullout from the dive. When the shuttle reached 15,000 feet, it was on a glide path to Crater Lake. One mile away from Crater Lake, Jerry lowered the hydrofoils. Twenty seconds later, the hydrofoils entered the water. The hydro-drogues deployed and rapidly slowed the shuttle to less than 40 mph. It settled into the water and floated on its hull.

"Smooth landing," noted Bule. "Let's go look at my caves."

"First, we have to prepare the helicopter for flight," responded Jerry as he opened the upper cargo bay doors. Next, Jerry activated the helicopter's flight operations deck elevator, raising it to its top position. "Let's go to the chopper," he said.

Mike, Moose, Jim, and Jerry deployed the helicopter's rotor blades and removed the clamps that secured it to its deck. Speaking to Jim, Jerry said, "You and Tonya located these caves the last time we were here, so I'll have you sit in the pilot's seat and Tonya in the copilot's seat."

"Hopefully, we can find them again."

"Is there any doubt?"

"That jungle is a dense sea of green with very little contrast. It's too bad we didn't leave a radio beacon there to home in on."

"As you recall, we left those caves in a big hurry last time. We had to go to Zebron to rescue Rex and his family, so it never occurred to us to leave behind a navigation beacon."

"We'll find those caves," stated Tonya. "My jungle instincts are pretty good."

"That's the kind of confidence I like to hear," responded Jerry.

Turning to Moose, Jerry said, "I need you to stay here and guard the shuttle."

"That should be easy. There's no one around."

"That might be a bad assumption. I was captured by aliens the first time I came here," stated Jerry while looking at Trang.

"Being captured by us just might be one of the best things that ever happened to you," responded Trang while grinning at Jerry.

"I can't argue that. You've given me the energy and vitality I had 15 years ago, and you've slowed down my ageing. Thank you."

Bule's curiosity got the best of him. "What was that exchange all about?" he asked Jerry.

Speaking in Bule's language, Jerry told him what had been said.

"You get me into my archives, and I will stop your ageing completely," Bule said.

Pointing at the open helicopter door, Jerry said, "Hop aboard and we'll go to your caves and see what we can do."

Looking skeptical, Bule said, "Is this thing reliable, or should I call in some pterodactyls to take us there?"

Grinning broadly, Jerry said, "We haven't had any mishaps yet."

"Okay, I'll put my life in your hands." Bule turned toward the helicopter, and he and Selene stepped aboard, as did everyone else, except Moose and Trang.

Speaking to Jerry, Trang said, "Just to make sure Moose doesn't get captured by aliens; I'll stay here and help him guard the shuttle."

"Things sure do change with time," commented Jerry. "The man who captured me is now one of my shuttle guards."

"I do know this area," responded Trang. "And I know what kind of tricks aliens might use."

"There aren't any aliens around here," stated Moose.

"This planet is so full of surprises that I don't take anything for granted," responded Jerry. "Just stay alert."

"You got it."

Jim started the helicopter's turbine engine and took off. He headed east at an altitude of 800 feet. This placed the helicopter about 200 yards above the tree tops.

Tonya was familiar with the jungle below because she grew up in it. However, it looked far different from the air than from the ground, where she was when she discovered the caves. But she remembered what kind of animals she encountered en route to the caves. Now she telepathically tuned in to the jungle below hoping to find some of them, especially the ones that were territorial and could be used as signposts.

While Tonya focused on her task, everyone else observed the jungle below. "What an endless sea of green," Selene said to Jerry. "We haven't been to our caves in several centuries. We know about where they are, but finding them in all that green is next to impossible for us."

"Don't worry," stated Jerry, "Tonya will find them."

Keeping her mind focused on the jungle, Tonya kept pointing where she wanted Jim to fly. When 20 minutes passed by, Tonya said, "I've located the monkey troop that lives in the cave area."

Using the helicopter's sound system, Jim announced, "We're near the caves. I need everyone to scan the sea of green and look for the opening that is above the caves."

Jim circled the area. After two minutes went by, Rex pointed to the right and said, "That might be it over there."

"Let's check it out," responded Jim while turning to the right.

When they arrived over the break in the forest, Tonya looked down and said, "We're here."

"I wish this opening were a little wider," Jim said, "then I could land. But since it's not, the winch is the only way down."

Jerry, Tonya, Bule, and Selene stepped onto the detachable center section of the helicopter's floor. Jerry deployed the safety rails and hooked up the cable from the ceiling-mounted winch. "Hold her steady," he said to Jim. "We're going down."

"You got it," responded Jim. "The trees here are 150 feet tall, and I'm 30 feet above them, so you have 180 feet to descend."

Using a portable control box, Jerry pressed a button to release the center floor section and a second button to activate the winch. As the small, open-air cage dropped away from the helicopter; Tonya, Bule, and Selene telepathically searched the surrounding jungle for predators.

Halfway down, Tonya said, "There's a pack of lupusaurs west of us that we'll have to keep tabs on, in case they decide to come this way."

"Do you have any idea how far away they are?" Jerry asked.

"My best guess is about a half-mile, which means they could be here in just a few minutes, if they pick up our scent and decide to investigate."

"Let's hope they don't," stated Jerry as he turned toward Bule and Selene with a questioning expression.

"I'm not detecting anything nearby," responded Bule. "But there is a pair of saber-toothed cats off to the north. I believe they're less than a half-mile away, but I think they're sleeping."

"I'm not detecting anything dangerous nearby," stated Selene.

"It sounds like it's safe to land," Jerry said, while slowing the cage's descent with only a few yards to go. Within seconds, the cage hit the cliff top with a gentle thud, and everyone stepped out. "We're clear," Jerry said into his communicator while placing the remote control box on the cage floor.

Mike brought the cage back to the helicopter, where he stepped into it, followed by Geniya, Rex, and Zack. Shortly, they were on the ground, and Mike sent the cage back up to the helicopter.

Speaking with Jerry via their communicators, Jim said, "Call me when you're ready for pick up."

"Will do, have a safe flight back."

Jerry visually inspected the cliff top that he and his party had just landed on. Because of frequent rain, it was covered with a thick carpet of moss punctuated by numerous ferns. Toward the west, the rock formation abruptly ended with a 60-foot drop over a nearly vertical cliff. Toward the east, it was buried by a jungle-covered hill that gradually rose nearly 300 feet. It was only 30 to 40 feet from the cliff to the hillside. From north to south, the rock formation stretched only 200 feet before the dense jungle took over.

Speaking to Bule, Jerry said, "I need some background information. A lot can happen in 120,000 years. What was this area like when you built the caves below us?"

"This planet was cooler back then, and weather patterns were different. This area was a semiarid desert. The rock formation we're standing on was barren. The jungle that surrounds us wasn't here. The area was populated by cactus plants and small hardy trees that could handle the dry climate."

"How did you live here with those harsh conditions?"

"Fresh water trickled out of a small spring at the base of this cliff. It provided us with drinking water and water to grow a vegetable garden and fruit trees. Also, there was a small river a mile north of here that originated in the mountains to the east. We caught fish in that river, and hunting was good along its shores."

"You also built a cave complex upriver from Mystery Lagoon. Why did you divide your people into two groups?"

"That area had a different climate than this area. It was much wetter there. Different things lived there than here. We were doing research into life in different climates with the goal of deciding where we wanted to live."

"I'm confused."

375

"Why?"

"I'm wondering why you decided not to live in either location. Why did your people go to the Solar System?"

"Some of my people settled down on Zebron. Those that came here were explorers at heart. They had wanderlust. After living here for 18 years, this planet became old hat for them. They wanted to go to the Solar System. They were convinced they would find a life-rich planet there. They wanted to explore it and come back here."

"But you and Selene decided to stay here, how come?"

"We enjoyed living here, so we elected to stay here and let our son command the mission to the Solar System, but he never returned."

"How come you never communicated any of this to Tabor?"

"We tried, but we were unable to connect with him."

"Any idea why?"

"You said that Tabor told you they were attacked by enemies from another star. If he was fighting an interstellar war, his end of our communication system may've been shut down by enemy action. After the war was over, there would've been a rebuilding period. If the destruction was horrific, the recovery might've taken decades, maybe even centuries. If he ever succeeded in getting his end of the communication system up and running, it didn't matter, because our end had broken down."

"And you were unable to fix it?"

"My son took my starship to the Solar System and never came back, so I had nothing to fix it with. But now, you are here, and you are a descendant of my son. So in a sense, my son has come back, so let's go get my communication system back in operation, so we can report to Tabor. You and I talking to him will be like a family reunion."

"We don't yet know that we are family."

"The proof will be available in a day or two."

"Then, I'll have to start calling you Dad, or Pops, or Grandpa, or something like that."

"I can live with that."

"Okay Pops, let's head for the caves."

Being the most familiar with the jungle, Tonya led the way through the forest at the south end of the clearing. Carefully picking her way through the thick vegetation, it took several minutes to descend a landslide to the base of the cliff, where she turned north.

Shortly, everyone was walking on the carpet of moss covering the rocky area at the cliff's base.

While looking at the face of the cliff and the cave entrance, Selene said, "This brings back old memories. I remember the day we moved in and the day we moved out."

"I do too," Bule said. "When we left, we took only what fit in our backpacks. Everything else we stored in our secret, sealed room, and when we came back years later, we could not get into that room. Some kind of breakdown had occurred, and we had no technical equipment to diagnose it and fix it. So we became nomads, wandering the planet and living off the land."

"So why didn't you go to your other cave complex and attempt communication with Tabor?" Jerry asked.

"That complex does not have a sealed room with interstellar communications equipment," responded Bule. "This was our primary base. All of our high-tech equipment was installed here."

"If we're going to contact Tabor, it looks like we have only two options," stated Jerry. "Either we fix the communications equipment that's here, or we go back to Zebron and use the equipment in the cave complex that is there. Since the roundtrip would take a month, it would be nice if we could fix what's here. So where do we start?"

"I have an electrical power failure, but I don't know why."

"Where does the power come from?"

"It's solar power."

"Where are your solar cells?"

"You're looking at them."

"I am? I don't recognize them. Where are they?"

"They're on the face of this rock formation."

"I don't see them. All I see is a granite cliff 60 feet high and 200 feet long."

"You're right. This rock formation is granite, but much of the western face is covered with an exotic material that looks like granite, but it isn't. The material is loaded with solar cells and tiny rechargeable solid-state batteries. The gatekeeper wall needs a lot of power to warm up and deform itself into an open doorway. That power comes from the face of this cliff."

"I get the feeling that your electrical system was designed to last for an eternity."

"It was."

"Any thoughts on how it might've failed?"

To answer Jerry's question, Bule walked to an ordinary-looking spot on the cliff face about ten feet to the right of the cave entrance. He put his hands on the wall and telepathically transmitted a sequence of thoughts into the wall. The wall turned warm and emanated streamers of blue light that connected to Bule's head. Within seconds, the wall opened to expose an electrical circuit box.

While pointing at them, Bule said, "These circuit breakers were put here to protect the system from a power surge, such as what could come from a lightning strike against the cliff. They are popped open, and I don't know why. They are supposed to automatically reset when it is safe to do so. But I can't diagnose the system because my testing equipment is locked up in the sealed room, and I can't get to it."

"Testing equipment isn't going to be a problem," responded Jerry. "We either have, or can make, whatever is needed. Our problem is to figure out what's needed, and I must say that I'm puzzled as to why your circuit breakers haven't reset. If a lightning strike fried part of your solar power plant, it seems like the rest of it should be operating normally, and the circuit breakers should've reset."

"That's the way I see it," stated Bule.

"Maybe the problem isn't out here," suggested Jerry.

"I don't know where else it could be."

"How does power get from here to the sealed room?"

Bule pointed at the large transparent plastic panel on the upper face of the cliff and said, "Light entering that panel follows a tunnel with side tunnels to bring light into the cave rooms. The tunnel has a mirror finish that allows light to follow its curves. For the sake of convenience, our electrical power cable is laid out in that light tunnel. Also, the skylight ceiling panels in each room are connected to the power cable. The ceiling panels are designed to be luminescent. With just a small amount of electrical power, they give off soft light to supplement the daylight brought in."

"That surprises me," commented Jerry. "When I first saw your ceiling panels, I thought they were just skylights. It didn't occur to me that they might also be electrical."

"We wanted extra light on cloudy days and at night."

"What if your power cable is shorted out? It seems like that could cause a huge power draw that could trip circuit breakers, and they would have to stay tripped because it would not be safe for them to reset."

"The light tunnel is sealed. I don't know how there could be a shorted cable in there."

"Inspecting that power cable is the simplest thing we can do. I think we need to do that before we look at other possibilities."

"It seems simple, but the problem we have is getting into the light tunnel. It also was designed to last forever and to never be opened. Those skylight panels are a thick rugged plastic and were glued in place with permanent cement."

"All of this is really surprising to me," commented Jerry.

"What do you mean?" Bule asked.

"When I picture cave dwellers, I see ancient humans with stone tools. When I left Earth, I never dreamed I'd meet a high-tech cave dweller, but you are certainly that."

"When you put it that way, the idea of a high-tech cave dweller does seem paradoxical," admitted Bule. "But when we built these caves, we expected to live here for a very long time, so we used our technology to build a long-life, trouble-free dwelling. Also, we didn't want undesirables to be able to easily mess up the inner workings of the system during times when we weren't around."

"We don't want to mess up the system, but we need to get in there and look at that cable. The easiest way in might be to drill a small hole through one of those ceiling panels and put a camera-carrying mechanical bug in there. Are there any defensive systems that would attack us if we do that?"

"No, and I think your plan should work."

Jerry turned to Mike and explained in English everything that he and Bule had just discussed. "Life would sure be easier if we all spoke the same language," commented Mike. "Then, I could've participated in your conversation with Bule."

"Bule and Selene have already started learning English, and I don't think it's going to take them very long. They already speak a number of simple phrases used in everyday conversation."

"I'll be happy when they're fluent in English. There are so many things I'd like to talk to them about."

"Be patient, it'll happen sooner than you think."

Mike nodded and asked, "Which panel would you like me to drill a hole through?"

"The one in the first room is probably as good as any, so let's go there."

When the party arrived in the first cave room, Mike opened his toolbox and removed his battery-powered electric drill. He fit a sharp diamond-tipped cutting tool to the drill that would quickly remove a one-inch diameter plug from the one-inch thick panel. The ceiling was only eight feet above the floor, so Mike was able to reach up and cut the hole without a ladder.

After opening a side drawer in his toolbox, Mike removed a camera-equipped mechanical dragonfly. Folding its wings back, he slipped it through the hole, and its wings snapped back into flight position. "It's your baby," he said to Jerry while handing him the control box. Mike handed video headsets to Bule and Jerry. Having only three video headsets, Mike saved the last one for himself.

Jerry activated the dragonfly and flew it to the main tunnel, where he quickly spotted the power cable. Turning right, he flew the dragonfly westward along the cable until it reached the circuit breaker box. "No obvious problems," he said while turning the dragonfly around. "Now, we'll follow the cable to the concealed room."

"Your optics are very good," stated Bule. "That dragonfly is giving us a good look at the power cable, and so far, it looks great."

Shortly before reaching the concealed room, Bule, and Mike exclaimed in different languages, "There's the problem." What they saw was a burned, shorted out cable and the skeletal remains of a small mammal.

"It looks like all of my technology and rugged construction was defeated by a ground squirrel chewing through the insulation and shorting out my cable," commented Bule. "But how did he get in there? I left no openings when we built this complex. Everything was sealed."

"You must've overlooked something," Jerry said.

"When we finished construction, we pressure tested the light tunnel, and it held pressure, proving that it was sealed."

"That's rather compelling proof that you didn't leave any openings," Jerry admitted. Turning to Mike, Jerry explained in English what he and Bule were discussing.

"It's obvious that Bule's design and construction methods were quite thorough," stated Mike. "So I don't think that squirrel got in as a result of a construction flaw."

"Then, how did he get in? This granite is pretty hard stuff. I don't think he dug his way in."

"Maybe he got in with a little help from Mother Nature."

"How?"

"Let's suppose that this huge granite formation isn't as solid as it looks. Let's suppose that it has some hairline stress cracks in it. A major earthquake could easily cause that kind of crack to open up a few inches, and that's all that a ground squirrel would need to gain entry."

"Your theory should be easy to prove. We'll inspect the rest of this light tunnel. If that large a crack exists, it should be easy to spot."

"A three-inch wide crack might not exist anymore. A second earthquake might've closed it."

"Okay, let's look for any crack in the mirror finish," stated Jerry as he put the dragonfly back in flight.

Three feet before reaching the transparent ceiling panel over the secret room, Jerry said, "There's our crack, and it's open less than a tenth-inch. So your theory just might be right on."

"The location of the crack worries me," stated Mike. "It may've allowed water to get into Bule's sealed room. The communications equipment we want to use to contact Tabor may be damaged."

"Everything in that room could be damaged. We need to get Bule in there so he can inspect his equipment. Do you have what you need to repair that power cable?"

"If I can get in there, I can repair it. We need to cut an access hole through one of the ceiling panels that is large enough for me to crawl through. I have a saw that should do the job. All I need is the okay from Bule."

"I'll discuss it with him." Jerry turned to Bule and explained what Mike wanted to do.

"I do need that cable repaired," responded Bule. "And I don't know any other way in, so we have to cut the hole. Would you mind closing the panel and sealing it when we're done?"

"We can do that."

"Which panel do you want to cut through?"

"Let's do the closest one to the fried part of the cable."

"Before Mike goes in there, I need to manually lock the circuit breakers open, so they don't automatically reset the instant Mike repairs that cable. We don't want him to get fried like that squirrel."

Jerry informed Mike as to what Bule said. "I need to go outside too," responded Mike. "Unless you and Bule want to lift me through the hole I'm going to cut, I need to make a ladder."

"You weigh about 220, and I don't feel like lifting today, so let's make the ladder. With all the wood lying around out there, it should be easy to put one together."

Shortly, the group was back outside, and Mike had his large tool-box with him. Mike visually surveyed the area and quickly spotted what he needed. While pointing at it, he said, "That downed tree over there should do just fine."

While Selene and Tonya telepathically searched the jungle for danger, Mike and Jerry went to work on the top end of the downed tree, where the trunk was three to four inches in diameter and straight as a rail. Using his hatchet, Mike quickly stripped the trunk of small branches. With a saw, Jerry cut two ten-foot lengths. Placing them side-by-side, 18 inches apart, he and Mike attached cross-members.

"It isn't pretty, but it's a functional ladder," stated Mike.

Jerry picked it up to carry it into the cave. "It's definitely heavy-duty!" he exclaimed. "It should certainly support you."

With Mike carrying his large, heavy toolbox, and Jerry carrying the ladder, the party went back into the cave. They walked to the back room, the room that had writing on its walls.

While pointing at the ceiling panel, Mike said, "The shorted part of the cable should be nearby."

Mike put the appropriate blade in his power saw and plugged it into the battery pack in the bottom of his toolbox. He reached up and cut a man-sized hole in the ceiling panel.

Jerry set up the ladder. Digging around in his toolbox, Mike selected the items he needed to repair the electrical power cable. "I'll have it fixed in no time," he said while climbing the ladder.

While crawling on the tunnel floor, Mike said, "This curved mir-ror finish is weird. It's giving me a very distorted view of myself."

"Don't let it get you disoriented," warned Jerry. "We do need that power cable fixed."

"I hate to admit it, but it's having a dizzying effect on me."

"You can use the power of your mind to tune that out."

After a few moments with no response, Jerry asked, "Are you still there?"

"Yes! I just needed to close my eyes for a few moments to get rid of my disorientation. I'm in a circular tunnel with a mirror finish all the way around. I feel like I've entered a fun house at an amusement park. My sense of balance is screwed up. I'm having a difficult time dealing with this weirdly distorted frame of reference."

"There is a way to deal with it. Just take your time and find it. We've got all day."

A couple minutes later, Mike said, "I think I've got it licked. I'm crawling along with my eyes focused only on the cable."

Shortly, Mike said, "Okay, I'm here. I'm looking at the shorted out cable. The two lines are welded together from the intense heat of the short. I'm going to cut away this part and replace it with a connector."

"Do you have the right capability connector to do the replacement?"

"Using what I have, I believe I can improvise a connection that will work. Let me think this through, and I'll get back to you in a few minutes."

True to his word, Mike called back in 15 minutes and said, "The job is done. I'm on my way out."

After Mike climbed down the ladder, Bule smiled at him and shook his hand. Turning to Jerry, Bule said, "Now, we're going to put it to the test. Let's go outside."

When they were outside, Bule went to the circuit box and returned the circuit breakers to automatic reset. Within seconds, the self-checkout was complete, and the circuit breakers automatically reset. Wearing a broad smile, Bule said, "The system is up and running. Let's go visit the sealed room."

"What if the wall doesn't open?" Jerry asked. "What I mean is that it has been shut down for a very long time. The artificial intelligence might no longer be functional."

"The wall's artificial intelligence comes from thousands of nano-processors able to communicate with each other. There are ten times as many processors as are needed to do the gatekeeper job. If a processor breaks down, the active processors will find a viable processor to replace the failed one. Even after 120,000 years, at least half of them should still be functional. That's five times as many as are needed."

"So the wall should recognize your telepathic command to open."

"It should, let's go find out."

A couple minutes later, everyone was in the room with writing on its walls. Bule placed his hands on a blank area on the back wall and telepathically transmitted a sequence of thoughts into it. Several streamers of blue light emanated from the wall and connected to Bule's head. Momentarily, the wall grew very warm, almost hot. Then, a small hole appeared that grew into an opening large enough to step through.

Bule walked through the opening, closely followed by Selene, Jerry, and Mike. Concerned about water damage, Mike looked for the crack that was discovered in the light tunnel. He spotted it in the floor, in the left wall, in the ceiling, and in the right wall. Jerry and Bule also inspected the crack.

After looking around the room for obvious damage, and not seeing any, Bule said, "Maybe I got lucky. Maybe back when that crack was open wide enough for that squirrel to get in, there just wasn't ever enough rain to flood this room. This area did have a dry climate back then."

"The crack is also in the floor," noted Jerry. "Any water that did leak in through the ceiling had a way to drain out. Even so, I think you're lucky that a second earthquake came along and closed the crack, because you do have a wet climate here now. Apparently, when the second quake hit, the debris in the crack was crushed tightly enough to form a waterproof seal, because it is dry in here."

"I'm going to assume everything is fine and test my communications equipment," stated Bule.

Jerry relayed Bule's intention to Mike, who responded, "I'm going outside then. I'd like to see that blue energy beam form."

"Before you do that, let me ask Bule if there's any danger in being too close to it."

After talking to Bule, Jerry said to Mike, "Bule said that an antenna will deploy from the highest point on the cliff top. An energy beam coming out of it will punch a hole through normal space/time and set up near instantaneous communication with his home planet, if it can find a receiver there that is turned on. If you get caught up in that beam, you will disappear from here. He thinks that you will be forever lost in what he calls the X-Dimension."

"Wow! That's a bit more than I'm ready for!" exclaimed Mike. "Did he say how far away from the beam I should stay?"

"At least 50 feet!"

"I'll give it more distance than that. I'm just not ready to explore some other dimension with no way to come back. Could you ask Bule to wait until I'm in position? I'll give you a call when I'm ready."

"You might take Tonya with you," suggested Jerry. "She'll keep you safe from jungle creatures."

Having overheard the conversation, Tonya said to Mike, "I'll be more than happy to telepathically search the jungle for you. Are you ready to go?"

"Lead the way," responded Mike.

When they were in position at the south end of the cliff top, Mike called Jerry. "We're ready," he said.

Mike stared at a mound near the center of the cliff top. It was 20 feet in diameter and five feet high at its center. It looked like a flattened hemisphere.

Things happened quickly. The moss and ferns growing on the central part of the mound disappeared with a sizzling crackling sound, and a blue beam of light about five feet in diameter appeared. At a 60-degree angle from the horizontal, it extended upward to the north as far as the eye could see. The blue color was intense and quite brilliant, but not too bright to look at.

"Wow!" exclaimed Mike. "I'm being treated to an awesome force that I just don't understand. I need to talk to Bule about this."

"It's inspiring!" exclaimed Tonya.

Suddenly, the blue beam disappeared with a deafening crack of thunder. Mike stared in stunned disbelief, because there was now a cylinder on the mound precisely where the blue beam had been. The cylinder was four feet in diameter and 20 feet long. It was at a 60-degree angle from the horizontal when it appeared with the collapse of the beam. No longer supported by the beam, it tipped over, hitting the ground with a thud. "What is happening?" Mike exclaimed.

He called Jerry. "You need to get up here!" he exclaimed. "Something unbelievable just happened. Apparently, a cylinder rode in on the beam. I don't know what's going on, but we may have visitors from the X-Dimension. Or it might be a bomb that an enemy sent here."

"Stay away from it! We're on the way!"

"You got it."

Tonya focused her telepathic powers on the cylinder. After just a few seconds, she said to Mike, "I don't think it's a bomb. I think Tabor's in there."

"How can that be? He's on a planet 60 light-years from here."

"Apparently, he's figured out a way to ride that beam into and out of the X-Dimension."

"That's hard to believe."

"I know it's hard to believe, but I think he's done it, and he's not alone."

"Can you contact him?"

"I'll try." Telepathically, Tonya transmitted, "Tabor, this is Tonya. Are you in the cylinder that just tipped over?"

"Yes, but where am I?"

"You're on Alcent."

"I am! Wow! That means we made it. I thought it was possible, but now, I know it is. Can you roll this thing over, so we can get out?"

"I'll try."

Turning to Mike, Tonya said, "Tabor is here. But he's trapped. We need to roll that thing over."

"Jerry said to wait until they get here."

"I know, but that was before we knew what we have here. People are trapped in there, and we need to help them out."

"Okay, let's go. I'm sure Jerry will understand."

Mike and Tonya ran up to the cylindrical capsule. Together, they pushed against it and slowly rolled it over. Then, two hatches popped open, like canopies on a two-seat fighter jet. A man and a woman who had been lying down inside the capsule sat up. They appeared shaken and bewildered. Blinking their eyes, they looked around. "It's hard to believe," commented the man, "but it appears that we really have made a giant leap to another world."

Turning his attention to Mike and Tonya, the man said in English, "Hello, I am Tabor, and this is my wife Karol. We are from a planet named Lucon. We are called Luconians."

"I am Tonya, and this is Mike. I was born here, but my people are from Proteus. Mike is from Earth."

At that moment, the people who had been in the cave emerged from the forest to the south and began running toward the capsule. "Who are they?" Tabor asked.

"They are friends," responded Tonya. "I'll introduce you and Karol to them when they get here."

When the party arrived, Tabor and Karol stared at Jerry and Bule for a few moments. Breaking the silence, Tabor asked, "Which one of you is our son?"

"I am your son," responded Bule. "And this is Captain Jerry Jerontis. He is our many times-removed great-grandson."

"The proof isn't in yet," stated Jerry.

"That might be," commented Tabor, "but you look like twin brothers."

"They sure do," added Karol.

"We can do the family reunion after we get the proof," stated

Jerry. "But for now, I'd like to know how you got here. Your presence is a shocking surprise."

"We're more shocked than you are," stated Tabor. "We were in this capsule doing a systems checkout; when all of a sudden, the lights went out, and we woke up here."

"Are you saying that you weren't planning to come here?" Jerry asked.

"We wanted to come here eventually, but we didn't know if it would be safe to ride this capsule through the X-Dimension. We were doing a systems checkout in preparation for loading the capsule with plant life and small mammals. It was to be a test flight to Zebron when you contacted us to report your findings on the mystery of what happened to Bule. We never expected that you would find Bule and turn on the beam from here."

"Finding our son alive is a wonderful surprise!" exclaimed Karol while climbing out of the capsule. Bule stepped forward to help his mother out of the capsule. During a warm embrace with Bule, Karol said, "I never dreamed that we'd see you alive after all these years."

Tabor climbed out of the capsule and was greeted by a big hug from Selene, followed by a bear hug from Bule. Turning to Jerry, Tabor said, "When I asked you to solve the ancient mystery of what happened to our son, I didn't expect all of this. I thought we'd have to come here and help you look for clues. That's why we built this capsule with the hope that it would work."

"To be honest with you, we didn't hold out much hope of solving that mystery," replied Jerry. "But sometimes the pieces in a puzzle just seem to fall in place. You might say we got lucky."

"I think there was more to it than luck," stated Karol. "It had to take some effort, and I want to sincerely thank you for that." Still emotionally charged about finding Bule and Selene, Karol involuntarily stepped up to Jerry and gave him a big hug that he returned.

After the hug, Jerry said, "I appreciate your gratitude, but you need to thank Jim and Tonya. They were primarily responsible for finding Bule and Selene."

Now it was Tonya's turn to receive a big hug from Karol and from Tabor. "When do we meet Jim?" Tabor asked. "And how do we thank you?"

"Jim is our chief helicopter pilot," responded Tonya. "And you'll meet him when he picks us up."

"But how do we thank you and Jim?" Karol asked.

"You can share with us the secret of long life."

"We're already planning to do that for everyone, but we want to do something special for you and Jim."

"We're planning to be married soon. You could do us the honor of officiating at our wedding ceremony."

"We would be honored to do that," stated Karol.

"Good, that will add a special touch to the occasion."

Mike pointed at the capsule, then at the mound where the blue energy beam emanated from. "I'd sure like to know how all of this works," he said. "The very idea of jumping across 60 light-years of space in a matter of seconds is mind boggling."

"You cannot make such a jump in the ordinary, everyday universe that you are familiar with," responded Tabor. "The physical laws that govern space/time do not allow that to happen."

"So how did you do it?" Mike persisted.

"I'm getting to that. Prior to the invention of the beam, our astrophysicists had long speculated that the universe contained far more energy than what was being measured by astronomical instruments. After a good many years of frustration over their inability to detect and measure this invisible energy, they concluded that it might exist in another dimension, which they decided to call the X-Dimension. They theorized that they might be able to punch a hole through ordinary space/time if they could tap into the energy in the X-Dimension and excite it at its natural frequency along a narrowly defined path. After decades of research, they found a way to do it, and the theory was validated. Simply put, when the energy in the X-Dimension is put into harmonic resonance, it can be used as a carrier wave for instantaneous communication across light-years of space."

"The concept sounds simple, but I'd sure like to understand how your equipment taps into the X-Dimension. Then, I'd like to know how you can get that X-Dimension energy beam to carry a capsule."

"We found a way to make the capsule part of the beam. Receptors in the capsule's skin are tuned to the X-Dimension energy beam. The receptors pick it up, and the capsule becomes enshrouded with the tremendous energy available in the X-Dimension. In essence, the capsule becomes a bubble in the energy field in the blue beam and is swept along by it."

"But how could you survive the infinite acceleration forces that you were subjected to?"

388

"There weren't any acceleration forces. We simply dropped out of ordinary space/time and reappeared at a different location in ordinary space/time. We disappeared from Lucon and reappeared here."

"I'd sure like to see a detailed design of all this equipment and then find out from you how everything works."

"There's a lot of technology involved that I can share with you, but I'd like to wait a few days before we get into that. I need to get reacquainted with my son and daughter-in-law, and I need to get acquainted with my many times-removed great-grandson. Also, I have a new world to get acquainted with, and we have a wedding to officiate."

"I can wait," responded Mike. "There's really only one question that we need an immediate answer to."

"What might that be?" Tabor asked.

"I am concerned that this X-Dimension beam gives people easy access to Alcent. We are no longer isolated. Is there a criminal element back on Lucon that might try to ride the beam to Alcent? Do we need to post armed guards here?"

"All societies have evil people in them, and Lucon is no exception. However, this capsule can only ride the X-Dimension beam safely if the beam is activated on both ends. If they launch a capsule when this equipment is turned off, then, there is no way to know exactly where in ordinary space/time the capsule will reappear. If this equipment is turned on, then, the capsule has a specific point in ordinary space/time to home in on. You probably noticed that the X-Dimension beam collapsed when we arrived here. That's because instrumentation in the capsule turned off the beam upon our arrival, so that we could leave the X-Dimension and re-enter ordinary space/time at precisely this time and place."

"Are you implying that time travel is possible in the X-Dimension?"

"We believe that it is, and we think that is why it looks like we jumped across 60 light-years of space instantaneously. When Karol and I entered the X-Dimension, it might've put us in a state of suspended animation. We may've been in that dimension for a good many years and not even been aware of it. We may've time-traveled to this point in time, as well as, to this location in space. To people in ordinary space/time, it looks like we made a very quick journey, but in the X-Dimension, the journey may've taken a good many years. We just don't know. A lot of research needs to be done. Also, I want to reiterate that we don't know how to navigate the X-Dimension without active equipment on both ends of the beam."

"Wow! You're hitting me with a lot of theory to think about. But if I understand you correctly, Alcent will remain isolated if we keep the equipment in these caves turned off."

"That is correct."

Jerry had been intently listening to the conversation between Mike and Tabor, but now that it had run its course, he said to Tabor, "That capsule and the X-Dimension beam have forever changed our situation. It is revolutionary technology. It is essentially an interstellar elevator. With it, people can travel between stars as easily as between floors in a skyscraper. I'm not sure that this is what we want. If this system were set up between here and Earth, this planet could be flooded with people. The life that's already here could be crowded out. We came here with the idea of respecting the life that's here and trying to live in harmony with it as much as possible. A massive influx of people from Earth could put that in jeopardy. We need to turn this thing off until we decide what to do with it."

"It looks like my arrival has created a big problem for you," commented Tabor.

"It's not your presence that's the problem; it's how you got here that's the problem."

"New technology always has benefits and drawbacks," stated Tabor. "We just have to learn how to take advantage of the benefits while limiting our exposure to the bad things that could happen. The easiest thing to do is to just keep this equipment turned off until we figure out what to do with it."

"We are in complete agreement on that," asserted Jerry. "Let's turn it off, close the open ceiling panel, and go home where we can relax on the beach and get acquainted."

"What do we do with this capsule?" Mike asked.

"We can close it and leave it here," replied Tabor. "If we decide to use it again, this is where we'll launch it from."

"I don't think that's a good idea," Tonya said. "It's covered with human scent, and lupusaurs don't like humans. They could attack that capsule. If they get it rolling, they could drop it over the cliff and wreck it."

"That's a good point," agreed Bule.

"How much does it weigh?" Jerry asked.

"About 300 pounds," responded Tabor.

"Let's take it with us," Jerry suggested.

"I am a stranger in this world," stated Tabor. "So whatever you locals think is best is fine with me."

"Okay, let's finish up here and go home," Jerry said.

Two hours later, Jim picked up the capsule and half the people. After flying them to the shuttle, he returned and picked up the remaining people. When everyone was onboard the shuttle and the helicopter was tied down, Jerry closed the upper cargo bay doors and started his takeoff run. Within a few minutes, the shuttle was above the atmosphere and in a ballistic trajectory that would return it to Pioneer Island.

Chapter Sixteen

After landing on Clear Lake, Jerry taxied the shuttle into South Bay. He saw that there was a welcoming committee on the dock with Dianne and Connie standing in front of the group. Word had gotten out that there were visitors from Lucon, a planet 60 light-years away.

Jerry was the first to step off the shuttle, followed by Tabor and Karol. In a loud voice, Jerry announced, "This is Tabor, and this is Karol. They are Bule's parents."

"They are also your many times-removed great-grandparents," stated Dianne. "The genetic research is nearly complete, and the computer says that there is a 98.7 percent probability that you are a descendant of Bule and Selene, and that makes you a descendant of Karol and Tabor."

"This is incredible!" exclaimed Jerry. "You've traced my ancestry to Lucon, a planet 60 light-years from here. And today, I've met my ancestors from the distant past, which is astounding. I feel like I should ride the capsule through the X-Dimension and visit the planet of my ancestors, just to see where I came from."

"I don't recommend that," stated Tabor. "Karol and I made a successful journey, but our success might've been a fluke. We need to send that capsule back and forth dozens of times to make sure that it works every time."

"Are you trying to tell me that one successful test flight does not make a proven system?"

"That sums it up very well. Besides that, we haven't yet decided what we want to do with this technology. We do need to evaluate the risks."

"Thanks for reminding me. My spirit of adventure just gave me the urge to jump onboard and enjoy the benefits."

"We are going to put a halt to your ageing process, so you'll have plenty of time for that, after we evaluate the risks."

"Very well put," agreed Jerry.

"Is anyone hungry besides Moose?" Dianne asked.

"I haven't eaten since this morning," responded Jerry. "And I am starving."

"Good!" stated Dianne. "We have a dinner buffet on those tables over there, so let's go eat."

Turning to Tabor and Karol, Jerry asked, "Are you ready for your first meal on Alcent?"

While grinning at Jerry, Tabor said, "Lead the way son. We'll follow you."

With Jerry and Connie in the lead, the group leisurely walked on the dock to the sandy beach, where they found tables decked out with a broad variety of delicious food. Selene tapped Jerry on the shoulder to get his attention; then, she said, "My motherly instinct was right. You are a descendant from me."

Jerry smiled at Selene, gave her a big hug, and said, "Yes, Mom, your instinct was right on."

"Now that it's been proven that you are a part of the family, and Tabor and Karol are here, I suggest that we sit down and eat. And I propose that this beach party be seen as a family reunion celebration. Lord knows we've all come a long way to be here, and a celebration is in order."

"It needs to be a big celebration," stated Jerry. "This is a family reunion like none other. I've met my ancestors from the distant past, and all of you are so healthy and youthful, in spite of your unbelievable age."

"You are also going to be youthful for a very long time, because we are going to roll back the clock a bit for you; then, we are going to stop your ageing process."

"That's another reason for having a big celebration. When I left Earth, I wasn't searching for the fountain of youth, but that is what you're giving us. Thank you."

"You've earned it. You've been a force for good in our little corner of the galaxy, and you need to live a long time, so you can continue your good work."

"Thank you for the compliment. I won't let you down, Mom. I have great plans for the future. A very long life will give me plenty of time to carry them out."

Jerry, Connie, and Selene filled their plates and sat down at a table with Bule, Tabor, and Karol. They were joined by Jim and Tonya.

Rex dropped by to join the group. Speaking to Jerry, he said, "General Kayleb sent us a message. He wants you to know that the nation building you helped him begin is proceeding smoothly. He thanks you for the communications equipment that you gave him, and he asked if we've made any progress solving the cave mystery."

"Did you send him a full report?"

"Not yet. I'm wondering how much we should tell him. Specifically, do we tell him that we have visitors from Lucon and how they came here?"

"I think we should, and I think we should talk to him about using the X-Dimension beam as a means of communication between here and Zebron. Also, we could test fly the capsule between here and there as many times as it takes to ensure that it is a reliable method of transportation."

"Aren't you worried about this planet being flooded with too many people from Zebron?" Tabor asked.

"There was a horrible war on Zebron, and most of its population was wiped out. The planet is so sparsely populated that there is no need for them to come here looking for open space. Earth is another matter. It's so overpopulated that we just simply cannot give them the X-Dimension technology."

"But if we did give them the technology, they still could not come here unless we have a turned-on receiver on this end," argued Tabor.

"But they could demand that we allow huge numbers of them to come here, and if we say no, they could send an armada of starships here with an invasion force to overpower us. Then, they could set up as many X-Dimension beam receivers here as they want. They could flood this planet with people, some of whom might not share our respect for the life that's here."

"I am surprised that you're so worried about the people who sent you here," commented Tabor.

"Earth has a very long history of struggle and armed conflict. If too many of them come here, we could end up with the armed conflict that goes on there."

"That just might be a valid concern," agreed Tabor. "But I suspect that there's also something else going on in your mind. Would you like to tell me about it?"

Jerry looked into Tabor's eyes and said, "You're right. I do have another concern. Maybe I'm just being selfish, but I like the way we are isolated from Earth. I like having the entire planet to ourselves. I like having the opportunity to build our own society here, a society built on a foundation of respect for the life that is already here. My dream is to build a nation here that is closely aligned with the nation that General Kayleb is trying to put together. We share many of the same goals and beliefs. Together, we can build an interstellar community."

"I like your dream," stated Tabor. "But you do have enemies on Zebron. If we test fly the capsule between here and there, won't that give your enemies the opportunity to come here?"

"General Kayleb has some very capable Special Forces soldiers who can guard the X-Dimension station on Zebron. But what about Lucon, are you going to want to test fly the capsule between here and there?"

"I have enemies there that I don't want to give an opportunity to come here. But Lucon already has this technology, so we have to be concerned about them. If my enemies manage to come here, they will not share your dream. They will have a very different vision for this planet. They would plunder what's here, rather than, harmonize with it."

"That's exactly why I don't want a multitude of people coming here from Earth. Some of them would be plunderers. But how do we prevent your enemies on Lucon from coming here?"

"The X-Dimension antenna that is here must be reoriented. It needs to be aimed at the one on Zebron. The one on Zebron needs to be aimed at the one that is here. If we do that, my enemies on Lucon will not have equipment here, or on Zebron, to home in on. We need to re-aim those antennas anyway, so that we can test fly the capsule back-and-forth between here and Zebron."

"I like the potential benefits the X-Dimension capsule presents," stated Jerry. "If we can develop quick, convenient transportation between here and Zebron, it will help tie our society together with General Kayleb's nation. My dream of building a local interstellar community will come to pass."

"Speaking about being tied together, I have an announcement to make," stated Tonya.

"What might that be?" Tabor asked, while displaying the as-if-I-don't-know kind of smile.

"Jim and I want to be united in marriage. Everyone is here. Everyone is happy. Everyone is celebrating, and you and Jerry have your interstellar business taken care of, so we'd like to be married now."

"This morning, you said you were planning to be married soon," commented Karol. "I didn't realize that soon meant today. Is it okay if we finish eating first, or does it have to be right now?"

"We can finish eating," responded Tonya with a glowing smile.

Speaking to Rex, Jerry said, "I trust that a full accounting of this wedding will be included in your report to Kayleb."

"You bet it will! But the report to Kayleb has to wait until the wedding celebration is over. My family and I have a special thing for Jim and Tonya. They played a key role in rescuing us, and Jim was nearly killed by the bullet he took in his chest. Celebrating their wedding is special for us."

Still wearing a glowing smile, Tonya said to Rex, "I'm happy you feel that way. How would you and Shannon like to play a special role in our wedding?"

"What do you have in mind?" Rex asked.

"You and Shannon could witness our wedding vows and sign on the dotted line that we actually did get married."

"We would consider it an honor to do that."

Using the public address speakers set up in South Bay's picnic area, Jerry announced, "One hour from now, there will be a wedding ceremony right here on the beach. Jim and Tonya are getting married. You are all invited to attend."

Trang and Geniya were seated at the end of an adjacent table that put them near the end of the table where Jim and Tonya were seated. After Jerry's announcement, Trang grinned at Jim and said, "It's not too late to change your mind. You have an hour to think this over. You can still get out of this."

Shocked by her father's comments, Tonya exclaimed, "Dad! Why would he want to back out?"

"Does he know that he's marrying the spirit of the jungle, and that you have a real flare for being independent, and that you like to disappear into the jungle for days and weeks at a time?"

Before Tonya could respond to her father's bantering, Jim enthusiastically said, "I'm not backing out! I fell in love with her on the day we met. I like her free-spirited approach to life. We're planning to disappear into the jungle together for days and weeks at a time. She will help me get acquainted with the plants and animals that live on this planet. It will be a fun-filled adventure. You might even call it a honeymoon trip into an exotic setting."

Pleased with Jim's highly spirited comments, Tonya looked into her father's eyes and asked, "Does that satisfy your concerns?"

"Let's just say that I got the reaction I expected, and that I'm happy with your marriage to Jim."

"Does that mean we have your blessing?"

"You sure do!" exclaimed Trang with a broad smile of approval.

"That goes for both of us," stated Geniya while warmly smiling at her daughter and at Jim.

One hour later, Jerry announced, "My fellow citizens of Alcent and distinguished guests, we are gathered together to celebrate the wedding of Jim and Tonya. This is a joyful occasion for all of us, but especially for them. Their marriage is based on love and a commitment to each other. For them, this marriage symbolizes a deeply personal relationship. For the rest of us, their marriage symbolizes what our nation is all about. We are an interstellar community. Tonya was born here, so she can claim to be a native of this planet, but her parents come from Proteus, a planet orbiting Delta Pavonis. Jim is from Earth. Jim and Tonya's wedding will be witnessed by Rex and Shannon from Zebron. The ceremony will be conducted by Tabor who is from Lucon. I'm not sure how Jim and Tonya managed to make their marital union so complicated, but people from five planets orbiting five different stars are involved in their wedding. Their marriage is truly an interstellar wedding that was born in our interstellar community. May their relationship and our community grow strong and last a very long time."

Tabor stepped up to South Bay's improvised podium on the beach and said, "Thank you Jerry for your thoughtful comments. You put everything in perspective."

Facing Tonya and Jim, Tabor asked, "Are you ready to get married?"

Tonya and Jim stood up, took three steps forward, and faced Tabor. "We're ready," they said in unison.

Tabor looked into Jim's eyes; then, he looked into Tonya's eyes; then, he said, "The union you are about to enter into will bring you joyful times and difficult times. The joyful times are easy. The difficult times will require patience and understanding, but if you will patiently work your way through the difficult times, you will have a stronger relationship and a brighter future. Keep in mind that marriage is loaded with responsibility. If you are blessed with children, you will be responsible for nurturing them in a way that develops them into strong, stable, responsible adults. On Lucon, we view the family as the basic social unit of society. Strong, stable families in which children have a father and a mother are a strong foundation on which to build a strong, stable society. Are both of you ready to accept the responsibilities that come with married life?"

Jim and Tonya looked into each other's eyes. After a few moments of silence, they faced Tabor and said, "We are."

"Are you prepared to make a total effort to resolve your differences when they come up, so that you can have a happy marriage for a very long time?"

"We are."

"Karol and I have been married for 123,000 years, and we are going to give you the medical knowledge to stop the ageing process. Do you think you can stay in love and stay married for as long as we've been married?"

"I can't imagine what it's like to live that long," responded Jim. "But I love Tonya, and I want to be her lifelong companion, lover, and soul mate through good times and bad times. I will be there to support her no matter what her needs are."

"I also can't imagine what it's like to live that long," stated Tonya. "But I love Jim, and I want to be his lifelong companion, lover, and soul mate through good times and bad times. I will be there to support him no matter what his needs are."

While smiling at Jim and Tonya, Tabor said, "I had some formal wedding vows prepared for you, but you've just said it all, so I now pronounce you husband and wife."

Speaking to Jim, Tabor said, "You may now kiss the bride."

After they lovingly kissed each other, Jim and Tonya turned to face the crowd and were greeted by loud cheering and applause. The new bride and groom slowly wandered into the crowd to receive hugs, kisses, and congratulatory handshakes from people wishing them well.

The joyful bliss exuded by Jim and Tonya touched everyone's heart, adding a special sense of joy to an already happy crowd. The people of Alcent had much to celebrate. The mystery of the Ancient Ones had been solved in a dramatic unexpected way that bode well for the future. With Alcent's twin moon's Nocturne and Aphrodite providing soft background light to go with the campfires, the party on the sandy beach of South Bay lasted well into the night.

Book Review

Thank you for reading *Mysterious Alcent*. I hope that you enjoyed it. This is my third book, and it is important to me to find out what you think of it. Please take a few minutes to answer the following questions:

Did you enjoy the story? _____ Why? _____

_____

_____

_____

_____

What did you like the most about the story? _____

_____

_____

_____

_____

If you could change one or two things in the story, what would you change?

_____

_____

_____

_____

I am currently writing a sequel. If you could have two or three things happen in the sequel, what would they be? _____

_____

_____

_____

_____

Would you like to be notified when the sequel is available for purchase? _____

If so, please print your name, address and phone number:

_____

_____

_____

_____

Thank you for completing this book review. Please send it to:

Daniel L. Pekarek
Alcent Adventures
P.O. Box 23781
Federal Way, Washington 98093-0781
DLPekarek@aol.com